THE
PLAYERS

Deborah Pike is a writer and academic based in Sydney. She grew up in Northam and Perth, Western Australia. Deborah completed an Honours degree in English at UWA and graduated with a PhD at the University of Sydney. She is an associate professor of English Literature at the University of Notre Dame, Sydney. Deborah has travelled widely, and lived in Paris for several years where she worked at Shakespeare & Company Bookstore, the OECD, and the University of Paris VII. She is author of *The Subversive Art of Zelda Fitzgerald*, shortlisted for the AUHE award in literary criticism. *The Players* is her first novel.

THE PLAYERS

DEBORAH PIKE

 FREMANTLE PRESS

For Mark

and

In memory of Tina

Contents

Prologue

1994

She sat in the shade of a salmon gum, watching the rest of the cast with amusement. There they were, in costume at last, composed like a tableau vivant, a blur of colour among the trees. But now Felix was yelling at them all. And it was hot. And she was parched.

She pulled a plum from her pocket and bit into it – sweet, delicious, warm on her lips, juice running down her chin.

Revolution in action, Felix had called their play, quoting Napoleon, apparently. But how could a play lead to revolution? Had Napoleon been referring to the power of wit, instead? She'd been reading about that.

The sun spiralled down through the leaves, making her woozy. The white glare. The baking dust.

Something was unravelling inside her. Susanna, her character, was slipping away. Felix had been upset, declared that the scene with Sebastian had *flopped*. He believed in her, he'd said, but he didn't have time to explain.

She had to outwit her oppressor, that much she knew. Wasn't that what revolution was all about? But surely a revolution entailed an uprising. A declaration of war?

Plum juice dribbled down her neck, dropping spots onto her apron. Dark flowers, spreading. Like carnations. Yes. The peaceful revolution. Gloria had spoken about soldiers marching through the streets of Lisbon with carnations in their rifles. Not one gunshot. The end of the colonial wars, but that hadn't been any good for East Timor, it had left them vulnerable to civil war and invasion.

There were so many stories of revolution, but they all seemed remote, stretched far away in time and place, when all around her was scorching, boring Perth.

But then again – she remembered Pinjarra, a town not far from home. Had there been a war there? A revolution? No. A barbaric massacre, more like it. Captain bloody Stirling. How *dare* he? Those English colonisers! It made her feel ashamed.

Heaving a sigh, she sucked the last fruit from the pip and spat it out. A line of ants scurried towards it.

What if history had taken a different turn? Australia, a French colony instead … After all, hadn't a Monsieur Baudin and his cronies skirted the rim of West Australia three centuries before, hoarding flora and fauna onto a ship? With astronomers … and draughtsmen? Hadn't they wanted to *capture New Holland*? … All that plundering and conquering! No different at all from the Count in the play.

Her mouth was sticky. She needed to wash her hands. She didn't care anymore if she was required, if her scene was next. She'd had enough of it all.

She hauled herself up and pushed through thick bush. The sun, a burning host.

A rocky path led through mottled shrubs and eucalyptus trees, hard sap teeming down their trunks. She dodged straw-like flying insects and termite mounds, inched her way over small stones, down the escarpment towards the creek, and leaned towards the cold water and splashed her mouth clean.

Then she stood on a bare, bronzed rock, loosened her dress and shook it off, and stepped into the water. When it reached her knees, she lowered herself, turned on her back and floated. Closing her eyes, she breathed in beautiful, cold, shuddering breaths and imagined she was drifting away.

Footsteps. A tumble of falling stones. She scrambled out of the water, tugged her dress over her wet body. A voice? No. Not a voice. Figaro. Her heart slowed. She lay down on the large rock facing upwards to the sun.

They didn't greet one another. It had always been that way.

'I'm not shirking,' she said. 'I just need a break.'

'I'm really worried about my lines,' he said quietly. 'There are so many, and I don't know how I'll remember them all. I don't even understand what they all mean.'

That was true. Figaro had a lot of lines. But she was struggling with her own.

'You'll get there,' she said.

It looked like he had come for a quick dip too. The sun was fluttering now, across her arms.

'Don't worry,' she said. 'I can't seem to get my part right, either. Haven't you noticed? I'm not very good.'

He didn't respond.

'What should I do?' she asked, feeling the sun on her lids. 'I've been reading up on revolutions in the *World Book Encyclopedia*, but it hasn't helped one bit.'

There was a long pause. She closed her eyes again and heard a pebble skim across the creek, then another.

'Think of someone you hate,' he said. 'Maybe someone you would even kill. And imagine he's the Count. Take it into every scene. See what happens.'

And then she saw Charlie in her mind's eye. Charlie. Charlie. Then the sun, bursting into fire. She could see it. Smell it: the humiliation. Charlie. Yes. She would do everything she could to outwit him.

She opened her eyes. Figaro was sitting near, fully clothed. He looked away. Reaching out to him, she just missed his hand. The crunch of his feet echoed as he climbed the side of the escarpment. Where does the heart go? she wondered.

ACT ONE Rehearsal

[1993–1995]

If love is not to fly away
Then what has Cupid wings for, pray?

– Pierre Beaumarchais, *The Marriage of Figaro*

1. Sebastian

Perth 1993

When he first saw her, she was wearing a sweeping skirt and boots, with a long woollen cardigan, hiding her hands in her sleeves. Eyes too blue somehow. He thought she looked like a moving sketch, all limbs and bones, nothing to hold onto. He imagined her slipping out of his embrace.

She looked at him. 'Veronika,' she said. 'Friend of Lucas.'

'Lucas?'

She pointed to the band. 'He plays bass guitar.'

She had a doll's mouth, full cheeks that softened her edges. A smattering of freckles under her eyes, like a stain of permanent tears. He felt a flush of warmth, the need to keep her close to him.

'Happy birthday, young Sebastian.'

Sebastian turned towards the voice. 'Uncle Frank.'

'Twenty-one today!' Frank thrust a bottle of whiskey into his hands. 'Another few years and you'll be an old geezer like me.'

'Let me introduce you—'

But Veronika had disappeared.

When would he see her again? See those bright, haunted eyes. He hankered for something alive in her. Something he couldn't quite name.

It was a year until he saw her again. Unexpectedly. Thrillingly. In a philosophy lecture, sitting several rows in front of him. She was scribbling in a notebook, and he noticed her long, slender hands and a yellow flower, a honeysuckle perhaps, tucked behind her ear. He watched her intently, waited for her outside on the lawn, asked if she remembered him. She'd been to his twenty-first, he said. She smiled, then told him she remembered the pink icing stuck to his lips. He asked her to join him for lunch, but she refused.

He didn't believe in omens, in luck or superstition, but seeing her azure eyes, the tousled red hair, her smiling refusal to give in to him, he couldn't shake the feeling that 1994, his twenty-second year, marked a new beginning. He would simply have to try a little harder. Try something different. Catch her.

2. Veronika

Ah, yes. The birthday party. She'd felt like an imposter, smuggled in by Lucas to see the lives of the idle rich: the delicate glasses, the meticulously crafted morsels on silver trays. Shiny people with neat edges and no stray threads, conversations trailing into nothing. The birthday boy standing too close to too many women, a toothy smile on his face.

But what she remembered most vividly, most painfully, was a cigarette falling onto her skirt, the rush of fire on the hem, a frantic splashing of water, and how it took her back, as she was always taken back, to Starfish Bay. The bonfire at the beach. Flames orange and blazing, people running and screaming. And then that fearful moment in time, alone and afraid on the beach, when she'd called out into the darkness and no-one came.

She'd been so young then. Barely an adolescent. And now she was on the brink of turning twenty. She still found it hard to believe she was studying at university. The only other person in her family to do so had been her great-grandfather, who had studied mathematics in Prague just before the century turned. Her father was the son of Czech immigrants, had bought fifteen acres at the age of twenty-six, made a market farm in Mundaring in the Perth Hills. Her mother, Angela, had grown up on a farm in the Avon Valley and was then courted by Michal Vaček with baskets of apples and pears. Her parents had liked his no-nonsense attitude, his thorough knowledge of business; her mother had liked to say that he was good enough for her family and strong enough to carry her through life. She'd raised two daughters, devoted herself to the orchard and to family life, but told Veronika she'd never expected a daughter to study French, philosophy and literature. It was, she'd said, *a bit of a surprise, a lot of a surprise, really.*

It was French that Veronika loved most of all, the way the words rolled, lilted, leapt. Some were dreamy, suggestive, chiming with her spirit. She was proud of having read an entire volume of Verlaine's poems without needing a French dictionary, but her mother was concerned that studying that language gave her daughter 'notions'. But it was precisely those notions that sustained her: the promise of Paris, of marvellous things to come. Galleries and the Opéra, chic cafés, the treasures of the Louvre, concerts at the Saint-Chappelle. Smoky bars. Seduction.

When Sebastian found her again and pressed her to talk, she was wary. She wondered if she could be serious about a man with such a pretentious name. But she had to admit he was handsome, in a conventional and reassuring way: square-jawed; broad-shouldered; thick dark blond hair; an even nose; amber-coloured eyes. And unlike other students she'd met, he was clean-cut, beardless. So she agreed to eat lunch with him on the lawn, let him lead her to the giant Moreton Bay fig tree near the lecture hall, let him take her arm to ease her onto the grass. Sun sliced the air and she clung to the shade. Students milled around.

'So, did you enjoy the lecture on Nietzsche?' she asked.

'Yes, I did. Although I must say, it was hard not to be distracted.'

He smiled at her, and she felt her face grow hot.

'And I *have* started the essay,' he said, 'although I *am* rather busy these days. It's my final year, but I'm still completing my other degree. I'm getting my teeth into political science and—'

'You're the president of the dramatic society, right?'

'How do you know?'

'Lucas told me.'

'Lucas?'

'My friend. He's my housemate. He was in the band at your party.' She played air guitar.

He edged a little closer. 'I have a proposition for you,' he said. 'I want you to audition for our next play. I mean, it's a couple of months away but we're already looking at our options. We could read through some plays together.' He smiled, as though pleased with himself. Let me tell you something,' he said. 'This play is going to be brilliant.'

Reading through a play together? What kind of ploy was that?

'But what about Nietzsche?' she said.

'Nietzsche?' He tilted his head. 'Well, there's a lot one could say about Nietzsche.'

She wondered if he'd started his essay, after all.

'I think he was a strange man,' she said. 'Full of his own bombast and gloom. So what if he lost God? Every generation loses something.'

He looked amused. 'What has our generation lost?' he asked.

'True art,' Veronika said decisively. 'It's all imitation now. Pastiche. Parody.'

She rose to her feet, dusting off the crumbs from her sandwich.

He kept seeking her out after lectures, and she had to admit she was flattered. At first there were jerky exchanges: banal observations about lunch and the weather, half-baked philosophical chit-chat. Then they moved onto more serious matters: the music of French for her, the attraction of reasoned argument for him. Stories about their families: his neurologist father and exuberant, doting mother; her orchardist father and a mother who loved to cook. He was an only child; she had an older sister. Sebastian was intrigued by her immigrant heritage: *Bohemian*, she told him – at least, Bohemia was where her grandfather had been born in a village called Lužany in the Hradec Králové Region, where his family grew apples. Her father had wanted a daughter called Veronika, with a *k*, to honour his great-aunt. Veronika's grandparents had escaped communism, fled in the dead of night, crawling on their stomachs through a forest to some kind of freedom in Germany. They'd come via ship to Australia in 1949 and her *babička*, Veronika's Nan, was sent to work in a slipper factory, her *dědeček*, grandpa, laying pipes.

When Sebastian called her family *real* and his own family *stifling*, she was aroused by some unspoken need in him.

And then without really planning it, without talking it through, they began to skip lectures, escape onto the Great Court, disappear into the shade. They would sit for hours under the dripping willows, books between their thighs, pretending to read. It was a place of quietness and beauty, this shady grove. It seemed to become *their* place. She imagined it was an outdoor cathedral, graced by magpies and willie wagtails, built from earth and wet black bark.

One day she watched Sebastian strip off his shirt and wade the length of the moat around Winthrop Hall. He was showing off, she knew, saluting the cheers of students. A week later she watched him launch himself in a hang-glider from the top of one of the towers. Astounding! Was all this for her?

And then, on a sunny, hot afternoon, lying entwined in their grove, he told her how much he liked her name and the little 'hook' above the 'c' in her surname, which Veronika taught him was called a *háček*, and pronounced *ha-check*. It rhymed with Vaček. He liked that her father was a farmer of sorts: authentic, a man of the land. And he liked that she wasn't like the other girls he knew, the Jessicas and Victorias who lived in big houses by the river, tall and strapping sportswomen with blonde ponytails. He called her a bright flower blown in from the wind, a bird who'd flown from a strange continent.

'And I love the sound of your voice,' he said.

He leaned in to kiss her, softly, on the mouth.

It felt like being kissed for the very first time. With Joshua. In their secret place, in the tree house, where the rest of the world fell away.

She felt Sebastian lifting her shirt, kissing her belly. Felt his roving hands. He knew what to do, and it pleased her.

One day he asked about her sister.

'She's overseas,' Veronika said. 'Nannying.'

'You don't like her much, do you?' he said.

Veronika shrugged. 'We don't have a lot in common. She wasn't really a reader, except for, you know, *Cleo* and *Cosmopolitan*. And she was … well, into boys from an early age.'

She pictured holidays at Starfish Bay – Ana lying on the shore, sitting up when Charlie walked past them; then her sister, leaning over, breasts brimming out of her red bikini. Then at night, watching Ana from their bedroom window, leaping onto Charlie's motorbike, clutching his waist, her skirt barely covering her thighs.

'I envied her, too,' she said. 'She was … kind of free.'

She didn't tell him how she'd pictured herself on that motorbike. Thirteen years old, with no idea where Charlie might be heading. The unspoken thrill of it, edged with fear. She snapped herself out of it. Needing to be *distracted from distraction*. That poem she'd studied last semester. She needed a new interest, a new passion. Something dramatic that might set her free.

3. Felix

Felix bought his kombi with four hundred dollars cash the day after he arrived in Perth. He saw it for sale parked outside the Northbridge Backpackers. It was sky-blue, painted with pink clouds like giant marshmallows. He took one look at the van and felt an oceanic sky open up inside him, a feeling that might propel him outwards and upwards into a cosmic expanse. He imagined himself driving along lonesome coastal roads past luminous rolling waves. He would disembark, spend the day in the sun and then sleep inside rocky clefts of cliffs. He could see himself zooming through vast deserts with hopping kangaroos all around, as he laughed himself into liberty.

At first, he couldn't believe he'd bought the van. Hadn't even checked the engine. The owners, two Irish hikers, convinced him it was in top condition. *Volkswagen. Can't go wrong,* they'd said. It had taken them across the Nullarbor without a hitch, after all. Felix wasn't sure what *a hitch* involved, but he was overcome by his vision. The promise of blue.

The van had cost him most of the savings he'd made from selling sausages at a football stadium in Karlsruhe. He panicked at the thought. But after he'd driven to Cottesloe Beach and sat under one of the giant conifer trees, he figured it had been worth it, just to breathe in the salty air of the Indian Ocean. It would see him through his one year in Australia, enrolled in an exchange program in the Faculty of Engineering at the university in Perth. Ready for all the freedom and wild heat he'd heard about back home. The kombi would be his ticket.

Long before his engineering days, he had taken to directing plays. It was an old talent he'd developed at the Berlin College of the Arts. How he'd loved his drama studies, and his distinguished tutor, Max Leiner, whose speciality was the theatre of Bertolt Brecht. After leading two successful student-devised shows, Felix had formed a tender and powerful bond with Max. The man became the model for the artistic and intellectual life which Felix longed for. *You remind me of myself twenty years ago,* Max had once said, after witnessing Felix in motion with a group of actors.

But Felix could still remember his parents' wary faces: their suspicion of *creative* things. They'd insisted he do something *nützlich*. Useful. So as soon as he finished his first degree, his parents urged him to head south to the Karlsruhe Institute of Technology to study Civil Engineering.

It had been a gruelling two years of learning hydraulics, quadratic equations and design modelling. Boring, repetitive lectures. Until a new lecturer caught his eye during a class on reinforced concrete structures. The man's impressive assurance, his theatrical gestures. His lecturer's passion was reinforced concrete, but Felix knew, then and there, that his own passion belonged to a script, to the moulding of actors, to the excitement of performance and audience applause. The thought of it made him come alive.

Now, in Perth, Felix sipped his espresso in the library coffee shop, pretending to consult his textbook: *Steel Designers' Manual*. The typeface on the front cover appeared like a blue-and-orange optical illusion coming nearer, then receding. He sighed, picked up the flyer on his table. It advertised the events for the last two weeks of semester: BACCHANALIAN BEER FEST. PHILOSOPHY SOCIETY SOIRÉE. SOLID GOLD DISCO CLUB. ARTY FARTY COCKTAIL PARTY. And then ... UNIVERSITY DRAMATIC SOCIETY (UDS) ANNOUNCING THE ANNUAL GENERAL MEETING, GREAT COURT UNDER THE FIG TREE. 1 PM. On this very day! Felix checked his watch: a quarter past one. He abandoned his coffee and dashed across the lawn.

He found an assortment of students splayed out in the dappled shade, listening to an extremely well-groomed young man reading from a clipboard. A young man with a serious air about him, proclaiming the responsibilities of office bearers. But no-one was paying him much attention.

'And now.' The young man looked around at the crew. 'We have been given a rare opportunity.' He paused, it seemed, for dramatic effect. 'To stage a production in *January* of all months.'

Felix tried to catch the gist of what he was saying. Something about having to begin rehearsals in exam week. And then something else about another society – the graduate dramatic group – offering UDS their summer spot.

There was a murmur from a girl draped in a ripped black dress stuck together with safety pins. Her lips were painted blue.

'I heard there was a *skirmish*,' the girl sang, 'between the actors and management. So the graduate dramatic society decided to boycott the venue. And that's why it's available.'

Felix understood 'boycott', but what was a 'skirmish'?

'Idle gossip. Who cares why? Let's just do it,' said the young man. 'We'll need someone willing to direct, I would do it, only—'

'Not again,' someone yowled.

The young man cleared his throat. 'Our production of *Sex and Death* last term was critically acclaimed in *Peafowl*,' he said. 'But we didn't get the audiences we'd hoped for. So, as president of UDS, I'm saying we need to mount a play that will attract greater interest and increase our revenue; get us out of the red.'

A snigger.

'We could even take it on tour.'

Some excited chatter. And then nothing.

Felix emerged from the shade and looked around the group.

'My name is Felix,' he said. 'I am an exchange student from Berlin. I offer my expert competencies for the direction of a play. I want to suggest *The Marriage of Figaro* by French playwright Pierre Beaumarchais.'

General muttering.

'During my studies in theatre in Berlin,' he said, 'I learned this was the most popular play in the history of Europe. The first time the spectacle was shown at the Comédie-Française in Paris, three people died in the crowd to get a ticket. This popularity will guarantee audiences for your society.'

He sat down quickly but realised he had more to say, so sprang up again. 'In addition, I have directed before with much successes. Notwithstanding my formation in Civil Engineering, I learned the Brechtian method.' Feeling self-conscious now, and a little out of breath, Felix pulled a cigarette from his pocket. He hoped he'd conjugated his verbs correctly. He wasn't sure if everything he'd said about the play was, in fact, true. But he knew it had been a crowd-pleaser throughout history. He lit up and puffed quickly in the shade.

'Okay,' said the earnest young man, 'who wants to do this? Any takers?'

'Brechtian – that means Bertolt Brecht,' said the blue-lipped girl, nodding with authority. 'Cool. He was a really cool guy. Into anti-realism. Montage.'

Felix looked around. It appeared to him that while not everyone understood what he had proposed, there were eager-looking faces in the group. Something had resonated. But then a frowning young man in a baseball cap marched up to him, introduced himself as Lucas. He was worried about the society's finances, he said, and thought *Oedipus Rex* would be a better choice. High school students were doing it for their finals so, *bums on seats*, he said.

Then a young woman introduced herself as Cassie, insisted that only *Antigone* would do. It had the best roles for women, she said, and everyone knew there were never enough of those.

'But my French play has many good parts for girls,' Felix said.

'I know which part I like,' someone said.

Laughter and groans.

The president shushed them, waved around his clipboard and declared that Felix's was the best proposal.

'People being crushed in a theatre crowd,' he said. 'It appeals to my latent capitalist inclinations.'

He shook Felix's hand.

'Not very democratic,' Lucas protested.

'Unconstitutional!' said Cassie.

'Typical Sebastian,' someone else said. 'Making the decisions for us.'

Cassie turned to Felix. 'Make me the star!' she said.

'Auditions will start right away.' Sebastian nodded at Felix. 'And we need to sell tickets. *Fast.*'

The blue-lipped girl shook Felix's hand. 'I'm Gwen,' she purred, 'and I'll play any part. I'm also the publicity. You know, designing posters and such – that's my thing.'

'And I'm Gloria.' She was dark-skinned and dark-eyed. 'I'm willing to try something new.'

Felix noticed another beautiful girl. Red hair, eyes radiant blue, but she hadn't said a word.

The group dispersed. Felix said he would advertise for auditions as soon as possible. The open-air New Fortune Theatre was only available for the first two weeks of January. If they missed it, that was it.

That afternoon, Felix attended his three-hour laboratory on soil mechanics. He watched his lab partner examine different kinds of soil through a magnifying glass, but all he could think of was *Figaro*. The logistics. He took out his notepad and sketched a schedule for auditions and rehearsals, then his plan for staging and costumes. He thought of Max – and the electrifying frisson of his tutor's intellectual provocations – and carved into the lab bench with a pocketknife *Felix B + Max L*. While no-one was looking, he chiselled *Vive la Révolution!* in tiny letters underneath.

He headed back to his house on his bicycle. He took the side avenue past Pelican Point. He was struck by the stench of seaweed. The twilit windsurfers were in sail, like bright tottering dots on the curve of the cove. He passed bunches of kids with their trousers rolled up. Some were flashing their torches into the darkening shallows; others had cast their nets over the brown water, their voices echoing off the surface. He could not fathom how free they were, talking and fishing, not giving a damn about a thing.

He cycled through Kings Park with gusto. The white necks of eucalyptus trees seemed to form a welcome arch above him. The cicadas became louder and louder, in time with his heartbeat. Maybe he would enrol in metaphysics, perhaps even religious studies or history. He'd seen a course, Witchcraft and Magic in the Middle Ages, advertised in the prospectus and wondered if they would accept his enrolment next semester.

Felix lived in a brick bungalow which he shared with two medical students from Penang. He enjoyed with them an occasional breakfast of nasi goreng. Someone had written *free sex* on the pavement out the front. Stolen road signs adorned the walls of the corridor. *Bad craziness* was painted on the door. An enormous yard was covered in crisp, brown grass. A punching bag hung in the laundry. After his lab, it was his usual routine to give the bag a few punches, but today he felt like opening a beer, sitting on the front veranda and greeting passers-by. He thought of his friends at home in Berlin in their cramped apartments in Kreuzberg, with their giant satellite dishes protruding from their balconies, freezing in their fingerless gloves, bent over the radiator, *Popstars* and hot sausage.

4. Gloria

All Souls Day. Good timing for old Mr Gomes to pass away like that, Gloria thought. Well. Not on the exact day, but near enough.

It was a year later, in the Gomes's backyard, when she met up with her friends for *Kore Metan*. For *festa*. There had been frenzied pipe music. Some of them had gone crazy with their dance moves. Rosária's two brothers were already quite drunk. Gloria found it disrespectful. One of them, Santiago, was howling to a ukulele. Rosária, her best friend, had lost her grandfather – but now she was so busy chatting to all the guests, Gloria wondered if she'd even seen her. It had always been their mission to have serious fun at events like these. Was it fun? Gloria wasn't sure.

She still felt sad for Mr Gomes. He had been a big campaigner for freedom for Timor-Leste. A political man, who also ran a lunch bar in town until it all got too much. Sad when good people pass on, Gloria thought. *Kore Metan* was meant to signal the end of the mourning period. It *was* astonishing to see Rosária's mother in burnt orange after a whole year of wearing black, but it wasn't like you could get over the death of your father as quickly as all that.

Gloria leant against the back fence, holding her paper plate, stomach full of chicken curry and fizzy drinks. The garden was jam-packed. The frangipani trees looked pretty all lit up. Everyone had pitched in, but it would have been expensive – the sound system alone. Gloria thought of her own father and felt sort of blank. Before they all turned up at the house, they had thrown petals on Mr Gomes's grave. Gloria's own mother, Sofia, had brought some beautiful stones. There had been loud cries. Kookaburras. Candles. Mrs Gomes clutched to her chest a tattered photo of her mother and father.

'*Tua mutin*? Santiago brought it. Heaven knows where he got it from.' It was Rosária, holding up a large plastic bottle.

Gloria said no thanks. She knew it was special. You couldn't make palm wine in Australia, but she'd tried it before and found it too sweet.

'I know you smoke, so you may as well drink.' Rosária gave her a big nudge. Gloria shook her head.

'Do us a favour and put us out of our misery, will you?' Rosária motioned over to the veranda where her brother and his friend Martinho were singing and playing ukulele. 'Take that microphone away from him. He sounds like … like …' She looked sort of pained. The two of them started to giggle.

'—Like he did at that fundraiser, where—'

'Like a total embarrassment. What a cringe.' Rosária shook her head. 'Just so as you know, my brother and I are seriously not related. C'mon, Glor. Your turn.'

'I don't really feel up to it.'

Gloria caught her mother's eye through the bodies in the crowd. She could see her huddled next to Rosária's mother on a twin pair of stools, the two of them conspiratorial. What were they doing? Psychoanalysing? Talking about things in the oven? Sofia winked at her daughter and then put a finger in the air. She always did that when she wanted Gloria to act proper, to put her back straight, behave. Had she been slouching against the fence? What was so bad about that? It was so unfair when your mother had extra sensory perception.

'I'd rather hear you sing Kyrie eleison to the organ than that … Oh, spare me. I can't believe Mum let him.'

'I dunno, Rose.'

'If you won't do it for me, then do it for my grandfather,' Rosária pleaded, and moved away.

Gloria felt guilty. She wasn't sure what the guilt was for. Probably a whole lot of things all squashed up together. She folded her oil-stained paper plate and straightened her spine. What would she sing? She took off her shawl and removed the stupid clips from her hair.

Okay, Mr Gomes. Okay, she thought, okay.

Game over, she heard Rosária say to her brother. She forced the microphone out of his hand and passed it over to Gloria. Santiago swore and shrank away. Martinho looked bemused and nodded and began to strum gently, slowly.

And so she sang '*Foho Ramelau*'. For Mr Gomes. For her father. A controversial song perhaps. But how good it was to sing … It was almost like crying, to sing, to sing like that, to sing loud. She could sing through her feeling. Maybe she was jealous of Rosária for having a father and a brother who were alive and a grandfather whose death could be celebrated.

And she could sing too, because she was proud, proud of something in herself, something she ... well she didn't really know what it was ... this thing that made her courageous. When she finished the song, she could see in their eyes that they had been moved and awed by what she had sung and how she had sung it.

5. Felix

The UDS rehearsal venue was attached to one of the campus theatres. After navigating the map Sebastian had given him, Felix found it by throwing himself against a great oak door which opened into a secret chamber of sorts, with a shiny black floor and beige walls. But it was airless and made him feel inhibited, closed in. He wanted to rehearse in the New Fortune to get the actors accustomed to projecting outdoors, but the theatre had been booked out with another show – a *Shakespeare for Drongos* production that ran matinées – so they had no choice.

Early one evening he stood in the studio watching Gloria's audition. She had been reciting Chérubin's song to her own improvised melody:

My steed was weary and slow
(Alas, but my heart is in pain)
Our heads alike hanging low
As we wandered over the plain

Excited by her transporting rendition, Felix forgot the rules about smoking, rolled up some tobacco, offered her one as soon as she had finished. She gladly accepted. Almost everyone was a smoker, and they were all trying to quit except Gloria. This made her even better, in Felix's books. He told her she had to jump out of a window in the play, and she said she didn't mind a bit.

'This is a part for an adolescent boy,' he said, 'but it is always played by a woman. You will see that Beaumarchais wrote in the character notes that he is *a charming young scamp*.'

Gloria pulled her oversized sweater over her drainpipe jeans and wriggled around.

'She is constantly upsetting the master's schemes,' Felix added.

'Sounds wonderful,' she said.

'Your singing is beautiful.'

'Church choir.'

'You study music, Gloria?'

'Teaching.'

Felix loved her nimble movements and her short curly hair. She fiddled with it occasionally, uttering her playful lines. This habit drew attention to her mischievous laugh, just right for the role. A true original, he thought. Some quality set her apart from the others who'd auditioned. She was candid. And it was as if you could confide in her your deepest secret and know you would never be betrayed. He was sensitive to such things.

A groundsman in a boilersuit and hardhat clomped into the studio.

'We'll have none of that here,' he said and pulled a cigarette out of each mouth. 'You'll set off the bloody fire alarm.'

He issued both of them with a ticket that said WARNING in big red letters. He told them that if he caught them smoking in the studio again, they would be banned from using any venue on campus. Felix was too excited to care.

He cast the law student, Sebastian, as Figaro, even though he had delivered a rather flat version of the revolution speech. But the other guy, Lucas, kept forgetting his lines. The casting of Suzanne, the young bride, was also not without its problems. Felix knew that Cassie had made her too sweet, while Gwen had made her too brooding and complex. He thought that a young woman called Veronika was rather icy in her delivery, but he figured she would manage after some defrosting. He cast Gwen as Figaro's trickster mother, Marceline, and Cassie as Countess Rosina. Felix wasn't sure what to do with Lucas. He was a very bad actor, to be sure, but he had a certain kind of presence. Should he be cast as Bazile, the musician? Or the comically odious doctor, Bartholo, where his gaucheness would come in handy? He would think on it. Experiment during rehearsals. There was no-one yet for the Count. Perhaps he could play that part. There were some minor roles yet to be cast, but people could play dual roles. They would make do. Rehearsals could begin.

6. Veronika

There was no mistaking his voice. Sebastian. Perched on the edge of a sofa in the Arts common room, coffee mug in hand, surrounded by a gaggle of girls. He was seemingly lost for words. Veronika hovered at the door. She met the eyes of a young woman who smiled at her dreamily, grabbed her by the arm and dragged her inside. She exclaimed in clipped English tones that she was *lovesick*, then flopped into a tattered armchair.

Veronika stood hovering. She was finding these encounters awkward.

'Who are you pining for?' she asked the lovesick one. Hoping she didn't sound sarcastic.

'Who else?' The young woman sighed and cast her hand across her brow like a tragic figure. 'Sebastian Harper-Jones.'

Veronika turned to look at him. He wore well-cut trousers, a pristine shirt and a look of vague confusion as a woman draped across the sofa tugged at his arm. She was showing a great deal of leg in those fishnet stockings.

'Sebastian, darling, please,' she buzzed. 'You've simply *got* to re-read Nietzsche.'

Veronika was incredulous. The place was crawling with women in love with him. She felt suddenly oppressed by this collective stirring of female desire and by the 1960s furniture: heavy wood in oblong shapes and hideous sofas of bottle-green leather.

The lovesick woman on the sofa held out her hand. 'I'm Cassie Fletcher,' she said.

They shook hands. A strangely formal gesture, Veronika thought, for such a loose gathering.

'You think I have a chance with him?' she said.

'As good as anyone else, I imagine.' Veronika turned to go, but Cassie refused to let go of her hand.

'I know you, you're Veronika. I saw you at the audition. *You* got the part I wanted in the play. I would have been wonderful playing opposite Sebastian—'

'Oh, forgive me—'

'As Suzanne.'

'Yes.'

'In that play. But Felix Baumann is a genius. UDS has been in drastic need of new direction, and our saviour arrived in the form of a German engineer. Who would have thought?'

'Not me.'

'But he didn't pick *me* for the part I really wanted.' Cassie pushed out her bottom lip. 'I'm the Countess. The jilted one. *Boo-hoo!*'

'He *is* an engineer,' Veronika said. 'Maybe he doesn't have a clue.'

Cassie shook her head. 'Believe me, Veronika, I have been in so many plays,' she said, 'and they were all *horrible* student-devised things.' She scrunched up her nose. 'Shocking, just *shocking* things. I have no desire to pop out of a suitcase naked and recite Plato's *Republic* backwards. I don't want to roll around on the floor and chant *ohhhhm* anymore! I am *tired* of having to perform Shakespeare in a Star Trek costume. And if I see another *bloody* shopping trolley—'

Veronika found herself smiling.

'I just want to be in a period drama,' Cassie said, and thrust out her arms. 'To play a wan and wonderful woman who wears long, puffy dresses and experiences forbidden kisses with wicked men.' Words were flying out of her mouth like ribbons on a pole.

'Isn't that the Countess's role? At least, sort of?' Veronika said, but Cassie didn't seem to register. She wanted to be adored, she said.

'Why shouldn't I be adored? I've got long hair, for God's sake.' She pulled out her bun and shook out a gloriously abundant head of hair – brown, wavy, more romantic than anything Veronika had seen.

'Your crowning glory,' she said.

'Oh, I *am* dreadful.' Cassie shrunk into her chair. 'You must think me dreadful.'

'Not at all, really.' Veronika couldn't decide if this Cassie was real.

'It's just that I have so much to give a man,' Cassie said. Almost whined. She looked around anxiously for Sebastian, who was still being pawed by the woman in fishnet stockings.

'Is that true, baby?' a voice called out. '*So* much to give a man?'

A young man with a thin yellow beard. Veronika had seen him sharing a joint with two other guys: one in a leather jacket with elbow patches was reading a book upside down, the other was lying on his stomach on the floor, barefoot, with a guitar slung over his back.

Yellow Beard sidled up to Cassie. 'Anything you gotta give, baby, you can give to me.'

Veronika saw Sebastian put his mug aside, then untangle himself from the woman, walk over.

'I'm glad you came,' he said to Veronika, squeezing her hand. There was no time to respond, as the man in the leather jacket grabbed her other hand and quickly shoved his book into it.

'You gotta read this, sweetheart,' he said. Veronika held it up.

The Unbearable Heaviness of Philosophy Made Lighter, the man said.

'That book ... that book.' It was Sebastian, pointing his finger. '... should not be tossed aside lightly. It should be thrown with force!'

'What? Out the window?' The fishnet woman appeared at his side. 'I've heard that one before, Sebastian, you'll need to be more original than that. Anyway, what's wrong with the book?'

There was a rush of vehement opinion from different people: patronising ... *I believe in God ... egotism makes people want meaning beyond themselves ... who made the world then ... the title is a play on* The Unbearable Lightness of Being ... *I just love Kundera ... this chateau cardboard isn't so bad ... do you realise we're facing a world which could go into terminal anarchy ... are we to regard this as a mere transcendental presupposition for the notion of contingency ... when we compartmentalise, we live with inconsistent mindsets.*

This was Veronika's first Philosophy Society gathering. She wasn't sure if this was glittering genius or unadulterated twaddle.

Then everyone scrambled for more mugs as they passed around the last cask of wine. Sebastian cranked up the music. Out came a Smiths song. Cassie started singing along, something about feeling wrecked because the twenty-first century was breathing down their necks.

'Less than a decade till the new millennium,' Cassie shrieked, 'and Sebastian can't even bring himself out of the third century.'

'Ah – the third century. Let me see. The time of Tertullian. *I believe it because it is absurd.*' Sebastian smirked. 'Cass, you are too cruel.' He mimed a stab in his chest and turned his back on her. But then he was taking Veronika by the arm, taking her aside, whispering, telling her not to mind Cassie. That everyone knew she was a *phoney*.

'She's never been to England but speaks with a plum in her mouth. Her father owns an art gallery, so she thinks she knows everything about culture in this city. She told me she read *Don Quixote* at the age of nine and then the collected works of Goethe when she was fifteen. As *if.*' He shook his head. 'We were on opposite sides of a debate once,' he said. 'She couldn't argue her way out of a paper bag.'

Veronika ignored him. Thought him a bit mean, actually. But she didn't want to get into petty squabbles. She opened a page in the book she'd just been given by the guy in the leather jacket. Nietzsche. *Thus Spake Zarathustra.* She read aloud: *Courage … and adventure, and delight in the uncertain, in the unattempted – courage seemeth to me the entire primitive history of man.*

Sebastian took the book from her hands. 'That's it!' he said, jumping up onto a chair. 'We shall henceforth be called "the Players", like Zarathustra's stage players.' He struck a pontificator's pose. 'Zarathustra shall inspire us – and all the players in our play. Courage indeed! We shall achieve great things in the summer of nineteen ninety-five. The Players will perform on a new stage, and wow them with talent.' There were a few claps. Someone whistled.

He hopped off his chair. Smiled, moved in closer. 'Did I tell you I love the sound of your voice?' he said.

She had prepared the scene in front of the mirror. *Look, Figaro. My wreath of orange blossom. Do you like it better so?* She'd gone over it with Lucas reading the part of Figaro while the two of them waited at the bus stop before the audition. She'd remembered every line. She'd made a garland of honeysuckle to wear at the audition, along with her favourite red corduroy dress. She'd been told that redheads should never wear red but she loved to buck a trend; she'd stained her lips crimson. *Resourceful, intelligent, lively,* so the stage notes said of Suzanne, *not brazen.* No. She hadn't been brazen, had she? Wooden at first, maybe. Stilted. She'd heard such words used to describe actors. Felix, the German director, hadn't seemed all that inspired, and she'd been racked by nerves at the start. But when he gave her the script to Act Four, something seemed to shift. Suzanne and her betrothed setting up a trap for the Count. She'd enjoyed reading that part, a scene she hadn't prepared for. Maybe that's how it worked: some spontaneity thrown into the mix. And something changed for Felix as well: he became animated, full of ideas, fun to work with. She enjoyed the chunky rhythms of his accent, his energy. She liked his delicate, pale features, his lively gestures, his tight striped T-shirt, his nimble limbs. Everything about him, as he sprang around her, flirted a little, and she'd flirted back: *Love and you? ... Fie! You rascal! Is there more than one sort? ...* Had they *really* been flirting? *When it comes to love, you know, even too much isn't enough,* he'd said. Surely not. Surely it was just the script. And yet she'd forgotten that she was Veronika, forgotten her own life ... *I shall love none but my husband.* And Felix standing in for Figaro ... *Stick to that and you'll be a wonderful exception to the rule.*

It was funny. And intoxicating. Something had happened. Yes, she had become Suzanne. All the deception, the disguise, the game she and Figaro were preparing to play – it was perfection, all of it. It was the maddest scheme, the craziest thing she'd ever done. *I love to hear you talk nonsense. It shows how happy you are.* And she wanted more of it, as much as she could get. Maybe it had started as a ploy, Sebastian wanting to keep her near, but it had turned into something else, something new. She was grateful. Grateful to be feeling more alive.

Sebastian continued to pursue her ardently and with apparent sincerity. It was his gaze perhaps, or the way his brows hung low over his eyes, which gave him a kind of guilelessness, despite what she suspected were his carefully crafted remarks. There had been more lingering kisses. Phone calls. Notes. Extraordinary flowers like giant art shows delivered to her door. And he liked to offer instruction on military history and international affairs. Veronika knew nothing about either of these things. He'd also begun to think about buying shares in a telecommunications corporation, was developing an interest in politics, and was already working two days a week for an insurance company *to get some practice,* he told her, *with the real world.* He'd recently doorknocked for the local Liberal Party candidate. Veronika heard it in Sebastian's voice: that he was confident of *bigger things* for himself. She'd had a couple of boyfriends before, but they'd been insipid, unformed, while Sebastian had – what was it? – a golden air about him. A halo. Deputy head boy at his school and vice-captain of the rugby team. A baritone in the school choir. He'd boasted that his school had been established by his great-grandfather, an Anglican minister who'd brought *pragmatic and puritan Anglicanism to the settlers.*

Veronika liked Sebastian's air of certitude. She liked the way her disorganised, scattered self could be received by him without effort. The way he contained all that floated around inside her – there would be no spilling over. She liked his voice: deep, modulated, with a muted accent, so different from her own. When she spoke with him, she heard in her own speech the intonation of her grandmother. The tones of earth, hands and body – words from the Swan Valley orchards, old Czech words of her father's. Sebastian used words and phrases she didn't understand, like *abrogation, filibustering, unicameral*. She would look up such words when she got home, then repeat them into her mirror. And while his days of singing in the cathedral choir as a boy had long gone, he entertained a vague notion of God, which Veronika could not bring herself to follow. Still, she thought, as long as one of them believed, she could make do with that as well.

He asked her to go with him to his father's surgery to collect an important book. She saw a waiting room full of canvases that looked like colourful insects exploding in all directions and beautiful kimonos set in glass on the wall. Gorgeous art books on a glossy table. Classy. But when Sebastian's father called them into his surgery, he completely ignored her and barely acknowledged his son. He disappeared behind thick glasses and pushed a book into Sebastian's hand: *The Measure of the Years*. It was only later that Veronika realised Sebastian must have dragged her there to show off. She even suspected he'd put the book in his father's briefcase.

He told her that the book was *an oldie but a goodie*, the biography of a former prime minister, Robert Menzies. *Sir* Robert Menzies, who'd led the country for nearly twenty years.

Veronika confessed she'd never heard of him.

'But he's famous, Ronnie.'

He'd never called her Ronnie before. Or used the word *famous* to rebuke her.

A formal invitation from Sebastian's mother followed to *attend* a Sunday afternoon tea. Veronika had never been invited to an afternoon tea before, but having seen his father's art, his books, his studied air, she suspected it would be a great deal more than a mug of Lipton's with a dash of milk.

The family home was in Cottesloe. An imposing stone house with a tennis court and an enormous swimming pool. Sebastian guided her into a spacious hall saturated with the scent of wild liliums, three vases full, placed artfully on a glass console. Mirrors in elaborate gold frames hung from various walls. She wondered how they could live like this, with not a thing out of place. Beige-coloured furniture filled the room. She saw plump lounges with patterned, fringed cushions, Oriental glass lamps, and more mirrors and cushions, more artfully placed ceramic ornaments, and tasteful wooden blinds that opened onto views of a sumptuous garden. It was all so splendid, so opulent, so unlike her family home with its old shabby furniture and fustian throws, its haphazard, fading rugs.

They sat under enormous striped umbrellas. Sebastian's mother, an angular fifty-something woman with bobbed hair and too much rouge, had ushered them into the garden. She offered champagne served in thick crystal glasses with thin rims. Vivienne Harper-Jones was an eager sipper of champagne, it seemed, even for an afternoon tea. After her third top-up, she laughed thrillingly, throwing her head back and gulping the liquid down. Bedecked in heavy jewellery and wearing an asymmetrical dress, she appeared almost sculptural. Regal. She served pumpkin scones and opened another bottle of champagne. Veronika liked the enormous Japanese pepper trees under which they sat. She thought how lovely it would be to live in a place where there was always the smell of the ocean and endless glasses of champagne.

A neighbour, Mrs Brierly, had also been invited and was talking incessantly about gardening and plant diseases. Lamenting that red cabbage and parsnips were no longer in season and that a politician she adored would not be in Cabinet this year. Now. What was Veronika studying at university? French. Ah yes, such a romantic language, although the French, it must be said, were inclined to arrogance.

Vivienne rattled on about a concert she'd recently attended. 'Imagine having to manage a double bass!' she said. 'A woman, what's more.' After each phrase, she raised her eyebrows.

'Women *can* play the double bass, mother,' Sebastian said.

'I am sure they can play, my dear, but whether they *ought* to is another question altogether.'

Mrs Brierly turned to Veronika. 'Do *you* play the double bass?' she asked.

'No. Not at all.'

'Oh, what a relief,' Vivienne said, settling back into her chair.

The phone rang. 'I'll get it,' Sebastian's father called out from his study. There was a dead moment as they sat there. 'Seb, it's for you. Your rugby coach. Wants a word.'

'If you will excuse me,' Sebastian said.

His mother shuffled forward on her chair: 'Do tell me, Veronika, what does your family *do*?'

'Well,' she began, with some trepidation, 'my father runs an orchard—'

'An orchard?' Vivienne exclaimed. 'Isn't he clever!'

'It's in his blood,' Veronika said. 'His own father cultivated fruit in Czechoslovakia, and his family, for several generations.'

'Well, I never …'

'They left everything behind, my grandparents. Their land. The orchard.'

Mrs Brierly pursed her lips. 'Australia was good to them, I gather?' she said. It didn't sound like a question.

'It was tough for them,' Veronika said. 'Neither of them had much English when they arrived. People used to shout at them or speak to them as if they were stupid. My grandfather learned more Italian than English because he ended up working with Italians.'

'Well. What an adventure it must have been for them,' Mrs Brierly said.

'And your mother?' said Vivienne.

'Oh, my mother … she works in the orchard too. She's also a housewife. Devoted to my father, to my sister and me.'

'Devotion.' Vivienne sipped her champagne. 'A lovely quality in a mother.' She eyed Veronika carefully. 'I'll expect you'll want children,' she said. 'When you're older. Exactly how old are you, Veronika?'

And so the afternoon dragged on in this polite and limpid way. When Vivienne turned her attention to Mrs Brierly, Veronika wandered out into the garden. It was crowded with earthenware seating and clay pots filled with voluptuous ferns and feathery plants. She felt suddenly overcome by all the pots and the talk and the heavy jewels and found herself falling softly on the grass. She looked up and saw stars beginning to dot the sky. It was cold but she didn't care. She didn't know why the world was moving, why she felt so odd and delicious and dizzy, or why things weren't quite how they'd seemed before. She began to laugh, breathing in the heady scent of jasmine. And then she saw Sebastian peering down at her face.

'So you had a good time?'

She nodded. Or thought she did.

He took a deep breath. 'God, you're beautiful.'

She'd been laughing so much there were tears in her eyes. She felt flush. Wanton.

'I know what I'd like to do with you,' he said. 'But I'm in my parents' garden. So get up now. Come on.'

Veronika couldn't stop laughing.

He gave her his hand and hoisted her up. She lost her balance and fell into his arms, still clutching her empty glass. He prized it out of her hand.

'Delicious pumpkin scones,' she said with sincerity. 'What's happening to me?'

'You're drunk.' He steadied her. 'We'd better take you home, missy.'

She was sober enough to know that she had embarrassed him. She'd done it all wrong, been too free with herself. She should have prepared things to say, had questions to ask. Sebastian knew how to make polite conversation. A handsome, well-built man, he stood solidly on the ground, and his solidity reassured her.

He drove her home in an old Saab his parents had given him because they no longer wanted it, he said. So much red leather, she said, but only two seats, not very practical ... where did he put all the shopping ... or random furniture from the curbs ...

She looked out the window as they drove along Cottesloe Beach. A beach. Starfish Bay ... Joshua ... by the sea. She could hear his voice as if he were right there, could see him dissolve in a rush of crashing waves. His thick mop of hair ... long arms and agile hands, forming pictures of his thoughts. His eyes, like chunks of ice, the colour of the sea, sea that was falling in front of him ... her ... and their feet had sunk into the sand under the moving white foam as they began to run, in and out, chasing the end of waves making zigzags across the shore, as if they'd always be running in the shadows of twilight.

The car stopped in front of the warehouse. Sebastian coughed.

'I suppose this is where I should invite you in,' she said.

'I suppose it is.'

She heard the hesitation in his voice.

Had he forgiven her? He must have forgiven her. He'd told her she was beautiful. That he wanted to do things to her. Was it her difference that he wanted? That she wasn't a Jessica or Victoria. That she didn't know the things he knew. The funny words she used, words about working the land and the sound of birds, such as *ručně dělat, úroda, ptačí zpěv* and, when she swore, with the occasional *ježiš marja!*

'Veronika Vaček,' he would say whenever he introduced her. Pronouncing her name with precision, guiding her with his hand on the small of her back.

He didn't come in, after all. Was he trying to make her want him even more? Or was he waiting for marriage? Did he want to do *the right thing*? But they were much too young to get married. Or maybe he needed a wife on his arm as he went about making his way in the world. She realised how little she knew about him, and he about her. They'd never talked of such things, and she wasn't sure how to begin.

So yes, she was relieved when he said he had to prepare for one of his final exams.

When she and Sebastian turned up for their next rehearsal, they found a glum-looking Felix waiting outside the door. They no longer had a space, he said. They had been kicked out. The groundsman had caught him smoking again, and despite Felix's pleas, the *Dummkopf* had made good on his warning.

'So where are the others?' Sebastian said.

'The pub.' Felix shook his head. 'Always the pub when things go wrong.' He sighed. 'It is my fault,' he said. 'I have been a disappointing.'

'I know a place,' Veronika said. 'My parents. I could ask them.'

7. Joshua

Josh had been weeding all day when Veronika entered the kitchen. They exchanged brief, startled hellos. She faltered, asking him how he was twice in a row, and brushed stray curls behind her ear. She was as lovely as ever, taller somehow, hair tied to the side, face fresh and freckled. Eyes – like wounds.

He wanted to give her a hug or at least take her by the hand, but he hadn't had a shower and his nails were rimmed with dirt. He poured her a glass of water and was so lost for words, it was a relief when Angela came in, urging Veronika to stay for dinner, asking Josh if he would like that too. *I see her so rarely*, Angela said. Veronika volunteered to fetch some herbs from the garden. Josh offered to set the table. Putting down the plates, he was hit with a sudden déjà vu: Starfish Bay. Dinner with the whole family at Old Mrs Vaček's. Felt like aeons ago.

Shit! He dropped a plate. It shattered all over the linoleum. He cleaned it up with the dustpan and newspaper. What a klutz.

He'd always thought he'd see Veronika back at the orchard one day, but he'd never imagined it would take so long. And now that she was finally back, now that they would be sitting down to dinner and talking, not talking, he realised he hadn't been prepared for this. For her.

'I think she's getting ideas, going to university, all the skinny girls who think curves are out of date,' Angela said. 'It's plain nonsense.'

Michal tucked into his roast pork, nodding in agreement; Veronika definitely needed *fattening up*. She's perfect as she is, Josh thought, but he didn't dare say a thing. Veronika mentioned an exam coming up.

'*Knedlíky*,' Michal said, digging into *the tastiest dumplings in the Southern Hemisphere*. Josh caught Veronika's eye at last and she gave him one of those looks that said *see what I put up with*? Her face was the sweetest refuge – even if she hadn't yet smiled. He would have to jolt himself out of staring at her all evening. Still, he felt like he could put up with anything as long as she was there.

Maybe she was upset, seeing how much he had changed. He noticed her looking at the scars on his arms and hands, at his grazed knuckles, and wondered whether she would ask him about the scars. About the ones you couldn't see, from his time in juvenile detention. But he was out now, free, had been for years. And just last month, Michal had given him a job. Tried to make him feel at home.

Angela delivered them some sort of cake fresh from the oven. Josh tasted poppyseed and pears hot and melting in his mouth. Angela asked Veronika to stay the night, but she said she had to get back to Perth.

Was there a man to get back to? Josh wondered if he'd get a chance to speak to her alone.

Veronika pushed her dessert aside and began to fiddle with her spoon.

Angela stood, walked to the sideboard, picked up a faded colour photograph, gave it to Josh.

'Michal's mother,' she said. 'Her *babička*, Tereza Vaček. Veronika has my reddish hair, you see, but the braids make her look so much like Mum.'

Josh squinted at the picture. True, Veronika and her grandmother had the same high forehead and cheekbones, and there was something ethereal about them both. Was Angela trying to make a point? That Veronika shouldn't forget about her family?

'Poor Babička died just before I turned sixteen,' Veronika said. 'You met her too, didn't you, Josh?' Josh nodded, unsure of what to say. It was too late to offer condolences. He recalled old Mrs Vaček – a gentle, talkative lady with a neck like a tree trunk and hair as white as moonflower. Angela put the photo back on the sideboard, turned to her daughter. 'Ronnie, do you ever think of Babička?'

Veronika put down her spoon. 'Of course,' she said. 'I remember her stories.'

'So many of them,' Michal added.

'Like the first time she went to church in Australia.' Veronika turned to Josh. 'Babička was living in an immigration camp and didn't know she had to wear a hat when she went to church. She said everyone stared at her. The foreigner. And then she and some friends from the camp went for a walk. They gathered up armfuls of purple flowers and decorated the church with them. And they got into trouble. They didn't realise they were weeds – Paterson's curse.'

'And her story about the long journey in the boat,' Michal said. 'A whole month jammed in with others, all the women and children stacked up together in beds. But there were games, too, and learning English, learning about the Australian animals. She was so disappointed when she landed and couldn't see an emu or a kangaroo.'

'She was given a piece of fruitcake when she stepped off the ship,' Veronika said. 'She was thrilled about that.'

Angela shook her head. 'She said the camp was horrible. Insects and rabbits and terrible heat. Awful food.'

'Boiled potatoes, I remember her telling us,' Veronika said. 'Stringy stew and tasteless soup. But she loved hearing other languages, and the way the children had to point at things to communicate. They made up a language of gestures. Poor Grandpa arrived on a separate ship which took six weeks longer. He got stuck in Gibraltar. You know, he was made to work on a pipeline for two years?'

'It was either that or being a lumberjack in Canada,' Michal said, chortling. 'He didn't have the physique for that.'

'I could have been Canadian,' Veronika said. 'Imagine, Josh. We would never have met.'

Josh wondered what she meant, but again he didn't dare speak.

'The Aussies got in first,' Michal said. 'In the refugee camp, in Moschendorf, a day before the Canadians. My parents wanted out. It was pure chance they ended up here.'

'Or maybe it was meant to be,' Josh said finally and smiled shyly at Veronika.

'Lucky Babička was trained as a seamstress,' Veronika said.

'A milliner, actually,' Angela said. 'In the refugee camp, they were taught skills. That's where she learned millinery.'

'But they were also bored, frozen and starving,' Michal said.

'They were proud of you,' Angela said, stroking her husband's arm. 'Getting the market garden growing, and then the orchard.'

'I miss Babička,' Veronika said.

Josh felt a sort of vertigo with all this family talk. He wanted to match their stories with some of his own. But all he had were broken threads and bruises. Not an anecdote to his name.

'She adored you,' Angela said.

Veronika nodded. 'She knew what kids wanted. Me, anyway. She let me play on my own.' She looked across at her father. 'Speaking of plays,' she said. 'I have a favour to ask you both. A big one.'

8. Veronika

'You look so different, Josh,' she said. His face was the same, but his eyes looked more knowing, somehow. He'd grown his hair, too, tied it back. And he'd filled out, looked less boyish. But his enormous grin hadn't changed, was still filled with skewed teeth.

He was leaning against the wall of the packing shed, watching her intently.

'Different?' he said. 'How so?'

'You look older.'

He frowned. 'It's been six years, Ronnie.'

She heard an edge in his voice and didn't know how to respond.

'Wait here,' he said. 'I've got a … kind of surprise.'

He disappeared inside while she waited in the warmth of the evening. All the trees she could see were bearing pale pink plums. It was the ideal viewpoint: the valley on her left, the eucalypts fringing the orchard on the other side. And it was quiet, except for the currawongs calling. Great masses of clouds gathered. All this too, was the same, with Fred and Ginger jumping round her ankles, glad to have her home. Her spaniels, her parents, the orchard and now Josh. Little pieces of her past all coming together, like a quilt being shaken out, showing all its patches.

Josh had seemed so shy over dinner. But then he'd always been shy, and she hadn't really known what to say to him, either. She hadn't even known that he'd be there, that he was working on the orchard.

He called her from inside to come into the packing shed. He beckoned her to climb a ladder and showed her what he'd made: a second-level bedroom of sorts, with a mattress and rumpled sheets, an alarm clock on the floor. A small ledge with piles of clothing, an old bookshelf crammed with large print books on travel. Five small square canvases of wild-looking paintings, great whorls of colour.

He handed her an object. A simple, rough sculpture of a girlish figure. She could make out the shape of a flared skirt.

'A ballerina carving,' he said. 'I made it for you. When I was put away. In Longmore.'

She didn't know what to say.

'You loved dancing,' he said. 'You wanted to be a ballerina.'

She shook her head. 'Not anymore. I grew too tall. Anyway, you were always the creative one. Good at making things.' She pointed to the canvases. 'Are those your paintings? They're so … dramatic. Eye-catching.'

'Nah. They're Warra's pictures. A mate in Longmore. I tried painting but I was rubbish. Sculpture was better. I did six weeks of it, and the teacher let me make this. For you. She brought in some sandalwood especially.'

'It's beautiful, Josh. Thank you.'

Josh shuffled about on the spot. 'Let's sit,' he said. 'No chairs, but.'

He pointed to the mattress with a flourish, as if making fun of the situation. Of himself. She felt a surge of pity wash over her.

They settled onto the mattress, leaning against the wall.

'Superbly comfortable,' she said and straight away wished that she hadn't.

'So. You're working for my folks,' she continued. 'How did that happen?'

'Well, after I got out of juvie, I had a few other jobs. Then I drove a truck up north in the mines for a couple of years till I got laid off. I didn't do anything … wrong, I mean … I wanted to come back to Perth. I've been out of there for four years, you know.'

He paused, looked at her closely, and she felt her body tighten. Did he come back for me, she thought. Surely not.

'I took whatever work I could find,' he said. 'Kitchen hand. Brickie's labourer. I managed to save some money. And then, out of the blue, I ran into your mum and dad in town and the next thing I know, I'm working here.'

'So, what do you do?'

'Spraying and fertilising, that kind of thing. Sweeping and cleaning. Netting the trees to keep away the possums and cockatoos. Helping your dad with the reticulation, the weeding. Oh, and I'm fixing the roof after this big storm we had. Your dad's been teaching me about the crops, the different plants around the place.'

'And do you like it here?' she said. 'The work?'

'It's good, yeah. I like being out of doors. The fresh air. Your mum's garden. Her cooking. And your dad's a good bloke. They've been … well, kind to me. Like family.'

She remembered his stories of a dead mother, a father who'd *shot through* when he and Charlie were kids.

'So, how's *your* family?' she said. 'Charlie, I mean.'

Josh reddened. 'Dunno. Somewhere up north. He sent me a fucking postcard. No contact details.'

Josh hardly ever swore, she knew. And he didn't get angry. Not often, anyway, as far as she recalled.

'You rescued me from your brother,' she said. 'You know that, don't you?'

He shrugged.

'When Charlie burned my hair. When he ...'

'Messed with you.'

She placed her hand on his arm, saw him flinch. 'He was just bragging, Josh. Trying to make my sister jealous. Nothing happened, honestly.'

Josh unclenched his hands, his scarred, gnarled hands, and turned to face her.

'When I was locked up,' he said. 'For a while there, you were all I could think about.'

'Oh. I ...'

'The thought of you.'

'Josh—'

'Kept me going, you know ... but ... you didn't come to see me.'

His face was tight with pleading, and again she was lost for words. This wasn't what she remembered: the ease of them together as kids. When words had been beside the point.

He turned his back to her and moved away some books from his bookshelf, retrieved something small wrapped in delicate white tissue and gave it to her.

'Josh! This is too much.' She tentatively unplucked the ribbons. She couldn't believe it: her grandmother's necklace. She had called it her harlequin rose from Czechia. It was an Art Nouveau design, almost antique, a string of tiny crystal roses that were green and yellow and cherry. The colours emanated a peculiar vibrancy.

'You left it in the tree house,' Josh said. 'Remember? When we ... the fire ... I went to get it. I knew it meant so much.'

Of course she remembered. She thought she had lost it.

He explained to her how he'd put it in a wooden trinket box, dug a hole, right in the ground underneath the tree house and buried it. He went looking for it when he came out of juvie and dug it up quite easily. He cleaned it and kept it for when he'd see her. He just didn't know it would take so many years.

She felt a terrible pang. 'How can I ever thank you?' She kissed it and bundled it into her pocket.

He looked down onto the ground, then up again into her eyes. 'So. You're doing a play,' he said.

She nodded, relieved that he'd changed the subject. 'I love it,' she said. 'I love acting. I feel like … how can I explain it? I feel like I'm being carried through this magical stream of time. It's like something's flowing through me … it's like a kind of forgetting, the best kind of forgetting.'

She could see he was trying hard to follow.

'And then I have to come back to the real world, the dreary old world.' She laughed. 'Does that make any sense?'

'I don't know anything about acting,' Josh said. 'But there was this play we studied … *Our Town*, it was called. And there's a line … this woman attends her own funeral, and she looks back over her life and says, *Oh, earth, you're too wonderful for anybody to realise you.* It kind of got to me. I wanted to know what that felt like. To feel that life was wonderful. I … I …'

She didn't know if he would keep going. Whether she even wanted him to keep going.

'I was in juvie,' he said. 'It was fucked up. I kept punching the asbestos walls, thinking if only I punched hard enough, I could get out. But then they moved me to a cell with brick walls, only I tried punching them out as well. Broke my right hand.' He looked away, looked back at her. 'But I never punched anyone, Ronnie,' he said. 'Some of the other guys would beat each other up, but not me. Just the walls.'

She gripped the sculpture tightly.

'Sometimes …' He stopped, started again. 'Sometimes people would stare at me. After I got out. Waiting for me to do something wrong. It freaked me out. Made me feel sick.'

She went to touch him but stopped herself. 'You're free now, Josh,' she said. 'You don't have to look over your shoulder.' And I didn't come to visit you, she thought. Not once. She could tell him that her parents thought she'd feel afraid, how they'd insisted she was only a child. But she was fourteen years old, hardly a child, and how could she tell him that she hadn't fought hard enough to see him? That in fact she hadn't fought at all. That she'd done as she was told. Taken the easy way out.

45

'It's so good to have you back,' she said, and jumped off the mattress, climbed down the ladder, said it was time to go home. Goodnight, Joshua, goodnight. With nothing else to say.

Lying in her own bed, unsettled, unhappy, she couldn't shake off the memory of Charlie. The brother who was always in trouble with the police, *the menace, the ratbag*, the locals called him. Hanging out with dodgy people, getting into fights. The day he'd lit a match, malice in his eyes, laughing in strange convulsions as he moved in closer, burned off the edge of her plaits. Still laughing, a muscular boy in a ripped singlet, a shark-tooth necklace, while she was screaming, screaming, terrified that all of her would shoot up in flames. And then another voice, another boy, Joshua, a tall, skinny boy, a rush of vile words and kicking and shouting and she could see the sky, sideways, imagined angels tumbling, sweeping up the clouds with sweet music. The angel boy with his dark hair, making Charlie disappear.

She'd kept patting her hair. Two smoky-smelling stumps at the end of elastic bands.

But then another memory came back to her: Starfish Bay. She could still see the bonfire. Charlie getting drunk and Ana getting angry, Charlie belching out apologies to *Ana's little sister … I've been such a bad boy, Ronnie …* Josh leaping up, wrestling Charlie to the ground, people egging them on, fists and blood, Josh pushing his brother away, standing, turning around, disappearing into the night. She had followed him. Into the darkness. Called his name until she was hoarse. No answer. It had been too dark, so she turned to trace the light of the bonfire. She found Charlie singing happy birthday to Ana, then kissing her right in front Veronika, after he'd lured her to the island on the catamaran only a day before. Charlie, reaching into a pile of branches, lighting them one by one, handing them to each person. He grabbed Ana's arm and the two of them trotted down the beach, each with a branch in flame.

They had turned into the national park, where Josh might have gone.

She tried to think of something pure, something bright and shining, before everything went wrong. Like when she was a child, collecting autumn leaves and placing small stones in matchboxes, talking to them, naming them, checking on them every day. The freshness of the afternoon breeze sweeping away the heat and all the feelings that churned up inside her. And the books. Babička's house at Starfish Bay. Her old books.

Peer Gynt and some plays by Chekhov and Czech writers with unpronounceable names. Veronika had studied the letters, imagining how they might sound. She liked the idea of a play best of all, as if characters could creep out of the page and begin to speak to her.

A play. She pictured Sebastian, in Perth, waiting for her return. He'd urged her not to stay away too long.

9. Sebastian

He was standing at the gazebo in Kings Park, surveying the Players while waiting for that damned smoking Felix to arrive and hand out their scripts. Sebastian wasn't pleased about the new arrangement: leaving at the crack of dawn, rehearsing in an orchard. It was a long drive from the city in the heat. And he was nervous about meeting Veronika's parents. It was as if she'd kept them hidden. As if she was ashamed of them. Why would she be ashamed of them? Her father was obviously a salt-of-the-earth kind, and a businessman to boot, and her mother couldn't be any worse than his own: the way she'd eyed poor Veronika up and down, put on her usual airs. He was fed up with his family, bored with hanging around in the heat, and now Cassie was carrying on about selling your birthright for something or other. She was such a poser.

He looked across the vista of the city, under a sky tinged with pink. Down by Barrack Street Jetty, a slow ferry slipped across the skin of the river. Cars like tiny ants crawled up Great Eastern Highway towards the hills. Skyscrapers mirrored in the gleam of the water. This is what the city has become, he thought: his great-great-grandfather's home away from home. A land of banks, steel and glass. Productivity and potential.

'It's all a façade,' Cassie said, as if she could read his mind. 'A façade of happy white patriarchal capitalism. But underneath all these symbols of masculine progress, there's the river. *That* – that is the city's repressed femininity.' She held out her arms as if presenting an exhibit.

Sebastian guffawed. 'Aren't we lucky then, that you haven't repressed yours.'

'I'm more worried about the fruit picking,' Lucas said.

Sebastian startled. Veronika gave him a wide-eyed smile.

'We won't need to pick the fruit until harvest time,' she said. 'We have three weeks until then. That's a good five weeks at the orchard. It will be bonding. It might even be fun.'

'What if it's too hot?' Cassie wailed.

'How come I didn't know about this harvest business?' Sebastian said, to no-one in particular.

'Because you got here late,' Lucas said. '*I* was on time.'

'For once!' Gloria said. 'Look, I'm not sold on this idea. We can't afford to spend the summer prancing around an orchard rehearsing a French play. I'm working at the Blue Moon three nights a week. Gotta pay the bills.'

'And I have some shifts at the bookshop,' Veronika said, 'but we can make it work.'

'You're not the only ones,' Sebastian said. 'I'm in the firm Thursdays and Fridays.'

'As if you have any bills,' Cassie said.

Veronika looked at each of them in turn, pleading. 'Felix has the schedule all worked out. It won't interfere with our work. With study. He knows some of us have exams and jobs and that we will come and go and stay when we can. And ... well, Dad is relying on us now.'

Sebastian shook his head. 'Where the hell is Felix?' he said, seething now, unhappy. Even, just a little, with Veronika. She was captivating, she was smart, she responded to his touch, but she hadn't deigned to set him apart. Made him feel special. Chosen. Just as he'd chosen her.

10. Felix

So sorry to be late, he said, but he couldn't get his kombi to start. He'd tinkered around under the bonnet, opening gaskets, checking oil, the water and various pipes and screws. He'd prayed in English, telling God that his car was *kaput*. Then he'd kicked the side of his van and it seemed to have worked. He'd nearly run down a couple of tourists in his hurry, he said, and then there were policemen on horseback blocking the way, piles of horse shit so high, he said. He couldn't stop talking, he knew: no breakfast, too many cigarettes, and the fear that the Players would all go away. Ruin his plans.

But once he handed out the scripts, everyone smiled. Well, most of them smiled. Sebastian was ... how did you say it? He was looking like daggers.

'Time to go,' Felix said, and they jumped into action.

A few of them piled into his van: Veronika, Gwen and Lucas. Sebastian slunk into his Saab. Gloria took Lucas in her car. Felix drove down the leafy promenade out of Kings Park, then past many shiny apartments as he dodged all the cyclists madly pedalling around the river. He checked the rear-view mirror. Gloria's car was still behind them. He knew nothing about her except her long, long journey as a child across a vast ocean, when she'd been more terrified of sea monsters than the soldiers left behind on the shore. She'd once told the group that she and her family lived in a bungalow by the river, had joined the local church and were disappointed by the tuneless singing. And then the family heard the news: her brother had been killed in Díli.

He crossed the Causeway, drove past ugly yards selling trucks and rental cars, past more apartments with spindly palm trees out the front. Still, at least there was space in this city and big fluffy clouds. The place continued to astonish him: such bright sun, vistas that seemed to vanish into endless light. A city of horizons. Then more ugliness along the highway: Tyre Centre, Liquorland, Barbecue Kingdom, Supa Valu, Flag Motor Inn. But still, this was a place of possibility, where space unfurled without end. It went to your head, as if you could climb the sky.

11. Sebastian

After an hour of driving, they arrived in a deep green valley with hills tilting to either side. Fruit trees rimmed with bushes: bottlebrush, he knew, and towering eucalypts, although the names of other trees escaped him. And then the house: a rather ugly building, modelled on the Hellenic style, complete with a fountain at the entrance. Two stone sculptures of nude angels kissing, their lips forming an energetic spout of water. Such extravagance, really, he thought, despite what he assumed were the family's modest means. He waved at Veronika once he'd parked, but she was too busy to respond, fossicking for things in the van.

They piled out of the kombi, pulled out their bags, their costumes, pieces of scenery. A man – tall, swarthy, smiling – came out of the house, greeted them with a tray of breakfast food. Sausages and pancakes. Announced himself as Michal. Veronika took the tray from his hands, pecked Michal on the cheek, then turned to face the crew.

'My father,' she said with a smile. 'But my mother is the cook.'

Sebastian waited to be introduced, but Michal was ushering them along, Veronika leading the way. A slim, titian-haired woman in a spotted sundress was standing by a long wooden tray laden with food.

'My mother,' Veronika said to the group. 'Angela.'

Again Sebastian waited to be introduced, but everyone was rushing to tuck in: muffins, grapes, bottles of cider. Gaudy napkins. He stood aside, made his way to Veronika's father.

'Mr Vaček,' he said, trying to sound decisive. 'I understand we'll be assisting with the harvest.'

'Too right. We should be ready to start picking in a few weeks or so. Two thousand trees out there.' He gestured to the orchard. 'Fifteen hectares' worth. One hundred plums per tree. Two weeks' work – maybe ten days with you lot going hard at it.'

Everyone stopped eating.

Felix cleared his throat. 'Is the cider from your apples?'

'From the bottle store,' Michal said. 'It's the same at the Sunday market.'

People ask me how to make peach preserve and plum jam. Ha! I don't bloody know, I say; I just run an orchard, not the CWA.'

'CWA?' said Gloria.

'Country Women's Association,' Veronika said and bit into a muffin.

Sebastian munched in silence.

After breakfast, Veronika led the way to a shed. A packing shed, she called it, big enough for all the Players to sleep in. Sebastian glanced around the space: a giant aluminium space. It was organised into different parts, everything *just so*. One section had been filled with machines and metallic contraptions, but Sebastian did not know what they were for. Hovering outside, wondering what to do, wondering what could be done in this strange new place, he saw two ponies and a horse out in the paddock. He heard the screech of cockatoos, raucous, bothersome, swirling high above him.

He heard footsteps behind him and turned.

'Bloody pests!' Michal said. 'I chase them with my tractor.'

Veronika's mother smiled. Sebastian had no idea if the man was joking.

Lucas grabbed a small apple from a tree near the shed, but Michal didn't seem to mind, launching into talk of California apples, how he mostly grew peaches, as well as apricots and plums, a special kind of plum that they mustn't eat before it was ripe unless they liked stomach-aches. Sebastian wanted to speak to Veronika's father. He wanted him to know who he was. But he didn't have a chance because the man kept talking … picking … Usually a couple of weeks picking, but maybe less with all of you here … waxing the fruit … putting stickers on them. Lucas groaned.

Gloria began rummaging through a large canvas bag. She drew out a lacy dress and some black velvet waistcoats.

'But they're stained,' Veronika's mother said. 'And they need stitching. Here, give them to me. I can fix them.'

'Oh, Mrs Vaček!' Gloria gushed. 'That's so kind of you. And … well, we need some costumes made from scratch. Cassie has all the material; her dad got it from Europe. Some of it's from Spain.'

Sebastian drew himself up. 'I'm sure Mrs Vaček has better things to do,' he said.

'Call me Angela, please.' She turned from Sebastian to Gloria. 'I'd love to make some costumes,' she said. 'My mother-in-law – now there was a woman who was good with a thread. A milliner, she was. Taught me a thing or two.'

Sebastian forced a smile, tried to look interested.

'Besides,' Angela said, 'I'd like to get a bit involved. In your play. Whatever it's about.'

'I'll help you,' Gwen said, twirling around in her tartan miniskirt. 'See this skirt? I revamped it from an old kilt. I'm pretty resourceful. I can get to work on the costumes after I'm done with all the posters.'

Sebastian looked across at Veronika, tried to catch her eye, but she was laughing along with Gwen, as though the sight of a tartan skirt was a source of great hilarity. Why didn't she take his hand and say: *Mother. Father. This is Sebastian. My boyfriend.* It couldn't be that hard.

'What's your play called?' Angela said. 'Veronika told me, but I've forgotten.'

Everyone chimed in: *The Marriage of Figaro ... French ... Seventeen seventy-eight ... otherwise known as The Follies of a Day.*

'And there's a wedding,' Gloria said, clapping her hands. 'Suzanne and Figaro.'

Sebastian grinned, and before he could stop himself: '*Veronika's getting married to me.*' He saw Angela's puzzled face. He twitched. 'I mean in the play,' he said. 'Veronika is Suzanne, and I'm Figaro.'

Angela nodded. 'Is there a wedding dress?' she asked. 'I can make one, if there isn't.'

Felix beamed. 'Wonderful!' he said. 'A wedding dress for a Spanish servant girl, but it must be in the style of the eighteenth century. That is the precise charm of the play.'

'Frills! Hooray!' Cassie squealed.

Michal looked Sebastian in the eye. 'So it's a love story,' he said.

Gwen smoothed down her skirt. 'It's a story of love thwarted,' she said. 'The Count tries to seduce his wife's maid. Suzanne. But ...' She twirled around once more. 'It's complicated.'

Sebastian felt angry the rest of the day. There'd been no special introduction, no introduction at all, to Veronika's parents. He'd been herded along with the rest of them, as he wandered without purpose in the orchard. Wishing he was drunk. Or back at his desk at the firm. Or playing rugby. His sneakers were getting dirty, and now some geese were approaching, menace in their eyes. He began to sweat.

Every time he'd tried to talk to Veronika, she was busy with something or talking to someone in the cast. As if she was avoiding him. He couldn't even find a time to ask her: are you avoiding me? How do you feel about me? I know as little about you as I know about Californian apples and some special kind of plum and chasing squawking birds with a tractor.

The geese were getting closer, and one of them nudged his hand, saw that it was empty. It bit Sebastian's thumb and honked.

12. Cassie

Sebastian, bitten by a goose! Cassie had to laugh. She was meant to be memorising her lines, but it had been far more entertaining watching him stumble about the orchard.

'Serves you right,' she called out across the trees.

Sebastian turned around and sighed. He looked defeated. Then the corners of his mouth curved up. He gazed at her for a moment, as if sizing her up. She could feel herself being noticed. She straightened her back. Shook out her hair a little, then left the shade.

'Are you alright?' she said, approaching him. 'Where are you going, Sebastian?'

'To get my things,' he muttered. 'I've had enough.'

'That's ridiculous!' He began to turn away. 'You simply *cannot* leave. Stop. Stay here.' He was rubbing his fingers, and she felt a rush of pity now, for his wanting to leave, for hurt the honking goose had caused him. 'Give me your hand,' she said.

'It's nothing serious.'

She took his hand and slowly traced her fingers around his palm, circled three small sores. The goose had *actually* drawn blood.

'Let me fix this,' she said.

And then ... was it possible? Was he giving her *that* look? She felt her heart thumping. She looked at him.

'It's not just the goose bite, is it?'

No-one seemed to be inside when they reached the house, and Cassie wasted no time. She dashed to the bathroom, then rifled around in a cabinet for a bandage, for anything useful.

'Eureka!' she said. 'A first-aid kit.'

She rushed back to the living room, plonked herself next to Sebastian on the sofa. She applied the Dettol to his palm, trying not to shake. She slowly wound the bandage around his hand. She could have wound and wound around all afternoon. She thought of Chérubin's stolen bloodied ribbon. Perhaps this bandage could be a love token, she thought. *Poor Sebastian.* She should ... maybe ...

'Trouble in paradise?' she said.

Sebastian grimaced. 'She *says* she wants to be with me. She *says* she cares for me. But her *actions*, Cass, her actions …'

Cassie kept her eyes on the bandage, kept her hands steady as she fastened the safety pin.

'There,' she said. 'All better now.'

Sebastian shook his head. He looked hurt, like a sulky little boy. 'She's so unfair to me, Cass. She doesn't even sit through my whole rugby match. She ducks off and goes for a bloody walk – God knows where to – and then comes back saying *well played*. As if I am stupid. As if I didn't know she'd taken off.'

Then – just like that! – he put his bandaged arm around her waist and drew her into him. So what else could she do but nestle her head into his neck.

'Don't quit the play,' she said quietly. 'Not because of some silly goose. Not because of any sort of … goose.' She tapped her finger on his nose, affectionately. She wouldn't do anymore, not yet.

'Please don't leave,' she said.

'Hey, what do you think of the poster?' A voice bounced off the walls. It was Gwen. She had finished her handiwork.

13. Felix

That afternoon, Felix made his way down the valley and found a clearing among the trees, next to a creek. It seemed to be the only flat piece of land in the orchard, apart from where the house was standing. It could be their stage, he thought. *Eine Waldbühne.* Their theatre among the trees.

He quickly summoned the Players to the space, hoping to get started. Hoping for joy. But they arrived looking distracted, moody: Lucas wanting to work on some scenery, Sebastian complaining of his allergy to dogs, sneezing relentlessly. Veronika standing with hands on hips, as though daring Sebastian to be quiet. Gloria and Gwen looking as though they'd rather be back in Perth.

'Imagine it's seventeen seventy-eight,' he told them. 'Just months after the discovery of Australia.'

'The *invasion* of Australia,' Gloria cut in. 'With the First Fleet.' She glared at him, as if he were personally responsible.

'But Western Australia wasn't *invaded* until eighteen twenty-nine,' Lucas said, looking round at everyone, as though waiting for applause.

'Actually, Europeans *discovered* Australia in sixteen sixteen,' Gwen said pointedly. 'They didn't officially *invade* until almost two centuries later.'

Felix sighed. 'Okay. I get it. In seventeen seventy-eight, Beaumarchais had just finished writing his play, *The Marriage of Figaro*. He was already famous from *The Barber of Seville*. But his next play – *our* play – made his reputation.'

'But Louis the Sixteenth hated it,' Sebastian said, with a look of disdain. 'I read about it somewhere. He said the play was terrible. That it would never be staged. That the Bastille would have to be torn down first.'

'But Marie Antoinette *loved* the play,' Veronika said. Felix could have kissed the girl.

'*Lots* of people hated it,' Sebastian said. 'And anyway, who's going to play the part of the effete aristocrat with loose morals?'!

'*I* am,' said Felix, trying to stay calm. 'Now come along, we need to rehearse Act Two. *Jetzt gleich!* No warm-up. We don't have all day.'

Sebastian nudged his arm. 'Beware of Veronika,' he said loudly. 'The vanishing woman. She disappears in an instant, and no-one knows where she goes.'

Veronika gave him an angry look.

'I've got a stomach-ache,' Cassie moaned.

'Lucas, bring some of the set out here,' Felix said. 'We need to work on the spaces. Is everyone ready? *Plätze, bitte.*'

14. Sebastian

Felix had called for a break. Late afternoon, Sebastian walked down to the creek with Cassie. They took off their shoes, dipped their feet in. He scooped up some water, sipping. Took more and drank. It came from the hillside, Veronika's father had told them. He tried not to think about Veronika. He splashed Cassie instead, and she screamed. Small droplets fell across her collarbones, a single droplet on the top of her breast. He watched it slide down the fold of her dress.

'I'm sorry I keep teasing you,' he said.

'I forgive you,' she said softly, staring at her knees. And then she gave him what you had to call a *bewitching* smile. 'You know, don't you, that people tease the ones they like.'

He wondered for a moment if that was true. Yes, he had teased her mercilessly in their uni debate: *Sport is a religion for Australians.* She'd argued for the positive side. He could still hear her declaiming her *three key points*, could still see her skirt clinging to her thighs. But did he *like* her? Well, he liked her more since she'd tended to his wound. Cared for him.

'Do you remember our debating days?' he said. 'They were fun, weren't they?'

'Oh God! You teased me to hell and back. You were a perfect beast.'

She splashed him, and he let out a mock yelp.

'As for the grand final,' she said, 'it was totally unfair. We were by far the better team. We should have won. We were just too radical.'

He grinned at her.

They sat silent now, slowly moving their feet from side to side in the creek. He could feel the cold water, the sun on his back, the closeness of Cassie beside him. He could even hear her breathing: a low, lovely hum. He held up his bandaged hand. 'Thank you for this,' he said. 'You may be second-rate at debating, but you're very kind, Cass. Very thoughtful.'

'It will be better in no time,' she said.

She leaned into him, bumping him gently, side to side, hip to hip. Her eyes were alive, and her lips were so plump, so close, and he ... no, he couldn't. He shouldn't. But before he knew what was happening, she placed a hand around his neck, pulled him closer and kissed him on the lips. She tasted of cider. He kissed her back and heard her moan and he had to stop; he had to move away.

He looked down at his wounded hand, then up into her eyes. 'We should be getting back,' he said.

She tossed her head.

'That didn't happen,' he said. 'Okay? It didn't happen.'

15. Joshua

He came across the girl in the garden shed and she offered him a plum from her pocket. He didn't quite know why, but he refused. He'd seen her earlier and wondered about her slight accent and beautiful skin. And now that she was standing right in front of him, smiling and relaxed, he asked her where she was from.

She rolled her eyes. 'Perth.'

'No, I mean before that.'

'What's it to you?' she said.

He shuffled his feet.

'My family comes from East Timor,' she said. 'From a town called Maubara.'

He knew nothing about East Timor, couldn't even find it on a map. But he couldn't say that, could he? Show her what a numbskull he was.

'Have you been here long?' he said.

'Fifteen years.'

'So why did you come here?'

'For peace and quiet,' she said, then shrugged. 'Anyway, are you in the play too? I hope you know your lines.'

He ruffled his hair, embarrassed. 'I'm not in the play. I work here.'

'Doing what?'

'Weeding. Maintenance. Harvest. That's coming up soon.'

And then, because she was smiling at him: 'I'm Joshua,' he said. 'People call me Josh.'

He dropped a bag of fertiliser onto a low shelf, and, unexpectedly, the girl held out her hand.

'I'm Gloria,' she said. 'Nice to meet you.'

'You too.'

He felt something had been settled between them.

'You're lucky,' Gloria said. 'The play's driving me nuts. Everyone keeps arguing when it's meant to be fun. And ... well, some people are just plain cruel.'

'Cruel?'

'Sebastian. He's so full of himself. Private school boy and all that. Entitled. Part of the lucky sperm club. You know, the kind of guys with fancy cars and a born-to-rule idea of the world.'

Josh nodded. He liked her *fight*.

'I bet he goes sailing every weekend,' she said. 'On a fancy yacht.'

'My dad had a sailing boat,' Josh said. He hadn't known he was going to say that. 'Not a fancy one, but. Just an old one. He taught me to sail. I ... don't know where he is. He kind of up and left me and my brother.'

He could see her watching him closely now. What was she thinking? That he was a soft kind of guy who'd spill the beans before you could blink? A mummy's boy?

'That's tough, Josh,' she said. 'I'm sorry.' Then she sighed deeply. 'I don't know where my dad is, either. He was in prison, but now ... no-one seems to know.'

'I'm really sorry. I ... I've been in prison, too. For two years. I ... I lit a fire.' He waited for her to recoil, to judge, to dismiss him, but instead she just kept watching him with her kind brown eyes.

'It was an accident,' he said, 'but it caused a lot of damage. No-one was killed, though, so I guess ... I guess that's lucky.'

'It's a blessing,' Gloria said. 'And you've paid for what you did. So ... was it ... I mean, was it hard? In prison.'

'It was lonely.'

'You'll be okay,' she said. 'You've got a job here in this nice place.' She smiled at him again. 'And you're not in the stupid play.'

'Chérubin, we need you!' someone bellowed across the clearing.

'That's me,' Gloria said. She yelled that she was coming, then turned to face Joshua again. 'I work at the Blue Moon,' she said. 'Making cappuccinos and other fancy drinks. Northbridge, you know. You should come and say hello sometime.'

Then she took off in a hurry. Josh climbed onto the forklift and turned on the engine. He sat there for some time. Turned off the engine. Then he put his head on the steering wheel and wept.

He sat reading under the trees, trying not to watch. But he couldn't help himself; it was just plain nuts, as Gloria had said. There was one guy tossing a pile of paper onto the ground, ripping off some kind of cloak, huffing and looking all high and mighty, marching up the hill and disappearing. It had to be Sebastian, the guy who belonged to the lucky sperm club.

Another guy, the one who seemed to be in charge, kept yelling all the time, waving his arms about. Another guy was sitting on a ladder doing who knows what. A couple of girls kept sniping at each other. Josh returned to his book.

He felt his arm being yanked upwards. Veronika.

'We need you!' she said urgently and hauled him off the ground.

And before he knew what was happening, someone was shoving papers in his hand, Joshua protesting ... knew nothing about acting ... shuffling the pages ... didn't have a clue about this kind of stuff ...

Veronika put a hand on his arm. 'Please,' she said. 'Do it for me.'

Her eyes were shining.

'Okay,' he said. 'Just this once.'

Someone clapped him on the back. 'I'm Felix,' he said. 'The director of the Players.' He took Josh by the forearm. 'Now, Act Two, Scene One. You are trying to help Suzanne and the Countess plot against the Count. You are aiming that the Countess should fabricate an affair with Chérubin.'

Josh had to laugh. 'But why?' he said.

'So the Count will get jealous and rediscover his affections for his wife. And so that he will stop trying to enact his *droit du seigneur* on your fiancée and finally leave her alone. You understand?'

'Not a bit.'

Felix sighed. 'Forget it,' he said. 'Just read the part.'

Joshua tried hard to follow the lines: Veronika and some girl saying something about windows and heat and how men were all the same. Greyhounds and doors and someone called Figaro. None of it made sense. And now Felix was snapping at Veronika, telling her to stop skipping about the place, to remember *destination, destination, no action without motivation*, then turning to Josh, telling him to read his lines.

Josh cleared his throat. *What could be simpler? Somebody thwarts one's plans so one gets one's own back by upsetting theirs.*

Who the hell says *one*? he thought.

He looked up to see Veronika smiling at him.

16. Felix

He had no idea where Sebastian had gone, but he was pleased to hear Joshua easing into his role. Words were peeling off his tongue as if he were a natural. It was because he didn't know the script, Felix told him, so the emotion was *new*. This should be the case every time, he told the Players.

'Now. Next scene, everyone.'

'Great.' It was Gloria, pouting again. 'I've been sitting through this for over an hour just so I can say my fourteen lines.'

Felix darkened. 'I can do without this kind of attitude, thank you, Gloria. And just because you're not speaking doesn't mean you're doing nothing on stage. You have to stay in character, fixate on your internal object.'

Gloria rolled her eyes.

And now Lucas was yelling down from the ladder, also complaining. How he didn't believe this part of the play. That the Count would know it was a set-up, and the audience wouldn't buy it. He lost his balance and fell to the ground. His water bottle flew out of his hand and spilled all over Felix. The cast roared with laughter, and Felix, enraged, kicked the water bottle hard.

'*Ernsthaft!* You are not taking this *seriously!*' he shouted.

Lucas staggered up from the ground. 'The idea was to have a bit of *fun*,' he said.

Felix pulled back his shoulders. 'I think in Germany we show the theatre more respect,' he said.

'This is *amateur* theatre,' Lucas said, his face crinkling up. 'You think we all have to be bloody Laurence Olivier and what's her name ... that woman.'

'Vivien Leigh,' Veronika said, 'is the name of *that* woman.'

Felix gave the cast a withering look. 'Amateur theatre is important,' he said. 'When I directed Bertolt Brecht's *Aufstieg und Fall der Stadt Mahagonny* at the Universität der Künste Berlin, all the actors were amateurs. They learned as they performed, as much as the audience.

It is about the process, not the product. I don't demand that you are professionals. In fact, I prefer it that you are not.'

'Could have fooled me,' Lucas said.

'I just want you – all of you – to take this seriously,' Felix said. He moved closer to Lucas. 'Tell me, please, what could you possibly be doing that is more important than *tay-arter?*'

Lucas sneered. 'I'm studying Geology,' he said. 'I have exams on geochem and petrology coming up. I want to be a *geologist*, not an actor. And I reckon Seb really left because he has his master's application due, and he doesn't have the time to put up with your crap.'

Felix was seething, but Lucas wasn't done.

'We've all done plays before, but this is madness,' he said. 'Gloria's studying Primary Teaching, Gwen's doing Advertising, Veronika's studying French or something, and' – he pointed at Josh – 'Christ knows what this fella does but I'm sure he has better things to do with his time.' He turned to glare at Felix. 'Do you think we have all day long to do the *homework* you set us?' he said. 'To prepare our scenes. To psychologically transmogrify into fictional human beings? We all have other demands on our time, Felix. Aren't you supposed to be studying Engineering? Isn't that why you came all the way from Germany? To do a master's?'

Felix felt himself redden.

'Don't you have a thesis to write?' Lucas kept on. 'On the circumference of wheat silos or something?'

'Please, just *halt den Mund!* Shut up, would you?' Felix's arms hung by his sides. 'I ... well, I am no longer studying. I still haven't told my parents. And so now ... I am not enrolled in anything.'

He walked to his chair, slumped into it.

But Lucas was still babbling on ... how Felix wanted them to stay in character all the time ... how stupid it was to talk to bus drivers in eighteenth-century verse ... and so on and so on. Until Felix looked at the rest of the cast for help.

'I thought I would like the beach culture,' he said, feeling his eyes moisten.

Veronika offered him a tissue.

'I'm out of here too,' Lucas said.

17. Joshua

It was time to do the mulching. Since everyone had gone back to the house. As he plunged his hands into leaves and twigs and dirt, he thought about how much he'd enjoyed reading his part. It had surprised him; he'd surprised himself, doing something new. He hadn't stumbled over too many lines, even though the words were sometimes strange.

Words can woo and words are weapons too some girl called Cassie had tried to explain to him. Woo? What a bizarre word! There was one massive speech, true, and that was hard, but Felix said he wouldn't have to memorise it all. He could start the big speech and let the others take turns in saying the rest. Trust Veronika to rope him into it. For an instant – the touch of her hand, her beautiful, open smile – he wondered if she still had feelings for him. But he knew it was impossible, with his patchy past and pieced-together life. Her going to university, learning French, looking … what was the word … *arty*. Billowing skirts down to her ankles. Bracelets. Her hair the colour of flames, tangled in plaits or tied up in a bun. Her body was different, too. She wasn't a kid anymore. But her face was still the same, the way it drew him in.

But still, he felt different about her now. Since she didn't understand him. Why he'd needed to see her in prison. Needed her.

18. Gloria

She was taken aback when Josh turned up at the Blue Moon. She'd invited him, sure, but she didn't really think that he would come. She had to smile at his red nose – too much sun today, he told her – and at his rough, powdery hands. She thought of the girl in *Great Expectations*, who'd shunned the boy with the coarse hands and thick boots. But she liked Josh's hands. And there was something about him that made her feel at ease.

He spent hours in the café, helping her out. Collecting plates, mopping the floor. She was aware of him watching her from time to time, and she liked it. He didn't seem sleazy, not a bit. When she was done, she handed him a newspaper, said she'd be ready in a minute, just needed to get changed. She couldn't believe he'd waited for three whole hours!

As she approached his booth, he looked up from the paper and frowned.

'Trouble in your part of the world,' he said.

'Always is.'

Should she tell him? What would she want to tell him? It was a secret, really. At least to outsiders.

'My dad is still there,' she said. 'And my aunt. My cousins. Don't hear from them much, either. They don't have a phone, and the post is unreliable.'

'Do you think they're safe?'

Gloria blinked. 'Nobody's safe.'

'So that's why you came here?'

'Yeah.' She beckoned to the door. 'My feet are aching,' she said.

She locked the front door, and they walked without talking, below the plane trees of James Street. She saw their shadows on the pavement and felt pleased to see the leafy shapes, and despite her aching feet, she felt pleased to be striding next to Josh.

'Where are we going?' he said.

'I just want to walk for a bit.'

She couldn't say: I want to keep you by my side.

It was nearly midnight, but the place was still throbbing. People were zigzagging in and out of the Neptune, the Libido Bar, the Pot Black snooker club. Gloria knew these places like the back of her hand. The outside, anyway. When they crossed the Horseshoe Bridge, she suddenly felt the need for coffee. Conversation. The Istanbul Café was open, and the hairy lady with black whiskers was still there, talking in some unknown language on the phone. Possibly Turkish. Josh guided her to a seat at a low brass table, and instantly the whiskered lady put down her phone and rushed to take their orders. Coffee. And yes, Gloria decided, she was hungry after all. Vine leaves, falafel. Hummus.

'So how do you like Perth?' Josh said. As if she were a tourist.

'Did you know it was almost once called Hesperia?' she said. 'I learned that in primary school.'

Josh shook his head.

'It means *land looking west*. So when the kids at school asked me why I looked different, I told them I came from *the far east*.' She giggled. 'Our teacher told me off for telling fibs.'

Josh frowned. 'I don't think that's funny,' he said.

'I liked using my imagination,' she said. 'And reading, I loved reading. One of the first books I read in English was a version of *The Thousand and One Nights*. Not very Australian, but it was magic just the same.'

'So what's your place like?' he said. 'Maubara, isn't it?'

She was pleased that he remembered. It was a coastal village, she told him, where people kept pigs and chickens and goats. She told him about Lake Maubara, where her father would take her fishing when she was a child. How they would hurl themselves through space on his motorbike, past dry open savanna, sandy expanses bordered by mangroves, akadiru palms and hibiscuses.

'How I loved it,' she said. 'The lake, the dead trees rising out of caked mud. The salt flats and the small shrimp my father pulled out of the water with his net. He'd made a raft, too, out of bamboo, and took me out in early mornings. My favourite place was the mangroves. I used to beg my father to find a crocodile, but he never did. I had to be content with rose-headed pigeons, parrots, black cuckoo-doves. And as I watched them, I'd make small figures out of clay. The honeyeaters, too, and the sunbirds.'

'You made sculptures?'

'I wasn't very good,' Gloria said. 'But I guess that's not the point when you're a kid. But one of the best things was our sacred tree.'

Josh's eyes were aglow. 'I had a sacred tree, too,' he said. 'It was in a forest near a town called Starfish Bay. I built a tree house and lived in it.'

'Lived in it?'

'For a few weeks, yes. And I shared it with a family of possums.'

Then he asked her about her own family, and she liked this, too: the way he asked her questions without seeming to pry. The way he seemed to enjoy sitting here with her, mopping up his food with wedges of flatbread, sometimes smiling.

Her parents spoke different dialects, she said: her father Mambai; her mother Tetum, a mixture of her own language and Portuguese. She still spoke to her mother in Tetum, but she'd forgotten so much, even though she tried hard not to.

She told him that after her family had moved to Australia and her father stayed behind, they knew they wouldn't hear from him. He couldn't write. It was expensive to phone. He used to speak every so often to her mother. She begged him to come home. He said it wasn't safe. That it was a waste of money. He asked them to keep waiting for him. It had been a long, long time since his last call. But there was one thing she would never forget.

'Something my father taught me. That the world was *the great big clamour of life*. The place where people and nature make a joyful sound.' She leaned across the table. 'Sometimes I feel like the whole world is whispering to us. The cosmos. My father's people, the Mambai, divide all things into two categories: silent mouths, *kuku molun*, and speaking mouths, *kuku kasen*. Silent mouths are all the non-human creatures, like rocks and trees and grass, insects and birds.'

'The great big clamour of life,' Josh said. 'If we listen hard enough to the silent mouths.'

'Exactly. My father told me how once upon a time, all the earth spoke. When you stepped on the ground, it cried. When you cut the grass, it screamed. All of creation made sound. But then our Father in heaven, He imposed silence on that world. He chose the youngest of His beings ... humans, us ... to be the speaking mouths. To use the rest of silent creation for our own ends.'

'Was that your God's plan?' Josh asked.

Gloria noticed. *Your* God, he'd said.

'We don't know His plan,' she said. 'But what speaking beings must do, what *we* must do, is pay our debt to the silent mouths. As restitution. As gratitude. Through rituals, through song and dance. We must make noise. The loudest sound. We must beat our drums and sing.'

'Maybe that's why you joined the play,' he said.

Gloria nodded. 'That's it. So I could make joyful noise. Make joy eternal. This is how I feel when I'm with my people here. A community, you know.'

'So, what do you do with … your people?'

'My friend Rosária does Tebe dancing – it's a group dance. Men and women. Traditional. It's for important days, you know, celebrations and all that. I prefer bush dancing, which I know sounds weird. I mean, who admits to enjoying the daggiest thing ever? Anyhow, we hang out together, make *katupa*, which is coconut rice in a palm leaf, it's pretty tasty. We sing, too, on special days, like when Martinho – he's a family friend – made his solemn vows. He's really good at soccer, too. The girls don't really play, though. I do enjoy the singing, but now you see, I am also *acting* …' She took a sip of the thick, dark coffee. 'But it's not always joyful, is it?' she said. 'Especially when Sebastian is around. I'm glad he left to go back to his boring job. And his yachts. I don't know how Veronika puts up with him.'

'Veronika?'

'Yes. His girlfriend.'

Josh frowned. 'I didn't know that,' he said. He straightened up. 'Tell me about your sacred tree, Gloria.'

She liked him saying her name.

She told him that the military had hacked it down. Tore off the branches, limb from limb. And from their *uma lulik*, they took the sacred ancestral heirlooms. She heard her voice begin to break. Her mother had held onto her *morteen*, her sacred beads, but that was all.

'We lost everything,' she said. 'Our homes, our way of life. But here we are safe … And frankly, there is an upside to it all. Marriage customs in Timor-Leste are full on. At least now my mother doesn't have to pay *barlake* if I get married. It's like dowry for the groom's family, only pigs and textiles instead of money. On the downside, I miss out on bridewealth, of say, thirty water buffalos.'

'Why thirty?'

'I can't remember.' She smiled at him. 'If I got married back home, I'd have to produce heirs. As many to match the buffalo.'

'Strewth. That would keep you busy. Do you have any sisters?'

Gloria shook her head. 'I had a brother,' she told him. 'He was killed. That's when my father got involved in the resistance movement. Fretilin. Fighting for our independence. My brother … We used to leave things at his grave. Coffee, rice, corn or spring water. A scarf. A ribbon. Prayers.

And then we left. Me and my mother. My father might still be there, in the mountains.' She felt her hands clasped tight under the table. 'I want to go back to be with my people,' she said. 'And I have an aunt, some cousins, still living in my village. But I can't go back yet. It's not safe. Sometimes I think, if only they knew. If only anyone knew what people did to one another.'

She could see Josh furrow his brow and felt a surge of guilt. Burdening him with her dark stories.

'I'm talking too much,' she said.

'You're talking just fine,' he said. 'I mean ... it's tough, what you're saying. But ... well, I'm glad that you're trusting me to say it.'

She felt her heart expanding.

'So, you don't know where your father is?' he said.

'No. And I want to find him. I *need* to find him. He fought against the Indonesians. He worked in secret. A missing person, one of many thousands, but he was my father. Caique da Silva. A man.'

Was she being much too gloomy again? And what about the things he had told her?

'You lost your father, too,' she said.

Josh looked away, looked back at her. 'Yeah, but ... well, he didn't do anything brave and heroic. He just ...' He shrugged. 'He just left us. Me and my brother. When we were kids.'

'Do you miss him?'

Josh shook his head. 'He beat us black and blue, me and Charlie. Only Charlie came out a lot worse because ... well, he tried to shield me, you know. Not that it always worked.'

Gloria reached out her hand, placed it on Josh's hand. She waited for him to say more, but he just sat there.

'Tell me some more about your sacred tree,' she said.

'My tree house,' he said with a pensive look. 'It's a long way south from here. It's ... I don't know ... Veronika can tell you all about it.'

'Veronika?'

'Yeah. We knew each other as kids.'

Gloria heard something in his voice. Regret? A touch of anger? She couldn't tell.

'So is the tree still there?' she said.

'Maybe.'

'You could go and find it one day.'

He began fiddling with his fork. 'Maybe,' he said. 'Maybe not. I mean ...
I lost my old life, like you. I know what that feels like.'

'Being in prison?'

He leant back against his seat. 'The fire ... I went a bit crazy,' he said.
'I caused a lot of damage. No-one was killed, but I ... it was dumb. Really
dumb.'

She thought he might tell her more, give her more of his sad story, but
out of the corner of her eye, she saw the old lady clearing up, clattering
dishes. Gloria looked at her watch and saw the time: one o'clock!

'Shit!' She sprang from her seat. 'My mum's gunna kill me!'

Josh insisted on paying, and as they hurried out the door, he insisted
on walking her back to her car. That was the moment, she knew, even
though it was late, and her mother was going to kill her. She knew she
had to do it. She had to turn his chin towards her and kiss him. Softly. He
kissed her back, and it felt lovely and gentle, but then he became more
urgent, searching her, and she had to stop. Move away. She wanted this,
she knew that, but she had to be a good girl.

'I have to go,' she said.

His mouth hardened.

'Let's ... let's just be friends,' she said, and before he could protest, she
hurried into the dark.

She knew what her mother would say. She would forbid her daughter
to see a boy who wasn't Catholic. It was as simple, and as awful, as that.

Rosária had phoned, according to her mother, and said she was keen to
meet. But Gloria was due at the orchard by noon.

She missed her friend, but it was Rosária's fault, really, that Gloria was
in the play in the first place. Gloria had just left her lecture on ... what was
it? ... diagnostic teaching or something ... when she had seen a poster on
the Arts noticeboard. A picture of silhouettes in black and white. A count
and countess in baroque wear. *The Marriage of Figaro*. She'd heard it was
the name of an opera, and she knew she could sing, although she needed
to improve. Maybe she'd get better at singing in public if she joined the
play. Auditioned. Although that sounded a bit scary.

She had been on the verge of forgetting all about it when she saw
Rosária waving from the lawn. They were meeting for lunch. And Rosária
must have seen something on her face, straightaway, asked her why she
looked so worried. So it all came out: the play, the singing, the audition,

and then Rosária getting all excited, insisting that Gloria could really sing, she *had* to audition. *No way*, Gloria had blurted out. Rosária really liked to taunt her sometimes. Said that if she didn't audition for the play, she'd have to sing at the organ restoration fundraiser. Gloria couldn't think of anything worse. She now wondered why she had agreed to the stupid bet in the first place.

She called her friend to say hi.

'Never see you anymore,' Rosária complained. 'You're always working, and now you're in the play. It's like you've forgotten us.'

'I haven't, it's just—'

'Come over. We can go and visit Martinho and his brother. Practise songs for next Sunday.'

'Rose, I have to be at the play rehearsal, and it's *miles away*.' She looked at her watch. There really wouldn't be time. It had felt like aeons since she'd been with them, though, going out to movies and hanging out, just mucking around.

'C'mon, you know I never lose a bet,' Gloria said.

'Sure, but you can't you take a couple of days off? Martinho's got this new synthesiser,' Rosária said, excited. 'I swear it sounds like Van Halen, Glor, you have to come and listen.'

Gloria took a deep breath. She heard the joy in her friend's voice, felt the lure of fellowship, but she couldn't miss rehearsal, could she? People depended on her. She couldn't let people down. And besides ... there was Joshua.

'You want to play Van Halen in *church*?' she said, trying to keep things light. 'That's a bit eighties, isn't it?'

'Yeah,' Rosária said, then giggled. Gloria giggled too. Felt the spark of connection.

'So what time on Sunday is the heavy metal mass?' she said.

They giggled again. And now Rosária was away with more gossip, chatting about Martinho being a bit weird, listing all the ways he was weird, but Gloria wasn't really listening anymore. She couldn't get the picture of Joshua out of her head. She'd been with him for hours, and it had felt like minutes. Yes. The warmth of his voice. The buzz, the ease, the lightness. Something exciting about him. New and familiar at the same time.

'Guess what?' Gloria said, breaking in. 'You wouldn't believe it. I did something totally wild last night.'

'Yeah? *Tell me!*'

19. Joshua

Next morning, he read the paper more carefully. *Massacre in Díli: Three Year Anniversary*. More than two hundred killed in Santa Cruz. Gloria's father might have been killed. Gloria still didn't know. She wanted to go back to her people, she'd said. What could he possibly say to her that would tell her how he felt? What could he say about something so unknown and far away? So dangerous.

She'd kissed him, then run away, and he didn't know what to do about that, either.

But she'd given him so much in that short space of time, huddled over a table, telling her story. The sadness, the horror, and those moments of joy with her father. He'd never heard stories like that before, from a place he couldn't begin to imagine. She'd trusted him with her past. Felt for him, too. Understood him. Kissed him. And then left him.

20. Felix

The lady of the house approached him by the fountain, wiping her hands on her apron. She offered to make him *a cuppa* – which he knew meant a cup of tea – but he asked her politely for coffee. He knew he must have looked flustered, out of sorts, and felt embarrassed that she was seeing him like that. Had she seen him before, through the kitchen window, pacing up and down, waving his hands, trying to figure out what to say? To explain to his parents his sad situation. Maybe the beds were too hard, Felix thought. His own had been quite comfortable, in some sort of lumpy sack that Josh had prepared for him. He'd woken up thinking he was back in Berlin, in his bedroom with the poster of Boris Becker and his collection of tennis paraphernalia. But he was, in truth, on the other side of the world, in an orchard. He was meant to be directing a play. It appeared that his cast had fled. And his new recruit hadn't shown up either.

The lady of the house returned with coffee in an elegant china cup.

'Thank you, Mrs ...' He had forgotten her surname. *Dummkopf.*

'Angela.'

He took a sip of coffee – instant, awful – then cleared his throat. 'I am leaving,' he said. 'The play is over now.'

She said nothing.

'I have failed to realise the play,' he said.

He went and sat on the edge of the fountain, peered down into the little fishpond. A giant goldfish swam past, looking bored, as if yearning for a dark seaweed cavern.

'I have been too much authority. *Zu streng,*' he said, then realised he was talking to the retreating fish. He looked up at Angela. 'I have lost the respect of my actors.'

She patted him on the shoulder. 'It was just a bad day, love,' she said. 'What's the play called again? The mad day? You just had a mad day.' She smiled at him maternally. 'You can do it. You're a smart young man. An engineering student, Veronika tells me.'

'*Ja, doch.*'

She sat down beside him.

'There once was an engineer,' she said. 'He designed a pipeline from Perth all the way up to Kalgoorlie. A magnificent work of engineering that brought water to the goldfields. The hot, dry parts of the state. It's still in use today.' Wasn't the whole country hot and dry, Felix thought. And he wasn't in the mood for a history lesson.

'But he took his life a year before the pipeline was finished and the water began to flow,' Angela said sadly. 'He thought he'd failed, but all he needed was patience. It was tragic.' She drew herself up. 'The costumes are ready,' she said. 'I have mended them all, ironed them all, hung them up in the laundry, and they're ready for the cast to try on. I made some new pieces from the material Cassie gave me. I even had some beautiful white satin in the linen cupboard to make a wedding dress for Veronika. My mother-in-law gave me all her remnants before she passed away.' She stood up, offered him her hand. 'Come on,' she said. 'Let me show you.'

He followed her into the laundry. And there they were: so many costumes hanging in the air, as if waiting for their actors, as if beckoning them to play. All the colours, the warmth, the frills and lace, summoning a place from two hundred years ago. He ran his hands across the lustrous satin, the velvet knickerbockers, murmured at the newly hemmed socks, the mended tears, the concealment of stains on a mustard gown. He closed his eyes and saw a picture of the closing scene. It was *wunderbar*.

He opened his eyes and turned to the wonderful lady of the house.

'I must gather my players,' he said. '*Ein neuer Start*. We must begin again.'

'That's the spirit,' she said.

'But I will need your … gardener, is he? Joshua. Can you permit him two more weeks with the Players?'

'I'll speak to Michal,' she said and brushed down her apron. Ready for business, like Felix.

He wouldn't have to make that phone call. Not yet.

21. Gloria

It was good to be back at work. It was good that Sebastian had gone. And the breakfast: something for everyone, spread out on a table under the lovely wisteria. Rows of toast, pots of strawberry jam and orange marmalade, peanut butter and Vegemite, tubs of yoghurt. Orange juice and mugs of tea. Excited chatter among the cast, about the dogs licking their faces in the night, waking people up; a dream about taking ecstasy; another dream about dancing in a nightclub. Everyone in good spirits. Except for Josh. Gloria watched him shove two slices of bread in the toaster, as if wanting to punish them.

She had told him she couldn't be with him. Except in the play, of course. But she hadn't told him why. And now he wouldn't even look at her.

Veronika had a book with her. She flashed it at Gloria, asking her if she wanted to read it. *Pocket Nietzsche* it said on the cover. No way, Gloria said, squirming, and so Felix volunteered to read it. Perfect, Veronika had said, *the Players needed a good dose of courage.*

After breakfast, Josh sat slumped against the garden shed, reading the script. Becoming Figaro.

It was midmorning when Felix corralled them to the clearing. He'd put on Bazile's tall black hat and read from Veronika's book in a commanding voice:

'And thus spake Zarathustra to the people. *I say unto you: one must have chaos in oneself to give birth to a dancing star.*' He showed them a winsome smile. 'We need to take the risks!' he declared. 'Like the tightrope-walker who plunges to his death. Zarathustra buries him with his own hands.'

He closed the book, clamped it under his arm.

Lucas shouted that the play must go on. Even *he's* ready, Gloria thought.

Then Felix apologised to them all. He had been too impatient for warm-ups and games at first, but now he saw that such things were important. A flurry of activity followed: trust exercises in pairs. Stretching. Warming up the voice. Swapping scripts and reading each other's parts, playing truth, dare or torture, with one turn each. Someone dared Veronika to jump into the creek, and soon they were all in there, soaking wet. Even Josh. They shouted out their lines in the water, icy-cold, thrilling. *How stupid clever men can be … when he gets me alone for a few minutes … enter some fellow's house at night, do him down with his wife … goodbye, dear Fi-Fi-Figaro, goodbye … what about a kiss to encourage me … what will my husband say …* They jumped in and out of the water. They ran in dizzy circles around the tractor and the shed. They shrieked and they larked, they jibed and they jested.

Gloria surveyed them all: panting, exhausted, happy. The borrowed words becoming their own.

22. Ana

She would say that she wanted to surprise them by coming home for Christmas, a month earlier than expected. She wouldn't tell them she'd been fired from her nannying job, then felt too ashamed to ask her old Uncle Jozef for help, to let him know she was there in Prague, jobless, without much Czech or even German.

It had happened so fast. She'd lost little Tommy in the market. It was cold and her shopping list was long. She'd had Martha by her side, but when she went to buy the ham, Tommy had somehow slipped away. She'd searched for him all over the place, round and round the square, down the side streets and back again, trying not to panic. Had asked the butcher to use his phone, tried to speak calmly to Tommy's parents. All of them searching for hours. Eventually they'd found him, at the pet store in the market, patting one of the rabbits.

Ana had been dismissed. She still thought it wasn't fair. They'd found him, after all, and she'd become attached to the children. She'd had to say a hurried goodbye, among tantrums and tears.

She caught a taxi from Perth airport, still in her winter gear and hefty with jet lag. Her bowels congested with too much aeroplane food. She was stunned by the brightness, by the bloated sense of space and time. It had been three years since she'd been home, but when the taxi pulled up, everything looked the same: the shed, the fountain, the house. Even the unknown people milling about outside, who must be the next crop of fruit pickers.

Her mother answered the door. Three years it had been. Gasped, as Ana knew she would. She had something draped over her arm that looked like a wedding dress.

She took Ana in her arms. 'Is everything alright?' she said, warm in her ear.

'Fine, fine, I just ... I was homesick.'

Her mother drew away, still looking worried. 'But *why* didn't you call?' she said. 'We would have come to the airport!'

'No matter,' Ana said. 'And it looks like you're busy. Harvest time, no?'

Her mother cupped her face. Told Ana she was as beautiful as ever, but paler. Her hair had grown. And no, the people weren't fruit pickers. Well, yes, they were, but they were here to rehearse a play.

'What? You're friggin' kidding me?'

'No, and they take it very seriously. Veronika's in it, too.'

'With her hippy, weirdo uni friends.' She had written to Ana about them.

'They're *nice* people, Ana. All of them.'

Ana tugged lightly at the dress on her mother's arm, asked if her sister was getting married as well.

'It's her costume,' her mother said. 'I haven't finished it yet. But I've done most of the others. I've—'

'Been slaving your guts out for them I see.'

Her mother ushered her into the house, fussed about with Ana's case, offering tea, food, opening the fridge, asking about Europe (*good*), the flight (*fine*), saying she'd make up the bed, offering food again. But Ana was *too pooped to talk*, she told her mother, hearing her voice sounding sharp. She looked out the window, but the hippies and weirdos had gone.

'I'm going to stretch my legs,' she said. 'It's a wonder I don't have deep vein thrombosis, the flight was so friggin' long.'

She walked slowly down into the valley, stood at the edge of the retaining wall. And there they were in the clearing: a bunch of loonies running around, all drenched and dripping, shouting at one another. A few people were stretched out on the grass. These idiots are gunna pick fruit, she thought, they wouldn't have a fucking clue. And there was her sister, standing next to – Joshua. Yes, it was Joshua. Grown into himself, with longer hair. She wondered how long he'd been out. Free. And back in her sister's life. She could see, even from a distance, that Veronika looked different. It was the way she was standing: her head held high, and her hair tossed over her shoulder, as if nothing could shake her. Sealed off, inaccessible. Ana hadn't seen her in years. Or Joshua. And here they were now, the two of them.

It gave Ana the chills, remembering. How she'd been late to the bonfire, and all the surfers and a couple of local girls were already woozy with beer. And there was Charlie, too. Of course. And then two figures coming out of the darkness, coming towards them, casting black shadows over the sand. Veronika and Joshua, hand in hand, their shadows growing larger, like those Balinese puppets in the school play. And as they drew closer, they changed into colour: Veronika's strawberry hair and swirling spotted dress, Josh in blue trousers. Standing in front of the bonfire, neither of them saying a word. The fight. The fire.

Ana felt like an axe had hit her on the head. She needed to lie down. She needed to sleep.

23. Cassie

Cassie checked on Josh to see how he was handling things. He'd looked like he'd been having fun with his part just the other day, but now he seemed out of sorts, as if he didn't belong. He was having trouble with some of the words, he'd said, pronunciation and meaning. And how would he remember them all? She knew what it felt like to be on the outer. She offered to help him with his lines, sat next to him at lunch, and insisted on piling up his plate.

She chugged down the cider, glass after glass, hoping that no-one would notice. There'd been too much sun and running around. She was dehydrated. She was hungry. And sitting at the rowdy table, scoffing sausages and onions, cheese melted over bread, soft ice cream, more glasses of cider, all she could think of was Sebastian. How he'd left because she'd kissed him, how he must have loathed her, repulsed him, because she was fat and ugly, sitting next to Veronika, beautiful, slender Veronika.

I might as well not exist, Cassie thought, biting into bread, chewing and swallowing, leaving the table and heading for the toilet. Behind the water tank, where only the ponies would hear her. She bent over the toilet seat. She put a finger down her throat, and it felt like an orgasm, this seizure in her stomach and throat, the release of vomit.

Should she take lovers? Would that make her feel better, less broken up? Less alone. She'd once fallen for a flautist, one of her father's friends who played in a string quartet. His name was Tristan and he was in his fifties and he'd had such sinewy arms, but the cider and sausages were better than anything she could stick her fingers into, like cold lasagne. Ah, yes. A peculiar sense of release. A pleasure of punishment.

When she'd finished, she felt full of disgust.

Sebastian didn't want her.

She wiped around the toilet seat, mouthing Marceline's lines:

You men, lost to all sense of obligation, who stigmatise with your contempt the playthings of your passions … what is there for these unhappy girls to do?

24. Veronika

She'd taken the horse for a ride, the placid, cookie-coloured one. Nanki-poo, but she couldn't remember who'd named him. Maybe it was Ana, although she'd never been into horses. Ana's passions had been River Phoenix, make-up and boys. Especially Charlie.

The horse refused to move, so Veronika kicked it in the side. She had to take care not to rip the wedding dress: her mother would be livid if she ruined it. She looked up to see a figure walking towards her. Joshua, waving and calling her name.

'Who are you marrying?' he said.

'The horse.' She patted its flank. 'Certainly not Sebastian.'

Josh shaded his eyes from the sun. 'Yeah. Gloria told me you two were together.'

'I was going to tell you, Josh.' She saw that her hem was stuck in a stirrup and gently loosened it free. 'But right now, he's pissing me off,' she said. 'Being so supercilious.'

'Super what?'

'Up himself.' She sniffed. 'I think it's over,' she said. 'Actually.'

'Maybe you can talk to him. Try to ... you know ... patch things up.'

Veronika gave him a look. Why was he trying like this?

'You look tired,' she said.

'Everyone's tired.'

'True. But ... oh Josh, come on, let's be friends,' she said. 'We're friends, remember? Why don't you jump up on my noble steed?'

He shook his head. 'You still talk funny,' he said.

He mounted the horse with ease, put his arms around her waist. He smelled of petrol and grass. They trotted down the fire trail and did a loop into scrubland thick with mallee roots and xanthorrhoea.

'Oh! My goodness, look, Josh! It's Ana!' Veronika leaned back to him. 'She's home early.'

She was coming down the slope towards them, draped in a scarf, like a shrouded phantom from the past.

'Great,' Josh said. 'She can help us with the harvest.'

'Yeah, right. She'll be filing her nails instead.'

Ana stared up at them.

'On your high horse again, I see,' she said, approaching. 'And getting married, too. Congrats and all that.'

Josh slipped down from the horse. Stood to face Ana.

'Just a tip, Josh,' she said. 'That op-shop shirt won't cut it for a wedding.' She looked up at Veronika again. 'So, am I gunna be the bridesmaid? Or … don't tell me, you've eloped.'

'Nice to see you too, sis. And the dress is for our play.'

Veronika slid from her horse, led him by the reins. The three of them walked slowly, stiffened into silence. Until Ana suddenly turned to Josh and took him by the hand.

'So you're out of that bloody place?' she said.

What does it bloody look like, Veronika thought.

'Sure am,' Josh said. 'And now I'm working on the farm.' He let go of Ana's hand.

She grinned at him. 'You've turned into a spunkrat. Got a lady?'

'How was Europe?' he said.

Veronika would have kicked her sister if she'd been within range.

'Europe mostly sucked,' Ana said. 'And now I might go back to hairdressing. Just Snips in the shopping centre. Don't care, really.' She eyed Joshua carefully. 'Have you seen your brother recently?'

'Can't say I have.'

'You haven't seen Charlie Simmons? Your own flesh and blood! Where is he? What's happened to him?'

'No idea.'

Ana picked at a fingernail. 'I saw him in London,' she said. 'On some business deal. Wasn't there long, but.'

'What?' Veronika stopped suddenly, and the horse snorted his displeasure.

No-one said a word. Veronika couldn't tell which was worse: the jabbing conversation or the uneasy, loaded silence. She looked across at Josh, then back to Ana, but their faces were shut to her, to each other, and to whatever it was they wouldn't say.

25. Ana

Ana was finding it hard to get out of bed. She'd been sleeping strange hours since she got back from Prague. Being home felt like a slow kind of strangulation. It was a different kind of jet lag, but a jet lag all the same, to be thrown back into her old life. As if she'd been in a time warp, with no-one there to witness it.

And she couldn't stop thinking of Charlie.

She'd said it so casually: I saw him in London. He didn't stay long.

And now her sister, with Josh. High on a horse together, their bodies close. When had she first seen them together? It was a few days after the burnt pigtails when Veronika brought him home. This tall ethereal-looking boy, who'd looked like he'd blown in from a world where unicorns existed. They'd laughed together, he and Veronika, their tanned arms almost touching as they played checkers on the veranda. Veronika kind of wild-looking, her freckled face made spectacular by the loss of her childish plaits.

Ana was angry at them, although she didn't quite know why. She'd started painting her fingernails to hide her feelings, asked Josh about his brother. And when he'd said he had no idea, Ana smeared the red polish on her hand. She hadn't seen Charlie in three days. Three whole days of boredom and reading her horoscope, making fun of her little sister and the book she was reading.

Until a small shell flew in through the window and shattered into tiny pearly pieces. It was Charlie, come for her at last. And she'd climbed through the window, run down the street, hopped onto his motorbike. She could still feel the hardness of his chest as she clung to him, riding to nowhere, the smell of him: leather, dried leaves, dust. And when they stopped and he'd turned to look at her, she'd put her hands in her hair to make pigtails, to remind him of what he'd done.

Another time returned to her. Two underage kids trying to get into the pub past a large bouncer at the door. Charlie telling her not to worry, he had connections, he'd said, but she'd suddenly felt anxious and cold in her little denim skirt and T-shirt. He must have seen it, felt it, because he told her to hop on his bike again. He'd taken her to his house, where she'd never been before. An old grey brick house with blue shingles. No garden. Just dirt. And inside, two deckchairs and a bare mattress, a kitchen littered with greasy bowls. She'd felt disappointed. Let down. And she was hungry, too. Until he took her to The Caravan, saying it in capital letters as if it mattered. And it did: a little kitchenette decked out in orange and yellow panelling. Spotless. A bed with a purple sleeping bag. A desk with a notebook on top and more records than she'd ever seen in her life. A rack with old work boots, sneakers, a pair of thongs. She remembered every detail and how she'd been touched by the homeliness of it all. His space. He'd put on a record and poured her a drink that burned her throat and then she'd lifted up his T-shirt and kissed him round his belly button, kissed his stomach, his chest, and they'd tangled together, licking, sticking to each other, finding and looking and kissing, cries and sighs and screams and ripples.

Later she found out he'd been expelled from school for sniffing cocaine. It had struck her as banal.

Then she'd seen him again, almost by chance, in London, roughly five years later, in one of those pubs where Australians go. *Once more*, he'd said. *For old times' sake.* She hadn't regretted it at the time. But rekindling things had somehow left her pining for him.

She ignored her mother's call for dinner and opened her laptop. Typed in Charlie's name. A list of titles and links. Charlie Simmons, football. Plumber. Information technology support. Racehorse owner. Maybe racehorse owner: he would probably be rich. She clicked. He appeared. Unmistakably Charlie. Heavier in the face, rings under the eyes, but cleaner-looking. Shaven. Charlie. Charlie. She would hunt him down. Ring the racehorse people. An association or something. She would pretend to be a relative. Or an old family friend. Because he didn't have a family.

26. Cassie

They had to share the stable with a pony, but there was plenty of room for all the materials. Cassie had been worried about getting it there: the headache of trying to fit the long plywood flats into the kombi, along with all the paint, brackets and tools, but they'd made it in the end, on a second trip back, shoving and squashing and using the roof rack. And now it was time to pull out the enormous planks and begin cutting sheets of canvas on top of them to get the right size for the backdrop. Cassie was glad to have Lucas to help her. She spread a sheet of plastic over the filthy concrete, swept around the straw. The pony shuffled out of the way, snorting now and then, flicking its black tail.

Cassie was amused. 'Sharing a stable with a pony,' she said. 'So much for occupational health and safety. And you, falling off the ladder the other day. Not good, Lucas.'

'My right hip still hurts,' he said. 'But I'm prepared to suffer for my art.'

He finished cutting the canvas, and Cassie passed him the drill and the hinges to join the panels. She watched him lay the canvas on top of the drop sheet and begin painting on the fireplace. He worked from a neat pencil sketch on a giant notepad.

'Impressive,' Cassie said. 'Where did you learn all that?'

'I built the set for *As You Like It.*'

She smiled at him. He smiled back.

'I got some tips from the pros,' he said, 'and some library books as well.'

He gave her a hand hoisting up the panels so that they stood up vertically. She got to work with more nails.

'And where did you learn that?' he said.

'Hammering nails? It's not that hard, Lucas.'

He looked a bit stung, then went back to painting skirting boards onto his canvas. He explained the problems ahead: they had to find a king-sized bed for Act One, then transport it to the theatre and work out how to store it offstage when it wasn't needed. Cassie had suggested painting some sort of *trompe l'oeil* or using mirrors as a projection. More Brechtian, she'd said. And painting a bed into the backdrop if they wanted to be *minimal.*

And then: 'Do you fancy me, Lucas?' she asked. Just like that.

He kept his eyes on the canvas. 'I haven't … well, I haven't really thought about it,' he said.

'Could you love me?'

'What?' He stood up, went to where she was sitting behind the panels, but she shifted so he couldn't see her face. 'Cassie, what are you on about? Are you reciting some kind of script?'

'Do you think I'm pretty?' she asked.

'I guess so. I mean … sure. You're pretty when you smile.'

'Then why don't you fancy me?'

He kept trying to see her face, but she kept shifting the planks around. She was feeling a little vulnerable now. But she'd asked him, hadn't she? And he was playing it cool.

She peered from behind the panel, wielding her drill.

'What are you looking at?' she said.

Lucas shook his head. Went back to painting.

'I can tell. You just don't think of me in that way,' she said. 'That's fine. I can handle it.' She began to drill.

He had to shout over the noise. 'Is everything okay with you, Cassie?'

'Let me think,' she said. 'Sebastian doesn't love me. I've just failed my philosophy essay. My mother and father are control freaks. They're divorced, but that doesn't stop them from trying to circumvent my freedom.' She put down the drill.

'I'm an only child, you know. But I feel like an orphan. My parents don't know how to love me or each other. My mother has an Electra complex. And did you know that my parents fuck other people?'

'That's heavy,' he said. There was a note of sympathy in his voice and then a matter-of-factness: 'Technically, they're no longer together, so—'

'My father's a corporate wanker,' she went on. 'Owns an art gallery too. My mother's a lawyer, and I think she fucks her clients. The blokes who've left their wives and complain about paying child support.'

'Not like my parents,' Lucas said.

'No? Tell me.'

'My dad's a boilermaker; my mum's a kindergarten teacher. They met at a Seekers concert, married, had two boys and a girl and three guinea pigs. They never touch each other and probably haven't had sex in years.'

She looked at him abashedly. 'Do you think love is a terribly burdensome thing?'

'I've never been in love,' he said. 'Except maybe with a harpsichordist when I was sixteen. But ... it doesn't have to be, does it? Burdensome, I mean.'

'Sometimes I think ...' Cassie sighed. 'I think I might *expire* with the weight of my desire.'

Lucas looked a bit stressed. He started wiping the paint marks off the concrete with an old rag.

'I'm actually not in love with anyone,' she said. 'And I'm not going to love anyone, ever. I would be broken, shattered, by the burden of loving someone. Oh, the demands of love, the subjection of the self, the subjugation of one's will. Know what I mean?'

Lucas furrowed his brow. 'That sounds pretty silly, to be honest. Shouldn't love be simple? You care for someone. You show it. And then you get on with things.'

Cassie drew herself up, put her hand on her chest. 'Let me tell you about the future of love,' she said. 'Since my full name is Cassandra, a woman from Greek mythology, who was blessed with the gift of prophecy. Trouble was, though, no-one believed her, so her gift was really a curse.'

Lucas tossed the rag into the corner and turned to her. 'So then tell me a prophecy I'll believe,' he said.

'Okay. Easy. Veronika will marry Sebastian.'

'Maybe not. He just walked out.'

'You can't have a maybe,' Cassie said. 'Okay, here's another one: Felix will fall in love with a man.'

'Huh? ... Hm ... Maybe.'

'I said you can't have a maybe, Lucas. Okay, here's one with a definite answer. You and your band will achieve outrageous fame and fortune.'

'I wish,' Lucas said. He shook his head. 'Have you even heard us?'

'Of course not.'

'Then come to hear Mud Cloud. Live. Next Saturday at the Last Drop. Nine pm. See you there?'

He told her that he liked her, after all. Said she was funny, didn't take herself too seriously. Or maybe she took herself too seriously in a funny kind of way. And he said he liked her big green eyes.

27. Veronika

She'd made a big decision. She'd skipped rehearsals and driven back to Perth for work with the hope of finding Sebastian and luring him back. To the play and to her. She had a nagging feeling that she'd hurt him and needed to put things right. What had she said? What had she done? She was inclined to be impulsive, she knew, but wasn't that why he was drawn to her? Lying on his parents' lawn, drunk as a skunk, so different from the well-mannered girls of his class. As she drove along the highway in her spluttering jalopy, she began to picture him: his eyes wide with surprise, his arms ready to hold her.

She glanced out the side window, turned her eyes back to the road. And in that instant, she wondered if she really cared for him. Well, of course she did, but maybe not as much as she thought. She could still feel Josh's arms around her waist: the warmth of them, the comfort. Or maybe her sister cared for Josh. Or for Charlie. How could you possibly tell the truth in other people's hearts? But one thing was certain: she wished Ana had cleared off forever, not come back into her life. Her superficial, selfish, boy-crazy sister.

She spent three hours working in the bookshop. She kept herself busy sorting, sandpapering edges, stacking books, trying to memorise her script. It was Thursday. Sebastian would be working at his firm. She would drive into the city and maybe find answers to the things that were bothering her.

She drove past Parliament House and swerved onto St Georges Terrace, spied a parking spot near the Anglican Cathedral and stepped out of the car. Halfway down the block, she remembered she'd forgotten to lock her car or feed the parking meter, shrugged, and kept walking. So many new buildings lining the street. So much metal and glass. And there it was: a boxy brown building with a large blue-and-white sign on the top: AXA INSURANCE. She entered a lobby with glass windows on all sides and giant black leather chairs. There was a painting. Abstract, huge. Maybe they paid for them by the metre. She looked at the list of embossed names on the wall: AXA LEGAL DIVISION LEVEL 7.

She popped out of the lift, her gold-speckled skirt swirling, and startled the grim-faced receptionist when she strode straight past.

A few men in suits sitting at desks behind partitions. They all resembled one another. Then she saw his feet first: yellow polka dot socks peeking out of a pair of brogues. She'd once teased him about those socks, called them *unprofessional*. He was tilted back in his chair at a dramatic angle, his feet on top of the desk. Was he trying to look like he didn't care a hoot for manners? Or had he seen too many movies about powerful men in offices? He had a pen in his mouth and was gazing into space, either thinking hard about a problem or not thinking at all. She had a sudden urge to dethrone him, embarrass him, make him want her even more. Sidling up to him, she grabbed his feet and flung them to the ground. He spun around, pen dropping to the floor, and stared at her, open-mouthed. He was unshaven, his tie askew, and Veronika couldn't help laughing.

'What are you doing here?' he said, tight-lipped.

'I've come to see *you*, of course.'

He sat up straight and straightened his collar. 'I am not permitted unsolicited visitors,' he said sternly.

Veronika hooted. 'Unsolicited?' She was oddly excited by the bristles on his chin. 'You were the one who solicited *me*.'

He rose from his seat, confronted her. 'Stop playing games,' he said. 'You need to leave right now.'

'Is that an order?'

'The office is alarmed. I'll call security.'

'Fiddlesticks!'

'Fiddlesticks?'

Veronika smiled in what she hoped was a seductive way. 'That was my grandma's expression,' she said. 'Because she was too polite to say bullshit.'

She took his hand, held it to her sternum. He didn't resist.

'I want you to come back,' she said. 'To the play. To me. I'm sorry for what I did. Whatever it was.'

He wrenched his hand from hers. 'I don't wish to discuss it,' he said.

'But *I* do.'

'I'm surprised that you give a damn.'

She was shocked. 'Of course I give a damn, Sebastian. I care about you.'

'So much that you didn't even bother introducing me to your parents. And then you spent the whole time ignoring me.'

Veronika took this in. Decided to change tack.

'I'm sorry,' she said. 'I was too involved with the play. *Immersed* in it. And ... well, we need you back, Sebastian, honestly. Truly. Felix's been playing the Count as well as directing, and it's all too much for him. We need someone ... to play the Count.'

He shrugged. 'Not my problem.'

'But you were *so* good as Figaro.' She resisted taking his hand again. Looked at his silk tie, his strong jaw, his steely eyes. 'What about directing the play yourself?' she said. What *was* she thinking? What would Felix say? She must be desperate.

He folded his arms. 'Too messy,' he said. 'I'm playing Figaro. *Was* playing Figaro.'

'Felix gave the part to Josh.'

'What?' Sebastian laughed. 'The farmhand? An illiterate fool?'

Veronika felt indignant. 'He's not. Not at all. He's actually very smart and sensitive. Not as good as you in the part, but ... well ... think about it, Sebastian.'

She waited. Watched him thinking. She could almost see his thoughts: *Director* written on his chair.

'I'll mull it over,' he said.

'So when will I know?'

'You'll know.'

She went to kiss him on the cheek but heard a coughing sound behind her. She turned to be confronted by the grim-faced receptionist.

'You don't have a security pass, miss,' she said. 'I need you to come to reception.'

Veronika smiled, brushed back her hair. 'It's quite alright,' she said. Simpered, really. 'I was just about to leave.'

Sebastian touched her elbow. 'I'll see her out, Janice,' he said.

He led her out of the room, his hand on the small of her back. He walked her in the wrong direction, stood her in front of an open office door. She saw a massive painting of a river on the wall and a sleek mahogany desk. And through the window, a sweeping view of the real river, with a single yacht sailing by.

'That'll be me one day,' Sebastian said.

28. Sebastian

So. She had lured him back. It was against his nature to give in to her, to anyone, but he'd let her win in the end. How had she done it, he wondered. Was it her voice: commanding, seductive? Her piercing eyes? Or the way she looked at him, almost past him, as if there was something about himself that she couldn't quite fathom. He always wanted more of her, and it was new to him, this feeling. She would always keep him guessing. And she'd told him she believed in him, but not like the other girls he'd dated and dropped, the ones who parroted the right line in order to catch a man. Veronika – bright and irrepressible, gorgeous, foreign, full of ideas. She'd had the whiff of the orchard about her too – ripe plums, sunshine. Intoxicating.

Would he go back to the play? His mind went blurry with the thought. Rehearsals had been chaotic. Veronika had virtually snubbed him. She'd said she was sorry and seemed to mean it, but he'd had to … share her with all those other people. And there had been nowhere proper to sleep. He wondered if he'd even caught nits. Or fleas. All that dog hair on his pillow! Everything had sort of stuck to him at that farm. Nettles in his clothes. Leaves and sap on the soles of his shoes. Cassie. He had warmed to her, true. But he regretted giving her so much attention and now she seemed rather too eager around him, biting her lips and pinching her cheeks. But then Veronika said she wanted him back. To be there. But how would he tolerate it with that irritating, low-class friend of hers hanging around? What could she want with him? And what would he do now?

When Veronika had appeared in his office just now – unexpected, beautiful, desirable – the thought of spending his life in insurance, even with a sparkling river view, made him feel empty. Hollow inside.

Later, when he got home, his father called him into his study. They sat in his leather chairs, whiskey in hand. Sebastian looked around the room: vermillion walls, maps, a compass, a globe, medical journals, books about art, fat spy novels. It all seemed too careful, played for effect. His father leaned forward in his chair. Sebastian noticed age spots on his hands.

'Sebastian.' His father coughed. 'Are you doing the right thing by this ... Veronika?'

Sebastian stared at the painting on the opposite wall, a bushscape: dimpled granite boulders and phallic trunks of gum trees. Rocks like buttocks. His mother had painted it. He wanted to laugh out loud.

'I'm not sure what you mean,' he said.

'It's very simple,' his father said. 'I mean that you should either marry her or let her go.'

Sebastian had known exactly what his father would say, but hearing him say it, he felt a stab of revulsion in his chest.

He managed to excuse himself.

He went outside, wishing he smoked, and lay down in the dark on the edge of the swimming pool. As a child, he'd once thrown their pet tabby into the pool, scooped it out, been gouged on the forehead for his pains. Why was he so spineless whenever his father spoke to him? Laid out a plan for him? Why couldn't he be his own man, free to be himself or whoever he might become? Was this why he was drawn to the play? Where he could be untamed but in control? Live in organised chaos? Maybe he'd return to be a Player, immerse himself, as Veronika had said. Lose himself or find himself, or both.

But then another picture came into his head: his lecturer in political science, who always dressed in black and who'd taken him aside, told him his essays were *brilliant*. That he should study abroad, cultivate connections, consider a career in politics. Sebastian had been ambushed, exhilaratingly so, and grateful for the man's shrewd advice. Maybe *abroad* was a better idea. A prestigious university. He could take part in debates, drink port after dinner, go skiing in the Alps. Shake off mediocrity, slavish conformity.

He rolled into the pool, fully clothed, and felt the cool water soothing him.

29. Gloria

Ah! He was back, damn him. They'd been halfway through the courtroom scene, all the lines remembered, people growing into their parts, when Mr Full-of-Himself decided to turn up. Bless them with his presence.

Felix sprang from his deckchair. 'This is very ... unexpecting,' he said.

They shook hands. Everyone else stayed silent and still.

'Let's draw a line under the events and circumstances of the past,' Sebastian said.

Always the wanker, Gloria thought. And now the usurper: Josh would lose his part as Figaro. She couldn't bear to think about it. She knew how hard he'd worked to learn his lines.

'But your part is taken,' Felix said. 'I am sorry.'

'Veronika informed me that you need someone to play the Count,' Sebastian said. 'Well, you can count on me.'

Cassie let out a loud *humph*. Gloria glanced at Veronika. What did she look like? Puzzled. Had she really been to talk to him? Or was Sebastian making it up? Had he been missing the chance to *perform*? Or maybe he was actually missing *them*.

Gloria winced at her own stupid thought.

She and Josh went back to the shed for another line drill. She wanted to keep him motivated. Wanted to keep him by her side. She complained about Sebastian, waltzing in like a king, thinking he could come and go as he pleased.

Josh frowned. 'Is he really that bad?' he said.

'Why are you taking his side?'

'Because ... well, I might be responsible for him coming back. I suggested to Veronika that she talk to him.'

Gloria felt stunned. 'So ... is there something going on between the two of you?'

'No. And what's it to you if there was?'

He turned his back. His rudeness, his anger, was surprising. A bit shocking.

'I'm sorry,' she said. 'It's none of my business.'

He turned to face her. 'That's not what I meant,' he said. 'I meant ... you said you just want to be friends with me, right?'

Gloria swallowed hard. How could she say: my mother wouldn't let me get involved with you, even if she met you and learnt how kind you are. But looking at him now – his messy hair, the freckles, the gap in his teeth when he smiled – she felt something loosen up inside.

'I'm thinking of moving out of home,' she said. 'So I can do my own thing. You know.' She took a deep breath. 'Living with my mother, it's like wearing this great big jacket of emotional manipulation.'

She waited. He didn't say a word.

'Well, now. Joshua, isn't it?'

Sebastian, standing at the door. 'Don't think we've met properly, have we?'

He held out his hand, and Josh shook it.

'A word of advice,' Sebastian said. 'Since I already know Figaro's lines. You're playing a Harlequin. Figaro has the *ésprit Gaulois*. He's cunning, an opportunist. A negotiator. A libertine in love!' He showed his teeth. 'You have to be less sincere,' he said.

Gloria wanted to give him the sincerest kind of shove, but he was turning to her now, still smiling.

'And Gloria,' he said. 'You'd make a much better Suzanne than Veronika.'

She snorted. 'You're not the director.'

He tipped out his palms. 'Just trying to help,' he said.

'Are we done yet?' she said. 'We're busy.'

Sebastian took his cue and left.

She and Josh exchanged looks.

'He belongs in a TV commercial,' Josh said. 'For whitening your teeth.'

He moved towards her, and she thought for a moment that he would move even closer. Kiss her.

'Maybe we could get a place together,' he said. 'Just you and me.' He blushed. 'Separate rooms, of course.'

Gloria felt an energy between them. You could almost touch it. 'There's a spare place above the Blue Moon,' she said. 'It's a bit run-down, but—'

'We can always fix it up,' he said.

30. Joshua

It seemed that each day had been borne out of a hot wind coming from the east. It rolled over the slopes like an enormous sigh and left piles of broken twigs and leaves scattered on the ground. Each morning he was forever raking bits of scabby heath and silver-topped gimlet gums, debris from the clay bank, yellow fluff from shredded wattle. But the bush persisted through this strange, erosive sculpting. It was something of a marvel, he thought.

And it was time, now, Joshua knew. They had been rehearsing for more than ten days, and already the trees were heavy with plump purple daubs of fruit, soft to the touch.

They'd gathered for an early evening picnic: chicken drumsticks and coleslaw, chocolate ice cream. He saw the slightest hint of a tangerine sunset, knew he had to get a move on to help Michal set up for harvest before the light disappeared.

Michal lit the citronella candles and called everyone to be silent. Using an old blackboard, he sketched out a plan with chalk, drew a map of the orchard, allotted them each a portion of the land. He drew names and stick figures, arrows and lines, explained how to manoeuvre the ladders and how to strap on the barrels. The tricky part was picking the plums, he said: pull at them quickly but make sure you get them off. He reminded them to cherish his *black diamonds* but to eat as many as they wished. Wear a sensible hat and shoes. He would be coming around with the cart of bins in which to empty their barrels.

'It will be hard work,' he insisted. 'It will take most of two weeks.'

He told them where to find the equipment and scoops.

'Scoops?' A chorus of voices.

'Long poles,' he said. 'You use them to collect the fruit too high for you to reach.'

Then it was Angela's turn to lay down some rules in her no-nonsense voice. Cooking so much food was becoming difficult; she had little time for other tasks, so she would set up a roster. And instead of using the shower, they would have to wash themselves with the hose pipes near the stables. Tomorrow she would hire a portaloo. The good news, she said, was she only had a few more hems of the costumes to take up, and once the harvest was over, the final fittings could take place.

Joshua looked at all the faces of this motley, untried crew. He heard a few mumbles and grumbles, then watched them drift away. Michal showed him a look of concern.

'Josh, you'll give them a hand if they need it, won't you? I'm not sure this lot knows what they're in for.'

The two of them chatted for some time, hauling harvest bags, scoops and gloves back and forth from the barn to the veranda. Josh was happy to be helping out. Michal praised him for his good work ethic – something Michal had learned from his own father – and Josh felt his face redden with pleasure. He listened eagerly to Michal's stories: memories of his father coming home from the railways, boots creaking, face marked with dirt. How it broke his heart to know that his father never returned to work on the land, how he'd laboured in a railway yard instead. His mother toiled away over smocks and shirts. They didn't have enough money for a sewing machine, so she would go to people's homes and use theirs, sew them the things they needed. Word got around that she was good. It hadn't been easy for either of them: the taunts and insults, the prejudice. The pittance in their pockets. Sharing a flat in Maylands with another family.

Josh could hear the pride and the pity in Michal's voice. He envied him, too, to have parents whom he loved and respected. Who loved their son in return.

'You know, Josh,' Michal said, his voice quiet now. 'My mother married for love, against her father's wishes. A *mere peasant*, he had called my father. To his face, can you believe that? But whenever I think of them, I don't see peasants. I see dedicated workers who suffered. Four years of Nazi occupation, and then the new Communist regime that took over my father's orchard. And then they fled, took a giant leap to give their son a chance at a better life. Me. They gave me a better life.'

The typical migrant story, Josh thought. The determination to help their children. He couldn't help thinking of his own father again, then tried to flick him away.

'It wasn't easy to begin with,' Michal went on. 'Five years I spent in the nickel mine, machine operator, surveyor until I had enough money to buy this land. Make my father proud. I wanted to bring him back his orchard on the other side of the world.'

Josh felt touched by these stories and by Michal's wanting him to know them, as if he were a son or even a friend. But the man was also his boss. And he felt the pain of exclusion again: there had been no such stories in his own house, even ones of hardship and peril. All he had were splintered memories of altercations, a gaping sense of absence. There was no-one really except Charlie. And Charlie was always in trouble. Charlie, whom he loved and reviled. Charlie, who taunted and terrified him. Charlie, for whom he felt a burst of love and a breathless panic at the same time. Charlie, who did the best he could when no-one else was there to care for him.

There was his mate Warra, too. Maybe he should give him a call.

31. Gloria

'A barrel of laughs this'll be,' Gloria said, patting the barrel strapped around her waist, Josh standing next to her. She called them Tweedledum and Tweedledee.

They all began working together, telling stories and making jokes under the hot summer sun. Snatching, pulling in and around spiky leaves, grabbing, reaching across branches, enjoying the drop of the fruit in their round pouches that grew heavier by the minute. Felix was complaining, though, about the wind blowing seed heads into his eyes and making him sneeze like a madman. He *despised* the insects, too, he said, the centipedes and crickets and beetles, and he was sure it was only a matter of time before he saw a snake.

'It is a kind of torture,' he said, 'but I must remain open to extremes.'

Cassie told him to save his breath for the work.

Gloria asked Josh how he was doing, and he gave her that gap-toothed grin.

'I've always liked hard work,' he said. 'I like that there is a beginning and an end. A job to be done.'

She liked it, too, this attachment to the land. She'd been on a family farm many years ago, taken by a school friend whose name she couldn't remember. It wasn't long after she'd arrived in Australia, and she could still see the sanded earth of salty flats and then the paddocks of chocolate brown and straw. Flocks of dirty white sheep, hundreds of them baaing and trotting about. They were going to be shipped to Iran, said her friend. For slaughter. And Gloria had tried to name as many as she could, had sung farewell songs to them, amusing her friend when she hadn't intended to be funny.

I won't sing to the plums, she thought, before they're chewed and swallowed and gone.

Still, she loved being in the open air. The sun. It was as if all the spaces inside her, all her broken feelings, could be made whole again, become one with the trees and rocks and leaves. She loved the wild bushland surrounding the orchard, the raucous call of birds, the lemony scent of eucalypts.

She picked more plums, her hands working fast. Her brother had killed pigs. Her family had sat on the ground and had eaten the animals, half burnt, with their bare hands. She'd almost finished her studies. Maybe she could teach English or geography or botany. She'd heard about all the orphans in East Timor-Leste. But she wouldn't go back with her mother. Her health wouldn't stand it. Maybe she would find her father. Maybe Josh would come with her.

Or maybe she'd wait until things settled down at home. Not that she knew what was really happening there. How many people did?

Sebastian. Coming towards her, his barrel strapped onto him. He looked like a bloated, comical figure straight out of a cartoon. So why did he want to talk to her?

'I still think you should play Suzanne,' he said. 'It's best if someone like you performs that character.'

'*Someone like me?*'

'From the Pacific Islands, I mean. New Guinea?' Resting his hands on his barrel, pompous and smug.

'I'm from East Timor,' Gloria snapped. 'To be precise.'

'Even better!' His eyes widened. 'It would be more politically astute to cast you as the maiden, the victim of the Count's *droit du seigneur*.'

'What are you talking about?'

'Well, it's Paul Keating's fault,' he said. 'He's a huge fan of Suharto, the Indonesian president, as you know, and he let our foreign minister sign that damned treaty which means that Australia and Indonesia are in bed together. We can guzzle up all of Timor's oil supplies. Don't get me wrong, I'm proud to be an Australian most of the time, but this Labor government ... no integrity, not a scrap of integrity.'

'What's your point, Sebastian?'

'Well, I'm playing the Count, and if you play Suzanne, the innocent maiden, we could stand in for national figures. You would be exploited Timor, and I would be Australia, the ogre. Audiences these days need that kind of thing, you know. To keep the play politically relevant.'

She slapped her barrel like a drum. 'You can go and get stuffed,' Gloria said.

32. Ana

A giant lizard, a fucking blue-tongued lizard, came darting towards her, ugly and scary and quick. She'd always hated the things. She let out a scream, and a man appeared from out of nowhere, lifted the beast by the neck, carried it outside.

'Take it far away,' she shouted after him. 'So far that it doesn't come back.'

The man returned, grinning, held out a hand.

'Eek, don't touch me!' she squealed.

'Sebastian,' he said, and made a bow, as if playing a courtly gentleman.

'Ana. Veronika's sister.'

That grin again.

'Pleased to meet you,' he said. 'I'm Veronika's boyfriend.'

'Really? I thought she was with Josh.'

He laughed. 'You must be joking. She's with me. But you wouldn't know that. Ronnie said you'd been away for a long time.'

'Three years. Hardly an eternity.'

He looked her up and down, as if she were a racehorse he was thinking of buying. She had a sudden urge to whip off her skirt and show him her thighs, laugh in his face.

'You didn't even thank me for rescuing you,' he said, with a swagger in his voice. 'I know your type.'

She kicked off a shoe, sent it scattering along the floor.

'Piss off,' she said.

She was at a loose end. Fraying at the seams. She hadn't even heard back from Charlie yet, let alone seen him. So she was glad when her father insisted she come with him on the truck, help collect the plums. They drove to each of the actors, players, students, whatever they called themselves. They looked a weedy lot, struggling with the work. Not like the muscly Italian backpackers who were also good at flirting. She preferred it when people didn't speak English.

Her father was looking tired these days, and his hair had turned grey in her absence. He had been curious about Prague. What did it look like now, after the Velvet Revolution? The peaceful revolution. Thankfully, he hadn't asked about her job. He hadn't made a scene, either, about her skipping a meeting with her grand-uncle Jozef. He was just glad she was safe and sound at home, and anyway, his mind was firmly on harvest. She offered to drive the truck by herself, and he agreed, looking relieved.

She drove along the terraces, feeling good to be behind the wheel. In charge. Fred was yapping at the side of the truck, so she slowed down, opened the door, let him jump in. He licked her madly, then settled down onto her lap. She had one ally, at least, in this stupid place.

What was that idiot's name? Bowing like he was in some dumb movie. It was only a fucking lizard. Sebastian. A posh name. Pretentious. Well, he and Veronika deserved each other. Still, at least her sister had a boyfriend, and he was probably rich as well. They'd get married in some beautiful church and live in a beautiful house and have beautiful kids and go to the opera and the ballet and whatever. She felt anger simmering in her throat. She caught sight of Joshua picking fruit and drove past. 'You'd better watch out for Veronika,' she said in a loud voice. 'She's a real user, roping you into this. Doesn't really care about you, you know.'

Josh said, *huh?* And carried on working. Ana left him to do his thing. What could she do? She'd phoned the salon, but they had no openings. So that was that. What was she supposed to do now? What was she ever going to do? Losing a job she loved, hating the cold and having no money and doing stupid things, and now she was back, and where had it got her? What had she actually achieved? She'd only learned a smattering of Czech, could barely speak her father's language. And now here was her sister in some dumb play and studying French. High-and-mighty Veronika, always the clever one, the beautiful one, even more beautiful now.

33. Charlie

The airconditioner rattled on like a machine gun. It had been on the blink all week but now that someone had finally fixed it, Charlie thought he'd rather swelter to death than to endure the racket it made.

No-one was in. Not even Narelle, the office manager. He turned on the radio to drown out the noise. Some sort of soppy tune burst into the office unit. Celine Dion. Charlie cringed. He frantically fiddled around, buzzing past piano music, then jazz (worse), talking, more talking (screeching ad about car mufflers), then 'Stand Up, Stand Up for Jesus' (Hell, no!) until he found 'Pump Up the Jam.' That was music for sheilas too, like stupid Celine, but at least *doof doof* would save him from that deathly air-conditioner noise and from having to think too much.

He'd come to headquarters to check his email before he hit the road. He was waiting for something from the big boss about a new tunnel they were digging. They were trying to figure out if this one needed timber shoring and whether the miners would need an air pump to carry out the job. There had been a headache about water coming in with the last one. He didn't want a fiasco this time. It was all a risky business; you had to play your cards right. Manage it all as deftly as you could, or people could be dead.

Charlie had stuffed up a couple of times already. Lost his cool with the site manager and was put on probation. A disagreement about a safety issue for one of the workers, an ex-prisoner who Charlie didn't like. The company had a program to recruit some of the best guys within the last few months of their sentence, but this guy was a complete tosser, refused to wear his head shield and mask on his first attempt using an air drill. Charlie had let him have it, and the guy complained. So the site manager called in Charlie for a disciplinary meeting and Charlie taught him a thing or two. It all backfired. Two fuck-ups. Three, and you're out. Charlie knew he had a bit of a mouth on him. Told himself he'd have to keep it shut.

The prison program made him uneasy. He half expected Josh to turn up one day. He knew it wasn't likely, Josh would have left detention three or four years earlier, but he still dreamed of him when he was on site at

Yallabatharra. Josh's little-boy face staring up at him underneath a head shield, wielding a pick and axe, as if he were coming after him. Then another dream, Josh crushed to death in a tunnel.

Charlie tried not to think of his brother. Kept him in a box snapped shut. Charlie couldn't afford a smear from the past. He'd made the mistake of sending him a note while he was on the inside but then thought the better of it after. He was trying to get beyond all that. His shit dad and shit old life. He already had a pile of money. He just had to keep going.

He found a spare computer, logged in and dialled up a few times, but the line was busy. He unplugged the phone cable and tried again, with no luck. He jumped on Narelle's computer, saw the popup *connection successfully established*, but he couldn't log in. Her password? What would it be? He'd already done a bit of nifty groundwork a couple of months back over dessert in the refectory. They'd been tucking into trifle and Black Forest cake. He'd figured Narelle was an easy target, it might be handy to access her stuff, so he asked her first pet's name. Her partner's name. Even the name of the street on which she grew up. She'd given it all to him and then told him stories about a pet lovebird that flew away. Christ.

Charlie racked his brains for the pet name. Right. Stevie Ray Vaughan the goldfish, for Pete's sake. But maybe. He typed it in, all one word, no luck. Then he remembered. Stevie was eaten by the cat. Then there was Barney the rabbit. Still no luck. What was her partner's name? Robert? Rex. Narelle was always whining about Rex. Rex the chef. Rex1. Bingo! And there was Rex right in front of him! An acne-scarred face that only a mother could love. A photo of the pair cropped into a heart shape.

Narelle's mailbox opened but he quickly shut it down and logged into his work mail. It was taking forever to load. He clicked onto the internet to check his Hotmail. Eventually his messages jumped into view. He waded through the sea of junk mail, advertising everything from discount holidays in Bratislava to pills for erectile dysfunction to bargain-basement cookware.

And then a message from Ana, of all people. He'd almost forgotten about her. Ana. Yeah, she was a bit of fun. A boozy evening in Earls Court. He'd been skiving off during some investment conference full of up-themselves wankers, and she was there for a weekender. A hook-up. Music. A bit of coke. She'd kept talking, talking, talking her head off about feeling free to speak English, being understood, no longer feeling strange and out of fashion and out of place. And now here she was, sending him an email. A bit of an ego boost, it was, having someone chase him around the globe like that. Ana. She was kind of funny and draining at the same time.

hi charlie

hows it going? really awesome to see you in london. Feels like a long time ago. hey why didn't you stick around to say goodbye???. i can't believe i lost my bag at that troubadour place anyhow, guess what???? I ended up leaving Prague, got bored and that guy was a total creep and dad needs help with harvest. So im back in perth, do you want to hang out if your around?? for all intensive purposes, i kind of miss U. send me an email if you wanna go for a drink or see a band or whatever cos id still like to see you irregardless of whats going on. ill send u my number.

fred says woof woof!

kisses from Ana
ps. come on you know you want to

The radio disc jockey blurted away: *next caller to guess the song wins one thousand dollars ...*

Ana. She was okay in small doses ... He checked his work mail. The boss had written. The tunnel would go ahead. He would have to get cracking on the timber.

Driving back to Perth, he kept remembering bits and pieces of his tryst with small-doses-Ana. Most of it a drunken blur. His stomach clenched. Something wasn't right. He had said too much. She knew too much. He would have to keep her sweet. Keep Ana sweet. He'd send her another note. Connect up. She wasn't that far away anymore. Besides, it could be worth it: she had that babe of a kid sister.

34. Joshua

His barrel of plums was half full, but it felt heavier than that. He was beginning to wilt. He stopped, placed the barrel on the grass. He drank some water from his hip flask. What is it? he asked himself and bent over the grass. *She doesn't really care about you*, Ana had said. That couldn't possibly be true. She did care. She had to care.

It came back to him: the fire. The ashen air. The filth in the darkness. Flying embers, brilliant and threatening. He'd tried to find Veronika. He'd run for his life, as far as he could in the mammoth wave of heat. He'd run, naively, all the way to the tree house, seeking some sort of refuge. He'd seen Veronika's necklace, seized it, buried it quickly and bolted. He'd scratched his legs from thorns and twigs, had jostled and hopped his way through. He'd heard birds cry and animals thump in the blackness. He'd fallen and hit his head. He'd woken to the sound of sirens.

He wanted to walk away, get out of the place. Without making a scene.

Josh stood up and strapped on his barrel again. He kept picking plums until his shoulders stiffened and the skin on his hands cracked. He didn't stop for lunch. He would help do the harvest, he would act in the play, and then he would leave. Perfect.

Except … there was Gloria. His heart tugged. What would he do? Was it all part of the play, he wondered, their connection? Was it real? She may have liked him, but could she really care for him? Her life seemed complicated in ways he could not fathom.

It seemed to him that for a brief moment in time, he'd lost his mind, agreeing to act in the play. He'd done it for Veronika. But how could he get over what she'd done? It came over him like a sudden shock: the abandonment. How was that alright? How would that ever be okay? And now … he would find a job at sea. Warra had mates who worked on fishing trawlers. They would help him if he asked.

35. Veronika

It was the end of harvest. The cast turned up for a barbecue Saturday evening in exhausted dribs and drabs after twelve days of picking, barely able to move. Felix lit the barbecue, looking pleased with himself, Veronika thought, as if this simple act made him more Australian. Over the table, Lucas reminded them of his gig at the local pub; he was playing bass with Mud Cloud. Sebastian yawned. Gwen shrugged. Everyone ate in silence. They'd run out of beer and cider and were forced to drink lime cordial.

Veronika took Sebastian's hand, whispered *escape*.

They slipped away to the creek, sat down on the bank. She welcomed the quiet, a different kind of quiet – serene, comforting – from the tired and grumpy silence of the cast. But she wanted to talk as well, needed to show Sebastian her feelings. She looked down into the rushing water.

'I'm glad you came back,' she finally said. 'We haven't had a chance to be alone, and I just wanted to say thank you. With all my heart. And the play's so much better because of you. The harvest, the play ... it's all working out.'

He took her hand, stroked her palm. 'You're welcome,' he said. 'And I enjoyed meeting your parents. Properly. They're fine folk. Your mother's got a big heart. And your father: an honest, hardworking man.' He squeezed her hand. 'Your sister, though ... she's a different story.'

'I thought going to Europe would improve her,' Veronika said. 'Tame her a bit. But ... let's not spoil this. Us. I don't want to talk about her.' She looked up at the towering trees. 'It's lovely here, isn't it?'

'It is.'

She heard a tremor in his voice. Asked him if something was wrong. He insisted he was fine, that everything was fine, but Veronika wasn't quite convinced. Was it her sister? she asked him. Had she said something that upset him?

Sebastian let go of her hand.

'She told me that the country bumpkin ... Figaro ... what's his name? ... Josh. She told me he was your boyfriend.'

Veronika grunted. 'Not in a million years,' she said. 'He was sort of my boyfriend when we were kids. I was thirteen, fourteen. Just silly adolescent stuff. That's all.'

'Well, that explains it,' he said. 'You're much too sophisticated for him.'

'Sophisticated? No-one's ever called me that before.'

'Well, you are. And you're beautiful and smart and you drive me crazy – in the best possible way.'

She leaned over and kissed him. Wanting him to kiss her back, to lift up her shirt like he used to. Find her. But instead, he moved away from her, wouldn't look at her.

'What's wrong?' she said. 'No-one can see us here.'

'Veronika. I like you a lot. But I have to tell you something.'

She watched him carefully. 'Go on,' she said.

'Not long ago. I ... well, Cassie and I ... we kissed.'

'You *what*?'

'It just sort of happened. It meant nothing.'

'Meant nothing? A kiss is a kiss.' She felt her cheeks grow hot.

'Veronika. Ronnie. I ... please, listen to me. *She* started it.'

'And you kept it going. *We* kissed, you said. *We*!'

'Look. I ... I could have ... I was tempted. But I stopped it. I told her we had to stop.'

'You were *tempted!*'

He held out his hand, his good hand, and she drew back.

'You'd been ignoring me,' he said. 'You made me feel like I didn't count for anything.'

'And now I know why.'

'Look at me, Ronnie. I think you should give me some credit. I controlled myself, didn't I? It was just a bloody kiss.'

She leapt up from the ground, began to walk, hurry away from him. She heard him calling her name. She waited for him to tell her that he loved her. Only her. But all she heard was some stupid bird squawking in the night.

'*Jdi do háje!*' she spat.

36. Joshua

Josh had seen Veronika run across the orchard barefoot. She had been so fast; he knew something was up. He would find her, speak to her, but first there was work that needed to be done: feed the horse and ponies, check on the geese.

Once he was finished with the chores, he knocked on Veronika's old bedroom door. All he could hear were rustling sounds until *come in*. A feeble voice. He cracked the door open and saw her puffy eyes, her face in the mirror. She had been crying. Scrunched up tissues everywhere. She was wearing her grandmother's necklace.

Veronika motioned for him to come in. He leant against the wall and clanged his head against a framed picture of the Taj Mahal.

'I couldn't pick another plum if you paid me,' she said.

'I thought you Vaček girls would be used to it,' he said wryly. 'Hey, I saw you earlier. You okay?'

'Can't wait for our break over Christmas. Two weeks Felix said. God, we need it. Can you believe it? We're almost done with rehearsing. Soon we'll be bumping in, doing the tech run ...'

Josh felt a sort of twinge. He wasn't sure what it was. He figured she'd had a fight, but she wasn't ready to talk. He felt a bit stupid just standing there as she chirped on.

'Thought I'd wear this tonight,' she said, hand over her necklace. 'It gives me strength somehow – knowing that it was Babička's. I don't feel like going to Lucas's gig, not at all, but I promised him I would.'

She started carrying on about being overdressed, but Josh found it hard to keep listening. He was feeling tired. Tired and a bit fed up.

'I still don't know why you did it,' she said suddenly.

'Did what?'

'Lit that fire, Josh. I mean, what got into you?'

Her voice was sharp, cutting into him. She'd changed in a flash. Everything had changed. A thick silence cloaked the room. Josh wanted to leave, but he didn't want to flee in a panic, look like he was chickenshit. He felt stuck against the wall, wrestling with this feeling in his chest, something he couldn't even name, didn't want to name, while she sat there at her dressing table, fossicking for stupid things.

Another knock at the door. This time it was open.

'Felix!' Veronika stood.

'I am feeling the need for retreat,' Felix announced, 'so I will say my goodbyes. No pub for me.' He gave Veronika and Josh a quick hug, then left just as quickly.

'He looks wired and tired, doesn't he?' Veronika said. Quiet now, kind, as if she'd never accused him. 'I wonder where he's off to. I do hope he comes back.'

Josh shrugged, trying not to show his anger, wanting to stay in control.

'I need a drink,' he said and strode from the room, slamming the door behind him.

37. Cassie

The pub was filling up quickly. The decor was old-world: faux-Tudor roof, rustic wooden stools and tables, various coats of arms mounted on the walls. The place stank of booze and piss, but Cassie didn't mind. She was listening to the music – a duo on guitar and keyboard, singing a few fey songs so badly they'd make Mud Cloud sound like rock stars. She pushed her way to the front of the swelling crowd; she was excited about watching Lucas play.

Thank God the duo was done. Mud Cloud arrived, set up their gear, heard murmurs of excitement building around the room. Lucas started playing bass in the dark: a rhythmic thudding shift of notes that made Cassie bump and grind her hips. The crowd was pressing in. She thought she spied Veronika in the distance. Then the lead guitarist joined Lucas in a melodic riff, the drums came crashing in, the lights turned rainbow and the crowd hollered, threw their hands in the air. She kept pushing to the front, close to the bar, longing for a drink. She saw Gwen wielding a jug of beer, Gloria and Josh holding out glasses, Sebastian holding two beers at once, taking alternate sips from each glass. What a wanker, Cassie thought, longing for a drink even more. She made her way over, someone thrust a glass of beer in her hand, and Gwen put her head down, pulled some folded-up alfoil from her breast pocket.

'Want one?' she said to Cassie. As casual as hell.

'What is it?'

'Does it matter? It'll blow off the top of your head.'

'I only need music,' Cassie said, hoping she didn't sound up herself.

'I'll have one,' Gloria said, and Josh touched her arm, holding her back.

'Nothing left for me?' Sebastian moaned.

Gwen kissed him on the lips, then dissolved into the crowd.

Sebastian took a swig of beer, wiped his mouth. 'I wish women would stop kissing me,' he said. 'It gets me into trouble.'

'You're pathetic,' Cassie said, drained her glass, and tuned in to the band. She saw Lucas move in close to the microphone, his long fringe falling over his eyes, his guitar slung so low that it almost hit his knees.

'This one's for the woman with the brown curls,' he said.

Cassie jolted. It was for her. The song. Lucas. The music was deafening, a blur of words and jangling guitars, acid rock, and she thrust out her chest, swung her arms, swaying and free, free in the wild drumming music. She was the woman with brown curls. She was something.

38. Veronika

Sebastian found her at the back of the room.

'I knew you'd be here,' he said. 'Trying to avoid me.'

'I hate you,' she said, resolute and grim, and edged her way past swaying dancers, loud conversations, packs of people she didn't know. Where was Josh? She needed to see Josh. Someone who'd understand her. She spied him dancing and thought he looked absurd, no sense of rhythm, but it didn't matter. What mattered was talking. Connecting. She walked over to him, tapped him on the shoulder, and he turned to face her, then turned away. She grabbed his arm, but he wrenched himself free, moved away, stumbled into the crowd. I mustn't lose sight of him, she thought, hating the loud music, hating the stench of old beer, hating Sebastian. She could see Josh's dark hair in the mess of the crowd, saw him duck outside and into the night. She followed him. Determined.

He swung around, told her to leave him alone.

She grabbed his arm again, but he pulled it away again.

'Come back to the orchard with me,' she said. 'It's our home.'

He looked like she'd punched him in the face.

'It's not our *home*,' he said.

'We're friends, remember? We used to ... you and me, we—'

'That was a long time ago.' Joshed gave her a remote stare and inhaled. 'And now—'

What? Wait. You mean ... you're seeing Gloria?' Veronika shook her head. 'But you don't even know her.'

'I know her a whole lot better than you.'

She drew back. She had no idea where he was going with this ... this hostility.

'Why are you angry with me, Josh?'

He let out a laugh. 'What do you think?' he said. 'You didn't once visit me in prison. Two years. Have you any idea what that feels like? To lose two years of your life?'

She reached out her hand, but he swiped it away.

'Why didn't you tell me this before?' she said.

'I did. But you weren't listening.'

'I was. I was. I just didn't know what to say. I was a kid, Josh, a stupid kid. I didn't know what to do.'

'You were my *friend*,' he said.

'I'm sorry,' she said. 'Honestly, Josh. I just … But you have a new life now, a good life. You have a job.'

'Thanks to your father, yes. At least someone in your family is kind. Thinks about other people.'

'That's not fair, Josh. *I* think about you. I remember all the times—'

'Cut the bullshit nostalgia,' he said and folded his arms across his chest.

'But I love you, Josh. Don't you know that?'

'You love that idiot Sebastian,' he said and laughed. 'Well, you *perform* your love … to a rich, up-himself prat.'

'And what are *you* doing? Playing with that refugee.'

He looked dumbstruck.

Then turned on his heels and rushed inside.

She didn't, couldn't, follow him. She hadn't known she could be so cruel, so hateful.

She didn't know how long she sat on the pavement. She didn't know how she could go on.

She felt an arm around her shoulder, looked up to see Sebastian, and slumped into his chest.

'What was going on with that farm boy?' he said. 'He didn't hurt you, did he?'

She shook her head. 'I hurt *him*,' she said. 'Badly.'

Sebastian held her close. 'It's over now,' he said. 'You're safe with me.'

She snapped. She writhed out of his arms and pushed him away. She didn't know where she was going, she just needed to get away, hurrying back inside, Sebastian rushing after her, grabbing her arm, shouting *sorry, sorry, please forgive me*, grabbing her by the waist, spinning her round. She saw his stupid mouth and drunken face and pushed him to the floor, beer spilling all over him. Someone stepped on his hand, and she screamed and then a voice shouted even louder, raised above the clamour.

'Lemme sort this out!'

Veronika stared. Her stomach lurched. She knew that voice. That face.

She stared at him, aghast, as Sebastian struggled from the floor, grabbed at her waist. She pushed him off as hard as she could, trying to stay calm.

'My God!' Charlie's eyes were on stalks. 'It's little Veronika Vaček. You're … my, how you've grown up!' He pointed to Sebastian. 'Hey, is this drunk giving you trouble?'

Someone tapped him on the shoulder, and he spun around.

'Well, well, it's my *good* little brother,' Charlie said and jabbed him in the stomach. 'What a night for surprises. You've grown up, too, but just as ugly as ever. And what are you doing here? Trying to find a girlfriend, are we?'

Out of nowhere, Josh lunged forwards, shoved Charlie hard on the chest. Veronika couldn't breathe. And then there appeared, pale and trembling: Ana.

'Don't, Charlie,' she said. 'Please don't fight. I'm pregnant.'

39. Gloria

Gloria took one look at her reflection in the warped mirror at the back of the portaloo door, and, yes, she was a hundred years old. Her hair was lopsided. She must have slept in the same position the entire night. Moving it back into something more respectable, she wondered what the hell had happened. What had she taken? She felt shit. There was no other word for it. It had been a strange evening of euphoria and then the inevitable let-down because there always had to be a let-down when you thought things were going well.

She barely remembered a thing. She'd been talking to some locals. Cassie. And a weird band groupie who said he lived in a bus. God, her head hurt. Why had Joshua blown so hot and cold with her? She liked him a lot. Maybe too much. But she'd seen him make fists at someone, get into a bit of a brawl. It made her feel deflated, disappointed. And it wasn't really practical. Being with him. Not in a romantic way. But she wanted to move out still. She would ask him. Maybe. When the show was over. Once she got her act together. She should really ring her mum and tell her she'd be home soon. But then she felt her stomach rumble, heard it gurgle, and bugger it, she thought, I'll eat some breakfast first.

She made her way outside to the big trestle table overlooking the valley. Sat down. It was still really, really bright, she could barely open her eyes; another warm day, but no-one seemed to be around. The usual breakfast rigmarole wasn't happening. It was almost eerie, the silence, and the fruit trees looking so forlorn, all picked and plucked. Something wasn't right.

She checked her watch: December 11. Harvest was finished. There was something about that date, wasn't there? A run-through day. The first full run-through of the entire play. No scripts. They had to do at least three complete run-throughs before the break. Before opening night. *Far out.* They were meant to start hours ago. And where was Felix? And why didn't anyone seem to care?

Gloria went back into the packing shed to wake up the dead bodies. Lucas was there, his mouth open, dribbling onto his pillow. Sebastian too, sprawled out on his back. And Gwen, tucked up in the corner, fast asleep, with her Doc Martens on. Her blankets had formed some sort of volcano. But where were all the others? She decided to check the house. She was still in her pyjamas, but why should she care, why would anyone care?

No-one was in the kitchen, but there were voices in the living room. Gloria went to find out, saw Joshua, Cassie and Veronika, each on the edge of a chair. Michal on the phone, a worried voice. Mrs Vaček – was that her name? – suddenly appeared.

'Gloria. Some breakfast?' The woman was too cheery by half, too loud for Gloria's aching head.

'I'm okay for now,' Gloria lied. She was bloody starving. But then she knew she couldn't eat a thing until she knew what was going on.

Veronika wished her a good morning. 'The schedule is very clear,' she said. Decisive; in charge. 'We need to do a run of the whole play. We need to see how the swing roles work, time the costume changes, make sure of the smooth transitions on stage. With the props. But we can't find Felix. He should be here.'

Joshua stood up, his face sullen, gloomy. 'Didn't he say that he was off on some sort of retreat?' Still brooding from the night before, Gloria could tell. But there wasn't time for all that. They had to get on with it, before the break, otherwise the play wouldn't work, might be a complete disaster. It was crucial to get ready, not just the actors but the lighting people, the stage managers, for their opening on the first of January. So many people depended on them.

'Retreat?' Veronika looked perplexed. 'I thought he meant a quiet evening – that's all. A little break from us. It *is* odd. I rang his house. He isn't there. Whatever happens, we must carry on with the show. But how?'

Gloria wasn't sure it was as serious as all that. Felix was always having trouble with his van; sometimes it wouldn't even start. Maybe he needed to swear at it more. Or maybe they should ring the RAC. Except they didn't know where his car was. Maybe she *should* be worried. She felt a churning sensation in her stomach now, slightly afraid. Her body kind of knew these things sometimes, even if she didn't want to know them. The problems. The disasters.

'I might have a boiled egg, after all, Mrs Vaček,' she said. 'I can make it myself.'

'You sit down,' Veronika's mother said. 'I'll put one on now.'

Gloria thanked her and sat up on the bar stool. Mrs Vaček placed an egg cup and spoon in front of her. Gloria stared at the paraphernalia on the fridge. A calendar with a picture of the local mechanic. A postcard from ... Taiwan? A photo of Ginger and Fred. Aw. *Cute.* Phone numbers. Grubby finger marks. What to do now? Practical solutions were needed. Classroom management skills, she thought. What were they called? Preventative strategies – *create a positive environment.* Instruction. Rules and routines. If it applied to seven-year-olds, it should apply to adults, surely? Ah, yes, and responsive strategies: identify disruption. Communicate calmly ... She couldn't remember the other bits and pieces. She wished she had a pen and notepad.

She drummed her fingers on the counter. This play *had* to work out. They *had* to find Felix. What would happen if they couldn't get the play staged? Gloria would lose her bet when she joined the Players, that's what, her silly bet with Rosária. It *had* to go on, she thought, tapping the egg with her spoon. And she'd been away from her usual gang for so long, she had to have something to show for it. Rosária would never let her live it down. She'd missed the Van Halen mass, for crying out loud. There had to be a good reason.

An egg. Protein. Thank you, Mrs ...Vee? Gloria would wash herself with that chilling hose, slap her face and get changed. Then she would get them all moving with her determination and her classroom management skills.

Gloria went back into the living room, told them about her plan.

'Why don't we just do a run-through anyway? In the clearing. Without Felix. Give your parents some peace. I'll wake the others.'

The run-through had already started when Lucas turned up, script in hand, and half a piece of toast in his mouth. A blob of jam landed on his shirt.

'Gross,' Gloria said. 'And you've already missed your entry.'

He looked baffled.

'Give me that.' Gloria snatched the script from his hand.

Cassie rose. 'Now, I've given this some thought,' she said. 'And I think it's because you bullied him, Lucas. You told Felix that he demanded too much from us. You didn't respect him as the experienced European director that he is.' She had her hands on her hips. 'And now he's gone, hasn't he? Deserted us. Well, maybe not deserted us, as such. More like standing up for an artistic principle.'

Lucas looked too hungover to speak or to take offence at the accusation. He stumbled onto their dirt stage.

'Sit and wait your turn,' Gloria said.

Dazed, Lucas moved to the side and sat down next to Gwen in the makeshift wings.

'That was a while back now,' Lucas said, having caught up the conversation. 'We were good. Felix and me.'

It wasn't too bad, coordinating the run-through. Lucas didn't drag too much, with Gloria bossing and prompting when she could. And what had Felix said about acting? *Don't block the offer?* At least Sebastian was cooperating and knew all his lines as well. Veronika was improving, more relaxed, comfortable with her lines. Even if she and Sebastian didn't seem to be talking, at least they were acting. And that was what acting did: it covered over the reality. It was fun and hilarious, being a naughty page, hiding under Cassie's skirt. Cassie was really coming into her own, too, except she and Sebastian didn't seem to be speaking. And Veronika was clearly ignoring Cassie, except in the play. Joshua knew most of his lines, but then he wasn't speaking to Veronika, except in the play. Gwen did rather well overall, but it was hard to tell if she was speaking to anyone at all or if she was just concentrating hard. What a tangle they all were.

But Gloria was talking to them all. At least *she* could carry on without too much bother. And where the bloody hell was Felix?

40. Felix

Everything had turned into slowness.

How could he tell them? There was no way. Imagine: your director can no longer assist you. His brain is colonised by a turgid fog. Safe return not guaranteed. All the best with the show.

He couldn't let them see him like this. He had to recoup somehow. Recompose. Try to focus on the essentials. Shelter: the kombi. He could go back to his share house in town, but ... no, the cast would trace him there. He didn't want to return to the city either, to the hurl of noise, the excruciating, rattling presence of the others. He would navigate his way to the national park, its route set out in the *UBD*. He would sleep in the van, and during the day, set up camp ... where? In a cave, yes, a cave, where he could be alone for a while, wander along the tracks, try to figure it all out. Wait for the clouds in his mind to float away and for answers to appear.

He would need food. That was a good sign, wasn't it, needing food? He loaded up supplies from Ezy Plus. He would have Tim Tams and bread rolls, sausage, bacon, and noodles and things he could put in the cooler for a few days and things he could cook on his camping stove. Then he filled up an empty car oil container with twenty litres of water. Would the water taste of oil? Would twenty litres be enough? Enough to drink and wash himself? And clothing. He had enough with him, for a few days at least. And then he remembered: the Count's costume, he'd taken it with him by accident. He'd worn it for the play. He didn't mind it. The high collar, he particularly liked. The gold thread around the seams was beautifully done. He might wear it, in fact, if the weather was cool. But would he look strange if anyone saw him? Would he look as strange as he felt?

He left his van in the car park and took his things with him. He spent the first two days wandering the tracks and taking in the landscape. He was surprised by the difference it made to his feelings. He loved the aridity, the air like chalk, and the soft haze of heat. The trees – thin trees poised in elegant sway, and bushes and scrub with cones and nuts that looked prehistoric, vaguely threatening. The unexpected valleys and rock formations, the sunset spilling sublimely all over the vista.

He couldn't say what all this meant to him, but he knew it was exactly what he needed. He didn't know how long he would be here or if he would make it back in time for the play. For the moment, at least, he would stay here, hold the beauty in his heart.

He rolled out his mat inside a cave, preparing to rest for a while. He had spent the day looking outward, and now he'd found the space to look inward. To his desire. His long, drawn-out fantasy liaison with Max. He would take it slowly: gazing into Max's russet eyes, playing with his hair, unbuttoning his shirt, feeling the contours of his torso, exploring every inch with his hands before he even dared a kiss ... *Autsch!* Mosquitoes! Whining in his ear, spoiling the reverie, his longing. He slapped them off, cursing them, cursing himself for leaving the repellent in the van.

And now something else to worry about. His parents said he must finish his master's degree, but he'd withdrawn without them knowing, with no idea what it might mean for him, whether he'd be able to tell them, whether he'd be able to manage. They'd paid for it, upfront, a whopping international fee. Would they lose it all? And where did it come from, their impulse to contort and curtail and insist? He could almost hear them telling their friends: Felix has his master's degree, did you know that? Isn't that marvellous? But that was mean of him, surely, to think that. They had his best interests at heart; he loved them, he really did, and he was homesick, horribly so. He pictured himself drinking his father's *Feuerzangenbowle*, eating his mother's *Weihnachtsstollen*. How he craved a piece of that sweet cake. And to hear the neighbourhood children singing carols in the square. It was sentimental, he knew, but the picture stayed in his mind, telling him to go home.

What had he gained, after all, from this excursion to the other side of the world? Some new friends among his housemates, perhaps even among the cast. He had been surfing, windsurfing and sand surfing, had tasted adventure driving across pristine dunes, seen limestone pinnacles in an endless yellow desert. He had seen art, walls of it, mesmerising dots and painted barks. He'd enjoyed a little theatre. But even as it pained him to think it, he knew he was also out of place. He had tried making jokes to add to the conversation, but people moved on too quickly. Sometimes it was impossible to understand what they said, their mouths half-open when they spoke. Maybe that is why he loved the play: he knew the words and what they meant. The words didn't rush on to an unknown ending. He was the director. He was in control.

How he yearned for his future to be in the theatre. To direct, or at least to be in the world that Max had shown him. But maybe it wasn't meant for him, after all. The cast were having fun but often fighting. He thought he had brought them all together, but now he wasn't sure. And it came to him again, the feeling, his body stiffening, paralysed by the fear of failure, of the show falling apart in front of his eyes. Why had he taken the whole thing on? It was huge. Too huge. And why was it that he always stood, somehow, on the outside?

It was twilight on the third day. He had taken off his shirt, sprayed himself with insect repellent, sitting in the shade of his cave. An image of Max, emerging from the sea, towelling his back. *Autsch!* He was sick of the squealing mosquitoes! They always ruined things just when he was about to reach the good part. Were these damn insects immune to Aerogard?

He looked up to see a figure coming towards him. Veronika. Wearing a sun visor, shorts and T-shirt, running shoes. She waved at him, called out his name, and began to run even faster, closer.

'Hey, Felix.' She was puffing like mad when she stopped. 'Just came to say hi. I am so glad to see you!'

She wrapped him up in a fierce hug. He could feel the sweat on her body, smell her pungent sunscreen. Then she drew away from him, looked at him closely. Being careful with him now, waiting for him to say something. Explain.

'Am I a theatre maker'? he asked.

'Of course, Felix. Look how far we've come. With the play ...'

He shook his head. 'I don't know if I can do this,' he stuttered, almost forgetting his English. He'd been talking in German in his head for the past three days – it took some effort for his English words to come out right.

'I understand,' Veronika said.

He wondered how she could.

'Sometimes it can all get a bit overwhelming,' she said.

'Ja.'

'And then it's hard to know what to do.'

'Ja.'

She moved closer, and he saw kindness in her pretty eyes.

'Come with me?' she said.

He didn't know what to say or do. He saw tan marks on her forearms and legs where her T-shirt and shorts ended. He figured that the harvest must be over. Had they all been out running, searching, hoping to find him? He felt bad. They must have felt worried about him. Even distressed. Maybe they cared about him a little. How could he have done that to them, just disappeared without a word? He must go back. Try to make amends, maybe start all over again.

The two of them began walking together. Veronika pointed to a sign: *Camping prohibited*. Felix hadn't noticed it. He didn't really register such signs, even when he wasn't in this crisis, this thing he was going through. The bad feelings. Was he prohibited? In his city, the place he was meant to belong, he knew from where he'd grown up that there were signs about going somewhere, not going somewhere, a divided city, oppressive. But he didn't belong in Australia either, even among all the beauty. Trespassing in the national park. He felt a quick shiver run through his body. Perhaps we are all trespassers, he thought and suppressed another shiver.

They came to a canyon that opened out onto another outdoor amphitheatre. In the distance, kangaroos stood in a semicircle: imperious, motionless creatures.

Veronika turned to face him. 'Aren't they magnificent?' she said. 'It's like they've come out to greet us.'

Felix nodded. 'I wish I had my camera.'

'There's something in the way they're looking at us, isn't there? As if they're cheering us on.'

'*Ja. Genau.*'

'Wouldn't this make a wonderful outdoor theatre?' Veronika said, opening her arms to the sky. Then took Felix's arm. 'Let's walk this way.'

She veered towards an abandoned railway tunnel, which cut through the escarpment. As they approached the entrance, they saw a plaque. Felix peered closely, hoping to understand the language. A railway had been built through here, he read, in 1908. It carried coal from the area down into Perth and ceased operation in 1930.

'Curious,' said Veronika, their voices reverberating off the tunnel walls. She turned to face Felix again, her eyes glowing. 'Hear that?' she said. 'Our voices have become larger. I want to act for a living, Felix, and you have inspired me to do that.'

Felix felt his heart settle. 'That is wonderful,' he said. 'And I want to direct. Thank you.'

Veronika beamed at him. 'No need to thank me,' she said. 'It's wonderful for both of us.'

The tunnel began to narrow, allowing them to walk closer. It is right to feel closer, Felix thought; it feels good to be walking with Veronika. The ground was covered in tiny wet stones. They trod on the drenched surface, their conversation punctuated by the sound of their feet. Then they did a full circle and arrived back at his prohibited camp site.

He stopped them in their tracks, touched Veronika's arm. 'How did you know I would be here?' he said.

'I didn't. I just went out for a run. To clear my head.'

Felix had noticed other joggers and walkers in the park. His collision with Veronika had not been such a strange coincidence after all. He hadn't even driven away that far.

'Come back to the orchard,' she said. 'Have Christmas with us. We can do this, you know, really.'

ACT TWO Performance

[1995]

'Don't let us be like some actors who never perform so badly as the day when the critics are all there in force. There's no chance of doing this better another time.
Let us know your parts properly today.'

– Pierre Beaumarchais, *The Marriage of Figaro*

41. Veronika

She wears her mistress's gown. Voluminous mustard silk, with white cuffs starched like flowers. She is pressing her hands on the rim of her breast, her mouth wide, laughing. She is no longer Suzanne the housemaid but the Countess of Almaviva of Andalusia. In the cool shade of the chestnut trees, she conspires with the Countess, who dons the dress of a maid.

This is the plan: they will trick the Count into believing that the one is the other. He will be made a fool of. He will get his comeuppance. No more dalliances with *autres femmes*. The Countess's heart beats through her ears. She removes a stray thread from her dress. May it all unravel.

Figaro, the Spanish dandy, emerges from the garden.

Suddenly she is no longer Suzanne, she is not even the Countess but Veronika. And he is not Figaro, but Joshua striding across the stage. How unlike himself, she thinks. How regal and commanding he looks in his topaz jacket. I have lost him, she thinks. I have killed him. She is fading away under this co-mingling of seams, the heaviness of the dress. She locks eyes with him, and there it is: the two of them, years younger, slipping off their clothes on the sand, entering the surf, the water rising around them, swimming until the cold is too much and they turn back to shore. She remembers a tawny sunset melting into the sea.

She moves to stage right, leaves the real Countess to meet her Count. She tries to catch Joshua's eye once more. Sees his puckered lip, his dishevelled hair. A pause thickens in the hot, still night, and she hears herself breathing. She is drowsy. Is it the tenth night in a row she's stood here like this? It's wearisome, this business. She peers into the crowd: three hundred and fifty tonight, apparently. She catches glimpses of faces but then can't see a thing, just a great stripe of blinding light. She is sweating where the dress gathers at her skin. She would run across the stage and kiss him if she could. It's the last night, after all. Surely some magic is called for, some reversal of expectation. The light recedes for a moment. It's her sister, Ana, in the front row. There's a vacant seat beside her. Ana's hands rest on the mound of her belly. But Veronika knows that she mustn't be distracted by the who and the why.

'Joshua!' she cries.

She moves her mouth, but there is no sound. She is still. Breathing. She feels the heave of her chest. But everything seems delayed, distended somehow. She is clammy, unsteady. She doesn't know what to do with her hands. *Why can't I speak? Or move?* Is it that she is far away, on the edge of a dream? Someone is running onto the stage towards her. She falls.

A slap on the cheek.

'Veronika, darling. Are you okay?'

Sebastian's voice. Willing her to return.

'Where am I?' she says. A searing pain at the side of her head.

'In the common room. You know. Our dressing room.'

'Ah. Was I ... was I out for long?'

'No. And you're fine now, aren't you? Are you okay, my love? Drink some water.'

'My head,' she says feebly. She hoists herself up on one elbow, looks around the room: costumes and props in heaps on the floor, empty takeaway food containers, polystyrene cups. She smells something sharp, possibly curry. A microwave beeps on the other side of the common room.

Sebastian looms over her. He looks ridiculous in close-up, with rouged cheeks and a black wig. Wearing a flash gold hunting suit.

'Shouldn't you be on stage?' she says.

He smiles. 'Gloria's improvising,' he says, 'with some song.'

A head appears around the door. Felix.

'Veronika.' His voice is urgent. 'Are you ready to get back on the stage?' He disappears.

Sebastian fingers her curls. 'You drive me wild,' he says.

Veronika suppresses a giggle, rises from the sofa, tells him in an icy voice to leave her alone.

He gets down on bended knee. 'Marry me,' he says.

She wrests a handful of pins from her make-up bag, fastens her wig.

'Where's the ring?' she asks.

He fumbles in a braided pocket, takes out a small velvet box. He opens it carefully. She sees a sapphire chiselled into delicate angles, a thin gold band. Exquisite.

'In that case, alright,' she says.

'So you'll marry me?'

'No, stupid.'

130

She steps past him, checks her make-up in the mirror one last time, adjusts her corset.

'It was my grandmother's ring,' Sebastian growls.

'Let's go,' she says and scurries down the corridor, enters stage left.

Gloria is singing like a haunting flute. Veronika stays still, looks at her, looks at the audience. They are spellbound.

She weaves around the scenery, resumes her place onstage, near the plywood chestnut trees. Sebastian strides towards Cassie, strapping and bold. Joshua as Figaro is ready to enact his clever design: to gather the crowd, walk in on the Count *in flagrante delicto*. He cups his hand to his ear, shakes his head in indignation, performs his heartbreak with exaggerated gestures. Gloria springs across the garden to meet her lover in the pavilion. She sweeps aside her cloak – a nice flourish, Veronika thinks – and bending towards Gwen in an extravagant embrace, whispers to her, puts daisies in her hair. Sebastian takes Cassie's hand. Quivering, she looks away. Sebastian's ardour lends pathos to the scene, indeed transforms it. I hate this, Veronika thinks. He does it so well. Is that how he kissed Cassie in another life, by the creek, the two of them alone and quivering? And three weeks later, Sebastian is asking her to marry him. Her head is hurting from the fall. There's a hum in her ear, a soft, persistent thud in her skull.

Joshua looks poised; his voice is confident, assured. *No, my Lord Count, you shan't have her, you shall not have her!* He has played his part so well that it's impossible to tell if his kisses hold any trace of desire. Her heart reels with the memory of her cruelty. The way she'd abandoned him.

On the other side of the stage, Sebastian is flirting with Cassie. Veronika barely recognises him beneath his layer of make-up. He seems cunning, convinced of his *droit du seigneur*, spouting his words of seduction:

Love is no more than a story of one's heart; pleasure is the reality that brings me to your feet.

Veronika wonders if he is acting. Whether he wants to make her jealous.

Cassie is a brilliant Countess. She even manages to blush, to make visible her coolness or her anger.

Veronika thinks: What if I married him after all? Her stomach grumbles loudly.

And now Joshua is approaching, hovering by the trees. Just as well it's the last night, she thinks. She is tired, barely able to stand.

Joshua sniggers. Gloria and Gwen join in. Veronika sees Lucas mooning them from the wings. There's a restless rumble from the audience. There have been pranks for almost every performance: fart jokes and obscenities, instructions for fellatio on the Countess's sheet music. Veronika mouths her lines, grows woozy at the ease with which Figaro gives his heart away. This part feels true. Josh speaks to her as if she were Gloria:

Madam, I adore you!

My hand is itching, she replies.

My heart is pounding.

It is Veronika, not Suzanne, who cannot abide the offence, who clouts Joshua on the head.

'It's me, Veronika,' she says.

Joshua mutters: 'You're Suzanne.'

They kiss. An exquisite kiss, coated in anger.

She runs into the pavilion, where the rest of the cast is assembled, in character, waiting for the end of the play.

Sebastian as the jealous Count is all flaring nostrils and clenched fists.

The real Countess loosens her veil, removes her wig. Her long brown hair unwinds around her shoulders. Sebastian looks stung by her deceit, by his own deceit, and by the sudden apprehension of her beauty. Falling to his knees, he begs for forgiveness.

Lucas begins his song, 'All in the Follies of a Day'.

Loud waves of applause tell them they are brilliant, they are loved.

The actors bow and bow again as the audience furiously claps and cheers.

Gloria shouts *woohoo!* Josh leaps in the air. Cassie is teary and smiling. They bow again. Clasped hands fly into the air. Felix takes a separate bow, and the crowd hollers.

So here we are, Veronika thinks. All of us together, lavishly attired, in the breeze of a summer evening. We've done it: staged a French play first performed in 1784, set in a baroque Spanish court, the words travelling across two centuries, two languages and three continents to reach an audience in the New Fortune Theatre in the dry heat of a West Australian evening. Elaborate, costly, impractical and worth every ounce of our energy.

We have made the poetry hold.

'Party at the Tropical Garden!' Felix cries. 'All invited.'

42. Veronika

They began peeling off their costumes, returning to the selves they had just left behind. Veronika was dying to remove her glue-on eyelashes: she'd felt as if she were conducting an entire orchestra with every blink. But she would miss being Suzanne; Suzanne was more certain of her future. She would miss having a script that guaranteed a happy ending.

She would miss Figaro, too. Joshua.

She was not yet ready to disrobe. The spectacular mustard gown had caught the light so beautifully. Every time she felt tired, inclined to quit the play, she thought of her gown: its lustrous beauty, the possibility of transcending her mundane life.

She knew her sister would be waiting at the front of the theatre.

Josh removed his loosely knotted kerchief from around his neck, and Cassie patted him on the back.

'Bravo! You had just the right combination of hauteur and swoon.'

'Thanks,' he said. Puzzled.

'I concur,' Sebastian said, holding out his hand to Joshua. 'You were a stupendous Figaro.'

They shook hands. A truce, Veronika thought, relieved.

'That was my swansong, I hope,' Sebastian said and looked around the room. 'I'm applying for a scholarship to study overseas.'

Veronika tried not to look startled.

'I had some other plans,' he said. 'But they didn't work out. Through no fault of my own.'

'Are you going to acting school?' Cassie gasped.

'I'm applying to Cambridge,' he said. 'One of the world's most prestigious universities.'

Veronika grimaced. Such pomposity.

'Cambridge?' Cassie laughed. 'You mean one of the universities that pillaged the colonies?'

But Sebastian wasn't listening, continued to swagger … Master's in Political Theory … magnificent library … important people … rowing club … throw off the shackles of family, respectability …

Joshua asked how long he'd be away.

'Two years,' Sebastian said. 'Maybe more if I forge a glittering career.'

'And what if you don't get a scholarship?' Cassie said, hands on hips.

'I'm confident,' Sebastian said.

He didn't tell me, Veronika thought. He didn't even drop a hint. And he hasn't once looked at me.

Was she angry? Resentful? Envious? She'd seen pictures of Cambridge: ancient colleges, cobblestoned streets, a river lined with daffodils, students in academic gowns. Sebastian punting on the river, courting English girls, not giving her a second thought. But she'd just refused his proposal, hadn't she? Did she think she was too good for him, even though he had money and class and a fine career ahead of him? Who did she think she was, really? A woman who wore a costume and felt lost when the play was over. Maybe she didn't care for Sebastian at all. Maybe she just wanted some drama in her life, Sebastian on bended knee, her haughty refusal, her sweeping back on stage.

But did it matter what she felt, to herself or to anyone else? She realised, in this rush of heated, unruly emotions, that what she felt most of all was alone. She couldn't keep her sister waiting any longer. She left the dressing room, took the corridor to the side exit.

'Veronika Vaček.'

She froze. Then turned back down the corridor, keeping her eyes on the floor, but he shoved the door open. She could hear his footsteps behind her and walked faster, pulled open the door to the fire stairs, climbed two levels in a hurry. She reached the walkway bridge leading to the library. She stopped, out of breath. But safe.

'Veronika.'

She swung round. 'I'm not avoiding you, Charlie,' she said.

'No? What are you doing, then?'

'I need ... a book. From the library.'

'It's closed.'

'Ah. Yes. I lost track of time. The play and all that.'

He moved closer. She saw his stubborn chin, his petulant mouth. The gap in his front teeth had gone. He'd gained weight, too. He looked flashy, sharp, but still with that hint of malice in his eyes.

'I wanted to make sure you were okay,' he said.

She leaned against the wall. It was cool to her touch.

'Did you pass out?' he said. 'Onstage.'

'I was fine,' she said, trying to breathe. He was in her face. 'I'm fine.'

Charlie sniggered. 'You're not,' he said. 'I know you, Veronika Vaček.' He grabbed her by the forearm, and she shook him off.

'I was actually looking for Ana,' she said.

'She's gone home.' He smiled. Leered. 'We came together. We're together, you know.'

Veronika knew she had to ask. 'I take it you're the father?'

'Twins, apparently.' Now he came even closer, his breath on her neck. 'Be nice, Veronika. You might see a lot more of me now that I'm in your sister's life. Now that she and I are what you might call *an item*.' He leant in even closer. 'Remember your lines. *Know thyself.*' He traced his fingers over the letter K, which was carved into the pale stone wall.

He pulled away, looked her straight in the eye. 'There was no-one on the stage but you,' he said, softly now, almost soothingly. 'If only you knew what you do to me.'

He was crooning at her, and something inside her snapped. 'I know what you *did* to me,' she said. 'And I was only a child.'

That day on the beach when he'd found her alone, taking her hand, saying things ... the blur of her feelings, the fear, the strange kind of thrill ... She needed to steady herself. She had to.

'What are you doing with my sister?' she said.

'I wheel and deal in stocks and shares,' he said, as if that answered her question. 'Corporate trade. Mergers. Uranium.' He smiled that smile again: smug, in control. 'I'm a changed man.'

'There's nothing changed about you,' she said. 'Just your swanky clothes. And you've had your teeth fixed.'

'I meant what I said about your acting,' Charlie said. 'You're star material. I could get you a nice job in a top theatre company. What do you say to that?'

A peacock appeared from nowhere, its long blue neck thrust forward. A headdress of soft green, whorls of blue across its breast. Charlie jumped at it, shouting, and the bird let out a cry, flapped away. Veronika wanted to hit him now, shout at him, tell him he was cruel, the lowest of the low, but even as the words began to form in her head, she heard herself sounding phoney. When the truth was, he wanted her, and he confused her with his wanting.

'I don't want your help,' was all she managed to say.

'Suit yourself,' Charlie said, and he strolled casually away.

43. Charlie

It had always been Veronika, not Ana. But somehow he got mixed up with the wrong one. The sister, the one that was easy. Too willing. Ana. All that dark hair. The pouting mouth. She'd been up for anything. It wasn't that he hadn't wanted her, it was just … she wasn't Veronika.

He drove back along the highway. Fast. Fuck the speed cameras, he thought. But where was he going? Not back to Ana, who'd burrowed her way back into his life. Into his bed. He'd arranged for a taxi to take her home. *I'll pass on my congrats and finish up some business*, he'd lied. Almost pushed Ana into that back seat. Had Veronika really been *fourteen*? She had transformed … that body … electrifying eyes … She'd always had something, but now … now … there weren't really words for how she made him feel. Unnerved. Provoked. Furious. He put his foot on the brake. *Too many fucking cops in this fucking city.* He pulled a finger sign to a police car turning the corner.

He must have been sixteen, skateboarding along the footpath bordering the beach, doing stunts to get Veronika's attention. It hadn't worked. He'd tried again when the wind was up, when the sea looked like flurries of snow, to show off on his board. Those girls on the beach. The sand changing colours with the sky. Those girls. Summers in that house on the edge of the headland. Enough to make him lose his head. But he wouldn't, couldn't lose it now. There was too much at stake. He didn't want some scandal in the news. He'd already been seen with Ana, at the Old Swan Brewery, and some journalist had made a fuss; he was gaining notoriety as a businessman, after all. And now he felt … left wanting … something … that breathtaking woman onstage. Talking to her so close like that. Far out. Trust her to blue-ball him.

He revved in front of Hungry Jack's and sped past fancy boutiques and even fancier schools for rich kids. He had to stop himself running a red light. It would be *her* fault if he smashed into a truck. Veronika. She'd made him do all kinds of dumb things.

He'd almost forgotten the surfboard, the one he'd stolen from someone's garage, walking home with it in broad daylight, barefoot, all the way through town, then onto a dirt track into the state forest, where the old caravan stood behind the house. He missed it, waxing the thing. All that getting high on cocaine, petrol fumes and the smell of tyres on bitumen, launching into the rolling water, bare-skinned, with a slick of zinc on his nose. Surfing the same way he drove. Not caring if he crashed the board on rocks, reefs or sandbanks. It was only Ana who seemed to notice him. That day after he'd been dumped by a mammoth wave and onto a pile of rocks, how could he forget? He'd chipped his chin. The scar, a pale gash, was still there. He ran his finger over it. It maddened him beyond belief just thinking about it. What would it take? He could be cunning. He could try to get to her through his brother. His sad pussy of a brother, in a play, of all things. Clearly he had the hots for her but it was obvious she wasn't putting out. He was always a bit soft, Josh. Wouldn't know what a woman needed. Wanted.

A blaring siren. Charlie checked his rear-view mirror. Another one. *Fuck this police state.* He had to pull over. A cop was waiting for him. Should he risk it and just burn off somewhere? But people knew his name, would see him in the news ... it wouldn't look good trying to outrun the cops. He was sick of cops.

But he wasn't a kid. He rolled down his window.

'Going rather fast there, sir. It's a sixty zone. May I see your licence?'

Charlie reached for his wallet and handed over the licence. The cop looked at it, then back at him.

'I had no idea I was going so fast.' Charlie spoke softly. 'My woman – she's pregnant. She rang to say she was in trouble. I'm desperate to get to her, officer. It's urgent.'

The cop kept staring, didn't say a word.

Charlie gave him a pleading look. 'We're expecting twins,' he said.

The cop shook his head, then whistled through the side of his lip as he gave Charlie back his licence. Then made him breathe into a plastic thing. He'd had a beer hours ago. He'd be fine. He was fine.

'This is a warning, sir. Speeding is against the law in *all* circumstances.'

Charlie thanked him from the bottom of his heart. Playing the game. Then he started up the engine, drove slowly, took the nearest right turn off the highway. The place was crawling with cops who had nothing better to do than ... *Fuck this.* He wouldn't go home. He started to drive back the other way, parallel to the highway, back to where? To the park? He slammed on the accelerator. His body jerked forward. There were too many stop signs. Was he feeling guilty? Not for speeding, surely? Guilty? Guilty about Joshua. Beetroot juice from a can he poured over his assignments. Throwing his schoolbag into the bushes. The headlocks, the insults. What else were little brothers good for?

How had it happened? Letting her slip away?

44. Veronika

It was Felix who came to find her, who offered to take her to the party. She told him she wasn't feeling well, that she was going to head on home.

'Do you mind if I have a smoko?' he said.

She felt a flood of affection wash over her: for his kindness, his courtesy, his bungling of a word.

'I like the way you Australians speak,' he said. 'Bikkie and garbo and barbie. Like little children. It is quite cute.' He looked over from where they were standing, side by side, into the Tropical Garden. 'This place has many happy memories,' he said. 'I will gladly take them back with me to Germany.'

'You are a very good director,' she said. 'And I'm sure you'll make a wonderful engineer.'

He waved his hand in the air. 'I will miss this beautiful campus. The elegant stonework, the enormous trees. And the river a few minutes away. I shall miss the ripples in the water, the barbecues, even the impertinent seagulls. And at night, the way the windows of the yacht club are covered in the shadows of the trees. They look like spiders, the shadows.'

'You walk there at night?'

'Sometimes my sleep is difficult … Come, let us walk,' he said. 'Into the garden.'

Veronika shook her head. She wanted nothing to do with the garden, wanted no memories of lying with Sebastian, legs entwined. The way he'd lifted her shirt and kissed her bare skin.

'Are you alright?' Felix asked.

She laughed thinly. 'People have been asking me that all night. And I'm fine. Honestly.'

'I am sorry you will miss the party. You are an important member of the Players. Nothing was possible without you and your family. The orchard. Everything.'

'Thank you.'

'And Veronika, you are a most fine actor. You have – how do you say it – it is instinct. In your bones.'

She flushed. 'Instinct?'

'Yes, instinct.' He took her hand. 'You know what to do without thinking all the time. And it comes also from the heart.'

She squeezed his hand. 'That's so kind of you, Felix.'

'I was not kind before,' he said. 'I shouted, *nein*? A lot of shouting. So now I am telling you.'

She steadied her breathing, looked up at the dark night sky.

'Are you sure you won't come to the party?' he said.

'I'm sure.'

'Let me take you home. Or find you a taxi.'

'Thank you, but I need to find my sister.'

He took her hand and kissed it, said goodbye. She watched him walk off into the night. And it came to her, sadly, that she might never see him again.

ACT THREE New Roles

[1996–1997]

'Intrigue! Plots – stormy interludes!'

– Pierre Beaumarchais, *The Marriage of Figaro*

45. Sebastian

They met on Valentine's Day a few months after he'd arrived in Cambridge. A party in the Blue Boar courtyard on an icy English evening. Tall fires in steel urns lit up the yard. The place that had once seen some of the most extraordinary minds in Western history was now alive with a fifties-themed party: girls dancing in spotted hoop dresses and boys making fumbling gestures of desire. Sebastian recognised a few people gathered in a circle: a tall guy with glasses who sang in the Trinity choir; a lean athlete from Kentucky he'd spoken to a few times in the Soci-Poli Library; a woman in striking saris whom he saw at breakfast each morning but had never once spoken to.

But it was the petite woman in the shirt dress pulled in with a thick belt who drew his attention. A cute bob, a blunt fringe. And when he ventured closer, he saw speckles in the pupils of her brown eyes. He watched her mouth open and close like a sea anemone when she spoke. Sebastian nudged his way into the group and introduced himself. He was so keen to make a good impression that he forgot everyone's name except hers: Lìjuān.

The group talked with seeming authority about the tech boom. About the remnants of British colonial power and the imminent return of Hong Kong to Chinese rule, just over a year away. When Sebastian ventured to commend John Major because the man would *never succumb to the Euro*, he saw Lìjuān's approving glance. He couldn't stop looking at her, no longer heard a word of other conversations. At some point, an announcement blared over a loudspeaker and the group dispersed, leaving him standing side by side with Lìjuān. He saw flames reflected in her eyes. They didn't say much. They didn't need to.

They went to bed together that night, fuelled by alcohol and basic need.

Over the next few weeks, they would often study late, then meet outside the colleges or in The Eagle. They would go to her room or to his. They hardly looked at one another when they joined other people in libraries, cafés or bars, but it was different behind closed doors. Vigorous. Intense. He'd never known a woman like her, so easy with her body. So free.

She asked him one night, the two of them jammed together in his narrow bed, if he had *a thing* for Asian women. He told her that he didn't think of such *things* in terms of race, although he did find her *incredibly hot*. She said she was disappointed but wouldn't explain why. He'd told her earlier that her hair looked lovely, and she'd automatically assumed it meant she hadn't looked lovely the night before. He felt put-upon: why did women put him in such impossible situations?

But she was also reflective, wondering aloud who she was: a Chinese woman, born in Beijing at the end of the Cultural Revolution, who moved to Shenzhen as a child, who loved America, had studied there, but now lived in England and was dating an Australian. *Weird, isn't it*, she told him. And she was playful, mocking him as *a colonial*, pretending to rebuke him because he was ashamed of her. He told her that nothing could be further from the truth, that it was *she* who insisted they act like brother and sister when other people were around.

One night she asked if his parents knew.

'No,' he said. 'Anyhow, it's not like we're ... well, you know ...'

'Together,' they said in unison.

She moved away from him, put her hands behind her head. 'I have a boyfriend,' she said.

'Ah.'

'Our families need to connect, for business reasons. And so, we are engaged.'

'Oh.'

'It's not as bad as it sounds.'

'Right.'

'He's a good guy.'

'A good guy.'

'I want to get married in Beijing, where I was born. That way we could have our wedding photos at the Temple of Heaven, but he wants to be modern and get married on Xichong Beach. Our parents would never allow that. Are you betrothed to anyone?'

There was Veronika, of course, but she wasn't his anymore.

A boyfriend. He did his best to ignore that, too.

Over mulled wine at The Eagle, a portrait of Oliver Cromwell looming over them, Lìjuān explained her dissertation in quantum physics. She was studying subatomic particles and had learned that electrons could be in two different places at the same time because they moved so fast. It was the theory of bilocation, she told him. He listened attentively, asked where her research was leading. She would extrapolate, she said, to other forms of matter, because electrons constituted matter, however imperceptible. Sebastian confessed that he'd always struggled with physics. He told her he'd once built a wooden windmill for an assignment on perpetual motion, but the contraption hadn't worked unless shaken vigorously. He was charmed by her laugh and by the trouble she took to explain her research. Romance did this to you, he thought: it stretched you, expanded your interests beyond your usual inclinations. It was a form of care, of attention. He was charmed, too, by her long, lacquered artificial fingernails imprinted with tiny American flags.

He found her intelligence arousing.

But then after the steak, after hot rhubarb pie, she ambushed him completely. Told him that her boyfriend from Shenzhen was coming to visit. That they would have to stop seeing each other. She must have seen something written on his face because she told him that the separation would only be for two weeks. He felt... what did he feel like? An experiment? One who was easily discarded?

He blustered. He railed. Then called it off. Whatever it was they had. They finished the meal in haste and in silence.

He cycled down Trumpington Street in a hurry, anxious to get back to his college. The roads were treacherous with slush and mud; he was pelted by rain that turned to sleet. He thought of the sunshine back home, and as the hood of his jacket slipped off and flew into a haze of traffic, he cursed the chilling cold. He arrived, sodden and miserable, back to his room, stripped off in front of the radiator, sat on it lightly until he burned his buttocks. He grabbed his flask of Bénédictine, stretched out on the carpet. As he guzzled his drink, he began feeling rather sheepish, like a child who'd thrown a tantrum. His father had once told him that he should *pull himself together*, find more productive ways to express his frustrations. But what had he really been feeling when Lìjuān announced a separation? Jealous? Affronted? Angry? Or was he pretending to feel more than he really did? Feelings are so unreliable, he thought; he'd learned that much from reading Adam Smith.

A week later, he was even more miserable, nursing a rugby injury in bed. A dreadful flu was racking his lungs, and the pain in his shoulder made him feel worse. His blocked nose throbbed. Tiredness pressed upon his skin. He pictured himself as old, bedridden, arthritic, his faculties blinking on and off like a faulty neon light. He lay in some complicated sling, fogged by doses of strong paracetamol, half-dreaming of bizarre visions that included sharp implements devoid of any context. At other times he struggled to breathe, stewing, writhing in a soup of sweat. He had no picturesque view to console him. His window overlooked Angel Court, but the sky was so drowsy and dark that the view became blurred, indistinguishable from night. And as the days wore on, he thought he might expire with loneliness.

Cambridge: he'd imagined medieval buildings with turrets and gargoyles, elaborate libraries, churches and chapels. He'd seen himself at high table, eating roast beef with carrots and beans, followed by steaming pudding. He'd pictured students in academic gowns scurrying to class as bells rang out in the mist. He'd dreamed of walks in wild weather, of sipping tea and munching on scones in cosy, carpeted rooms. And he'd planned to visit museums stuffed with classical sculpture, art, archaeological treasure. He'd planned to punt on the river with some curvy, pink-cheeked English girl. And he would write the most earth-shattering dissertation. He would analyse inflation in former Eastern Bloc countries with the prospect of Euro integration. He would be published. He would meet like-minded peers, earn their unstinting praise.

But lying on his bed, weighed down with pain and disappointment, he knew that he'd been foolish. He'd pursued a puffed-up fantasy of the Cambridge life. His rooms in college were draughty and damp; the roast beef in the refectory was rubbery and bland. And while the chapels and churches were beautiful, almost spiritual, his spirits were sapped by the drizzle, the low-hanging grey clouds. Even worse, the only girl he'd managed to get it on with had just given him the boot. And worst of all, he was making slow progress with his dissertation. If he were ruthlessly honest with himself, hardly any progress at all. He felt weighed down with regret for the life he'd left behind. He'd abandoned what was real and true.

In this moment, Veronika returned to him. He saw their limbs entwined in the Tropical Grove, felt again the softness of their kisses, the feel of her breasts, her touch. He wondered why they'd never … actually done it. Had she been waiting for reassurance, a sense of certainty? Or had she been too complicated, found him too simple? Or did the fact that they'd never gone all the way make him long for her even more? Not like Lìjuān, who'd rushed into bed without a second thought. And she'd been more solicitous than Veronika ever was. Lìjuān had come to the hospital to visit him when she heard the news of his accident. She'd brought him hyacinths, which now hung over the rim of a small vase by his bed, their stems like limp muscles. She'd pressed a book into his hand – *The Art of War* – and told him to read it before he went back onto *the field*. She meant the rugby field, of course; perhaps she'd meant the book as a joke. Whatever the case, he'd turned page after page, unable to grasp concepts, nothing sinking in.

He'd been tackled in the maul. The fullback from St Andrew's had clamped him round the chest. Sebastian could still remember his head and neck smashing against the lawn. He'd been knocked out flat. Woke up in excruciating pain, as if a jagged branch had pierced his neck, and with the feeling that his head had somehow shifted off his body and was sailing away without the rest of him. But he hadn't broken his neck, that was a blessing; however, his atlas vertebra had received a blow, it was now a swollen lump at the base of his skull. It was his own fault, of course. He'd been off balance, lost his focus, because his mind had been on Lìjuān and how he'd called it off. Not that he was going to marry her, even without *the boyfriend*. He'd never entertained the idea of something serious.

Veronika had been serious. She'd refused his proposal, even refused to see him before he left. He hadn't said that to his father, of course, who'd wanted to know what was happening with *that girl*. Sebastian had been shaving on the morning of his flight when his father's face appeared in the bathroom mirror. *It's off*, he'd told him. *At least, it's on hold*. Then he'd flicked the white foam into the basin with several sweeps of his razor, just like his father had taught him years ago. His father had sniffed through his moustache, then turned away.

On hold. Who was he kidding? He'd written Veronika a letter: newsy stuff about the architecture, the river, the weather, his studies. He'd waxed lyrical about singing in the Trinity choir, how it had overwhelmed him: the strands of sound coming from all the voice parts, weaving in and out of melody. It made him feel as if there were tiny birds flying out of his diaphragm. It was the absence of ego that appealed to him; he'd hoped that would impress her. He asked what she was doing, how she was. And then, before he could stop himself, he'd written that he missed her, *terribly*.

She didn't reply. She might not even have read his letter. He never wrote again.

A few days later, he was languishing still, tired of being unwell. Increasingly convinced that he would rot away in his bed, his fly-eaten carcass discovered by a horrified cleaner.

He heard a knock on the door and then a muffled voice calling his name.

'It's Alistair. Haven't seen you round for a while, colonial boy. How are you doing?'

Alistair. The tall guy from the choir. Sebastian managed to hoist himself out of bed. He was hardly dressed for visitors – a coffee-stained nightshirt, underwear and socks – but someone was taking the trouble, checking up on him. He hobbled across the floor, opened the door.

'Christ! You look shocking.'

'Don't come too close,' Sebastian warned.

Alistair fished a handkerchief from his pocket and blew his nose loudly. 'I've probably got it, too,' he said.

'It's not just the flu,' Sebastian moaned, feeling the need for sympathy. 'I had a bad accident at rugby. Double whammy.'

Alistair nodded. 'Sometimes all the excrement lands on you at once,' he said. 'Hindus might see it as good luck.'

'Comforting. Thanks.' Sebastian waved him into the room.

'I won't stay. Just thought I'd drop by to see if you'd like to come back to the choir. We desperately need some baritones. I've heard your Aussie twang but we can get rid of it with a bit of vowel work. Some pharynx exercises.'

'I'm not sure, Alistair. There's not much to sing about at the moment.'

'It'll do you good, old chap. Why don't you come to the all-choirs event? A few of the college choirs come together, it's a big sing-in.'

'Still not sure.'

'Look, you can do the goldfish if you like. Just mouth away if you don't know the part. Bulk up the team, as it were. And there's only one rehearsal, at Clare College Chapel. Oh. I forgot to say. That girl of yours will be playing the cello.'

'Who? You mean Lìjuān?'

Alistair winked. 'Yes, you lucky devil,' he said. 'You beat us all to it.' He pulled out some paper from his knapsack, unfurled a scroll of music. Spiral-bound; as big as an art folio. 'Have my score, old chap. I'll get another one. I'm conducting this one, by the way. Some harebrained scheme of mine.'

Sebastian thanked him, then smiled. It must have been weeks since he'd smiled. He looked at the music. '*Spem in alium nunquam habui*'.

Forty parts. But which one was his?

He decided that he didn't want any part. Not when *that girl of his* would be playing the cello.

A free computer in the middle common room. A marvel indeed. And he couldn't believe the length of her email!

> *Guess what?? I'm at an internet café at Victoria Station in London. Don't you love it? They call it a café but it's not really. It's just lots of orange computer screens with people madly typing. I don't see any coffee.*
>
> *Someone told me that you actually made it to Cambridge. That's wonderful, Sebbie. I'm really sorry for giving you a hard time about it back in Perth. I still stand by my comment that places like Cambridge are founded on dirty money but I was mad at you for what happened that day at the creek. I know that's all in the past now, but if I am completely honest, I was motivated by spite as much as my political convictions. Anyhow, when I heard the news about you in Cambridge I thought, how fabulous! You did it! So – have you joined Footlights? Or are you a swot? Do the spires inspire you? Have you lingered in libraries and fingered the pages of medieval manuscripts? Are you reaching the heights of intellectual ecstasy? Have you sighed under the Bridge of Sighs? What's it like to wander among those glorious old buildings, as one of The Chosen?*
>
> *And as for me, I'm in London! Lucky me. Daddy got me all sorted out with a job in a gallery in Notting Hill, but I couldn't stand it so I left and now I'm selling things at Oxfam. Sometimes I find the gems and then jack up the price and sell them at a market stall on Saturdays. I'm living with the daughter of Daddy's business partner, her name's Anne Sophie. She's half-French and I like her enormously. She's a no-nonsense sort who boils her vegetables and she's very well connected and important and doesn't seem to need to work. The ceiling in our place is so high and hardly any water comes out of the taps in the bathtub. The toilet doesn't flush properly and it's awfully damp but at least there's a roaring fire.*
>
> *Sebbie, I am really, really bad at typing and this is taking me*

simply forever to get right. I'd much rather see you. It's been ages! Can I come over? What do you think? Two old pals from Perth. So shall I visit you, just as a pal, you understand? Tell me when suits and I'll jump on the train. I don't care how long it takes. I've got my Walkman and my knitting, so I'll be fine.

Love from Cassie.

Sebbie, indeed! No-one called him Sebbie. But there was something refreshing, endearing, about Cassie, and she'd been honest with him about her motives. He had to give her that. It was quite decent, really. Noble even.

He remembered her kiss by the creek, and how a droplet of water had fallen down her dress and how he'd been flattered by her interest. But now she was being a friend. It was a long time since he'd had a friend, a real one, in this place. Someone from home to reassure him, to connect him to some kind of truth, to offer him a touch of kindness. How he longed for a touch of kindness.

46. Cassie

She was astonished! To see him lifting up his walking stick and shaking it all about. He said he needed help to stay upright when he walked. And he had a stiff neck on his right side as well, a shifted vertebra like a Frankenstein bolt, which meant he couldn't really keep his head straight. She couldn't help feeling sorry for him. She leaned in and kissed him on the cheek.

There. Done. No big deal.

He loved her new hairstyle, he said. Cropped short, like a boy. And blonde? He would never have picked her for a blonde.

They passed two orderly queues at the ticket booths, a newsagent and a mini Marks & Spencer. Cassie was surprised at the smallness of the station: shouldn't Cambridge have a grand entrance, something lofty and *superior*? Still, the Victorian façade with its arched windows, that was kind of special ... but what was it with all the bicycles outside? Mountains of bikes! She was relieved when Sebastian said they would walk.

'Didn't Germaine Greer used to study here?' she said. 'In the *hallowed halls*. I bet she didn't ride a bike, though.'

Sebastian was amused. 'She used to lecture actually,' he said. 'Newnham College. Lived somewhere on the way to Grantchester, I think.'

'Well, if you ever see her, say hello for me. A friend loaned me *The Female Eunuch*, the ideas kind of blew my mind. My friend said, *I can't believe you haven't read this book, have you been living under a rock for the last two decades?* I said I was too busy trying to hook up with a man and feeling sorry for myself and ... well, anyway, Sebbie, the book had a huge effect on me. I am no longer the woman who castrates herself. I own my body, and I refuse to be a slave to a *man*. I am getting to know myself, you know, and it's not as scary as I thought.'

'Glad to hear that, Cass.'

'I have dispensed with certain ... social constructs, shall we say ...'

Sebastian coughed.

'Certain repressive constructions of femininity,' she said. 'I've been reading heaps more about how women's lives have always sucked ... the white picket fence … the claustrophobic trappings of heterosexual coupledom. Oppressive familial structures. All those *apparatuses* supported by the agenda of Judaeo-Christianity and the machinations of late capitalism.'

Sebastian stopped in his tracks. 'My word, Cassie, that's impressive,' he said. '*You* are, I mean.'

She grinned at him. 'I *can* read, you know.'

He blushed. 'Sorry, Cass. I mean … well, look, I'm not opposed to equal rights for women or women's emancipation. J. S. Mill, one of my greats, believed in it thoroughly. But, you know, I believe it should all be about the *individual*. Freedom of *choice.*'

She looked at him closely. He was handsome, yes, still rather formal, but he seemed more attentive. Less full of himself. She was happy, walking beside him, all the way into town, even as he used his stick. The station was far away from the colleges, he explained, so that the students wouldn't be tempted to escape from their studies into the *wild vortex* that was London.

He told her about a concert that he would like to take her to. And she must stay overnight, of course.

'I have a trundle bed,' he said. 'Is that okay? Very basic.'

'Oh, I hear everything in Cambridge is basic,' she said, wanting to tease him now. She took his arm. 'Gosh, it's about to rain, Sebbie. I love it when the sky is plump with black clouds and the air is tinged with cool, soft and ready for the downpour. It's that honouring of the gloom of England.'

He laughed but she hadn't meant to be amusing.

'It's the triumph of the weather,' she insisted. 'Telling us *I know your tears.* Isn't it wonderful to be where the sky is so grey? It makes me feel so happy.'

47. Sebastian

Milling around after the concert, Cassie nudged him conspicuously. 'Wasn't that the cellist?' He flinched, and he realised he must have been staring.

'Don't you want to talk to her?'

'No, no, not at all,' he said.

'Liar.' Cassie promptly took him by the hand and led him to where Lìjuān was standing. He had no choice but to do the introductions.

Cassie clutched her hands to her chest. 'Your cello playing was gorgeous,' she said to Lìjuān. 'I love Bach, I adore him, but I've not heard that piece before.'

Lìjuān inclined her head by way of thanks, then introduced the tall Asian man standing beside her. *The betrothed*, Sebastian thought and tried not to grind his teeth. Wāng Yántāo, who extended a hand and, speaking in a suave American accent, asked them to call him Shaun. He suggested they all get a drink somewhere. Sebastian would rather be anywhere else, a walking stick in his feeble hand, still smarting with pain, but Cassie was bubbling, urging Sebbie to come along. Lìjuān raised an eyebrow.

'*Sebbie?*' she said.

They ambled along to The Eagle, Sebastian bringing up the rear to hide his embarrassing limp. Some of the choristers had already gathered at the pub, lustily singing '*Spem*', changing the Latin words into English obscenities. Undergraduate idiots, Sebastian thought, his mood darkening even more, squashed into a booth, wishing he could leave. But then everyone would see him hobble: Sebastian the rugby star, laid low and lamentable.

Lìjuān leaned in to Cassie. 'You sound Australian,'

Cassie nodded. 'But London is my home now,' she said. 'Far away from my draconian father.'

Shaun topped up her glass of wine, asked if she and Sebastian were together.

Cassie paled. 'No, we're just old pals from Perth,' she said. 'And what do you do, Shaun? I mean, for a living. Since we all have to live.'

Sebastian silently blessed her for changing the subject.

'I'm doing an MBA. A Master of Business Administration,' he said, hammering each word.

'And what is your college, Shaun?'

'I actually live in the other Cambridge,' Shaun said. 'Massachusetts. Harvard.'

Alistair appeared out of nowhere, squeezed into the booth without asking, a large pint of Guinness in his hand.

'Brilliant conducting,' Lìjuān told him. 'Even if you are a general relativist.'

Alistair grinned. 'I take that as a compliment. Especially coming from a quantum mechanic.'

'Seriously.' Lìjuān leaned towards him. 'When the F had that argument with the D. Positively orgasmic.'

'Ah, yes. That F. The ecstatic F.'

Shaun shook Alistair's hand, called his work *totally amazing*, asked how he kept all the parts together.

'It's nothing, really.' Alistair took a swig of his beer. 'And it was Sebastian's girlfriend who stole the show with her beautiful performance—'

'Who?' Shaun looked puzzled. Sebastian ducked his head.

'Me. *I* stole the show,' Cassie jested. 'I coughed at the wrong part! Right in the middle of that blissful pause. Gosh, I *am* sorry about that. I nearly ruined everything.'

Shaun narrowed his eyes. 'You're Sebastian's girlfriend?' he said. 'That's weird. You just told us you were old pals.'

Cassie raised her glass, took a slow sip. 'I meant to say ... I just wish I was his girlfriend ... I mean, Seb is in love with a woman called Veronika. He wanted to marry her. He still might. Veronika is his one true love.'

Sebastian swallowed.

'That's interesting,' Lìjuān said, in a monotone voice. 'I didn't know that about Sebastian.'

They lay in his room in the darkness. He'd insisted on taking the trundle bed, said it was the least he could do.

'You rescued me, Cass, thanks a million.'

After some talk about Soviet puppet dictators, the black market, his dissertation on the eurozone and *looking eastward*, and his supervisor – *a seriously smart fellow* – they fell into silence. He thought Cassie would drift off to sleep, but instead he heard her from across the room.

'What was it with Lìjuān?' she said. 'Or what *is* it?'

'We had a thing for a while. But she's marrying that Harvard cad.'

'Oh well. I'm sorry. But there's plenty more fish and all that. Especially for you, Sebbie. You can have any woman you like. I say that as a friend, of course. An old pal.'

He groaned. He heard Cassie cough.

'You can go back, you know. Go back and get her.'

He sighed. 'I have to finish my degree,' he said. 'I need to publish my thesis and start building a career. Maybe politics. Maybe the law. And ... well ... I don't want to go back.'

'Why not?'

'Just don't.'

More silence.

'You miss her, don't you?'

He didn't reply, turned his back to her.

'Are you in touch at all?'

'I wrote to her, but she didn't reply. I ... have you seen her?'

'Sure have. Her acting's going pretty well. The Old Mill Theatre, good reviews for *Hedda Gabler*. But she won't do film or TV, apparently; too much of a stage snob, I think. She still lives in that run-down place in Shenton Park. And ... well, I don't think she's seeing anyone.'

Sebastian stirred. 'So she's not with that farm boy, Joshua?'

'They fell out.'

'So did he run off with ... what was her name?'

'Gloria. No, they fell out too.'

'Sounds like everyone fell out,' he said and laughed, grimly.

'Except Felix. I heard he's back in Berlin somewhere, started work for a construction company. You never liked him, did you?'

'He was a good director, I'll grant him that.'

Cassie snorted. 'You kept wanting to take over.'

'Was I really such a prick?'

'You were. But you weren't half-bad as an actor. Done any acting since you got here?'

'Nope. It's too ... hierarchical. The director. The stars. The minor roles. *Figaro* was never really my thing. I ... well, I was more interested in Veronika.'

'You always come back to Veronika,' she said.

'I do?'

'You do. It's … well, it's kind of lovely in a sad sort of way.'

He felt grateful that Cassie was here, grateful to be talking in the darkness. Finding things out.

'What about you, Cass?' he said. 'Sounds tough rubbing two sticks together in London.'

'I like the weather,' she said, 'plus I'm a world away from my father. Funny, isn't it, how you care about the opinion of people you despise? I'm pathetic, really. Anyway, I'm trying hard to get him out of my head. And well, I've met someone. My roommate. Anne Sophie. It's a slow-burn kind of thing. Nothing's happened yet, but I can feel that it might … one day. You know … there's a tension.'

'Cass. I didn't realise …'

'I like women,' she said wistfully. 'Men are so hard. And square. Women are lovelier. Just nicer.' She sighed. 'I'm not a lesbian, though, I know that. It's about the person.'

'The person.' Sebastian turned over again to face Cassie. He could just make out her bright blonde hair in the dark. 'Do you really think I should go back?' he said.

'I do.'

'Like this?'

'Like what?'

'My neck, the limp, the headaches.'

Cassie sat up in bed. 'You'll be like Rochester in *Jane Eyre*. Veronika will love you more for your injury. Your weakness. She can take care of you. For some women that's a turn-on, you know.'

'You have an answer for everything,' he said. And then because he heard the sharpness in his voice: 'She refused to marry me, Cass. Why would she want me the second time around?'

'The question is: why do you keep wanting *her*?'

Sebastian thought for a minute. 'Because she was unexpected,' he said.

48. Veronika

She'd had a stroke of luck from the start. The director of the Old Mill Theatre Company had seen *The Marriage of Figaro*, and impressed by her performance, had urged her to audition for his next play. Viola in *Twelfth Night*, to be performed in the amphitheatre by the sea. The role, the location, the pleasure of the invitation: Veronika had been elated! Her first real gig. She loved being shipwrecked into another role, a role about playing another role: *Disguise, I see, thou art a wickedness.* She loved being a woman who becomes a man who becomes a woman again, just for love, all for love. All of it was for love. She loved carrying the entire play, becoming its beating heart, its glorious momentum. It was more than she could have hoped for.

And then another plum role as Medea! At the Regal Theatre, with its velvet curtains and beautiful Art Deco fittings and a history: everything from Shakespeare to *South Pacific*. But she'd had to work hard to create sympathy for Medea, a woman who killed her two children.

Rehearsals were exhausting and her studies were suffering – she'd gone from As to Bs and even Cs – but Veronika wouldn't have it any other way. She didn't mind the small audiences, either: a few hundred people, tops, in a theatre that seated a thousand. She didn't mind that she wasn't paid for any of it. There was still the applause, the compliments backstage, the fabulous review in the local paper: *stunning ... chilling ... more complex than we've ever seen before.* Her performance gave people pleasure, made her parents proud of her. Cassie, Gloria, Lucas, they'd all come to see her, told she was wonderful. But not Josh. He'd never once come to see her. At least, she didn't think so.

Buoyed by her success as the semi-divine goddess, the child-killer, the woman who used words like a weapon, Veronika plucked up the courage to audition for WAAPA, the Academy of Performing Arts. Without success. She'd cried for a bit ... a few days, actually ... then gave herself a pep talk, told herself she wasn't formally trained, was lucky to have had any roles at all. She thought about those other competitive acting schools over East but couldn't bear the thought of more rejection. So she kept remembering

Felix's encouragement, the two of them standing in the darkness of night, when he'd told her he had trouble sleeping. She knew what to do without thinking, he'd said. Her acting seemed to come from the heart.

She managed to pass at uni, even scored a B in French, but by that stage she didn't really care. What mattered was snagging another role: playing a barmaid in *The Three Bandicoots*, a historical play about the early settlers, which the company was taking to Geraldton. Where her sister lived. Ana had told her that the move was Charlie's idea. That his business interests in mining made Geraldton a *strategic* place to settle. Veronika had tried not to scoff: Charlie had always been good at *strategic*. Relations with her sister had thawed: Ana had softened with her pregnancy, even seemed a little vulnerable, as if the changes in her body made her character less brittle. Less spiky. But Charlie remained Charlie. Veronika hated the way he talked down to Ana, sometimes mocked her, and endlessly bragged about his pursuit of the mighty dollar, as if money was the measure of a person's worth.

She'd been relieved when he left Perth, a pregnant Ana in tow.

She hadn't spoken to her sister since she left. Somehow the time had slipped away: she was busy with her bourgeoning career, Ana with her two little kids.

Could she slip in and out of Geraldton without seeing her sister? And Charlie? Highly unlikely, given that her face would be posted around town. Her name: Veronika Vaček as Pearl, the barmaid in *The Three Bandicoots*, who according to the poster was a bright new star from Perth. She'd cringed when she'd seen it – *The Three Bandicoots* was hardly *King Lear* – but that wouldn't stop her from giving it her all. She owed it to her audience and to herself.

An eruption of high-pitched noises in the background. Ana's muffled voice … just a sec … Mummy's on the phone … no, no, don't do that … just sit and watch TV … won't be long, I promise …

'Veronika? What do you want?'

Veronika was taken aback by the snap in Ana's voice. Maybe she wouldn't visit after all.

'How are the kids?' she said.

'Yeah. Good. Little brats. But good. Yeah, little devils.'

As though she were pulling off daisy petals: I love them, I love them not.

Veronika steeled herself. 'I'd like to meet them,' she said.

Silence. Then Ana began shouting into the distance: 'You guys wanna meet Aunty Ron?' She whooped. 'Nuh. They're too wrapped up in *The Wiggles* to care.'

Veronika took a deep breath. 'So ... tell me about them. Who do they look like?'

'Charlie, of course. Who else would they bloody look like?'

Veronika felt defeated. Playing *nice* wasn't getting her anywhere.

'Tobias Lampert,' her sister added.

'What? What do you mean?'

'Lampert. The man I worked for. Minded his kids in Prague. You know, the rich Austrians? He's ...' She lowered her voice. 'He's the father. Of my kids.'

Veronika couldn't believe it. All this time, without saying a word. And now she would have to respond. She knew she had to tread carefully.

'Does Charlie know?' she said.

'Yeah. He figured out the dates. That's why ... why he left. He's gone, Ronnie. He left us.'

One of the oldest tricks in the book, Veronika thought, trying to fool a man about paternity. Her stupid sister. Her desperate sister. Had she really thought that shacking up with Charlie would solve her problems?

'He let me keep the house,' Ana said. 'And ... well, I miss him. I love him, Ron, I really do.'

Veronika was lost for words. As though she'd missed her cue and didn't have a prompt.

'Can you ... would you come and see me?' Ana's voice was a whimper.

'Of course. As a matter of fact, I'm coming to Geraldton in July. I'm in a play.'

'So that's why you called me? To come and see your play?'

'Don't be ... I called because I want to see you. But you can still come to the play and bring the kids, too. Okay?'

'Okay.' Ana's breath was a rasp. 'And Ronnie, the real father doesn't know either,' she said. 'Nor do Mum and Dad. They'd be devastated. I can't ... I just can't ...'

Veronika thought that her sister might cry, but there were no tears on the end of the phone. There was nothing left but to say *goodbye, take care, see you soon.*

49. Ana

The Three Bandicoots. What a stupid name for a play. Not that Ana knew what was going on or who was who because Ben was being a real pain, smearing bubblegum he found under his shoe onto the back of the seats, prodding the chair in front of him until the man turned around and glared, snapped at Ben to behave himself. Ana was mortified: it was one of the local councillors, and a good-looking one at that. She could see it written on his face: a mother who can't control her child. At least Meredith was quiet, asleep in her pram, but Ana was so worried that she'd wake up and scream that she couldn't enjoy this rare outing.

What had happened to the young woman who'd lived in a sumptuous house in an old European city at the heart of the continent? She hadn't bargained for this struggle, or the loneliness in a blustery, blistering town far away from anything she knew, anything she cared about.

She heard clapping and cheering and figured the show must be over. She saw Veronika, the star, take a few bows. She was wearing a black velvet jacket with lace trims and a long, grey bustle skirt, her hair tied up in a black ribbon. She had been very good, Ana had to admit, even if she didn't know much about acting. Veronika had managed to convince her that she was Pearl, a bold and plucky barmaid. You could forget it was your sister onstage. And how did she remember all those words, where to move, what to do with her body?

But then, Veronika had done it before. Ana had seen her in that other play at the outdoor theatre; she'd been so transported by all the events on stage it really made Ana wonder about the father of her children. Had Tobias used her, like that Count had tried to with the maid in that play? Or had some of it really been her own fault? Plays. Veronika had found *her thing.* Anna wondered, what's my thing? Not just being a mum, surely. There had to be more, didn't there? Some way to get a crowd on your side, clapping and cheering just for you.

Veronika wanted to *meet the children*, she'd said, as if she were offering them an audience. But by the time she made it to the house the next day, both children were mercifully asleep in their beds, their tiny faces flushed with exhaustion. Ana loved seeing them like that, rosy-cheeked and innocent. She'd read somewhere that it was nature's way of urging you to keep breeding. She knew it was meant as a joke, but she didn't find it funny. She loved her kids, yes, but she was constantly tired, often irritated and always short of money. Maybe Veronika could help her with some money. If she could find the courage to ask.

The doorbell. Her sister, at last, half an hour late, trotting out apologies. She arrived, flustered but elegant in a snug pair of jeans and a loose peasant shirt, her hair falling down to her shoulders. She looked taller. Luminous. They hugged awkwardly.

'You look lovely,' Veronika said. 'Sort of ... complete.'

Ana sniffed. 'You mean *fat*.' She stood back, brushed the hair from her forehead. She needed a haircut, needed to lose weight, needed not to cry.

'The kids are asleep,' she said.

'Can I have a peek?' Veronika made her way through to the lounge.

'Wait till they wake up.' She knew she was being snappy, but she couldn't help herself. With her sister looking so pretty, so free and easy. 'I haven't made any lunch,' she said, 'but I can make you a drink.'

'Tea would be lovely,' Veronika said.

Tea would be lovely. Ana suppressed a scoff. She fussed around with teabags and cups, watched Veronika looking around the room.

'Didn't have time to clean up, sorry,' Ana said. There were toys strewn about, several mugs on the coffee table. Ana quickly tossed the TV remote aside and pushed the toys into a corner. Then she and her sister sat down on the sofa, knees together, like their mother had taught them to sit.

'So tell me your story,' Veronika said.

'My story?' Ana shrugged. 'Well ... this story, the one I'm living now ... it's all about Charlie. When I had the twins, they were so obviously not three months prem, so he did the sums, got really mad and walked out.'

She saw Veronika grimace.

'I know what you're thinking,' Ana said. 'That it was a really dumb thing to do. But ... I panicked, didn't I? I knew I couldn't tell the real father. He was married and a big deal in Prague, so I ... well, I just couldn't say a word.'

'Was he ... I mean, did he ... take advantage of you?'

Ana's face tensed. 'He spoiled me,' she said. 'Champagne breakfasts while his wife was away. Back rubs every Sunday morning when she went to aerobics. I was flattered, I suppose. And excited. He was ... you know ... experienced.'

Veronika set down her cup. Ana feared she was in for a lecture.

'And where's Charlie now?' Veronika leaned forward. 'Does he give you any support?'

'I don't have a clue where he is, and no, he doesn't send a cent. He did give me the house, though. He did say I could stay here. He must have heaps of money, don't you think? All the stuff in the papers. Investments all over the place, schmoozing with important people. They call him an *entrepreneur*!'

Veronika frowned. 'So how do you manage?'

'I get some government money, and I work a bit at a petrol station, at the café. But I have to leave the kids with the old lady next door, and I feel guilty all the time. And I hate the smell of greasy chips and petrol. Maybe I'll ... there's blokes on the mines, you know ... and I reckon I can find myself one, get some support.'

'Really, Ana?'

'Oh, don't look so shocked, Veronika. You don't know what it's like, trying to raise two kids, living on the bones of your bum.'

Veronika drew herself up. 'Well, I'm not exactly rolling in money, Ana. My bookshop job and Austudy barely pay the bills.' She took Ana's hand. 'Look, why don't you go home? I'm sure Mum and Dad will help.'

'I'm not so sure about that. They came for a visit once, and apart from complaining all the time about the heat and the flies, they found it hard looking after the kids. And besides, they think the kids are Charlie's, and they kept cursing him for leaving me.'

Veronika gave her sister a fixed look. 'So why do you still love him?' she said.

Ana shrugged. 'Who knows? He's always had this ... well, like a kind of spell on me.'

'Sex, you mean?'

'It was ... it's more than that. It's ... well, it's kind of a secret.' Ana's teacup wobbled, and she set it carefully on the table.

'What do you mean, a secret?'

A child screamed. Ana rose from the sofa, glad to escape. She'd said too much already.

'It's Meredith,' she said. 'Come and say hello. She's a real cutie.'

50. Gloria

It was Gloria's second term in her first year as a primary teacher at Our Lady of Consolation, Kardinya. She was still trying to work out the job, her class, herself. Occasionally she got the hang of it, and sometimes it even felt right, as if she were actually being useful. She knew she had to give it time, be patient, keep learning.

Year Threes had been given a new class pet, an axolotl that lived in the long fish tank at the back of the class. The kids named it Axel. Not very original, but they were so thrilled when the fascinating creature arrived, they had already decided on the name.

Gloria had been so busy with spelling tests that she hadn't had much time to read up on the new pet. But she did know it was an amphibian, which meant Axel would shed his skin, metamorphose at some point in his life cycle. Gloria saw this as an opportunity for themed learning. She really enjoyed themed learning, it all made sense, and you could keep the class focused, absorbed. This new pet was the perfect chance to learn about change. Transformation. Metamorphosis. Gloria would apply the theme to science class and reading practice as well, and just about everything else they had to cover that term.

Me-ta-mor-pho-sis. There. On the whiteboard. It was a pretty big word for a group of seven-year-olds. But Gloria broke it down into its five syllables and told them to say each one aloud, match the sound with the letters and write the word down on their pads. They all managed to do it, well, apart from Matthew, who'd been bouncing his leg nonstop and looking through the window. He was doing okay until the *ph* sound, which really seemed to frustrate him; he kept saying *metamorposis*. Gloria gave some other examples of *ph* as an *f* sound, like *phone* and *photo*, but he got muddled, and the class was getting a bit rowdy, so she had to leave him and pay attention to the kids who were mucking around.

Then she tried a bit of musical chairs and moved Matthew away from the window so he'd pay attention. She sat him next to Katrina, a studious girl who might be a good example for him, but still he kept craning his neck, swinging on his chair, trying to see what was happening in the outside world. He was getting agitated about something, and before she could stop him, he fell off the chair, went *thump* on the floor. Had he injured himself? Oh hell ... that wouldn't be good, wouldn't look good for her ... but no, he seemed to be okay, getting up and looking around, grinning as if nothing had happened.

But now Katrina was complaining that he kept leaning over and copying her work and he kept borrowing her ruler and chewing on it and why did she have to sit next to him? And why did he keep pinching her pens and it just wasn't fair, she said. Poor Matthew, Gloria thought. She knew he could be a pest, but he was a nice boy at heart. And she shouldn't have sat him next to Katrina, who was Miss Perfect really, a bit annoying in her perfection. But it was too late to separate them now. The term had started, and their names were already stuck to the desk.

At recess, when Katrina sidled up to Gloria and repeated her complaints, her nose in the air, Gloria knew she had to take her seriously. She thought of a tactic that might work: would Katrina mind *helping* Matthew, just until the end of semester, because she was good at so many things and maybe she could spread that goodness around a bit. Gloria thought that flattery might smooth things along, but Katrina looked sterner than ever.

And it was Katrina who threw a spanner in the works three days after the new pet arrived. Gloria was explaining the different kinds of transformation and change when Miss Perfect put her hand up in the air and said, primly:

'Miss da Silva, an axolotl doesn't shed its skin. It has gills. It doesn't go through metamorphosis.'

Was the girl right? She probably was because she was almost always right. Gloria was stumped. Tried not to look stupid. She cleared her throat.

'Isn't that *interesting*?' she said. That handy, overused word that could sometimes solve or at least stall a problem. Questions of authority, of stupidity. But she was thrown, no doubt about it. Why couldn't she just admit she was wrong? Corrected by a seven-year-old in front of the whole class. She needed to distract them from Axel and metamorphosis; she needed to change tack.

'Heads down, thumbs up,' she said.

The kids cheered. She asked Neil to come up to the front and pick the thumbs.

While the class played the game – even Matthew joined in, kept his focus – she sat at her desk and tried to think of another way to talk about metamorphosis.

'Miss, can I go to the toilet?'

'Yes, Linda.'

Maybe she could throw it back to the class.

'Can anyone name an animal that sheds its skin?' she asked.

A few hands shot up.

Gloria chose Yù Míng, who looked like she was about to pop with the answer.

'A snake,' Yù Míng said.

'Yes,' said Gloria, 'A snake sheds its skin. It's a reptile. Well done, Yù Míng.'

'A snail,' Matthew said. He hadn't put his hand up. 'A snail sheds its house, its shell.'

'Well, that *is* a big change,' Gloria said. She didn't want to upset Matthew. 'Katrina, what else sheds its skin?'

'A butterfly.'

'Yes, a butterfly. An insect. That's an animal. As we know, it starts as a worm, then it goes into a cocoon and then it me-ta-mor-pho-ses.'

'I wrote a story about a butterfly,' Katrina said. 'It's called "The Butterfly". Can I enter it into the creative writing competition?'

'I wrote a story, too,' Matthew cut in.

Katrina shot him a dark look. 'I bet you didn't,' she said.

'I did too,' Matthew protested.

'What's it called?'

He hesitated. Looked around the room. '"The Axolotl",' he said. 'And it's about metamorphosis.'

Wow, Gloria thought. He'd pronounced it correctly.

She didn't remember mentioning the competition. Katrina's mum must have found out and pushed her into it early. She was a bit like that, Katrina's mum; no wonder the child ... but it didn't matter now because the kids were looking excited, chattering about writing a story, entering the competition. Why stop them now? A butterfly. Metamorphosis. Anything they liked, so long as it gave them pleasure and maybe kept some of them quiet for more than ten minutes.

A prompt. Stimulation. That would help. Gloria flicked through her things in the resource cupboard and found a picture of a huge colourful butterfly. She nipped across the corridor to the library, hoping no-one saw her leave the class unsupervised ... it was only for a minute. She copied the picture onto a transparency, then put that onto the overhead projector. To inspire them. When she returned, they jiggled in their seats, took out their writing pads, started writing away to their heart's content. About metamorphosis. Or change. Or butterflies or whatever. Anything.

Gloria did the rounds and checked on their work; there had been some creative *spelling* rather than creative *writing*, but she wasn't going to correct it now. She sat at her desk again, surveying all the heads, and saw on her monthly calendar the class had to present at assembly in two weeks. A short piece of theatre, the principal had asked for. Gloria sighed. There were already so many things to keep up with: finishing the reports from last term, the parent–teacher night, Jump Rope for Heart and Multicultural Day – well, at least that had been and gone. Gloria hadn't enjoyed it.

The principal had pressured her into dressing up in national costume, like all the children *from other lands*. At first Gloria hadn't thought much about it, went to find her mother's tais, so beautifully woven and dyed. She put it on for school. But the whole thing, Multicultural Day, other lands, the lunchtime parade to celebrate your culture ... it made her stomach turn. It was stupid, performing their culture as if they were quaint curiosities. As if culture were consumable, static, instead of complicated and dynamic. She wanted to share about East Timor and some of her family's customs, but she didn't want to parade around. There was no other word for it: ridiculous.

And now she had to think about assembly. A theatrical piece, the principal said. Gloria had never done assembly before, and she wished she had longer to prepare. She had sung in front of three hundred and fifty people on an outdoor stage, but somehow this felt more intimidating. The principal was a bit uptight and always going on about *standards*.

At the last assembly, the Year Sixes had performed a liturgical dance for Easter, and they'd been pretty darn slick. Some of them had enacted the Passion dressed in liturgical gowns, used expressive hand movements to mime the whole Passion, while the rest of the class stood behind them, singing and swaying to the music. And when Jesus in his white robe popped out of that cardboard box, Gloria had felt oddly moved, uplifted even, despite the cardboard box. Hard to beat that kind of stuff. But she had to. Well, she didn't have to *beat* the liturgical dance, but she didn't want her class to put on something second-rate, embarrassing.

She could do this, couldn't she? She'd survived *Figaro*, after all. She smiled, thinking of all the fiascos; what could be worse than that? But it had been exciting. Yes, something had changed in her after *Figaro*, she wasn't sure what, but it had made her more confident, like she *could* stand up in front of a class, keep them on track. She wondered how everyone was doing and thought wistfully about Joshua. She should send an email to Cassie, see how her travels were going. When she had some time.

She heard squabbling, returned to the present. Went to check.

'Miss, Miss!' Katrina, screwing up her face in annoyance. 'Matthew hasn't got his pen, he keeps asking me for a pen, and I need my pen and he puts his hand in his pocket and he scratches, *scratches* himself—'

Gloria had just about had it. But she needed to stay calm, needed not to reprimand a boy scratching his balls.

'Can't you two just work together?' she said. 'Maybe you can *help* one another? Write your story together. And why can't you give him your pen, Katrina, you have so many there! He will give it back, won't you, Matthew?'

Matthew nodded. Katrina looked like someone had just winded her or else made her eat lamb's brains for breakfast.

'But, Miss, I can't give him my spare pen because ... because Matthew hasn't got his pen licence yet.'

A pen licence! Gloria strode to her desk, pulled a pencil out of a drawer, went back to Matthew.

'You can write with a pencil,' she said.

Gloria felt she was barely managing. She tried to recall her training and drew a blank. All these theories. Vygotsky. Piaget. Nothing *practical*. It had been a long day, a very long day. She saw the time and announced that they would be presenting at assembly in two weeks. In front of the whole school. And parents. She told them it would be *fun*, but they would have to work together ... someone screamed. Someone was crying. It was Matthew.

Katrina folded her arms across her skinny chest. 'I refuse to work with him,' she said.

Refuse. Poor Matthew, Gloria thought. And damn Katrina. How could I defuse things, she thought. And then she saw it. Katrina loved to be the best at everything. Gloria brightened. 'Why don't you write a play for assembly, Katrina, and act it out?'

Katrina's scowl immediately transformed into a smile.

'Yes, yes,' she said eagerly. 'I can make my story into a play. My story about the butterfly.' 'Great. Done. You'll have to work with Matthew on it. Work *together*.'

Katrina went cross-eyed. Not a good sign. And now kids started talking, complaining ... *What about me? ... I've got a story ... Bet mine's better than yours.*

Gloria put on her calm face again. 'You will all be part of it,' she said. 'Everyone will have a special role to play. There are costumes and painting and the set, acting, maybe music ...'

They started chattering again, but this time it was happy talk, excited talk.

What an afternoon!

At the end of the day, when Gloria was packing up her books, Katrina approached her. 'Matthew and I have an idea,' she said. 'The Year Threes will present the best assembly ever.'

51. Veronika

Travelling back to Perth on the bus at the end of July, the cast was a buzz of chattering: elated, exhausted, keen to get home. But Veronika had chosen a seat at the back, wanting to be alone.

She could still picture the rosy little girl and boy, could still see the pride in Ana's eyes. But what she saw more clearly was Charlie. Her tormentor. She'd gone to the beach to collect shells, to make a collage for Joshua's home in the trees. She remembered a shadow crossing her face, crossing her shells laid out on the sand. A shadow, then Charlie's strong body. Had he said sorry for burning her hair? Had he ever once said sorry? Instead, he'd coaxed her to the island with a promise of much better shells, cowrie and abalone, and giant birds like eagles. She couldn't remember the name of that bird, but she could still see the blisters on Charlie's feet, feeling sorry for him … but infuriated by him, too, and somehow wanting to forgive him, all mixed up together.

He'd beckoned her into a boat, and she could still see this, too, his arm in close-up, and how the strength of it made her feel something new, something strange. On the boat he'd teased her about little Veronika growing up, and she'd covered the bumps on her chest. Girls learn it so early, Veronika thought. This awareness of their bodies. The edge of fear. Because everything changed after that. There were no shells on the island, he just wanted to be with her, he said. Alone. He pulled off his shirt. The gleam of his chest, his flat, tight stomach. The endless blue of the sky made her dizzy; she said, *take me home, Charlie*. But he grabbed her around the waist and lifted her up, and *you're beautiful, Veronika, I love you, Veronika, say you love me, Veronika*, and she beat his chest, and *I hate you, Charlie, I hate you*, struggling out of his grasp and falling on the rocks and hitting her head. She remembered blood. She remembered lying very still in the boat. The drone of the wind, the lisp of the waves. And then reaching the shore and Charlie was gone. And she was safe.

'Daydreaming, Ronnie?'

It was the stagehand, Fran, with her cat-like hazel eyes. 'Wanna slice of cake?' she asked. 'Apple and cinnamon. Fresh from the bakery.'

Veronika shook her head. 'You're really kind,' she said, as Fran made her way back down the aisle.

She was on the verge of tears now, seeing herself stumbling, running to find Josh, calling out to him. Watching him climb down from his house, wanting him to hurry, seeing his thighs, his chest and finally his smiling face appear in front of her. The shock when he saw her, the warmth of his hand as he led her to the creek and gently washed the blood from her face. How he'd given her space to talk but hadn't pressed her. She'd fallen over, she said, running too fast, but she was alright, really, fine, just wanted to see him. Making up a story to save herself. And then his gift, his marvellous gift, wrapped up in a plastic bag: a beautiful silk dress, crimson, intricately beaded. It was his mother's dress, and Veronika wanted to tell him it was beautiful, but all she could hear was *you're beautiful, Veronika, I love you, Veronika*, and she was swinging back and forth in the boat again, and all she could say was *thank you, Josh, thank you*, and how she was leaving soon for school and how badly she would miss him.

She never wore the beautiful crimson dress with the dropped waist. Her sister had spied it soon after, held it against her, twirled around. Demanded to know if she'd stolen it. *Charlie gave it to me.* And her sister had laughed because she knew it wasn't true, and anyway, Veronika wasn't invited to Charlie's bonfire. They didn't want a little kid like her hanging round. But she'd gone anyway, to spite Ana, to spite Charlie, and to see Josh one more time. She remembered: she'd worn the necklace Babička had given her, to make her feel pretty and grown up.

And that's when she saw it again. The bonfire at the beach. Flames blazing and alive. Charlie and Josh wrestling, punching, people laughing and getting drunker. Josh disappearing into the bush. Then fire. Buildings destroyed. Animals, too. Dead. The earth had been scorched, and the forest devoured. The wild wind carried the fires up and down the coast.

She'd seen Josh's face when he was loaded into the paddy wagon later that night. *Blank. Just blank.*

It was a welcome distraction to be cast in a radically different play. She'd had a good month's break, so she could throw herself into it, get on with things. Forget about men. She'd had one quick fling that briefly made her think of Sebastian, but that was it. She had no time for entanglements, even fleeting encounters. No time for thinking about anything but work: it was only the work that mattered. And since the company had actually made some money from their Geraldton tour, they could afford to try something avant-garde. Samuel Beckett.

Veronika was cast as Nell, and she felt strangely happy to dwell in a dustbin, speaking blackly comic lines to her husband, Nagg. She enjoyed her transformation into a dried-up crone: the white pasty make-up, the muck and the rags. The play was hilarious, but rehearsals had been serious. *Exploding the paradigms of traditional drama,* the director said. They must *destroy the image of a character.* Her homework was to spend her day in the life of Nell. How would Nell eat breakfast? Converse? Catch a bus? And then, in rehearsals, she would speed it up, slow it down, exaggerate gestures while speaking the text. She and Nagg had to imagine the process, the feeling of losing their memory, their physical agility. They even took a turn on a seesaw in the park, enacting Beckett's power games. They made up a circular dialogue with no discernible plot. It was terrifying. It was funny.

Finally, it was opening night. She surprised herself by feeling calm, steady. Before the curtain opened, she flashed a quick smile at Nagg, then disappeared into her dustbin. When it was time, she raised the lid, turned to face the audience. Then she saw him. In the front row. Charlie. She couldn't remember her lines, heard the lid crash to the ground, but she somehow managed to pull herself together. Run on instinct. Ignore the audience.

Kiss me! she heard Nagg command.

She found her place. She stretched up her neck like a turtle and puckered her lips, but she couldn't reach Nagg.

We can't, she cried, looking at Nagg, trapped in his own dustbin.

Try, said Nagg.

Why this farce, day after day? she heard herself say.

As she took her bows, she peered into the audience but couldn't see him. Had she conjured him up from her memories? Had her strength of will forced him to leave?

Or maybe he just didn't like Beckett.

'Not so fast.'

Charlie: grabbing her by the arm. She spun round.

'I saw your name on the poster,' he said. 'I couldn't resist. Well done.'

People jostled them in the foyer. Veronika wished she wasn't wearing jeans and a hoodie, that her hair wasn't still powdered white. He looked smart: an open linen shirt, white pants. Still the same heavy brow but with fine lines around his forehead. Almost handsome.

'Strange play,' he said. 'But I think I got it.'

'You're not meant to *get it*.'

He smelled of alcohol. 'Fancy a drink?' he said.

I can do this, Veronika thought. I need to. For my own sake, and for Ana's. She propped herself on a bar stool, waited for him to sit. He ordered two gin and tonics without asking her.

'You haven't changed a bit,' she said. 'Still doing whatever you like.'

He stared at her. Compelled her to look at him.

'I *have* changed, Veronika. And ... the way I treated you ... it was my way of showing that I liked you.'

'A psychopath's way, you mean,' she said and sipped her gin.

'Come on, don't be like that.'

Veronika tossed her head. 'I saw my sister,' she said. 'Not long ago.'

His face fell. 'She broke my heart,' he said.

She couldn't tell if he was sincere.

'Knocked up by some Russian guy,' he said.

'Austrian, actually.'

'Oh, yes. In Czechoslovakia,' he said.

'No, it's called the Czech Republic now. And the Slovak Republic. She was in Prague, working for an Austrian family.'

'But he was *married*, Veronika. The Austrian dude.'

She barely suppressed a laugh. 'Didn't think you'd care about such things.'

'For your information ...' He leaned towards her. 'I don't go messing with married women. Look, Ana didn't even tell me about the affair. I had to prise it out of her. With two tiny babies lying in the palms of my hands. I *literally* had the future in my hands, and then she wrenched it away from me.'

Were those tears in his eyes? Because a good actor knew how to manufacture them on cue.

'So you saw her, hey?' he said. 'I'll be heading to Geraldton myself. I've invested in a garnet mine there. Not the jewellery kind but garnet for making abrasives.'

'How apt,' Veronika shot back, but he didn't seem to get it. 'So will you go and see her?'

'I don't want to talk about Ana. I came to see you.'

'Sorry you thought the play was strange. I take it you didn't like it?'

'Veronika.' He placed a hand on her arm, and she flinched. 'Be nice. I made an effort, didn't I?'

She narrowed her eyes. 'Ana told me a secret about you,' she said. 'Well, she started to tell me.'

He grinned. 'No secrets with me,' he said. 'I'm an open book, Ronnie. Remember what I told you? That you were beautiful. That I loved you.'

She bristled. 'I was a child, Charlie!'

'Old enough to know what you were doing.'

She slipped off her seat. Wanting to shout at him, slap him hard. Knowing she mustn't make a scene.

'You make me sick,' she said and hurried from the room. Back to her shitty house that she'd lived in for years. Shit, shit, shit, she screamed, all along the highway in the dark.

52. Gloria

The principal announced them at the assembly.

'*The Axolotl and the Butterfly*, directed and performed by Year Threes.'

They were all there, the parents, the kids all in rows. Sitting in the back, Gloria unclenched her hands, tried not to feel nervous. They'd been rehearsing for almost two weeks, making costumes, learning about the animals. It looked pretty good. Maybe it *would* be good. Brilliant even.

Matthew crawled onto the small stage in his papier-mâché cylinder. His feet and hands were webbed in plastic; the black spikes on his head looked spectacular and his gills, finely painted. Then Katrina entered the stage and fluttered about in her magnificent rainbow wings (just like the picture on the overhead projector) – arrayed in glitter and tulle.

'Can you help me?' the axolotl said slowly, in his lowest voice.

'Help, you? Why, of course,' said the butterfly in a high voice, quickly, darting here and there.

'I can't fly,' the axolotl said. 'I want to be like you. Fast. Beautiful. Free.'

'Free?'

'Yes, free. Can you help me fly?'

'Help you fly? Let's see what I can do,' said the butterfly.

And so the butterfly danced around the axolotl and tried to lift his feet, but they were too heavy. 'Keep trying,' the axolotl said, in his low, slow voice. The butterfly ran to his back feet, but they couldn't get lift-off either.

'How about these?' she said, pushing at his gills. She pushed and pushed the gills. They moved a little, but they wouldn't flap. The poor butterfly flopped on the floor in defeat. (But Gloria knew exactly what was coming.)

'I'm sorry,' said the butterfly.

'It's okay,' said the axolotl.

The butterfly looked across the stage. 'I can't swim,' she said, sadly. 'Can you help me?'

'Why, of course. I can help you,' said the axolotl. 'I can help you swim. Follow me,' he said, and so she flittered around him as he trudged slowly to the pond. 'It's easy,' he said, slowly wading into the stream made of blue crepe paper. (Some of the children had spent hours making that stream, Gloria thought.)

The butterfly kept flapping and fluttering and trying to settle on the water. She tried, and tried and tried again but all she could do was flap.

'I can't, I can't,' she said, distressed. (She's doing a great job, Gloria thought. And so is Matthew: who would have thought the boy could act?)

'Land on me,' said the axolotl. And so the butterfly lay her wings on his long, helpful back.

(Matthew had wanted the axolotl to eat the butterfly at this point, as that probably would have happened in real life, he had said. But Gloria insisted on them using Katrina's ending.)

The butterfly began to cry. 'I want to go back,' she said. 'I want to go back to land. I'm scared.'

'I'm sorry,' said the axolotl.

'That's okay,' said the butterfly. 'Thank you for trying, though.'

'I wish I could be free like you,' the axolotl said.

(Here comes the beautiful part ... Gloria leaned forward in her seat.)

'I wish I could swim like you,' the butterfly said.

'But you're beautiful, and I'm not,' said the axolotl.

'That's true.'

'And you're fast, and I'm not.'

'That's also true,' said the butterfly.

'It's not fair,' said the axolotl. 'It's not fair.'

'But you know what?' said the butterfly. 'None of it matters. It doesn't matter that I can't swim. It's better to have a friend.'

'It doesn't matter I can't fly,' the axolotl said. 'It's much better to have a friend.'

(Nicely done, Gloria thought. Even if they weren't friends in real life, they were putting on a damn good show.)

'I'm feeling really tired,' the butterfly said. She stopped fluttering, sat for a bit on the hard wooden floor.

'How long do you live for?' she asked axolotl.

'Fifteen years,' he said.

The butterfly frowned. 'That's not fair,' she said.

'Why? How long do *you* live for?'

'Fifteen days.' (She sounded on the verge of crying ... also convincing, Gloria thought. Maybe the child did a lot of crying at home.)

'Fifteen days?' the axolotl said. 'That's not fair. Not fair at all.'

The butterfly got up, flapped her wings sadly. 'Nothing's fair,' she said. 'That's why we have to help one another, don't you see?'

'I see.'

'I have to go now. I need some nectar to gain some strength. I'm hungry.'

'Don't go,' said the axolotl.

'But … I'm worried that you might eat me.'

'Of course I won't eat you.'

The butterfly nodded. 'It's okay, I know you can't help it. That's just who you are. It's okay. And now I'm going to say goodbye.'

'Please don't go,' said the axolotl. 'I promise I won't eat you.'

'Bye, bye,' the butterfly said and fluttered off the stage.

All was quiet. The children looked stunned. Sad. They elbowed each other in the ribs, shook their heads, not knowing what to think. A couple of teachers started to clap when … yes, the butterfly whooshed back on stage.

'Will you help me?' she said to the axolotl.

'Why of course,' he said. 'Of course, I will help you in any way I can.'

Suddenly, spontaneously, everyone clapped and cheered loudly. All the Year Threes swarmed onto the stage, and each one took a separate bow. The set makers. The costume makers. The writers and actors. Boy, was Gloria proud, so proud.

She really felt like taking a break, what with all the worry and then the hope and then the elation … but there was no time for that. They had to go back to class, open their books and focus on religious education. Their first reconciliation in a few months. *Re-con-ci-li-a-tion.* Six syllables, Gloria counted on her hand. Well, they'd already managed five with metamorphosis; this next one would be a piece of cake.

53. Felix

It was three pm on a Saturday afternoon when he came home from a night out. His mother was sitting on the sofa, wearing her satin dressing-gown. She wore it all the time and would only ever change if a pupil was coming for a piano lesson. Or if she had to go out, which wasn't often. Felix wondered if she was depressed or just loved the dressing-gown, which was, in fact, quite fine and lovely, its fuchsia pattern, its delicate folds.

'*Du bist spät dann.* A big night?' she asked.

He nodded shyly.

'You can tell me, you know,' his mother said. 'I know. I've known for a long time. It's not a problem for me. But you must tell your father.'

Felix had known for years that he was gay, he'd had a number of involvements and encounters but hadn't told his parents. He figured they knew, that there was some sort of unspoken understanding.

Feeling relieved, he sat next to her on the sofa. But then, a pang of irritation. You must tell your father. She was telling him what to do. And then what? He was a grown man living in his parents' house for the first time in six years.

'We worry about you,' she said. 'Your late nights, your smoking all the time. And now you have a new job, how can you keep staying out so late and working the next day?'

Felix said nothing.

'I just want you to be happy,' his mother said. 'I hope there's someone special, a man who makes your heart stop, who—'

'Enough, Mama.'

She was prying now. She was too open. It had always been that way. When he was a teenager, she would share with his friends details of her sex life with his father. His sister found it hilarious, but Felix was mortified. Without the courage to tell her to stop. Stop embarrassing him. She would point: *We haven't done it yet on this table, but over on that lounge.*

She went to make coffee. He wouldn't tell her about Max, he'd never hear the end of her prying. He hadn't seen Max in three years, anyway; it wasn't going anywhere, would never go where he wanted. Max was twenty years older than him, and their contact had been entirely platonic. But for Felix it had been charged, meaningful. For him. But what did it matter if Max didn't feel the same way? He was probably already taken. There were attractive men everywhere. He tried not to think of Max and the whole theatre world. Max and Karlsruhe. As if leaving Berlin could have stamped out the memory of him. It had only made it more vivid. Was he in love with the man?

His mother returned with two cups of coffee, smiling again at the son she loved. Because she *did* love him, he was sure of that. She *did* want him to be happy. And he loved his father, too. They supported him, wanted the best for him. And, yes, he *would* tell his father, despite the man's massive ego. An architect, who designed what Felix thought were hideous skyscrapers, but Felix kept that opinion to himself. He would tell his father he was gay, but he'd stay silent about those concrete monsters.

Later that evening over dinner, Felix tried several times to tell his father. He tried when they finished the soup and waited for the next course. He tried in moments of silence, but his father started up again about his various important projects. Felix did his best to express his interest but he was waiting for the right time, the best time … And now his father was going on about his designs for some new hotel in Mitte. Felix couldn't stand it any longer.

'*Ich bin schwul, Papa.* I'm gay,' he said. 'I wanted you to know that.'

Neither parent said a word. Felix looked to his mother for support, but she was looking down at her plate. The clink of knives and forks sounded loudly.

'I'd like to stay here for a bit longer,' he said. 'Until I save enough to get my own place.' He looked at his father. 'Are you okay with that? Just for a while.'

His father stood up gruffly, retrieved another beer from the fridge. He plonked the bottle on the table, sat down again.

'What are you doing at Arup?' he asked stiffly. Click of the bottle top. Furious sip. Felix bit his lip. His father was avoiding the subject. Okay, I will tell him about Arup, if that's what he wants to know. So he told him about the new bridge between Copenhagen and Malmö, how he'd just received samples of the concrete, how he was monitoring the pours.

'We have to place the concrete into a mould, where it's cured for seven days,' he said.

His father said nothing. Felix battled on.

'The concrete survived what we call the destruction machine,' he said. 'Which means the concrete was strong. Fit for a pylon.'

His father raised his brow. 'And do you like it?' he asked.

'Do I like concrete? Well, no, Papa. Not really. To tell the truth, I am bored with the work. But you wanted me to do this, so I am doing it. And soon I will be making good money.'

His father frowned, leaned forward. 'Being gay is not the issue!' he said, his voice raised. 'Not the issue at all!' He smacked his napkin on the table.

Felix waited.

'A man has to earn a decent living,' his father said.

'I don't understand, Papa. I have a good job, in the middle of a recession.'

His father leaned back, looked at Felix's mother. She was still silent. *You must tell your father*, she'd said.

'I am sad, in fact,' his father said. 'Sad for you, Felix, not for me, not because you are gay, but because you will never experience the joy of having a family, of raising children.'

Was the man sad for his son or sad for himself? At least Felix's sister, Johhanna, had a steady boyfriend. *They* could reproduce. Make the old man a grandfather. He was on the verge of saying something, anything to break the silence, when his father threw his knife and fork down on his plate and trampled out of the room.

Felix looked at his father's bottle. He took a grateful swig. The beer would go flat anyway. He supposed he should do the dishes. He began to gather the plates, then dared a glance at his mother. She looked smaller, defeated.

While soaping the plates, he could see through the kitchen window his young neighbour, Anke, slicing rye bread. He waved. She waved back.

54. Veronika

She kept in touch with some of the cast from *Figaro*. Just the odd coffee and a chat. Gwen was working in a boutique (she'd quit dressing like a goth); she'd heard that Lucas had found work as a geologist in Coolgardie. Gloria loved her job teaching at a school in Kardinya. One of those new suburbs, she said, where all the houses looked the same and the median age was eleven. The last time they met, Gloria had joined a choir. She told her she wanted to go back to East Timor once the hell died down. Veronika nodded politely. But when Gloria added she had to search there for her father, it gave Veronika pause. She couldn't imagine it, she said. She would be lost if her own father disappeared. Josh had disappeared as well, according to Gloria. Somewhere up north, she'd said. Veronika said nothing.

She'd kept up with Cassie, too. Or more like Cassie had kept up with her, sending her postcards from her travels. She'd walked through the Himalayas and made her way to Dharamshala, where she'd visited temples and shrines. She'd lived off street food in Indonesia and had learned to do yoga. She'd bicycled through Cambodia, given painting lessons to kids in a village. *So much for my degree in philosophy and fine arts.* The last postcard was from London. She'd been to visit *Sebbie* in Cambridge and she was *sorry about that kiss and I don't fancy him anymore.* He'd taken her to hear *the most heavenly choir* and he wasn't such *an arrogant prick* anymore. Veronika didn't bite. What could she say, anyway, since she hadn't answered his letter? She was glad he hadn't tried to phone her or send one of his lavish bouquets. They were oceans apart, lives apart, and she figured it was all for the best.

No-one had heard from Felix.

As the year drew to a close, Veronika knew she'd reached her limits. She'd auditioned for Ibsen's *Ghosts* with the state theatre company, hoping to be cast as the maid, Regina. Young, strong-willed, ambitious, with nothing but her body to get her ahead in life. But she'd failed, just as Regina failed, and she'd tried not to feel disappointed. It was the state theatre company, after all: professional, the big time. The director had been encouraging but advised her to get some training. *You mean a degree in French literature doesn't cut it?* she'd said. He recommended a special workshop run by a man in Paris at the École Pierrot in Pantin – Antoine Fouquet. If nothing else, Veronika thought, she could speak with Antoine in his native tongue.

Nothing else. Was there to be nothing else in her life? Paris. Fancy living in Paris. She'd even thought about growing old there, dying happy there. She'd pictured it in close-up: her grave at the Père-Lachaise, not far from Colette's. Colette, who'd given people permission to *do foolish things as long as they did them with enthusiasm.* It was a city blessed by writers, all of whom she'd read: Madame de Sévigné, Corneille, Molière and Racine. She'd even tried to plough her way through Proust but had become lost in the semicolons. Baudelaire, on the other hand … *To be away from home and yet to feel oneself everywhere at home; to see the world, to be at the centre of the world …* She would walk the streets of Baudelaire's Paris, the centre of the world, the winding alleyways, the gracious boulevards. She would dance there, dart into cafés, dine with street musicians. She would roam through the Gothic Notre Dame Cathedral, with Victor Hugo's giant novel clutched to her chest. She would go to Paris, yes, she would. She would die there.

She phoned about the cost of the workshop, and there was no way in the world she could afford it. How could she have been so stupid, let herself get carried away with her useless fantasies, quoting famous writers in her head? She wasn't going to die in Paris after all; she wouldn't even make it to the border.

The receptionist's advice made her feel even worse: had she thought of applying for a scholarship to work with Antoine in Paris? *Spatial awareness,* she crooned. *The International Method.* But Veronika knew it was pointless. There'd be hundreds of hopefuls like her but with much more impressive credentials: graduates from drama school, people with professional experience, people heading for a glittering future. And then the receptionist's final blow: *Have you considered psychotherapy? It's a wonderful way to improve your acting skills.*

Veronika considered crawling back into her bin.

Then her housemate asked her to fill in for her at work. A corporate fundraiser, a cocktail affair, in a trendy restaurant by the river. A celebrity chef. Veronika hated the idea of serving wealthy, snobby guests pretending to be charitable, but the money would certainly come in handy. So she donned black trousers and a crisp white shirt. The evening was worse than she'd imagined: forced to listen to earnest chat about the best vinegar to use for ciabatta, or rapacious talk about investments, as she glided about serving wine and unknown specks of food.

It took her back to the birthday party. To Sebastian. When she'd offered her hand and introduced herself. And then later, when she'd refused his hand and an exquisite sapphire ring.

Maybe she should have married him. With his view of the river, the prospect of easy money.

She waved off the thought of Sebastian. Turned to go back to the kitchen.

'Little Veronika Vaček.'

Fuck! Was she always destined to meet him lurking in corners, lying in wait? Was he stalking her? In his immaculate black suit, blinding white shirt.

'I thought you were running a garnet mine,' she said. Acting cool. 'Abrasives.'

'You look very fetching.' He flashed her a smile. 'And yes, the garnet mine, but a whole lot more, Veronika. Lithium. Gold. Copper. Uranium. You name it.'

She said nothing.

'And here I am, supporting a worthy cause,' he said. 'In fact, I organised it. I do quite a bit of this kind of work, you know. Charity stuff, sitting on a few boards. It's important to give back.'

'And it's important to refill my tray,' she said.

He looked her up and down. 'Short of cash then, are we?'

She was tempted to lift the empty tray, smash it on his head.

'I'm saving up to go to Paris,' she said. 'To train in an exclusive drama school with a wonderful teacher called Antoine. I'm going to be—'

'Famous?'

'Better,' she said and edged her way past him.

She felt belittled. Humiliated.

She would try for that fucking scholarship. She would ring the cheery receptionist and ask for the relevant details. What did she have to lose, after all, but a little more hope for her future?

She phoned back to Paris. The receptionist was brisk. *Send us your CV ...*

'But when are the auditions?' Veronika said.

'CV first. So we don't waste your time.'

'I don't understand.'

Veronika heard a long sigh.

'We need to weed people out,' the receptionist said.

So I don't waste *your* time, Veronika thought. She was a weed. Her father knew all about weeds. A plant growing where it wasn't wanted. A plant in competition with cultivated plants.

But she would apply.

A terrible review in the paper and she was feeling in the pits. *Lacked maturity and conviction.* She kept drinking wine and feeling heavier and heavier and a stranger asking for her autograph groping her bum and now Charlie always Charlie, sweeping her away, kissing her neck, her breasts, and she wanted his mouth on her mouth and Cassie shouting at her to make him stop, *stop, Veronika, stop.*

Veronika jolted awake. Shaken. Sweating.

She rose from her bed, stumbled to the kitchen, made herself a cup of tea. *Have you considered psychotherapy?* drumming in her ears.

55. Charlie

He'd wanted to wait for her to finish work, take her out for a drink, but she'd given him the brush off. It made him mad, mad enough to have another drink, and then another, sitting alone in his apartment. But he liked it too: her fire, her passion. Even dressed as a damned waitress. Especially dressed as a damned waitress, come to think of it. More exciting, all covered up like that, not giving an inch away, hair pulled back, telling him where to get off. She was nothing like the women who rattled around him, fawned all over him, the women in bling.

And maybe ... was there something coming from her side too? Veronika. A vibe? But then why was she so hostile? Maybe she'd sought him out to wind him up, get something going. But then why wouldn't she have a bar of him? Maddening. He loved that she was maddening. And he was sorry for her, too, having to work a shit job like that, earning a pittance. Saving money to follow her passion. He'd seen something in her look, almost ruthless. Clawing away at something. He didn't get art, but he *did* get her will to succeed. He admired it. That's what he would have said, if she'd given him half a chance.

He poured himself another cognac, swilled it round. You and me, Veronika, beautiful Veronika, we're more alike than you think. I got out of Starfish Bay, worked in the iron ore mines till I got jack of it, saw the light, quit the coke, faked some papers to get a better job. The mine manager, a rich guy, he really liked me. That's how you do it, Veronika: knowing how to charm people, get what you want from them. He gave me a job as a plant operator, taught me all I needed to know about investments. So that's how it all began. My road to success.

He'd wanted to bring her home. Show her his flashy apartment. He wanted her to see what he'd made of himself. But what was the point of talking out loud if she wasn't listening?

56. Sebastian

He'd spent two whole weeks in a state of anxious indecision. Should he call her or not? Drive round to her house, knock on the door and say: I'm back, Veronika, I'm back. When he'd finally found the nerve to phone, when she'd agreed to meet him (sounding casual, almost off-hand), he'd been overcome with relief. Just hearing her voice on the phone, he'd fallen into a dumbfounded silence, had to stop himself from pouring out his love and racing round to her house (*yes, still living in that dump*, she'd said) and holding her in his arms. He was back from Cambridge, he'd managed to say, an articled clerk in a prestigious law firm. He hadn't told her he was back with a second-class degree or that his father's connections had wrangled him the job. What he'd really wanted to say, what made him burn with longing, was that he'd never stopped thinking about her in those two years away. That his body had been in Cambridge, but his heart had remained in Perth. Bilocation, he might have called it.

She'd invited him to see her in a play. It wasn't what he'd meant by *meeting. A Midsummer Night's Dream*, apparently.

He'd tried to sound enthusiastic.

But then she'd offered to meet him after the show and his heart raced and he thought he would take her to a bar and just look at her. Then kiss her. Touch her. Belong to her.

He checked his watch. He was half an hour early. Not a good look, skulking around alone outside the Victoria Hall. Hangdog; waiting. He thought he'd kill time with a lap around the old town. He passed the Fremantle Oval, where he'd won a game or two of rugby years before. He felt a momentary rush of pride until the inkling of doubt seeped in. Was he wearing too much cologne? Had he overdone it with the shirt? Too loud, maybe, the Liberty print. He had cut himself shaving and hoped she wouldn't see the small abrasion on his neck. And then he remembered: she'd always liked him better unkempt, unwashed. He smiled. Eccentric girl. He strode past the markets, all closed now, towards one of his favourite pubs where bearded youths were sipping beers. He wished that he could just meet her there. Now. Nice and easy. Face-to-face. No fuss.

But no, she would be dressed as a fairy queen. He would see her on stage. *A Midsummer Night's Dream.* Even *he* knew it had been done to death. But he would endure the play, for her sake.

He headed to the park on the Esplanade and passed the antique train café. Shut. Trust the whole town to be in some sort of narcotic slumber. There were white cockatoos teeming from the tall pine trees, screeching into the dusk. Nothing had changed. Places closing early. The disconcerting cleanness, the burst of boisterous birds. The dull lull of things. But *he* was not the same. He had been to Cambridge, done his master's, followed by a summer clerkship in East Anglia. No longer a student but a man of the world, an accomplished professional. If only he hadn't messed things up with Veronika. The proposal. He'd wanted it to be memorable, sensational, to do it after the show on the final night. So he asked his mother for his grandmother's ring. He was all prepared. But it just came out, in the middle of it all, when he thought she might be ill. *Marry me,* he'd said, absurdly, as if she'd been on her deathbed. The cursed timing. And then her refusal. Was it that stupid kiss with Cassie when it wasn't even his fault? Or maybe she'd been looking for a way out. He knew he'd come on too strong, but some women liked that, liked to be … possessed. But this time he wouldn't pressure her. No proposal, not even living together, if she wanted to lead an independent life.

He felt his heart stop, remembering how she'd led him to her house, her shambles of a room covered in half-read books. Wind chimes. A giant blue sofa. *A rare roadside find,* she called it. And she'd thrown him down on it, kissed him passionately, his hand beginning to inch up her thigh. Then she'd pushed him off. Why? Why?

But now he was seeing her again. This time he would make it work.

It seemed like an eternity before she appeared onstage with her entourage of fairies, under a great, red, pendulous moon, dry ice piping at her feet. She looked to him like a Mucha painting: a royal blue robe showing one shoulder, flowers fastened to her belt. Feet bare. Hair adorned with more flowers. There was shimmer on her cheek and lips, or maybe it was fairy dust. Her neck … He could hardly bear to look at her beauty. He focused instead on the set. He noticed the shabby proscenium arch, the stark green branches to sketch out a forest and a fairy kingdom. He squirmed in his plastic chair. Like a high school gym, he thought. Still, it was almost a full house. Not a bad show, really.

And now Veronika's husband was addressing her: *Tarry, rash wanton. Am I not thy lord?* Rash. Wanton. Sebastian hid a smile. If only, he thought. And now the fairy king Oberon was getting angry about something and Titania was accusing him of jealousy and Sebastian was hoping it wouldn't go on for too long. He needed to pee. He flicked through the flimsy program, as if that might hurry things up, but there wasn't enough light to see. He looked back at the stage, and there she was: holding a child. But it was too much to keep looking at her. Thank God the scene ended at last. Puck, the sprite, sprinkled her eyes with the juice of a flower. A spell was cast. *What angel wakes me from my flowery bed?* she cried in her musical voice.

Sebastian had to stop himself from calling out: *An ass!*

The Ass serenaded Titania. Veronika, a ravishing Titania, looked pleased.

And soon Sebastian was laughing at the madness of it all. Losing himself in the dizzy plot of mistaken lovers, the slapstick mechanicals, laughing so much he shed tears. Hearty applause. A good show, after all.

He darted out of the theatre. A cool September evening for a play about midsummer. Where was he meant to meet her? They hadn't quite firmed up the details. He didn't want to be presumptuous, going backstage, so he waited at the entrance to the theatre. Hoping she would call him. She *had* to call him. He looked this way and that, peering inside, waiting. Ten minutes. Fifteen. Twenty. He checked his watch again. Thirty minutes and most of the crowd had gone. Surely, he could go backstage now, find her in the dressing room. He went back through to the theatre, climbed up on the stage, waited in one of the wings. He asked around for Veronika. A few whispers and stares and then: *She's gone home, you've missed her.*

Sebastian went outside again. Had she disappeared down a trapdoor? Driven off in a mysterious car like a Hollywood starlet? Was she waiting somewhere else? *Meeting* someone else? He stormed his way to the parking lot. *Shit*, he thought, *she's ditched me again. No*, he must be wrong. She wouldn't, couldn't be so cruel, to lead him on and then … But maybe – and it struck him like a blow to the chest – she'd forgotten him. She'd simply forgotten him. And it came back to him, how she just up and left him, turned him into no-one, a nothing. He kept walking with no idea of where he was going, seething now, ready to strike something or someone. People passed him in a hurry, and he wondered if they could see him or see right through him or not bother seeing him at all.

He threw himself back into work. A man always had that. The city was growing; Perth was on the up and up. He'd heard talk of a new convention centre, rumours of skyscrapers taller than the Central Park Tower, the refurbishment of Council House. Plans for a bell tower in Barrack Square. And he could see it happening outside his office window. His work suited the times: civil litigation, construction disputes, contributing to the march of progress, to the economy, to the smooth and efficient running of a functioning society.

It made a lot more sense than dancing about on a stage. Or falling in love with an ass.

He'd given her his phone number, hadn't he?

He returned to the contract on his desk. Another new building, near the stadium, but this one was a major problem: the builders refused to keep working until they were paid, and the owners called their work *substandard*. Sebastian scratched his head, put his feet up on his desk, put them down again. Agreements on timelines and standards were important. Essential. He and the owner agreed that the builders were getting too big for their boots. They would call for an external review.

The phone rang.

'Sebastian, I am *so* sorry.'

That's all it took – the sound of her voice, warm, even inviting – to return him to joy.

'I didn't mean to disappear,' she said.

'Just like old times,' he said, joking, then immediately regretted his words.

Silence.

'*I'm* sorry, too,' he said. 'It's just that ... I ... I was disappointed. I wanted to see you.'

'But you did. I was a magnificent Titania, wasn't I?'

This, too, he heard in her voice: mocking herself but needing to be praised.

'You were very good,' he said. 'I mean ... I've only ever seen you in *Figaro*, but last night, you were so confident, so ... so right. You really inhabited the role.'

She laughed. 'You were always good at that, Sebastian. Laying it on thick.'

'I meant it,' he said. 'I honestly did. I really did like your performance.'

'*Like?*'

He laughed. 'Okay, you were magnificent,' he said. 'Scintillating. Superb. Heart-stoppingly excellent.'

Silence. And then, her beautiful voice again: 'Would you like to meet for lunch? Today?'

'How about ... you can meet me at my office. I'll show you round.'

'And show me what a big shot you've become.'

There was no mistaking her tone this time. Her voice was dripping with sex.

57. Veronika

She looked in the mirror. Who had she become? *Figaro* seemed a lifetime ago. She'd done many roles since she'd seen him last. She eased into her slip dress, looked in the mirror again. Was she showing too much skin? She turned around. The back was cut low. Maybe a pair of flats to make it look less like an evening dress. It was sunny out, but cool. It was only lunch, she reminded herself, as she threw a scarf over her shoulders. Peacock blue. Her best colour. This could work, she thought. She could carry on with her art without worrying about the bills. She twiddled with her hair, rearranged the tendrils. She knew that if she met him now, for lunch, for talk, for meaningful glances, there would be no going back.

One last glimpse at her reflection, and she gathered her things. She looked around at her worn furniture, the cracks in the wall. The tired blue sofa. All this could change. If only he wasn't … what was it about him? Something cloying. A sense of expectation. She sat down for a minute and took a breath. That was it. She would always have to give him her attention, flatter him. And what about his parents? His patronising mother and intimidating father. How could she endure it? To perform an interest in things … it would madden her beyond belief. Maybe she could persuade Sebastian to move … to Melbourne or Sydney, even overseas. But he'd want stability, wouldn't he? And children. Not that she didn't want them, but she needed to feel ready. But would she ever be ready? Could she bear the dirt and the noise, the constant tugging at the skirt that she'd seen with Ana's kids? She would be at the mercy of a baby, a child.

But she needed money, too, and the freedom that money could buy.

She cast a last look at her room. The cracks were still there; the sofa still looking worn. She summoned her energy, rose from her chair and walked out the door. She closed it with a decisive thud.

As she walked down the stairs and onto the driveway, she saw something poking out of the letterbox. A large envelope. She pulled it out, held it up to the light. She saw her name. She turned it over. She saw the sender: École Pierrot. What … why …

She ripped it open.

Dear Ms Veronika Vaček,

We are delighted to inform you that you have been accepted into the École Pierrot, Pantin, for our three-year program in Dramatic Arts commencing in October 1997.

But she hadn't even auditioned.

We have recently established a new scholarship for promising newcomers. Your curriculum vitae impressed us for …

She couldn't read the rest. She screamed and ran back inside.

ACT FOUR Foreign Selves

[1998–2001]

'There's nothing in taking risks, but to take risks and at the same time to turn them into your advantage – that's something!'

– Pierre Beaumarchais, *The Marriage of Figaro*

58. Veronika

A sultry day in Paris. The heat had caught the city unawares: arms and legs were bare, necks exposed. Businessmen peeled off jackets, loosened collars; bejewelled women in tiny dresses chinked their heels past Veronika's table. There was an air of relaxation. Veronika gazed at the sun-seekers clotting the banks of the Seine: people munching on chunks of cheese and baguette, gulping wine, reaching for bunches of grapes. A few plinked lazily on guitars, couples played chess or cards. Lovers formed loops; women read books.

A picture-postcard view, and yet she longed for some drama, for something to make her feel less detached, more than a mere onlooker. It was as if someone had drawn a box around her and coloured it with silence. She needed to walk along the Seine. Walking gave her energy; it took her out of herself, made her skin burn, her throat ache, heightened her sense of being alive as she broke into a run, felt the world stretch out like a canvas, the river flowing through her. But when she stopped, the feeling would return: the sense of estrangement, the lassitude.

Her back against the chair was wet with sweat. She took another sip of wine, then gathered her hair into a knot, rolled up her sleeves. She emptied a few gold coins on the table and left the café, wove in and out of the throngs on Pont Louis-Philippe, dodged a clown on a unicycle. She made her way to the tip of the Île Saint Louis and leaned over the railing, stared down at the currents of the Seine, longing for a gust of wind to fill her skirt, sail her away. On days like this, drifting and unsettled, home would often return to her: the dry summer, the rush of the sea, the salty breeze whipping her ankles, the waves lashing the cliffs. Was it Starfish Bay she longed for? And Joshua? For this, too, would happen. The memories, her guilt. Here, in the city of romance, where she ought to be free, unburdened. She'd disappointed him, she knew. Made him angry, made him turn away from her. Just as she'd disappointed Sebastian, who'd written her a pleading letter: he felt like *a flimsy cut-out … he saw a nothing face* in the mirror … he was *no-one* without her. Was this melodrama, theatrical self-pity? Had he been trying to convince himself, as well as her, of his undying love?

But Joshua's pain was real. She had no doubt about that.

She couldn't tell her family any of this in her letters and postcards. She also didn't tell them either, how after ten months in the city, with summer break just around the corner, she hadn't made a friend. Sixteen people in her workshops, all of them French natives except for a Japanese student, Akito, and Joëlle from Martinique. Oh, there'd been invitations for coffee, to a bar, to dinner, frenetic conversations after class about acting techniques. Parisians were sociable, she knew, but she didn't want to mix work with pleasure, especially the pleasure on offer from Gaspard and Hakim. Not that they weren't attractive, with their dark brown eyes, their lithe, agile bodies. And as for the girls in the group: intelligent, all of them, even funny like Celeste and Yaël, but all of them ruthlessly competitive, some of them dripping in privilege, with their talk of holiday homes in Chamonix or villas somewhere along the Côte d'Azur. Celeste's diamond bracelet alone would have cost more than Veronika's scholarship. There was no way in the world she could invite them to her apartment, with its tiny bed shoved up against the corner, its kitchenette with a camping stove, a bathroom that was merely a toilet with a portable shower fixture on top. She had to be a contortionist to perform her daily ablutions.

She remembered Cassie's email, news from out of the blue, picturing Veronika in *a romantic garret with a velvet divan, a voluptuous bed, the wavering light of a candelabra.*

She still owed Ana a letter, too. Ana: *doing it tough* with the kids, still working at the petrol station, no family around, no child support, the heat was abysmal, the kids were getting on her nerves. On and on and on. At least she'd stopped pining for Charlie, no longer even mentioned him, and Veronika would never ask. She wanted nothing to do with him.

She gazed into the inky dark waters of the Seine and vaguely thought about dinner. Boiled eggs on crackers, or lentil soup. A glass of Bordeaux. At only ten francs a bottle, she had to make sure she didn't drink herself into a stupor, fall asleep in front of the TV, watching France 2: talk shows with cheesy hosts interviewing B-grade French celebrities, or some American teen show, abominably dubbed. She longed for bouillabaisse or steak frites, or bœuf bourguignon, in a trendy bistro. She looked up at the sky, at the gathering dark clouds, heralding rain. She might risk it, hurry along the Boulevard Saint-Germain, then up the back streets towards the Luxembourg Gardens. It was her favourite walk: past smoky cinemas showing Jean Cocteau retrospectives, and endless cafés teeming with tourists and youths looking nonchalant, elegant ladies with pooches, scruffy-haired men. Or if it started to rain, she could shelter in a bookshop or one of the old record stores; study the maps and botanical drawings at the *bouquinistes* lining the Seine.

She heard the drift of a faint accordion, and the old feelings – the wistfulness, the creeping sadness – welled up in her again. She told herself to stop. Stop feeling sorry for herself, to be grateful for her unexpected, miraculous stroke of good luck. An *impressive CV*, the letter said. *A promising career.* And she was learning, after all, working so hard with Antoine. Before meeting him, after she'd won her scholarship, she'd imagined someone formidable – remote, unforgiving, a sneering *gendarme* conducting his baton – but she was instantly charmed when they met. His shock of silver hair and wide smile, his thick black spectacles perched on the end of his nose; the way he pronounced each syllable of her name: *La bel-le Vér-on-ique!* His grand, expansive gestures, as if offering her a bright jewel, and the way he broke into English when he sensed her struggling with her French. She'd nearly sobbed the first time he'd done that, when so much else was *impossible.* Trying to enter the library without proof of her address: *impossible.* Trying to pay with a credit card at the cinema: *impossible.* To select her own grapes from the *épicier: impossible: Arrêttez! Arrêttez! Mais qu'est-ce que vous faites?!*

She thrust her hands in her pockets, as if to anchor herself in this beautiful, vibrant city in which she remained a stranger. It seemed to be different for Cassie, who'd written about *a brand-new life* in London, working in a market, sharing an old house, *divinely happy.* She'd been on *a treasure hunt*, too, trying to get in touch with the other Players: Lucas was saving buckets of money in Laverton as a geologist, Gwen *fluffing about* in a fashion house. No-one had heard from Gloria or Josh, or knew anything about their lives. Same with Felix. Cassie had tried to find him, she said, but he seemed to have disappeared off the face of the earth. What *marvellous fun* they'd all had. And how was Veronika doing with her *acting career.*

There was also an update about Sebastian, who she said was getting itchy feet. Veronika remembered him kissing Cassie at the creek. On her parents' farm. How he'd resisted temptation. What a pompous ass. She shook her head. Why dwell on it now? It seemed so adolescent, no, childish, to have become so undone by a simple, stupid kiss. Thinking back on it now, and not for the first time, Veronika wondered if she'd been looking for an excuse to break up with him. And she couldn't help feeling for Cassie, who for all her craziness and gush, had been so desperate for affection. A crumb of affirmation.

What could Veronika tell her about her life in Paris? That she was living off the bones of her *derrière*? That she had no *career*. She had to focus on her classes. Workshops on movement: how they'd all thrown themselves onto the stage, exploiting space, testing their limits. They'd been taught how to *flow* like water – liquid movements in a circle – and then to *mould the air* as if it were a clay-like substance. And then to feel *beauty*, the energy of the earth while lying down, to play 'yes' and 'no' in pairs, to feel *the whole*. Did she know that emotion could be obtained through action, from the outside in, rather than the other way around?

She could tell Cassie about voice lessons from Madame Arnaud, a Reebok-wearing local TV star. Their terrifying first activity: drawing a picture of their own voice on butcher paper, then choosing three words to describe it. Articulating their fears about using a voice, in three words only. They were learning now how to breathe, pause, project. And then there was improvisation with Monsieur Coquelicot, an elfin person with fronds of pale hair, a big-time slapstick comedian. Anything could happen then. It was tame to begin with: *What if* you had to straighten your room before guests arrived? *What if* you had to cross a river during a winter storm? *What if* you're locked in the house when a fire breaks out? There was always a flash of panic before she strutted her stuff in his class, but the fire had really set her off. She'd rushed out to the bathroom.

But it was Antoine who stole the show when they had to prepare for scene work. He'd told them at the start that they must begin from *a place of courage, to share without hesitation your intimacy with the audience*. Grand-sounding words, but they also made Veronika feel a little anxious: how much would she have to reveal, even if it wasn't *her*, exactly? Didn't she want to forget herself, give herself away? Wasn't that the point? *Let the character lead*, Antoine told them. *Let it speak*. But there was always the trepidation, wasn't there, that the character might invade you, and then what would be left? She still didn't know if she was good enough to get better. Antoine's feedback was cryptic, he delivered her phrases such as *go moment to moment*, and *we should feel the inner acrobatics of your subconscious* ... And finally: *It's all up here*, pointing to her head. She couldn't be sure what it all meant, these scraps of advice. Was she good enough not to need more? Or was he largely indifferent to her progress? But she couldn't ask him that, could she? She was afraid of what he might say.

It was late one afternoon in October, and they were all cold and complaining. Madame Arnaud had at first insisted on *l'air frais*, but when it got too cold, they didn't have the wherewithal to shut the windows. While the windows were easy enough to open, they needed a ladder to shut them, the ladder was locked in the janitor's cupboard and no-one could find the key. When Antoine whistled in, they all protested that it was far too cold to rehearse and that they should all go out for *vin chaud* instead. But he jumped up wildly like a gymnast and shut the windows, one after the other, then turned around to face them.

'The *force* of the body, of muscle, of the *soul* in space,' he said. '*Preparation* ... is everything ... you prepare and this way you will have more *force*! I know this, I know what it means to *prepare*, as a young man – I worked in an *abattoir*!'

It had been months of *preparation* and now it was time.

He handed them all their scripts. A medley of different plays, he'd explained, scenes from some of the classics, all variations on a theme: mothers and sons. Veronika was given two extracts from Racine's *Phèdre*, a play she had studied at university. She had begun rehearsing with Hakim, who was playing Hippolyte. Sitting behind the curtain on the platform, he kept staring at her as she started tentatively to read. She began to feel uncomfortable, kept looking away, looking back, seeing his brooding face, hearing him throw away his lines and then: *Tu as un petit accent.*

'*Oui, évidemment!*' she snapped, impatient to get on with the scene. '*Et alors ...?*'

'*Je trouve ça charmant,*' he said. He reached over and tugged at a stray curl near her mouth and put it behind her ear. '*Voilà!*'

He sat back, sniffed at his script, began crucifying his lines with the wrong poetic metre. And this is how it continued, with his stares, choppy rhythms and suggestive remarks. Her speeches were soon so long that Hakim eventually lost interest.

'What is it?' she asked, exasperated. 'Is this some kind of game? Or are you having trouble connecting with your character?' She wanted, needed, to succeed. She refused to be thrown off by his careless attitude, his annoying innuendos.

'I'm running out of energy,' he said.

'Me too.'

'Ramadan,' he said. He got up and left her and gazed out the window. She could hear the voices of Akito and Celeste carrying on downstairs. *Oh! Ne parle plus, Hamlet. Tu tournes mes regards au fond de mon âme.*

Antoine came over and sat down at her side, crossed his legs.

'I have been watching you all this time,' he said airily. 'And listening. Your voice is melodious … beautiful … like a cello or a clarinet. But this can only take you so far. Your technique needs work.'

Veronika felt a flush of embarrassment. She nodded, hoping for something more specific. He asked her to stand up and carry on. And so she read out her lines for the third time, quite proud of her French, managing the hexameter and the feeling of *vraisemblance*. They had worked on rhythm, she knew it. Antoine observed her closely with his hand over his chin. He tapped his feet to the metre as she spoke her lines:

J'aime! Ne pense pas qu'au moment que je t'aime,
Innocente à mes yeux, je m'approuve moi-même.

He held up a hand, took the script from her.

'Where is the terror and pity, hm?' he said.

Veronika pressed her lips together and tried to think.

'She is in your head,' Antoine said decisively, tapping his temple, 'but she needs to be in your thorax, your hips, your hands, your legs, your toes, or the soles of the feet. You know, once you know this part and play it well, you should feel *intense streams of power coming from your chest to your fingers*. The words of a famous man: Michael Chekhov, the great acting teacher.'

Another famous man, Veronika thought. Shakespeare, Racine, Beckett, Ibsen, all the male French poets she had learned by heart. Maybe that was her problem. Bowing down to the great men. She tried to picture those *intense* masculine *streams*, but nothing came into her head.

'I've only just received the script,' she said, trying not to sound feeble.

Antoine took her hand and looked into her eyes. 'To radiate you must go beyond the words. To affect the audience, to transform a moment.'

Desire is at the root of everything, Antoine explained, as they huddled around after their scene runs.

Who exactly is Phèdre? What does she want? He gave them all a strict prescription of character work. He instructed them to score the script with transitive verbs. What is your character trying to do? Persuade? Beg? Manipulate? Seduce? Destroy? They would also have to research, go to the library and find out more about the world of the character, the playwright. Immerse themselves in the context. Veronika would have to find Phèdre's blueprint. Figure out what made her tick. That poor Phèdre, wife of Theseus, she'd been victim to the gods, falling perilously in love with her own stepson. Ah! Poor woman, whose *passion furieuse* had led her to her ruin.

Sometimes Veronika longed to feel such passion. But she was here to work, wasn't she? She had come here to learn, hadn't she?

But sometimes she dreamed of Joshua, and the chasteness of their kiss. Where it might have led. And once she dreamed of Charlie. The rousing strength of his arms. She must remember to fill out her prescription for the pill. For all the good it would do her. There was no time to be involved with anyone, let alone to fall in love.

Veronika walked back to the Métro along the Canal de l'Ourq. Pantin was an edgy part of town, much more exciting than the safe Latin Quarter where she lived in her little studio. Here it felt like a carnival: she passed a puppeteer and a few kids on skateboards, another bunch of youths playing *pétanque*. And in the midst of all this liveliness, the pleasure of movement, she found herself thinking of Joshua again. It wasn't an immoderate passion, like Phèdre for Hippolyte. And yet ... Poor Phèdre! She'd married someone much too old for her, and Theseus was unkind.

As she watched the crowds drifting, marching, talking, people winding bicycles through the throng, she told herself she wouldn't substitute from memory. Joshua was too pure to draw on. She must find something, someone else. Antoine would teach her how.

59. Joshua

Voices.

He shrugged them away. Turned in his bunk. Heavy head. Stale sweat. He closed his eyes again, swam back into his dream: a woman bending over him. Her warmth.

Red. A light stung through his eyelids.

'Josh! Your turn!'

He winced.

'Nar,' he moaned into his pillow. Pulled the covers closer, stretched out his legs. He'd flung about for hours on the tiny bed. Never enough room for his impossible limbs. All night he'd been like this. Or was it day? He'd lost track of time. He might as well have been drifting in a spaceship, spinning off the edge of the world.

'Up ya get.'

Josh felt Warra prodding him. Heard the tug and slip of a perpetual wave above him.

'Christ. Don't feel so good,' he said.

'She'll be right.'

Josh didn't move.

'My turn to sleep, mate. C'mon, time to get up.'

He still couldn't move.

'Been at it nineteen hours straight, Josh. C'mon, you bastard.'

'Christ!' Josh sprang from the bed. Wonky. Skull flooded dizzy.

'I'm done,' Warra said, lips barely moving. He brushed off his beanie, unzipped his jacket, kicked off his shoes, dived into bed.

Josh was starving. He stumbled into the kitchen, grabbed a couple of meat pies from the freezer, shoved them in the microwave. Shook as he ate them, almost swallowed them whole. He squirted condensed milk from a tube into a mug, added scalding coffee from the urn. He drank, then rinsed his face. Felt as ready as he would ever be.

He climbed up onto the deck. Night-time. The wind was up. Chill hit him like stones. Stench of bait everywhere. Diesel fumes. Rancid fish. Bird shit. The others were in front of a winch, hauling in a big swordfish, must be close to six feet. Josh caught a glimpse of a glassy wave hovering behind the boat. Three men reaching forward with their long gaffs. Someone was cheering. The lights of the boat spilled out onto the ocean like rippling columns in the dark.

Josh had once imagined the splendour and solace of an evening at sea, the brilliance of stars, but here, on this stinking boat, clouds clogged the dark sky: the stars and the moon were barely visible. Without light he was merely a pair of hands, a breath. Wordless, exhausted. How long had he been on the boat? As long as it took to stop feeling the pain: jamming squid onto hooks, dropping buoys, hoisting up fish, hands bleeding down the gaff. He remembered things, too, images flashed like negatives. His father's looming, angry face. Veronika's gentle kiss. But then the bonfire. The way she'd looked at Charlie. And now she'd gone to Paris, doing her own thing like she'd always done, her mother so excited when she told him the news. He'd pretended to care. Well, he *did* care, but what good did it do him? What good had it ever done? He'd had no luck with women. On the point of moving in with Gloria, he'd chickened out. Didn't know if he could bring himself to be with her and not be with her. She'd let him into her life, then pushed him away. When he'd liked her. Warmed to her. She'd kissed him. But he'd made the right decision in the end. Made a clean break from her and all the Players, whatever they were called. It felt like a lifetime ago.

He made himself snap out of it, focus on the work, join the men in jabbing the huge fish with his gaff. Dragging its great body towards the hull, this slick silver animal with its lethal sword. It flapped furiously. Died. They rolled it on top of a dolphinfish, and Josh felt his gut convulsing, food crawling up into his throat, exploding out of his mouth onto his face, hands, feet.

'You have to keep your food down,' someone said. 'No good being seasick.'

Josh shivered. He'd been sick for nine days. He had another five and a half weeks to go, with no sense of how he would endure it. Someone threw him a water bottle, told him not to get dehydrated. Josh chugged down the water, washed off the sick. Somehow managed to finish his shift.

60. Veronika

They did more character exercises over the week. If Phèdre was an animal, which one should she be? A lioness, no doubt. And so she'd spent the morning acting like a lioness, and the warehouse had become an animal kingdom filled with actors noisily pretending to be horses and dogs, foxes, elephants and mice. She'd also been instructed to close her eyes and feel her way into the character's *centre*. Was the character led by her nose? Her chest? Or her throat, perhaps? Was her *centre* coming from her gut, her genitals even? Was it the head or the heart? *The heart,* always the heart, Veronika knew that much. Always the heart. Phèdre. Led by the heart. And so, slowly at first, and then more fully, more confidently, she learned to immerse herself, with each of her five senses, in Phèdre's world. It was as if she'd created an imaginary body by sculpting her in the air and then stepping inside. This, she felt, was where acting, real acting, began: not through creating an illusion, but by inhabiting a body.

At the end of one rather intense session, all the more satisfying because of the intensity, Antoine took her aside. Veronika was surprised, a little wary. Would Véronique like to come to his home for dinner? To meet his wife and to taste his *cuisine délicieuse.* She felt both childishly nervous and immensely flattered and not a little puzzled by this unexpected invitation.

It took her hours to choose what to wear, how to *appear,* but she finally settled on the look of an old-world ingenue: feathered hair, kohl-rimmed eyes and deep red lips, like split plums. A turquoise suit made of mohair she'd bought from Emmaüs, her favourite thrift shop in the 10th. She'd given up lunch for a week to buy it. And then, to complete the look, she pulled on black knee-high boots. She stared in her small, cracked mirror and thought she looked suitably dramatic.

She allowed herself one glass of wine before she left. Just one, to bring out her best French. Two glasses and she would forget her verb conjugations. Three and she wanted to cry. But she would make an effort over dinner: she didn't want to bore Antoine or his wife. But she didn't want to *perform* either, especially the role of a foreign curiosity. She scanned *Le Monde* as she sipped her wine, hoping to be *au courant* with current affairs (Chirac and Jospin, jobs, unrest in Cergy-Pontoise), equipped with interesting conversation.

She arrived at Antoine's home, running late, feeling flushed from a brisk evening walk across the two islands and up the Boulevard Henri IV, peering in the tiny shops along the way: the *crèmerie, boulangerie, charcûterie, chocolatier*, with its chocolate sculptures of owls and rabbits and witches, the luthier at work on a viola. Maybe one day she would buy a chocolate viola. On her last day in Paris, maybe, as a parting gesture. But she didn't want to think about parting gestures, about anything beyond the here and now. It was altogether too daunting, too riven with the unknown.

Right now, she was in Le Marais, near the Bastille. She'd reached Antoine's apartment, and saw that the gate was open, saw a long, narrow courtyard leading to the entrance. Baskets spilling over with colourful phlox and freesias, bird cages and old bicycles covered in ivy, rusted lanterns. And on a barrel of burgeoning jonquils sat a poster-sized photograph of a young Antoine and what must have been his wife, Madeleine: strikingly young and handsome, both of them, embracing on a motorbike. Veronika felt a pang of envy, remembered lingering kisses, entwined limbs, the urgency of passion. She pulled herself up. Heard the murmur of voices and the clink of glasses from inside. She was ready.

Antoine met her at the door, took her bouquet of ranunculus and kissed her on both cheeks. The European kiss. He led her through a narrow hall lined with a bookshelf stuffed with *livres de poches* and into the kitchen, and she was instantly overcome by the crowd of pots and pans, rows of ladles and ingenious-looking implements whose names she didn't know. Plaits of peppers and garlic; crammed spice racks; an aromatic smell of roasting. Antoine stuffed her flowers into a jar of nasturtiums, as though life was too short to fuss with flowers, then extended a hand to a man who suddenly appeared from behind the pots and pans. A stout man in his forties, wearing an old-fashioned pinstriped suit.

'Our American friend, Eddie,' Antoine said, in his lyrical English. 'He plays the piano.'

'*Enchanté!*' Eddie declared in a grating accent. He shook Veronika's hand, firmly. 'Are you an American, too?'

'Australian. And Bohemian before that. Sort of. On my father's side.'

'Say, that's pretty cute! Here, have some kir royale.' He thrust a small glass into her hand. 'So. You speak English or French? Or Russian?'

'English and French, with a dash of Czech.'

'Oh yeah? Is that the language of Dvořák?'

'It is – and Janáček too.'

'God, I love that guy. His music is so damned evocative of winter forests.'

'My grandmother loved Janáček. Her generation.'

'Well now, how about that?! Don't s'pose you do Thanksgiving in Australia?'

'Ah.' Veronika nodded. 'So this is a Thanksgiving dinner? In Paris.'

Antoine reappeared, a wooden spoon in his hand. 'I can see Eddie is boring you already,' he said.

She noticed a splotch on his apron of what looked like pumpkin soup, and it made her feel more relaxed. She watched as he removed his apron with a studied air, as if preparing to assume another role. Then he motioned them out of the kitchen into a spacious living room. She felt like she'd entered a surrealist gallery: immense wooden pillars; walls adorned with framed poems and curious dolls' heads; sculptures of pseudo-Greek busts on the mantlepiece, either side of an enormous fireplace. And facing her, in the back corner, was a grand piano, on top of which sat a huge folding camera, and elaborate speakers in the shape of giant cochlea. As she made her way to the table, she caught a glimpse of a photo, adults and children frolicking naked by the sea. She wondered if this was the family; she knew the scene was very *French*.

Ah. This must be Madeleine, seated at a large walnut table. In her sixties, like Antoine. She looked gamine: large brown eyes, and wispy hair with aubergine highlights. Sitting next to her was Philippe, one of Veronika's classmates: dark-haired, ludicrously tall and skinny, rearranging himself on the chair and moving his hands like a shifting pair of inverted commas. She knew him as inarticulate and agonisingly shy, but on stage he was transfixing, brilliant at mime. He looked uncomfortable right now, wouldn't meet her eye, and she wondered, with dismay, if Antoine was trying to matchmake. Had he sensed that she was lonely? Hence the invitation to dinner? But she wasn't interested in Philippe.

Madeleine rose from the table and took Veronika's hand, said in staccato English, *such a pleasure to meet you. Mais, quelle jolie ensemble!*

'What a beautiful home you have, Madame Fouquet.'

'Madeleine, please. Oh, but I am anxious for more wine! Phi-*lippe!*'

He rose immediately to fill Madeleine's glass, and Veronika's too, then stowed himself back in his seat. Madeleine's face shone up at her, said in a strong French accent that *I am very interesting in Australia.* How she longed to see *the big reef.* Veronika confessed that she had never seen it, that Australia was too big to see everything.

Madeleine tilted her elegant head to the side. 'And what do you come to see in Paris?' she said. 'Apart from studying with Antoine, of course. I am meaning ... why did you *really* come?'

Veronika startled. They hadn't even started their meal, and now this question. So personal. So ... implicating. She considered. Took a sip of wine.

'I needed to escape,' she said quietly.

'Ah. From a man?'

Veronika nodded.

'Was he a cruel man?'

'No, no, not at all. He was ... well ... he wanted to marry me. Settle down, you know. But we're much too young and I want to do other things in my life and—'

'He was ... how do you say it? *Chiant?*'

Veronika paused. 'Dull,' she said. 'Yes. A little.'

Madeleine raised her glass. 'Then how fortunate you are here in Paris,' she said. 'Here, everyone is escaping from something. Work, family, children. Our memories. This is what I do with my photography. I capture the faces, so we will not forget.'

Veronika kept silent as Antoine ladled out soup. Madeleine smiled across the table.

'You are young, Veronika,' Madeleine said. 'You escape, and then you find.'

'And what kind of faces have you found?' Veronika asked, needing to change the subject. 'In your photography, I mean.'

'Ah. Yes. *Tu sais,* I am not looking to find anything when I take a portrait. It's more of an encounter with a person. My latest ones are of the steel factory workers. Such intensity. Such poise. These men. I love this phrase *Live free. Or die.* I want to capture them as free so that they will never die.'

And so the evening passed: conversation over turkey, a salad of crisp leaves in tart vinaigrette, and cheese so viscous, so delicious, that it seemed like liquid gold. Eddie told stories of America: growing up in a Queens brownstone, playing saxophone on the subway, studying jazz piano at the Manhattan School of Music. He'd met Antoine while working as an accompanist for the New York Dance Theatre. Antoine hurried in with talk of his career as a dancer, performing at a festival in Rio, but discovering that his passion was acting. He'd met Marlon Brando in the days when he was the most sought-after actor in the world. Even gawky, shy Philippe spoke of his ambition to one day open up his own *péniche* – a floating circus on the Seine, complete with a cabaret.

They asked Veronika questions about her family. What could she say that would possibly compete with studying at the Manhattan School of Music, performing dance in Rio, meeting a famous movie star? All she had was her heritage, really, to set her apart, make her sound interesting, if only by default. So she told them stories of Babička, who, having never seen an ocean in her life, had to endure the long journey on a decrepit ship from Genoa to Fremantle. How she'd felt both brave and terrified. How she'd been pregnant with Veronika's father, had given birth to him in a crowded immigration camp amid flies and filth and noise.

'She left behind her country,' Veronika said. 'She left people she loved, who she knew she would probably never see again. But she had no choice, really. She needed to escape the communists.'

'And the Nazis before them,' Madeleine said.

'And before that, the Austro-Hungarians. Babička once told me that her country had endured centuries of oppression. She must have understood what it meant to *live free or die*.'

'So did she live free in her new country?' Antoine asked.

'She did. It was a chance to reinvent herself. She made friends easily, learned the language, worked as a milliner, making beautiful hats for women who adored her. She knew how to make life liveable.' Veronika felt cheery, remembering. 'She even discovered acting in her fifties. The local Czechoslovakian club cast her in some amateur plays. Did you know that the current Czech president is a playwright? Imagine living in a country where the president writes plays! I can't imagine an Australian prime minister ever doing that.'

Madeleine shook her head. 'But what is Australia, anyway?' she said. 'You are a country of foreigners, no? And here, in Paris, you are also a refugee.' She leaned across the table. 'Do you have plans?' she said. 'For after Paris?'

Veronika had to confess that she had none. That it was enough, for the moment, to immerse herself in her work.

'I want to improve my acting, of course I do,' she said. 'But ... sometimes I feel ... stuck.'

She felt the weight of Antoine's gaze.

'What do you find so hard?' he said.

'The scene I'm doing with Hakim,' she said. 'From *Phèdre*.'

'And your Phèdre is stuck,' Antoine said. 'I have to be saying it, you know that you are not convincing me, or anyone. Not even yourself.'

Veronika felt her cheeks burn.

Madeleine put her hand over her husband's mouth.

'Antoine! Enough!' she said. She turned to look at Veronika, a tender smile on her face. 'Sometimes the *psychanalyse* can be very helpful,' she said. 'If you are feeling ... how you say ... stuck.'

Philippe tapped her on the arm. 'If I may, Madame,' he said. 'I think the *psychanalyse* interrupts the creativity. Things that are not *résoudre*, can bring tension, energy to a performance. You bring it all to ... the stage to ... transform onstage.'

Antoine flicked his palm. '*Boff!*' he said, loudly. 'Philippe, this thing you talk about. This is pure voyeurism. Spilling these guts onstage. This is not theatre. It is self-indulgence.' He turned to look at Veronika again. 'Forgive me, Veronika, to speak so frankly, but maybe there is some blindness ... some wounds. So when you come to playing a character in similar situations – of *traumatisme* – well, you cannot be convincing. *Ça veut dire* – your own limitations become the limitations of the character. It's not fair to Racine. To the script. It makes for an incomplete performance. *For bad* acting.'

Veronika could hardly breathe.

Antoine placed his hand on hers. 'You have the strength,' he said. 'You work hard. But I need you to be working harder. To face yourself.' He frowned. 'What am I meaning to say? You must ... *vous devrez affronter le passé.*'

She *must confront the past*. Veronika felt a wave of indignation rush through her. Was this why he had invited her? To berate her? To pick her apart in this safe, congenial setting?

And then, mercifully, Eddie – loud, brash, American Eddie – rose from his chair and announced he would play the piano. He lumbered over to the instrument, sat down with a flourish. Veronika expected the worst. But then she heard quiet, rippling music. Debussy, perhaps. Like gentle rain falling on her shoulders. A balm. Some relief from instruction and questions, from her anger and doubts, from the touch of Antoine's hand, trying to soothe her, failing to soothe her. She let herself loosen in the peace of the music, let the sound carry her to another place, beyond the jabbing words, to be nowhere and everywhere, to be still in her heart.

Antoine gave her a slight nod.

'Eddie surprises us all,' he said. 'It is good to be surprised.'

She walked home just as the sun was waking. It had been a long, entirely unexpected night. She paused on the Pont de la Tournelle and looked out at the city lining the Seine: the white buildings and the soft smear of the sky. The hazy light was peaceful; she almost felt she could reach out and touch its softness, or twirl slowly, gracefully in the street. Had it been the food and the wine, the music or the conversation? All of them together? Or was it the feeling of people taking an interest in her at last? Was it meeting a photographer, a musician? True artists. Madeleine had invited her to a *vernissage*. Was that meant to be compensation for Antoine's harsh words? No matter, she had been invited. And she would strive to be better. Isn't that what she'd wanted? Some tough feedback? But thinking back to what Antoine had told her, *feedback* sounded so puny, so shallow. He hadn't been asking her to change her technique. He'd been asking her to change herself.

Looking up at the blush of the morning sky, she found her mind drifting back to Starfish Bay, Joshua and her lying close together in the sand, listening to the waves, neither of them saying a word. She'd been happy then, or at least she thought she'd been happy. Before the fire started. Before everything went wrong.

61. Felix

Felix saw him again at a mutual friend's gathering. It wasn't exactly by chance, since the friend was someone Felix had maintained contact with from his directing days. Berat, the stage manager. He knew Berat would likely be in touch with Max and so ... this evening, Felix's plan, his secret hope, had blissfully worked. An afterparty for the play *The Interrupted Act*. It started just before midnight on the weekend of the Ascension.

Berat's apartment was covered in wood panelling, French New Wave movie posters and acrylic carpet of a maroon and dirty green. There were other men there and two or three women with wildly coloured hair.

And there *he* was. A vision too lavish to believe: Max, across a crowded room. It had been four long years since he had seen him. Max had shaved off the moustache. He still had thick brown hair with a charming cowlick, but it was now silver-flecked. Still the same broad face, straight nose, like a carving. A firm and muscular body beneath a fitted blazer. Felix glanced at Max's enormous feet and unflattering pointy shoes. He was some sort of dilettante, to be sure. Too athletic to be academic. Not the wiry, nervous type that filled the Berlin libraries. This man of his incessant imaginings. After all this time, Felix couldn't quite believe he was here, sitting across the room. Max pushed his glasses up his nose when Felix caught his eye. He gave the faintest hint of a smile.

Felix made his way through the room, sat next to Max. Warily. Hopefully. Max rolled some tobacco, lit up and smoked, then offered the cigarette to Felix. He found the gesture tantalising, intimate. Berat was talking about footballers with mohawks and how midfielder Marcus Urban was not, how would he say it, *typically handsome*, but he was *admirable*. The three of them argued over which players were handsome and why. When Berat left to welcome another guest, Max and Felix kept talking, disputing the handsomeness of men they only saw on TV, laughing about not going for the same footballer. As they joked and pretended to be serious about going on a date with muscle-bound and no doubt brainless men, Felix relaxed. The conversation was surprisingly easy. They could be friends.

And Felix was no longer Max's student. Those days were long gone. Yes, he thought, friends.

When Max asked him about Australia, Felix told him about *Figaro*. Max seemed impressed, particularly because Felix had managed all that in another country, in another language, with so few resources. Felix mentioned his *adventures*, which now seemed to him rather boyish and immature, sitting on an ottoman across from this cultured intellectual. Felix mentioned the Øresund Bridge. It would make history as one of the longest bridges in Europe. But he was so bored with the work, he declared, that he might not survive at the job. But he adored the clubs, he told Max. He was in the thrall of electronica and punk. Max showed his strong, neat teeth in a winning smile and spoke about his classes, the passion of his students, the gratifying success of his latest play (why hadn't Felix seen it? – Tadeusz Różewicz, a Polish playwright, a new German translation, pure anti-theatre), then turned the conversation to politics, to the need for solidarity and political action.

'You can't take your freedoms for granted,' Max said. 'You haven't experienced the same struggles, you know. Besides, I feel more vulnerable since the Wall came down. Targeted. There is still a long way to go.'

Felix pondered all this. He'd naturally assumed that growing up in the West had been easier, he'd known nothing else, but Max, who'd spent most of his life in the East, was suggesting otherwise. Felix told Max his story: how he had just turned fifteen when he saw the *Montagsdemonstrationen*, on TV. Then the Wall came down. The peaceful revolution. He hadn't been allowed out, his family had been glued to the news. Visions of the impossible, the unthinkable, the Wall being bulldozed, then thousands of people – neighbours, even half the people on his street – had all been there. The attempts to cross had all made headlines: ziplines, balloons, meat hooks, lying under stuffed pigs and slaughtered animals in a refrigerated truck. But it was the people running through, en masse, without impediment, that really blew his mind.

'I was desperate to go outside, but instead, my parents sent me to bed with my Nintendo Game & Watch. Remember those?'

Max looked sympathetic, amused.

'You always inspired me,' Felix said. 'You fought the good fight, marched in the streets, protesting against that horrible provision that criminalised people like me—'

'Which is why Brecht continues to matter,' Max said. 'The need for a social conscience, theatre that's not for entertainment and escape, but so people will not look away. *Verfremdung*. A fundamental artistic principle that—'

'Shakes people out of their complacency.' Felix nodded. 'Theatre must inspire people to take action.'

A few girls piled in the room, and one sat on Max's knee. They squeezed him and congratulated him on the play, showered him with compliments. Amid the fuss, Max reached out and brushed Felix's hand. A frisson. A phone number. He already had his office number from years ago, although he wouldn't disclose the fact. Disclose his desire. He wrote his own number on the back of a cigarette rolling paper and passed it on to Max.

'I'll call you,' Max said and gave Felix a half smile. An inviting smile? Felix felt a charge run through his body, his heart knocking in his chest.

And so, the ball was in his court. Felix tried to distract himself as he passed his time at work. He didn't mind the site visits. At least he could talk to people, be out in the fresh air, do something practical, but the office work felt tedious, pointless, emasculating.

He came alive at night. He would happily wait three hours to get into the best clubs. He also knew the optimum time to arrive to avoid the queue; five am on a Sunday was just right. He would wear leather pants, scowl at the bouncers, a sure way to be admitted. The crowd was often tattooed, pierced, dressed like winged creatures in black. Sometimes there were many men in shorts, women in spandex. Women in sparkling violet boots with silver spoons strapped over each nipple. There were people dressed in police uniform and army clothes. He loved it all. But it was the music that really got him. It was transporting, even spiritual. When he was dancing, he lost time. *Free yourself from the prison of the grasping mind*, he would play it on repeat in his head as he danced, and so he would, jumping, flying, catapulting across the floor.

They saw one another again. A drive to the Schlachtensee. Max picked him up in his 1968 Audi 100; the car wheezed and shuddered, burped curls of smoke. They exchanged pleasantries in the car. And that was it. Silence. They drove through sunny Berlin.

Max pulled up in the parking lot. They got out and ambled along side by side, following a stretch of lawn by the mahogany water, which was tinted with the cerulean sky. People were about, swimming, cycling, picnicking. The conversation did not flow as seamlessly as it had done before. Had Felix been mistaken about Max giving his number? Had he been wrong about that parting look?

Max started talking about Georg Büchner, then some philosopher, but Felix found it hard to listen, caught glimpses of Max's face; his brows arching as he waxed on about … what was it? *The origins of tragic drama* or suchlike. The man's hands, his beautiful, long, knotted fingers. Max carried on, the thump in Felix's chest drowning out the words. He was distracted by Max's loose flannel shirt, slightly rumpled, open to the breeze, exposing his clavicle. Sleeves rolled up unevenly, Max's brawny arms. Felix felt a strange sort of force surge through his love-starved body; it went right to his groin. He just couldn't stand it anymore, the doubt, the urge. Before he uttered a word, knew what he was doing, before his brain told him to stop, he drew Max into some dense bushes, away from the crowds, and kissed him.

A gentle kiss at first, tinted with tobacco and toothpaste. But then Max pulled away, checked furtively if anyone was around.

'I'm flattered,' Max said, 'But …'

Felix reeled. Had he made a terrible blunder? Misread the cues?

'You may no longer be my student, but it feels …' Max was speechless for a moment. There was a hum of traffic in the distance. 'There's quite an age gap.' He stood back.

'None of that matters to me,' Felix said, his breath quickening.

'You are a beguiling … talented young man …' Max said with a pained look. 'But this is not a good idea.'

'I disagree.' Felix said. He could have burst. 'And no-one can see us, not a soul.' He took Max's hand, guided it across his torso, up along his throat, pressed it to his mouth and kissed his palm. Max did not resist, and taking a deep breath, closed his eyes. Felix seized him, and grunted with desire at the firm, fit feel of him; shoulders, chest, stomach and thighs against him. He kissed him again, full on the mouth. This time, Max responded … darting tongues, gasps, wrestling. They fell to the earth, kicked off their shoes. Felix undid Max's shirt, explored his neck and nipples, traced the trail of hairs down his chest, then the tufts of hair around his belly button and then, without speaking, they both wrenched off their trousers. They kissed and moved and met one another with a certain, carnal ferocity. Underwear came off. Touching themselves, and one another. One, just after the other, climaxed. Felix's ear, planted in the dirt. He thought he heard the tremor of a tectonic plate far below the ground. The murmur of something deep. Joyful. The air jostled. Dead leaves blew about. Max wrapped himself around Felix. The two of them, exhausted.

One week turned into another.

Enjoyed was too small a word for what he and Max had together. It was ecstatic, overwhelming at times. Felix had never had sex like that before, but then he'd never felt such a connection to a man, how when they touched, they were touching something … deeper. Souls? Even if he didn't believe in souls. He couldn't really explain it. It was admiration he felt for Max, deep and sincere, for the man's beliefs, his convictions. It was talking long into the night about what mattered to them both: the theatre, politics, freedom, the freedom to be themselves, utterly and entirely. It was lying in bed with Max's head on his shoulder, feeling him breathing. It was Max's sympathy for Felix's feelings of boredom in his job, his sense of entrapment. *You must follow your heart,* he said, even if he didn't have a concrete solution. *A concrete solution!* Now that was funny. Max joked that young Felix would wear him out between the sheets, but there was no sign yet that he was fading.

There was only one moment, a false step that made Felix shiver with fear, which made him curse himself for his stupid, youthful mistake. It was the third week of their being together. Felix knew it was their third week because Max had given him a card: *The most magnificent two weeks of my life. Thank you.* Felix had been slightly alarmed at first: the words sounded like a parting was near, that the two weeks had been wonderful but now it was time to move on. But then Max had blushed, called himself a sentimental fool, and told Felix he didn't want this to end.

Excited, energised, and keen to show Max to the world, keen for people to see them as a couple, he urged Max to come to a rave at a squat inside an abandoned tunnel, right by the Kurfürstendamm. Something new, something different. I want so badly to dance, he told Max, for us to dance together. But as soon as Max saw the strobe lights, Felix saw his discomfort and the angst in his lover's face. He couldn't persuade him to join him on the dance floor, but determined to celebrate, needing to move, Felix jumped and hopped under the lights, bumping into other bodies, other men, until he looked across the room and saw Max sitting at the edge, talking to a man. He rushed to Max's side, disappointed, faintly anxious. Max didn't look up when he approached, kept talking to the man, he was older, Felix could see that now … the two of them shouting above the music … *fundamental conservatism to reunified Germany, even for gay people … a false democracy … legislation of the individual.*

Felix wanted to join in, make a joke, be acknowledged.

'Have your Wall back then,' he said.

Max glared at him. 'That was never the question.'

His voice was calm, but Felix could hear something underneath. Controlled anger, perhaps. Even spite. He turned on his heels and went back to the dance floor, tried to let it go. All lovers have disagreements, he told himself. We'll figure it out. I'll say sorry. We'll move on.

It was past midday when Felix arrived at Max's apartment. He knew he looked dishevelled and sweaty; he'd done nothing but dance and drink, consume a peppering of amphetamine. Still, he opened the door carefully, suddenly on edge. This was Max's home. Felix had been out for hours. He stood in the doorway, watching Max reading a paper, cigarette perched on a glass ashtray, the cinders dropping bit by bit. Then Max shook out his copy of *Der Spiegel* with considerable agitation. On the front cover, a woman peering over a brick wall and the headline AUSBILDUNG: GENERATION OHNE CHANCEN. Generation without chances. Was it some kind of omen for *his* generation, and not Max's? Felix knew he had to move, say sorry, he wouldn't do that again, rushing over to embrace him, but Max grumbled, brushed him away.

'You could do with a shower,' he said curtly. He put down his cigarette, picked up a coffee cup, took a sip.

Felix felt the bloom of sweat across his shirt and under his arms, could smell the staleness of his body. His trousers felt hot against his skin. A metallic taste in his mouth. His ears were ringing. He had been dancing nonstop for … how many hours? He moved away, tentative. Troubled.

Max looked up at him. 'You take for granted certain freedoms,' he said.

Felix thought better than to say anything. He had made Max stern, unyielding, unhappy. But then Max unexpectedly asked him to sit beside him, said they needed to talk.

'Of course,' Felix said, feeling vaguely curious yet somewhat resigned.

'I've been thinking,' Max said. 'About our time together.'

Here it comes, Felix thought. The break-up. His stupid dancing all night; his even more stupid joke about the Wall.

'I know it hasn't been long,' Max said. 'But we both want the artistic life, don't we? A stimulating life.'

The tone was reassuring.

'Why don't we move in together? In Prenzlauer Berg. We could open an independent theatre company.'

'An independent theatre company?'

'Yes.' Max put his arm around his shoulder. 'We have models we can learn from and consult. The nationals, like the Berliner Ensemble, but other independents, like the Ratibor, die Brotfabrik. Groups who can inspire us.'

'Inspire?'

Max frowned. 'Are you having trouble understanding me?' he said. 'I can't be any clearer.'

Felix dared to move closer. 'I'm having trouble believing this is happening.'

'If you want it to,' Max said, and began to stroke Felix's hair. 'But only if I don't have to get up on a dance floor.'

He kissed him. Kissed him again, gently, then more fervently, and Felix lost track of time again. They went to bed. They talked. Details. Legals, insurance, a board, actors, a director, a repertoire, marketing, a mission statement, rehearsal venues, lighting, a choreographer, set design, props, a stage manager, costume, auditions, scripts. Felix was dizzy with the possibilities.

Max rested his head on Felix's shoulder. 'But we won't give up our day jobs,' he said. 'Not yet. So you see, *lieber Freund*, you'll still be stuck in concrete for a while.'

62. Sebastian

Sebastian would always remember the prediction in his school yearbook, underneath his confidently smiling photo: 'Most likely to become an MP.' But now, amid the store of other memorabilia – rugby trophies, academic prizes for history and music, even a tennis cup he'd won at the age of fifteen – it was clear that *the most likely* was becoming less and less.

His work as an articled clerk on construction disputes had been equally disappointing. After another year of 'restricted practice' in the firm, he was finally admitted as a solicitor. There'd been such a fuss: photos and cake, buckets of champagne, his mother boasting to anyone who would listen. But none of this had felt like a life; it merely was a dull, repetitive and entirely monastic existence. He secretly decided it was time to ship out, head off, remake his future. Shake off Veronika for good. She'd stood him up. Made him angry again. Wouldn't even answer his calls. Every time someone mentioned Paris, he'd felt like throwing a glass of whiskey in their face.

He'd been reading the UK papers for some time. The condensed weekly editions of *The Telegraph,* bought at the newsagent at Wellington Street Station. He thought it was just the European news he'd missed – the quality editorials, the nuanced journalism, the closer connection to the world at large – but he had to admit, if only to himself, that he'd been looking to escape. Go back to England, the place where he had made his own connections, not his father's, the place where he was free from puppet strings, out of parental reach. London, yes, but to do something more in line with his interests. He wanted, needed, something bigger than building disputes in provincial Perth, the most isolated city in the world. He'd told no-one, not even his father, that he'd applied for the British Civil Service. A position as an assistant legal adviser in the Legal Directorate, the Foreign and Commonwealth Office.

It had taken months for a letter to arrive, announcing he'd been granted a thirty-minute phone interview. At half an hour short of midnight! But he'd been primed, had even dressed for the part. He'd spoken about his master's, about his keenness to work in an advisory capacity, the essential elements of sound international policy, his knowledge of European matters in the face of the new currency, the new Union, the implications for trade. He'd been on top of it all. He thought he'd done well. Superbly well, in fact. Then a second, even more confident interview, in which he was sure he'd impressed with his handling of a legal problem about the European Union law on public health and the trade of tobacco in Great Britain. It was all looking good. He also managed to provide proof of British citizenship: he'd acquired a British passport in Cambridge, thanks to his Sussex-born grandfather on his mother's side. Then the second last hurdle to jump: a two-hour interview in person with the Foreign Office HR team. He was offered a pre-interview discussion over the phone – *as an exception*, he was told – and he took this as his cue and booked a ticket.

His last hurdle was the security clearance since the job entailed access to top-secret documents. *Developed vetting*, the process was called, which meant interviews and phone calls to his parents and several friends, and three referees to vouch for him: his Cambridge supervisor, his current boss and his former boss at the insurance company. He had to complete questionnaires, provide bank statements, a police certificate. At the end of which he felt suitably vetted. Ready. He thought the job was as good as his.

He'd also had to endure energetic resistance from his mother, who'd threatened him with hysterics, pleaded with him to *think of his poor dear mother*. Finally, mercifully, she resigned herself to visiting him in London. Which had its attractions, of course. His father had waved him off with a list of names and phone numbers, but Sebastian had ripped them up as soon as the plane lifted off, bore him to another world. He felt excited, on top of the world. Grown up at last.

And so there he was, in London, in the last months of the final year of the century, sharing a flat in Chelsea with a Colombian, Julio, who made a mysterious living trading stocks and shares on the internet. He had the smallest bedroom on the second level of a four-storey Victorian building in Cadogan Gardens. He paid extortionate rent on a salary much smaller than the one he'd earned in Perth, but that didn't worry him, not a jot. Because he'd made it on his own. Because according to the HR team who asked him to join the force, to *assist in the protection of British interests*, he was *impressive*.

An impeccably dressed man had shown him to a desk in his very own room in the India Office on King Charles Street, Whitehall, an opulent building, according to the man. Opulent? It was as big as a bloody palace, Sebastian thought, newly refurbished, plush furniture, and full of important people on a mission. He looked out onto the spectacular Dunbar Court, marble floors and granite arches, replete with the busts of governors-general and the names of Indian cities. A lot for a junior, one might say. But there was also the possibility of moving up in the world. Literally. A posting overseas where the rest of the Foreign Office was based. Seventy countries across the globe: it was enough to make him dizzy.

He could still remember his face-to-face interview, when, as he told his mother, he'd *aced it*. He'd had just enough time to describe it to her before his phone card credit ran out. And best of all, funniest of all, he'd 'warmed up' for the interview by using techniques he'd learned from a UDS rehearsal. Some balding man running a local theatre had taught them games for becoming *solid on the ground*. Imagine yourself filling up with sand, he'd said, or visualise yourself becoming a tree growing roots beneath your feet. Sebastian had even used some of the man's vocal exercises, yodels and lip-wobbles. And what was the result? An assured and articulate response to all of the questions: *Will a written constitution be to the answer to the EU's problems? What are some principles of good legal advice in international situations? Describe your interest in EU policy. Can you come up with an example of a workplace conflict and how you resolved it? What unique qualities can you bring the Europe division of the Legal Directorate?*

Sebastian hadn't blinked. It had given him an edge, no doubt, being in all those plays. So much of life was a role play anyway, and he'd already played half a dozen or so powerful figures. Maybe something had osmosed.

He quickly accepted a handful of invitations from his old Trinity College chums: a table tennis tournament in Hyde Park (he'd come third), then a day of pedal boating in Battersea Park (just for fun). He cycled with a couple of friends on Wimbledon Common. There were the occasional after-work drinks held at Westminster pubs, a cocktail reception in a salubrious hotel. The Foreign and Commonwealth Office advertised courses in academic diplomacy, all possible to complete during work hours. After his first few weeks, he'd been casually invited on a weekend trip to fashionable Dubrovnik and then to feasting on Indian food in Brick Lane in local London. He would consider the former offer, once he got a grip on his role: a juicy one to begin with, working with an advisory team on the Schengen Agreement. How the abolition of border controls within

Europe could now be applied to the jurisdiction of the European Union.

In all this work, this activity, the striving for opportunities, he couldn't muster the energy for a girlfriend. His focus was squarely on his work. Until he found himself tangled up with his housemate's sister, Lucia. She was a waitress at the nearby Oriel. He had been out for a beer with Julio, and she'd joined them at the Queen's Arms after her shift. Julio left for some late-night trading, and Sebastian, on the verge of getting drunk, was taken with Lucia's soulful eyes and flawless olive skin, her irresistible accent. The way she said his name, 'S-Heb-ahstiahn', as if it began with an 'H'. She whispered in his ear in breathy Spanish, put her arm around him, and one thing led to another.

He awoke with her splayed out in his bed and left her there snoring as he scrambled off late for work. He noticed, stupidly, as he rushed out the door, that he was wearing odd socks. When he came home in the evening, expecting to find her gone, she was still in his bed, curled up with a magazine, then looking up at him, expectantly, as he walked through the bedroom door. He thought he might try again, have a bit of fun, but then she asked if she could move in! He'd been ambushed, tongue-tied, managed to nod, knowing this was all a huge mistake. And then, after a week of her watching TV, pouting, going to and from her shifts, singing in the shower, eating beans on toast, brushing her teeth, leaving long black strands of hair on the bathroom floor, a week of not knowing what to do with her, or how to get rid of her, she had a fight with her brother. Harsh words were exchanged – *hijueputa ... malparido ... puta!* A beer bottle was thrown against the wall. A glass shattered on the floor. Julio bought her a ticket to Bogotá. There were tears. And then she was gone.

He thought he was done with women for a while, but then Iris came along. She was working as an intern for three weeks for one of the desk officers, a new scheme they'd introduced to enhance diversity and opportunity, and she'd scored the gig above many others. A nineteen-year-old from Reading, plump and freckled, wholesome. She'd even survived the vetting process without a hitch, bright as a button she was. He met her by accident on the Clive Steps, some sort of collision over a dissembling briefcase. *Geopolitical research*, she'd explained, and as she'd anxiously reached down for the escaping pages, Sebastian's hand had touched hers. They laughed awkwardly; she gave him a quivering smile, and so he asked her out to lunch.

Iris wore long plaid suits that her mother must have given her; he found himself touched by how unfashionable she looked. She explained over lunch how she was following Mr Higginson's instructions assiduously, yes, the desk officer she was eager to please. She'd gathered documents and written letters, made many phone calls. She was doing her best, she told Sebastian. She'd even sourced the legislation and had found important papers. She showed him her collection of highlighter pens, insisted on calling him *Mr Harper-Jones*, keeping things strictly professional. It was a hierarchy, after all. He couldn't help noticing the damp curls clinging to her cheeks and the beat of the pulse in her throat. And how could he not love the way she laughed at all his jokes, even the bad ones?

So one thing led to another ... again ... when she'd sat next to him in the Red Lion after work, giggling nervously, her eyes glued on him. He found himself going back to her place after a swanky reception in the Locarno Suite. She'd been sick with excitement to have been invited, a mere intern. And so, he was doing the gentlemanly thing, escorting her home late at night. And what did he find? A room in a women's college in Bloomsbury; a temporary dig, clearly, for the internship. Even worse, the college was filled with gawking students slamming doors or talking conspiratorially in the corridor, like children.

The sex was disastrous. Iris's thick stockings were almost impossible to remove, and by the time he'd found a condom in his wallet, he had trouble getting aroused. He felt comical somehow, insensitive, in the way he touched her, kissed her. He went through with it like a chore, not really knowing why, wishing he could undo it. It wasn't, one might say, his finest hour.

Catching the Tube home, he couldn't help thinking that he'd broken some sort of code. Lost his compass. Not that it had been illegal or non-consensual, but still ... he'd taken advantage, really, and he was worried, too, that word might get out, damage him somehow. As he alighted from the train, he made a firm decision: he needed a break from women.

Making that break was worse than he'd imagined, with Iris working across from his room for her final week. She hadn't been able to look at him. Even worse, he managed to take her aside and tell her that she was too good for him.

He kept remembering how, in their terrible, botched encounter, she'd covered her naked body with her hands.

63. Joshua

They were docked in Port Darwin, in between a barge and a naval ship. Josh had been deliriously happy to see land, even if they still had to sleep on the boat. He stood on the deck, felt the air as thick as soup, saw modern buildings in the distance, jetties and palm trees, a stretch of ochre-coloured sand. Yellow and purple light leaked across the horizon. The smell of – frangipani, was it? – blew in the wind. But his pores were teeming with sweat, just standing there doing nothing. He wished he could dive into the water, but Warra had warned him off – the deadly jellyfish and stingers.

He heard a movement behind him.

'Letter for you,' Warra said, and Josh turned to see his friend holding a handful of mail. 'It's from the office, addressed to the shipping company. Don't know how long it's been here.'

Josh took the letter. Looked at the postmark: France. He almost jumped. He turned over the envelope and saw her name: Veronika Vaček. He opened the envelope carefully, unfolded the paper inside, and felt a surge of emotion rush over him.

Dear Joshua,

My parents gave me the name of your company but I have no idea if this will reach you. I have no idea where in the world you are. I wanted you to know that I haven't forgotten you, that I wonder what you're doing and how you are. Hoping that you're happy.

I know my mother told you I'm in Paris now, studying acting. I won a scholarship, it's just enough to keep me going. The director at my school says that I won't improve unless I look at something squarely in the face. Something in the past, he means. And I know what it is, Josh, and I'm sorry. I'm sorry for being so careless with your feelings, for abandoning you. I can't begin to imagine how you must have felt in prison because even though you told me, it's not the same as living it. All I can say is that I'm sorry. I hope you'll find it in your heart to forgive me.

I'll understand if you don't reply, but here's my address if you do.
I would love you to write.

Veronika

He folded up the letter. His hands were shaking. The letter was written some time ago. It had taken months to get to him.

What could he say to her? Should he even reply? He was no good with words like she was. She was sorry, she'd said. Could he find it in his heart to forgive her? When the truth was, he'd expected more of her and found out she was less. But he'd loved her, too, if love meant knowing she understood him. Believing she felt the same about him.

That afternoon in Starfish Bay, the two of them in his blow-up dinghy, floating in the flat sea, growing dizzy in the sun's reflection, making ripples in the water with their feet. He'd told her about his mum dying of cancer when he was nine. She'd listened. She'd held his hand. *I'm so sorry,* she'd said, *you must miss her.* All he could hear was the waves as he felt the heaviness lifting. He remembered how the sky had changed, how the clouds had broken apart and the brilliant light had seeped through.

After tossing it around in his head for a week, he decided he would write. He hoped it might offer some kind of peace in his head. He told her he was in Darwin right now, but most of the time he was at sea. That it was tough work but also boring, and he didn't want to waste her time being boring. He asked her to write to him again. Tell him about her life and what made her happy.

He remembered one of his lines from the play: *A man ... must laugh at the world lest he should weep.*

Dear Josh,
Thank you so much for writing to me. It means more than I can say. But you hardly told me anything about your life. I'm not criticising you. I would just like to see you. Will you do that, for me?

He had to take a deep breath after that. She would like to see him. She meant she wanted to know about his life, but maybe she meant something else as well. He checked the date. It had only taken a couple of weeks to get to him. So the news was recent. He kept reading, pages and pages. Like she was talking to him.

You asked what makes me happy, here in Paris. The snow. I've never seen it before and it's so magical, so white. I know it's a cliché, but it turns the world into a fairy tale. And I've bought a bicycle – probably the worst time of the year! But I love cycling to my classes in the cold, flying past the gold-tipped dome of the Académie Française – that's the building where important people discuss the French language, how to preserve it, how to accommodate its changes, and it's a grand building with imposing columns and graceful arches.

Cassie's in Paris for a few months doing an art course. Last night we went to the opera. She paid for our tickets with her father's birthday money. She told me she hates him but she won't refuse his money! The opera was sublime, Gluck's Orphée et Eurydice. Cassie and I both cried at the end when Eurydice died. Her body draped over Orpheus as he wailed his final song. Her cloak too red, a spreading petal. How is it that tragedy can bring such pleasure? I've never heard anything so magnificent, the drowning sound of the chorus, the strings, the trill of the soprano, I had it all spinning round in my head today as I cycled through the cool, grey air. I feel drunk on this city. It's like someone's whispering in my ear: Art is all that matters.

Afterwards Cassie took me to Bar Hemingway, it was full of rich Americans in white jackets. All the women blonde, beautifully coiffured. Soft lounges. We were served hot roasted almonds on a silver tray and cocktails in tall glasses. Such luxury. The bar is named to honour the American writer. He hung out there but survived on a pittance, all for the love of Paris, where he wrote his stories of intrepid adventures.

Cassie and I are stretching out our money. We never eat out, we don't buy glamorous clothes. We shop at the Arab market, eat eggs and baguette. Porridge. Frozen spinach and spaghetti. In cafés we only ever order 'un petit café'. We try to walk everywhere, or cycle, so we don't have to pay for the Métro. And if we're wise with our francs, we sometimes have enough to go to a gallery or buy a cheap seat at the Comédie-Française. We've seen a lot of theatre (the student discount is quite good). A claustrophobic and terrifying Macbeth at the Théâtre des Bouffes du Nord and an edgy Bulgarian play at the Théâtre Malakoff. Challenging, it was, with the French subtitles. Weekends, we go to fabulous old films at the cinemathèque.

When we have no money at all, we sit in the finest parks and watch *the world go by. We see it all: old couples canoodling, young couples having tiffs, toddlers playing with puppies, office workers eating hot crêpes, joggers, the vagabonds scavenging. The hustlers. So much life, Josh. I think you'd love it.*

I'm taking acting lessons, as you know. I have to do all my scenes in French. Even if the play is Russian! Some of the French is hard, written in what is called the past-historic tense, and no-one speaks that anymore. There's also this complicated rhythm to the poetry. It's one thing in French and then another in English. Talk about difficult! At the end of the year there's a showcase called a représentation publique de scène. *That's when all the casting directors come and see what we've done and how good we are. They might cast us in the next film, or for a season at the Odéon or some other national theatre or company. I've been working hard on my scenes. I love the role I'm playing at the moment, but Antoine doesn't think I'm there with it yet. He has a psycho-physical approach to theatre – it's quite something – and he's quite clear that the 'psycho' part I must work on as much as the 'physical'.*

I'm also trying to practise my everyday French, although Antoine called my French exécrable! *(which means dreadful). It's mostly pronunciation – the 'en' and 'in' and 'ain', things like that, I seem to mix up them up. I've had to learn phonetics to get it right. I can't believe it! After three years of studying the language, it doesn't really stick until you get here. He and his wife Madeleine invited me to dinner, and then she asked me for afternoon tea, where we sipped something exotic with lavender and cardamon. It's called* pôetes solitaire, *which means solitary poets. Isn't that lovely? Their friend Eddie is a pianist and his passion is jazz. He invited me to hear him play, and so Cassie and I have spent late nights in jazz bars meeting musicians with names like Jumpin' Jerry and Bad Mary Brown.*

So, this is how we live, Josh. I try to imagine what your life looks like.

Yours,
Veronika

Yours.

But he knew they were worlds apart. All her talk about preserving a language, drinking fancy tea, using elegant French words, going to the opera, or enjoying jazz in some swanky bar.

What the hell could he tell her in return? That the ship had docked but the ground was still moving. That he might spend his life seasick. The afternoon sun throbbed like a blister. The exhaustion. All that kept him going was Warra. But he wouldn't tell her that either, about his mate from juvie. He didn't want to take her back to that time when he was lost, and she was lost to him. He had to stay in the here and now.

But he sent another letter, anyway, beginning with light-hearted stories. How his mate never shut up but he would give you the shirt off his back. How his mate had found a stray dog and fed it beer with steak in HP sauce. The dog was a blue heeler crossed with God knows what but acted like a prince. The work was hard, he wrote, but he was getting better, faster, and he was earning decent money. He was set for another six-weeker on the liner: more hard work and as much sleep as he could grab. No plans for the future, but he'd heard there was building work in Bunbury, so maybe it was time to come home. He was sick of the sea, in any case. He finished by telling her how much he'd loved her last letter.

They'd been out through the Beagle Gulf, into the Timor Sea, and he was glad to reach land, with three weeks off work to look forward to. He couldn't help hoping there would be another letter. It was like being close to her, reading all her stories, hearing her passion, and the way she'd asked after him.

He was elated to find that she'd written again, grabbed the letter from someone's hand. He waited until he was alone, wanting to be alone with her.

He saw straight away that the letter was short. He began to read ... it was very different from the brightness of before.

Dear Joshua,

I feel like I'm getting nowhere with my acting classes. Antoine has been critical of me before, but today he hit the roof. He actually told me today I was hopeless. Hopeless! He said I was no good at 'subtext' (the meaning beneath the script) and that this makes me underprepared for my character. I thought he was so charming, so kind, but when he got so cross with me, I had to stop myself from crying because I'm trying, I really am. I need a friend, Josh. Cassie's here in Paris but it's not the same as being with you. You were my best friend, and we could talk about anything. I know it's not fair to ask and you probably can't afford it and you don't have the time but if you can come to Paris it would mean the world to me. You can stay in my shabby apartment, for free, of course, and I'll cook for you and show you the sights. Will you?

Always,
Veronika

64. Veronika

Josh had phoned her from London, out of the blue, to let her know that he'd like to see Paris. To see *her*. She'd wanted to rush out of her apartment and shout out the news to the world. Such goodness, such kindness! And all for her! But she had to stay calm, keep steady. She'd told Cassie that *an old friend* was coming to visit, and Cassie had squealed *Sebastian!* Veronika had instantly corrected her: it was Joshua she wanted to see. But she knew she would have to take care. She hadn't asked him how long he planned on staying or what he would do after Paris. She was grateful for his kindness, and she didn't want to use him, either. She just wanted to … she didn't quite know what she wanted except to feel his arms around her. Be with him. Together again.

It was really him. Joshua. Walking into the café. She couldn't quite believe it. He was a year older than her, about twenty-seven, but tanned and still attractive in a boyish kind of way. Almost pretty. Tall. His hair was much shorter, his forehead and mouth had a few lines but there he was, here he was, and she had to hold back the tears.

He caught sight of her at her table, and she rose to meet him. He stopped in front of her, gave her the shy smile she'd always loved.

'Good to see you,' he said.

'And you too.'

'You've grown your hair.'

'And you've cut yours. At last.' Veronika smiled.

'Happy new millennium!' he said and shuffled forward slowly, a large backpack strapped to his back. They hugged, stiffly, then disentangled themselves.

'I need a coffee,' he said. 'It took me twenty-four hours to get to London. And the place was crazy. The Tube. It was a nightmare.'

Close up, he looked exhausted. A little dazed. Veronika told him to take off his backpack, sit, relax. They sat across from each other at a tiny table. She became conscious of the way he didn't look at her. She was glad to see a waiter hovering by their table, anything to break the tension. Josh ordered a black coffee, and Veronika ordered tea in French. The waitress didn't smirk for a change.

Veronika reached out her hand, hoping that Josh would take it, but he kept his hands out of sight. And it struck her: his worker's hands, marked by the rigours of months at sea. She suddenly wished she hadn't ordered *thé au citron*.

'I'm so glad you're here,' she said. 'I don't know how to thank—'

'It's fine, all good,' he rushed in. 'Hey, you promised you'd cook for me. I haven't had a decent feed in months.'

So he'll play it light, she thought.

She felt a presence behind her, turned to see a slender African man approaching their table. Oh please, not the red roses, she thought, as she watched him take a flower from his basket, pass it to Josh.

'Just ignore him,' she whispered.

Josh fumbled in his pocket.

'Don't, Josh. Please. I don't want a rose, and—'

She watched with dismay as Josh handed the man a twenty franc note, then took his change and the flower. She cringed when the man beamed and bowed then moved on to the next table.

'Josh, it's best not to give them money,' she said. 'The word will get out and they'll keep pestering you.'

'Who's *they*?' Josh looked away, looked back at her. 'They have to earn a living,' he said.

She felt her face tighten. A few minutes in and she was telling him to toughen up. And he was telling her ... what? That she'd grown hard in the big city? She wished their drinks would arrive.

She felt their table shaking, heard the sound of clanging bells.

'Roadworks,' she said. For something to say. 'Those jackhammers have been going on for weeks now. Enough to drive you mad.'

'Specially for the people who work here,' he said.

Was this why he'd come here? To keep rebuking her like this?

'You were thinking of doing building work,' she said. 'Bunbury, wasn't it?'

He nodded. 'Maybe,' he said. 'I'm not sure of anything right now.'

The girl returned with their drinks. Veronika thanked her profusely, in French; the girl smirked.

Veronika turned to Josh. 'They hate people garbling their language,' she said. 'I mean ... the waiter does. French people generally.'

'You sounded pretty good to me,' he said. 'Although what did your teacher say?'

She groaned. He smiled. Would this be a better beginning?

'I'm sorry you're having a hard time,' he said.

'Well … I feel better already, having you here. And … you came halfway round the world to see me.'

He didn't respond. They sipped their drinks, said nothing for some time, until she couldn't bear the silence any longer.

'So London was a nightmare,' she said. 'I can imagine it. All those people crammed in the Tube. What's the population, anyway? It must be ten times the size of Perth.'

Josh frowned. 'It wasn't just the crowds,' he said. 'It was all the homeless people lying on the footpaths. In laneways. All the people begging for food, some of them just kids. I thought New Labour might have turned things around but it's been nearly three years in government and—'

'I didn't know you were political, Josh.'

He scratched his chin. 'I'm not really. I just notice things.'

They drank. They muttered platitudes. Then they rose from the table in silence. Josh kept bumping into people with his backpack, kept apologising in English. Veronika took him by the arm and steered him onto the street.

'Let me show you some of the sights,' she said. 'I don't mean the bloody Eiffel Tower, either. I mean things along the way to my apartment.'

She loved the city in its autumn colours. The trees had already turned yellow, as if Paris was turning into a sepia photograph.

'Isn't it beautiful?' she said.

'It's busy,' he said. 'And all these people sitting in cafés. I mean, are they here all the time?'

'I guess so.'

'Bloody lucky, then,' he said. 'Or bloody useless.'

He kept walking, kept staring at all the people on the pavements, sipping their coffee, laughing, talking earnestly. But she wouldn't counter his attack; she didn't want a fight. She wanted to be … happy. She pointed out the intricate balconies. Hip-hop dancers in full swing right in front of the Place Saint-Michel, making acrobatic leaps in time to a boom box. She pointed to her favourite Algerian patisserie that made pistachio slice and violet cake.

'And here's the best thing of all,' she said as they turned a corner. 'Notre Dame Cathedral. It's more than eight hundred years old.'

The beautiful sandstone, the imposing front spires. The engraved faces across the edifice; above the door, the Last Judgement. Look, she told him, pointing, *the dead revived from their graves!* She pointed at the Gallery of Kings, the martyr of St Denis without his head. The brilliant gargoyles.

'You can see them up close if you climb the spiral staircase,' she said. Pleased to see Josh looking so impressed. 'Once upon a time it was polychromous – you know, painted in different colours – but the paint has faded through the centuries. If you turn the corner and look up, you can see the twelve apostles descending the spire. Each one is different, each one has his own dramatic posture.'

Josh pushed the hair back from his forehead. 'It's Gothic, isn't it?' he said.

'Yes. And in Gothic cathedrals, revealing the structure is the key.'

'The key,' he said, as if handling the words like a smooth stone. 'It's amazing. I mean, the pictures on the net don't do it any justice.'

'We'll go inside sometime,' she said.

She felt something sharp bump into her leg, turned to see a young couple lugging a mattress, hogging the footpath, dark looks and mutterings from people around them. Josh looked amused.

'Remember trying to get the bed on stage in our play?' he said. 'Cassie and Lucas, tripping all over the place.'

'The bed fell apart three times,' she said.

'I think I drilled on some hinges somewhere,' he said. 'So they could fold it, store it. Jesus. We not only had to act, we had to bring on all the set and props with us too!'

'Can you remember your lines?' Veronika said. '*How stupid clever men can be?*' She began to recite. She skipped in front of him, twirled around a lamppost.

'*So they say.*'

So he remembered. He halted in front of her. She liked him like this. Whimsical.

'*Yes, but some people are unwilling to believe it,*' she went on.

'So, am I stupid for a clever man?' he asked. 'Or clever for a stupid man? That is ... for coming here ... to see you?'

'I don't remember that part of the script,' she said, grinning at him.

They walked past the Place Maubert. The market was finishing up: she could smell the rotten fruit and sour milk. Dirty lettuce leaves blew along the pavement. Men were shifting cardboard boxes into vans, and there were stray cats gleaning from toppled bins. They turned up a street with a steep incline and cobblestones, with the roof of the Panthéon peeking out at the end. When they were almost at the top, they entered a building with a large red door. They crossed a courtyard, passed through glass doors, then up four flights of a narrow stairwell. It was as familiar to her now as breathing, and yet every time she thought of the thousands of feet, millions, who had walked this way before her.

'Here we are, Josh,' she said as they approached the apartment door. 'And I forgot to mention. You'll be sleeping on cushions.'

'Cushions?'

'More comfortable than my own bed!' she said. 'Which is a thin mattress attached to the back of a dismantled door.'

'Luxury!' he said and leaned into her, tousled her hair.

He stood back to look at her. Take her in. She waited. Then he took off his backpack, dumped it on the landing, and moved towards her. Held her in a gentle embrace. The smell of his sweat aroused her. His body felt taut. Ready.

'I've missed you,' she said softly. 'So much.'

His hands moved down her spine, her waist, caressed her hips, both of them holding their breath. Then he stepped away from her, grabbed his backpack and pointed towards the stairs, and she felt it too, the charge, the need, as they moved, urgent now. She pushed open her door and pulled him inside. She turned to face him. Told him to close the door. He did as he was told.

65. Joshua

She tore off her jacket, pulled her shirt over her head, and took off her bra. He was transfixed. Her breasts were so lovely, so pert and lovely, and he moved towards her, but she was moving too fast for him, ripping off her skirt, her tights. And then she stopped. Took off her knickers slowly, as though she were teasing him, wanted to keep him waiting, all the time watching him, driving him crazy, and he couldn't wait, seeing her there naked and ready for him, unbuckling his jeans, taking off the rest of his clothes, and *I'm wet*, she said, and he lost it. He rushed towards her, cupped her face, her breasts, kissed her breasts, her stomach, her thighs and *ah,* she cried out, calling his name and they fell onto the floor and he rolled on top of her and kissed her mouth, wanting her, wanting all of her, he'd been waiting for years and years. And then he stopped. Just in time.

'I don't have anything on me,' he said, feeling his face turn hot. 'I mean, I wasn't planning—'

'It's okay,' she whispered in his ear. 'I'm on the pill.'

Now it was her turn to kiss him, hard on the mouth, pulling him into her, taking him in to her and he was in so deep and she was calling his name again and *come,* she said, *come now,* he'd never felt so hard in his life and my God, the release, the joy … she was trembling below him, her hands around his face and *divine, just divine,* she said.

It could have been a minute or a lifetime.

He laid her gently on her side, put his arms around her.

'Don't go to sleep,' she said. 'Promise?'

'Promise,' he said, and kissed her.

She'd made a fresh salad, she said. She was starving, she said. It was the tastiest salad ever, she said. She could have said anything, and he would have loved her, treasured her, held her close. She'd slipped some kind of singlet over her body and he wanted to take it off, slowly, touch her again, come inside her again.

'Spinach leaves, apples and tomatoes,' she said. 'Plus cucumber and goat's cheese and a fresh baguette.'

She walked over to where he sat on a pile of cushions. He was still naked, feeling good and right, and she was so beautiful. She handed him a glass of something fizzing, and he took a careful sip.

'What's this French rubbish?' he said and smiled.

'It's Italian, actually. Prosecco.' She leaned down to kiss him, then drew away. 'I'll get the rest of lunch, shall I?'

But he didn't want her to leave him, not now, not ever. He put down his glass and reached out for her hand. Pulled her down to his side, put an arm around her shoulder.

'I thought I'd lost you,' he said and pulled her closer.

'Lost me?'

'When you were with that Sebastian guy.'

'I ... we didn't work out,' she said. 'He was too demanding. Too glossy.'

She laughed, a happy laugh. He was just so damn thrilled to be with her again. He began to stroke her face.

'Do you remember our first kiss? he said softly.

'Our *only* kiss, you mean. The tree house. Yes. I do remember. Leaves. Fallen leaves all about the place. The singing of skin upon skin.'

He gave her a bashful look. 'I'd never kissed anyone before,' he said.

'What?' She leant back, smiled into his eyes. 'Fifteen! And you'd never kissed a girl before?' she teased him. 'So ... what did it feel like? Tell me.'

'Your breath was so light,' he said. 'And your fingers on my skin, they were so soft. God, I thought I'd die with wanting you.'

'But you held back.'

'We were young. Much too young.' He smiled. 'And ... well, the truth was ... I was scared.'

She kissed his chest. 'And now you're fearless,' she said. 'And perfect.'

He'd never heard a woman talk like this before. Her openness, her sweetness, after making love. He'd been with a couple of women before, but it was over as soon as it began. Just sex and relief and nothing more.

He was pensive for a moment.

'It was that night – remember? Before we went out to the bonfire. You took off your grandma's necklace. Or it fell off. In the tree house. Don't you remember?'

Veronika went quiet. He wished he hadn't brought that up. He changed the topic.

'I remember you doing ballet on the beach,' he said. 'I'd never seen anything so beautiful. And I remember thinking: Veronika Vaček. She's

235

real delicate and a bit wild, and I'd like to keep her by my side forever.'

Her eyes widened, as if she'd had no idea. Well, now she did, and he was glad he'd told her. That he wanted her beside him forever.

They forgot about lunch and made love instead. This time in her bed, looking into each other's eyes. Then he rolled her over and kissed her slowly along her spine, bump by beautiful bump. It was as if he knew what to do with her body; she made him feel ripe with something ... with grace. Love. She shivered, turned over, and nestled into him.

'Shall I tell you about Paris?' she said.

Well, you already did, he wanted to say, but she wasn't waiting for his answer, telling about some opera she'd been to – *The Marriage of Figaro*, in fact, Mozart's version – with Cassie, in *the most lavish theatre* she'd ever seen ... chandeliers ... a famous painting by someone he'd never heard of ... how she and Cassie had sat way up high *in the gods*, the cheapest seats, she explained, but when the lights came on she'd looked down, seen all the empty seats in the stalls, and the two of them had darted down the stairs to take them.

'How is Cassie, anyway?' he said. 'Still mixed up?'

'She's fun, always fun. I don't mean in a superficial way. I mean she enjoys life. Drains every drop. Moving to London seems to have done her a lot of good.'

Paris. London. It all seemed beyond him. What mattered now was this closeness: the life they had already shared and the hope of life to come.

'Do you miss Perth, Ron?' he said.

'A bit. I miss Mum and Dad, although they ring me now and then to ask how I'm doing. Translation: are you eating well, not being mugged, not catching a cold or some terrible disease. And Ana's having a hard time. Sometimes I feel guilty that I'm not there to help, but most of the time ... well, I'm relieved I'm not there.' Then she took a really deep breath, as though she was edging towards something new.

'Did you know about Ana and Charlie?' she said. 'That he's not the father of her twins?'

Josh nodded. 'He called me in a rage one day. And ... well, I can't say I blame him. Her tricking him like that. It was pretty low.'

Veronika pulled a face. 'I know Ana was stupid,' she said. 'But she was desperate, too. She had nowhere else to turn.'

'That's not really an excuse.'

He felt her body tense in his arms.

'I didn't say it was an excuse, Josh. It's an explanation.'

He wished she would relax. He wished she'd never started down this road.

'She was crazy about Charlie, Josh. Had been for years, although God knows why. He's such a ruthless bastard.'

Josh nuzzled into her hair, relieved that she didn't like Charlie. 'He's not all that bad,' he said. 'Honestly.'

She pulled away, looked into his eyes. 'You must be kidding, Josh. Don't you know what he's like?'

'Of course, I know what he's like. But … well, he took a lot of blows for me. From our father. He copped most of the punches.'

'Maybe he deserved them!'

'He was trying to protect me. Look out for me.'

She laughed, a mocking kind of laugh. 'Well, that's very noble of him. Charlie, the great protector.'

He was beginning to feel rattled now. Why was she … spoiling things like this? He needed to calm her down, needed to soothe her, soothe himself. He drew her into his arms again.

'I want to tell you something, Ron,' he said quietly.

He felt her body tighten.

'Charlie got mixed up with a bad crowd,' he said. 'He made a lot of enemies, and—'

'Why am I not surprised?'

'Ron. Just listen to me. Please. He got beaten up a few times. Rival gangs, that kind of stuff. And he had a lot of anger inside.'

'*You* had every right to be angry, too, Josh. The way your father treated you. But you didn't turn out to be so rotten. So cruel.'

He knew what she was saying. He'd thought about this before without coming up with any answers.

'It's a funny thing,' he said. 'How brothers can turn out so different. All I know is that my father hurt us both and Charlie … I don't know … sometimes I think he had to prove he was a hot shot, you know. To prove to himself that he wasn't a hurt little kid. That he wasn't damaged by our father.'

She stirred in his arms. 'But he hurt other people, too,' Veronika said.

Josh had to tell her. It was now or never. He wanted there to be no secrets between them.

'I knew Charlie wouldn't last a day in prison,' he said. 'Adult prison. His enemies inside … they would have beaten the shit out of him. All the time. Killed him, maybe. The guys from the Bay. A few of them were in there.'

She drew away from him. 'What are you saying?'

'That … that it was Charlie who lit the fire.'

'He … what?'

'He lit the fire. He just … went crazy. Out of control. I later worked out that he'd even doused the trees with petrol – the ones in the park near the beach. He was in some sort of rage.'

Veronika let go of his hand. But he needed to go on.

'I left the bonfire because I was afraid of what I might do to Charlie. I didn't want to lose it in front of you. I went to cool off, into the forest, to the tree house. When I got there, I threw the branch into the river. I could see trees burning in the distance. I heard sirens. I was petrified when I saw the police, I thought they were coming to rescue me, so I went with them. They handcuffed me. My saddest moment was looking at you, through the back window of the paddy wagon. You could not imagine what I saw in your face.'

Her eyes were blazing now. 'What the hell, Josh? What do you mean?'

'I told the police it was me. He was scared, Ron, really scared. I pled guilty because the Legal Aid lawyer said to. I had already spoken to the police. I told them we'd been running around with branches lit. The police said I had admitted it, but I hadn't really. The lawyer said she'd spoken to the police, who had overwhelming evidence against me. Someone had reported the dousing. Mixed me up with Charlie. She said the evidence was so significant that it meant that I would receive the lightest penalty by pleading guilty. I was in a mess. I did what she said. Twenty-four months. No bail as I had no home … The worst bit about detention was rehabilitation. I had to visit burn victims in hospital so that I would face the impact of my crime. It messes with your head. I started believing I had done it.' He was out of breath. Sweating. Relieved.

But Veronika gripped his hands and squeezed them, as if she was trying to hurt him. 'I can't believe this, Josh. You … you what? You spent two years in prison to protect *him*?'

'It's not that simple,' he said and looked away. Why wasn't she listening to him? Hearing him? He turned to look at her again, and she was glaring at him now, like he'd done something wrong, and he hadn't, he just hadn't.

'I don't get it. You saved him, you cared about him, but he doesn't care about anyone but himself.'

'Except you,' he said quietly.

'What? What does *that* mean?'

'He was in love with you. He told me.'

'*In love with me?* I was fourteen years old, Josh. What on earth—'

'And you fancied him.'

She shook her head.

'I saw the way you looked at him. At the bonfire.'

'You're kidding! He disgusted me. He made me feel sick.'

He started to speak, then stopped. Started again. He needed to get this straight.

'Look, I know Charlie comes across as ... like he's so full of shit. He comes across all nasty but—'

'Oh, so he's really soft and kind underneath.' She was pounding on his chest now. 'Josh, you have to go to the police, you have to set the record straight. It's not fair. You can't let him—'

'It was my choice.'

'Then I'll go to the police myself. Clear your name. Make Charlie pay for what he did.'

'It doesn't work like that. And anyway, it doesn't matter anymore.'

'Do you know how vile he is? Do you? At Starfish Bay ... he lured me to an island and started pawing me all over. And when he saw me again, after our play ... he cornered me, propositioned me. And then he came to my workplace and—'

Josh felt a cold seeping come over him. 'So you've been seeing him?'

'He has been fucking stalking me, Josh!'

'Did you see him while I was in prison?'

'What? Are you out of your mind?'

'How would I know what you were doing, Veronika? You never came to visit me.'

'I said I was sorry. Sorry, Josh, I'm sorry. How many times do I have to say it? I'm sorry, I'm sorry, I'm sorry.'

Now she was shouting at him. He'd had a gutful of this ... this mess, not listening to him, not hearing him, telling him what he should think, what to do. He pushed her away, picked up his clothes and got dressed in a hurry. He couldn't bring himself to look at her. He scooped up his backpack and headed for the door.

'Josh,' she called out. 'Don't go. Please. Let's talk.'

He opened the door, walked out of her apartment, slammed the door behind him.

Walking down the street to God knows where. It was only then that he remembered: the rose she'd left behind in the café.

66. Veronika

He'd gone. Within the space of four hours, Josh had returned to her, made love to her, then left her. She hadn't chased him down or called his name through the window, and she knew she wouldn't, couldn't, write to him. She couldn't abide the thought of him ripping up her letter in anger, in disgust, in despair, whatever he'd been feeling when he walked out the door, whatever he was feeling now.

And now a month had limped by and she still hadn't heard from him. She would walk to the end of her street and enter the medieval church, not to pray, but simply to sit silently, alone. At night she would lie in bed naked, feeling the shapes of her body, feeling Joshua inside her. Wanting him still. But cross with him, too, for his pointless sacrifice. The waste. He'd told her that prison had been a kind of hell. He'd saved his brother but damaged himself. His brave, stupid gift; his secret. Was that the secret that Ana had almost told her? The one that Charlie had deflected with his smarmy grin? What had he called himself as he'd looked her up and down in the bar? *An open book.* A coward, more like it. A filthy, rotten coward.

She was angry, ashamed, confused. Consumed by regret.

Cassie had asked her *why the gloomy face*, and she'd told her that Josh had walked out. How she didn't want to talk about it. Cassie had simply nodded, asked no questions, didn't nudge or pry. Until the morning they took a walk along the Seine, when Cassie turned to her and said: *You have to get out of this funk.*

She stopped, grabbed Veronika's arm, brought her to a halt.

'You should try psychoanalysis,' she said. '*Psyche* means butterfly in Ancient Greek, so psychoanalysis means letting the butterfly go free.'

Veronika sighed.

'It's worked wonders for me,' Cassie said. 'My therapy in London has been so *illuminating*. For one thing, I've discovered why I used to starve myself, why I wanted to crawl out of my flesh because it felt like there was too much of it. I can get on with things now, get rid of bad habits, unconscious patterns.'

Veronika tried not to snap; she knew Cassie wanted to help. She also knew she couldn't afford therapy, and besides, she lacked the energy to even get started.

'Or you could do something creative,' Cassie said. 'Not acting, Veronika, that's too cerebral. I mean something like dance, pottery or painting. I find painting really helps me clean myself out, if you know what I mean. I'm not very good at it but that's not the point. I just slosh away to my heart's content and ... hey, check this out. I bet it's a Picasso.'

They stopped to inspect a large white sculpture. A woman contorted into a square, her breasts stuck to her back, her legs positioned upside down.

'I'm wrong. It's Agustín Cárdenas. The surrealist. And it's called *La Grande Fenêtre*.'

'Hm.' Veronika turned her head sideways. 'Looks more like his *femme idéale*.'

'His *Ideal Woman* alright!' Cassie exclaimed. 'Just look at her! She's an impossibility. She has to be unnatural and twisted to satisfy a man.'

Veronika gazed at the statue again, then turned to Cassie. 'You can't read surrealist art naturalistically,' she said.

'I can and I will,' Cassie said. 'And look at you. You're spending half your life tying yourself up in knots, pining for some guy. That's no way to live, Veronika. You have to find some meaningful purpose. Become independent. Become more *you*.'

Veronika stiffened. Looked away.

'Okay. Alright.' Cassie squeezed her hand. 'Why don't you write him a letter?'

'I can't see the point. Nothing will change his mind.'

'Just try, Ron. You never know. I'll read it, if you like.'

It took two glasses of cheap red wine to compose the letter, another one to show it to Cassie.

Dear Joshua,

I am trying to find the other side of silence. I've been sealed off from the world since you left. I feel lost without you. I'm going to hear a string quartet at the Sainte-Chapelle tonight. Maybe I'll find a place for you in between the notes somewhere. A sound to wrap inside of, a note to sigh with, to slide down, to carry me somewhere to slip around and hold me since you are not here.

I had a dream about the sculpture you made me – the ballerina. It was made of clay instead of wood. It was transforming out of shape into another object.

I enclose here an eyelash that has fallen upon my cheek as I write. You may keep it if you like and put it in your pocket with all your falling stars and lost eyelashes and birthday cake wishes.

I miss you,
Veronika

Cassie kept her eyes on the letter, didn't say a word.

'What do you think, Cass?'

'It's ... poetic, isn't it?'

'Poetic?'

'Well ... it's ...' She turned, looked at Veronika. 'It's ... look, I know your pain is real. But this letter ... it's ...'

Veronika pulled back her shoulders. 'Go on, say it.'

'It's mawkish drivel,' Cassie said. 'And it's all about you.'

67. Gloria

It was a role she could now play without thinking – Miss da Silva of 4D – the entertainer, encyclopedia, agony aunt, motivator, peacekeeper, you name it. She was a one-woman band. Her fourth year of teaching at Our Lady of Consolation, and she'd kept giving it her all.

It was a hellish sort of devotion, dealing with kids with specific and difficult needs: poor eyesight, short attention spans, literacy delays. She designed them separate lessons in class, encouraged them as much as she could. It had been a lot of work, taken a lot of patience, and progress was glacial. Sometimes they went backwards, wouldn't listen, or they screamed, fought with one another. It was tough, too, managing parents who were overanxious, neglectful or interfering. And tricky trying to keep things smooth with the other teachers, with their allegiances, allies, enemies. The staff room a battleground of gossip. She much preferred playground duty.

Gloria had introduced the kids to fractions with a real apple pie and they'd been beside themselves with glee. She'd sung them 'Yellow Submarine' on the guitar. They loved it when she read them stories after lunch. They were quiet then. Rapt. She had read them *Underground to Canada*, but she was beginning to lose her voice, beginning to feel tired all the time, so weary with responsibility. Of being Miss Teacher. Where was Gloria in all this? And where was the balance between giving yourself and keeping something for yourself? *It is in giving that we receive,* according to Saint Francis. But was that really true? Was there no resolution in all this? There was no-one really to talk to about such things. She'd wanted to ask the other teachers: *When do you stop giving?* But she already knew the answer.

She glanced around the classroom – giant drawings of bright insects, vivid finger paintings, and projects on polar bears pinned to the walls. Grubby walls dotted with old Blu Tack, and the summer rain splattering the windows.

She drove home after school, talking out loud to the empty seat next to her, rain assailing the windscreen. She knew that some of this – her feelings of depletion, and wondering what her job, her life, was all about – she knew enough to know that some of it was guilt. She'd survived invasion, escaped the occupation. She was one of the lucky ones, alive, living somewhere safe, with a well-paid job. A reputation as a good teacher. But it wasn't just the guilt pushing her on, she knew that too. What was calling her? She didn't believe in the self-sacrifice of saints, stupid stories of morbid martyrs, it wasn't that. It was a sense of belonging that she craved. Soul retrieval.

She'd once gone into a New Age shop at the Subiaco Market, gave a woman with wiry hair and dark glasses fifteen precious dollars. The woman had told her she'd lost a piece of herself, and she needed a shaman to get it back. Gloria had left in a hurry, knowing that it was all bunkum, that it would only lead to disappointment.

But still.

Work filled her days, and sometimes her nights, when her thoughts would drift to Joshua. His gentle presence. He'd had a way of tuning in and hearing her out. They'd shared things: missing fathers, a childhood habit of sculpture, sacred trees. Such different backgrounds, yes, but there were also those connections. He had a way of treading lightly yet leaving an impression. True, it had been only a matter of months: but there it was, the thought of him persisted. The things left unsaid. With too many other people around, too much going on. Emotions running high; everyone on a knife edge.

The kiss still haunted her. Her turning him away.

But most of all, in the darkness of her nights, she thought about her father. Whether he was alive or dead. And if the unthinkable had happened, if the worst had come to pass, whether she'd be able to find his body. She'd already tried to find out where he might be. There was a lot of communication between groups in Timor-Leste and solidarity groups in Australia, but nothing which had given her any useful leads, any hope. The human rights groups in Perth hadn't been able to be help, either. She'd seen lists, names, reports but nothing with her father's name on it.

He might have been buried in a forest or thrown over a cliff. She had read about the mass graves, too, of people who'd starved in camps and been tossed into forests. And she had heard, too, about the restlessness of the dead, how those who had died without ritual would haunt their families until they found peace. Her mother believed in such haunting.

He has not come back to me, she would say, because he hadn't appeared to her in a dream to tell her he was gone. He would be wandering forever, her mother lamented, denied the eternity of sleep.

Just months before, there'd been a UN vote for independence in East Timor. Indonesia had finally left her country. And for some time now – months, years, maybe a lifetime – Gloria had felt a disquiet. She had her community, her people, good people who clubbed together when times got tough, like when her mother lost her job. Birthday cakes. Lifts to school. But she also felt like part of her would never settle until she returned to the place of her birth and to whatever she might find there. Or not find. She missed her father, her brother. She longed for equatorial light. For the way she'd once moved through space, unfettered, singing in her own language. Not having to explain herself. Why she looked 'different', what she believed in.

People sometimes asked her if she felt Australian. She would nod and say of course she did because that was so much easier. What she really wanted to say was that she didn't know.

68. Sebastian

She was blonde. With a ponytail. Pale skin. A checked shirt, fawn slacks. Nice body. She was sitting next to Alistair. He hadn't seen Alistair for nearly three years and had never laid eyes on this woman. Al's punching above his weight, he thought, and I've told myself to take a break from women.

Alistair rose from his chair, shook Sebastian's hand firmly. 'Tremendous. Tremendous to see you, Sebastian. Happy new millennium. This is my sister, Sarah.'

She smiled, showing perfect white teeth. Said *how do you do* in a posh English accent.

'Lovely to meet you,' Sebastian said, meaning it.

'How's tricks?' Alistair said as they settled down with their drinks.

'Good, good. Working in the Foreign and Commonwealth Office.' Sebastian drummed up the enthusiasm. 'I love it. EU stuff. Very exciting.'

'Bravo, you. A good future ahead of you, I'm sure, with all the European fuss going on at present.'

'And you, Alistair? What's the physicist doing, then?' He felt a pinch, thinking of Lìjuān.

'I'm not a physicist, old chap. I'm a quant.'

'A quant?'

Sarah leaned forward. 'A quantitative trader,' she said. 'They make loads of money. Didn't you know? All the mathematicians and physicists are becoming quants these days. I mean, just look at Al's clothes!'

An olive jacket and brown tie. Sebastian remembered Cambridge: Alistair's perennial tracksuits.

'Derivatives. Futures,' Alistair said. 'Quantitative analysis. Industrial Maths. You know, quantum finance. I work for Lloyds Bank.'

Sebastian felt somewhat embarrassed. 'Oh. Of course.' A penny had dropped. 'Well done, Alistair.'

'We're all doing it. The others I graduated with are at HSBC. We're catching a bit of a wave. A lot of demand for us at the moment. It's not that hard.'

'Not as hard as conducting *"Spem in alium"*?'

Alistair smiled. Then he looked at his sister, looked at Sebastian, and smiled again.

'My sister's been thrashing me at snooker,' he said. 'Why don't you take over?' He handed Sebastian his cue.

'Nice try,' Sebastian protested. 'I just got here, haven't seen you for years, and now you expect me to beat your sister at snooker?'

'Got it in one! I'll just sit here and watch.'

Sebastian suddenly felt put-upon. Trapped. But he took the cue from Alistair, then offered to get Sarah a drink.

'Lovely. An orange and soda, thanks.' She laughed. 'I know what you're thinking,' she said. 'She must be the only woman in London who doesn't drink.'

She has a nice laugh, he thought. And a *very* nice body. He wouldn't mind her thrashing him at snooker.

But then her phone rang and *sorry, have to dash*, she said.

Sebastian gritted his teeth. She sounded too much like Veronika, except for her fruity English tones.

He hadn't spent much time in Pall Mall. In the Oxford and Cambridge Club. The Billiard Room. The Smoking Room. It was Alistair's suggestion. The place was roomy and plush, full of chesterfield lounges and draped curtains with giant tassels. It smelt of cigars, leather and wax. And then who should walk in but Sarah. Looking lovely in a dark blue skirt, a ruffled white blouse. As she sat down, close to him, he could just make out the line of her bra, the curve of her breasts. He made himself look at Alistair.

Sarah stood up and perched on the arm of her brother's chair. Sebastian caught her lingering scent. Something musky and deep.

'Alistair tells me you're musical,' she said. 'What do you like, Sebastian?'

Hearing him saying her name ... and what did he like? He saw her sprawled languidly in his bed, stroking his chest.

'I like ... a lot of things,' he said. Stupidly.

'And so you're an Aussie?' she said. 'A wild colonial, then?'

Was she teasing him?

'I've been there, you know,' she said. 'I backpacked with two girlfriends. Had an absolute ball.'

'Highlights?' Sebastian asked.

'Oh, definitely the Rock at dawn. And Cape Tribulation – the rainforests. Fabulous. And I *really* liked Melbourne, too, *great* cafés. Not as pretty as Sydney, though.'

Sebastian laughed nervously. Was Alistair making fun of her or setting the two of them up? And then Alistair rose from his chair, muttered something about a meeting that Sebastian didn't catch. He really *was* setting them up. Wasn't he? He turned to Sarah, wanting to hide his uncertainty, feeling his heart begin to skip.

'Did you make it to my part of the world?' he asked her. Surprised by the calmness of his voice. 'Western Australia?'

'No, but I'm sorry I didn't.' She had the most magnificent blue eyes. 'I hear it's beautiful there. In Perth. I'd love to see it one day.'

'Right.' Sebastian tugged at his collar. Why was she making him so twitchy? The last time he'd felt this way was ... Veronika.

'Are you a graduate too?' he asked. 'Oxford or Cambridge?'

'No. I'm here as Alistair's guest. I went to business college. Studied events management. PR, you know. Gosh. To have his brains! I'd love that. But we can't have it all, can we?'

Sebastian liked her modesty. It sounded genuine. He even liked the way she said *gosh*, like an unaffected girl.

'Events?' he said. 'Tell me more.'

'I'm a functions manager. The Cavalry and Guards Club, in Piccadilly.'

All these clubs, Sebastian thought. Secret societies. Would Veronika have mocked him?

'It was easy to get the job,' Sarah said. 'Our father's a general in the British Army, retiring soon. Lots of contacts. But according to some people, I actually know what I am doing, so nepotism can work a treat if it's done well. Banquets, weddings, lunches, that kind of thing. Extravagant.' She smiled. 'Sounds just like my home – the one I grew up in, I mean.'

'Sounds rather like the one I grew up in too,' he said.

'Is that why you came to London?' she said. 'To escape a wretched family?'

She wasn't holding back. And he liked this. He liked it a great deal.

'There was a woman as well,' he said.

'Ah.' Sarah settled in her chair, as if settling in for a talk. 'Was she too much for you?'

Sebastian took this in. 'I think I was too much for *her*,' he said. 'Too pressing. Too ...' He heaved a sigh. 'Too extravagant.'

He was aware of her watching him intently.

'She wanted to do other things with her life,' he said, 'and I wanted her all for myself. At least, that's how it strikes me now.' He loosened his collar again, beginning to feel warm. But now that he'd started, he needed to say more. 'I could say I was young and foolish, but it wasn't that long ago. Maybe foolish will do.'

She kept fixing him with her look. She was eating him up with her big blue eyes.

'It's your turn to ask me now,' she said.

He wanted to reach out and cup her face. Kiss her.

'Are you … with someone?' he said. 'Or running away from someone? Or not wanting to run?'

She rested her chin on her hand. 'In the order in which you asked me. No, I'm not with someone. No, I'm not running away from someone. And no, I don't feel like running.'

Then she rose from her chair, just like that. 'Shall we try snooker again?' she said. She didn't wait for an answer, simply walked towards him, stood in front of him.

'Let me give you a tip,' she said. 'The aim is to snooker the other player, so you want to make it as hard for me as possible.'

Was that … an innuendo? He felt himself blush. Made himself walk over to the snooker table, Sarah striding in front. He picked up a cue, bent down, lined up. He felt, rather than saw, her lower herself next to him.

'It's about finesse,' she said. 'You need the right amount of force, not too fast, not too slow.'

He carefully positioned his cue and hit the white ball into another ball. It bounced off and went into a bare patch of table. Damn. He looked up to see her smiling. Not making fun of him, just smiling. He was beginning to wish that she drank to make it easier, to make whatever they were doing here … move along. But he made himself do it. Put down his cue and looked her straight in the eye.

'May I call you?' he said.

'Of course,' she said, as if she'd been expecting it. 'I'm often busy,' she said. 'But not too busy for you.'

69. Cassie

She still felt bad about getting stuck into Veronika, more or less calling her a narcissist. A self-pitying narcissist. But every time Cassie thought of that letter, she cringed. Not a word about how Josh might be feeling, just lots of soppy stuff about poor Veronika being hurt, boohoo.

She couldn't remember much about Josh from the *Figaro* days, except that he'd seemed sweet, a bit shy, surprisingly good on stage. Maybe Veronika had trampled on his sweetness. Who knew? But Cassie knew she wouldn't email or phone her. She'd let Veronika stew for a while, have a think about her letter. About herself. She really *should* see a therapist. It's done wonders for me, Cassie thought. I'm not taking a rotten cent from my rotten parents anymore, and I've stopped feeling sorry for myself. Most of the time.

In her *nicer* moments, when Cassie told herself to be more generous, she would remember the fun of being in Paris, she and Ron enjoying the beauty in a holding-your-breath kind of way. The Sacré-Cœur, the opera, the romantic sidewalk cafés. And especially the paintings, like the Matisse right at the entrance to the Musée d'Art Moderne de Paris, with all the bodies reaching and bending over like they were rolling off the edge of the sky. The way Matisse began with the blue paint and then didn't finish it, as if he didn't care. The energy. The incompleteness.

And then in the Musée d'Orsay, that amazing Vlaminck in a blinding kind of yellow. The Miró in the Centre Pompidou, where the red paint shivered across the canvas.

She'd told Anne Sophie all about those paintings, over dinner, on her first night back in London. When they hadn't spoken a word about the phone call. You said you missed me, Anne Sophie, she recalled. You said you wanted me to come back. You just can't say that and then not say it anymore.

Cassie wondered if she was going slightly crazy.

The bus screeched to a halt in Bayswater Road, right in front of Sainsbury's. A woman in a burqa rushed on, dragging a caddy of shopping and a folded-up pram in one hand, in the other a baby in a blanket. The driver, oblivious, jolted the bus into gear again. The woman reached for a handlebar and her caddy toppled over; the pram slammed against the bus door. There was jostling, a collective *oh* from the passengers.

'Let me,' Cassie said, standing and reaching across. She took the quivering bundle and sat back in her seat. The woman ducked down and collected her groceries – broccoli, a bag of walnuts, frozen chips, a couple of broken eggs. A mess.

Cassie stared into the baby's face. It looked like a 'he'. She couldn't remember when she'd last held a baby. This one had the faintest wisps of brown hair framing his forehead, little dark pools for eyes, curling black eyelashes. He gurgled at her. She put her finger into his tiny fist. He crinkled his nose. Broke into a smile. Little chubby cheeks moving, tiny hand waving. He smelled of milk and powder. He was too perfect for words.

'Excuse me.' The voice was soft. The mother.

'Of course, here you go,' Cassie said, handing back the baby. Cassie stood and let the woman sit down. An egg yolk slid back and forth across the floor.

She looked through the window at the pretty street, with its leafless trees and all the big white houses with bay windows, all neatly lined up. But it was cold outside, eight degrees it had said on the radio. She patted her bag of groceries, the food for dinner. She was the shopper, Anne Sophie the cook; the arrangement seemed to suit them both. Except Cassie kept forgetting things since she'd come back from Paris. It was as if her brain had been upended, scrambled.

She listed off the things she now remembered she'd forgotten: a bag of potatoes for Sunday roast; milk; telling Anne Sophie she was going vegetarian; paying the electricity bill at the post office.

She pictured Anne Sophie serving up the meal: her insinuating grey eyes and dark wavy hair that fell about her shoulders at different lengths, her fringe that never stayed where it should. Okay, maybe we're just friends, Cassie thought and rested her head against the window. Good friends. Shopping for clothes, eating out, going to the cinema, feasting on chocolate late at night, talking into the early morning in front of the fire about everything under the sun, from eyebrow shaping to the greenhouse effect to the melting snows of Kilimanjaro. Drinking in Soho bars, stumbling into karaoke singing 'I've Never Been to Me' at the top of their lungs. And more than that, Anne Sophie was a *good person*. She volunteered at the Royal Free Hospital, would tell her stories at the end of the day: visits to patients in different wards – geriatric, cancer, coronary care – where she would read to them, whatever took their fancy, although it was often just the newspaper. Sometimes they wanted to talk, and sometimes, if they spoke no English, Anne Sophie would just sit with them, *be with them*, she said. And she went to long training sessions, too, for volunteers: hygiene, counselling, intercultural communication.

Once, when Cassie had tried to tell her in a roundabout way that she was a good person, Anne Sophie had shrugged, said *it's the least I can do*. She didn't need to work, she'd said, and she needed to *do something useful* ... And then there was her lilting Northern English accent and her laugh, generous, full of heart. Large, like her body and her generous curves.

Cassie alighted from the bus, hugging her parcel, wanting a thicker coat. She lugged her way to their tiny house, climbed the stairs to the front door. She turned the lock, went inside, shrugged off her coat. She always loved this moment of arrival: the scent of books and the faintest smell of embers. She loved the *oldness* of the place: its green flaking taps, a rusty sink, a prehistoric bathroom with cracked tiles. It felt trapped in time, furnished in French antiques of dark brown wood: creaking furniture Anne Sophie's mother had given her. But Cassie was glad to call it home. Where she and Anne Sophie could be friends. An image came to mind: she and Anne Sophie at the women's pond. Anne Sophie naked. Anne Sophie – sensual, stately – sliding into the water, floating gracefully. *You're beautiful.* Cassie wished she could say that.

Dinner that night felt awkward, and Cassie couldn't work out why. Had she overdone it with the praise, calling the meal *delectable, cooked to perfection*? Anne Sophie had told her to *cut it out*. She knew she gushed too much, but still ... *cut it out* was hardly a prelude to something more intimate. They'd talked in jagged bits and pieces, about Anne Sophie's father, who was recovering from pneumonia, about Cassie's forgetfulness and how maybe she needed to go back to therapy. Anne Sophie's off-hand remark about her volunteer work getting her down, but *I don't want to go on about it.*

Nothing *flowed* in their conversation.

But then Anne Sophie put down her cutlery decisively.

'Have you heard from your Australian friend?' she said. 'The one in Paris.'

Cassie's face tensed. Was there something in the way Anne Sophie said *friend*?

'I think she's still there,' Cassie said. 'She hasn't been in touch for at least a month. I'm pretty sure I offended her.'

'You couldn't offend anyone.' Anne Sophie stretched her hand across the table and placed it on Cassie's hand.

Cassie flinched. Should she press further?

'I told my friend that you missed me. That you wanted me to come home.'

Anne Sophie squeezed her hand. 'And I'm so glad you did.'

Cassie could hardly breathe. She removed her hand slowly.

They finished their meal in silence. Then, Anne Sophie leaned back in her chair, looked Cassie in the eye.

'Have you enrolled in art school yet?' she asked. 'You told me you were going to.'

'Not yet. I ... I just haven't got round to it.'

'You should, you know. You have an artist's eye. I've seen you at that market. A good eye.'

Cassie chuckled, more loudly than she'd intended. 'Oh, you mean I have a good eye for pilfering?' she said. 'Odds and ends and vintage clothes from Oxfam, then reselling them. That doesn't make me an artist. Anyhow, I've already looked into it, and I can't afford it.'

'Oh, come on, surely—'

'I'm not taking my father's money anymore. Or my mother's. I'd rather eat gruel for breakfast.' She tossed her head, just a little. 'It's time I grew up,' she said. 'Even if I'm poor. If I keep taking their money, I won't—'

'Be a good person.' Anne Sophie smiled, a kind, sweet smile, then leaned across the table. 'We could make some money together, you and me.'

'Ha! What did you have in mind?' she said. 'Armed robbery?'

'I'm serious, Cassie. I'm thinking of a market stall. A good one, not the makeshift thing you've got going in Shoreditch. A real money maker. At Portobello Road.'

'But those spots must cost a fortune!'

'We'd have to apply to the council, but if we have a good business plan, a good product, we—'

'We'll be put on a really long waiting list. And what about the rent?' Cassie said.

Anne Sophie smiled again. It was … what would you call it? A mysterious smile.

'Just you shush now,' she said.

And then they went quiet again, both of them. Should I clear away the plates? Cassie wondered. Should I cut the strawberries? She lowered her head, unable to speak, unable to look.

'I want to talk about the phone call,' Anne Sophie said quietly.

Cassie met her gaze.

'Cass, I know I said I missed you. But that didn't … it doesn't explain how I feel about you.'

Cassie waited.

'This house, all of London – it was so dreary without you. You bring everything to life. Including me.'

Cassie took the deepest of breaths.

'And I admire you,' Anne Sophie said. 'I really do. You've done so much with your life. You left your country, travelled all over the world on your own. You opened a stall all on your own. And you're a real artist. You'll be a jolly good one, I know you will.'

'Thanks. Thanks. I mean—'

'And when I'm around you, Cass … The way your mouth moves slightly to the side when you're talking about something you love. And your shoulders hunch up, and your eyes have this fire in them. And then I feel – I feel undone.' She leaned forward, her grey eyes shining. 'Is this a bit weird for you?' she asked.

Cassie nodded dumbly.

'I just wanted you to know,' Anne Sophie said.

Cassie could think of nothing to do but clear the table, plonk the dishes in the sink, scrub them vigorously.

She felt a hand on her shoulder.

'Leave the dishes,' Anne Sophie said. 'I want to show you something.'

She took Cassie's hand and pulled her into the hallway. Pointed to a ladder.

'Let's climb up to the attic,' she said.

Cassie had poked her head in once, when Anne Sophie had asked her to bring a glass of water. She'd glimpsed unpacked boxes and a broken chair, had felt choked by all the dust. But now, as she clambered in, she felt the freshness of the room, the spick-and-span of it. The absence of boxes and that broken chair.

'I painted it,' Anne Sophie said. 'While you were in Paris. Do you like it?'

Cassie took in the walls: two bright red ones, two deep blue ones.

'It's beautiful,' she said.

'It's yours, Cassie. I want you to have it. To paint.' She ran her finger along the wall. 'Not the walls, I mean. Your own painting. Your real life.'

Cassie's hand fled to her mouth. 'That's so—'

'Good of me,' Anne Sophie said. 'Just take it, Cass. Will you? I want you to have it.'

Cassie looked up to the skylight, saw the clear, inviting moonlight.

'And no strings attached,' Anne Sophie said. 'In case you're wondering.'

Cassie reached out to hug her friend. Felt the warmth of her body, felt the lightness of a kiss on her neck.

'Thank you,' she said. 'You're … you're wonderful.'

Anne Sophie pulled away, laughed her loud, generous, hold-back-nothing laugh.

'I know,' she said.

She turned to leave, then turned back to face Cassie.

'I nearly forgot,' she said. 'Some guy called Sebastian called. He's living in London, apparently. He sounded Australian. Anyway, he wants you to call him.'

'Sebastian!' Cassie shrieked.

'An old flame?' Anne Sophie said. 'Or a new one?'

'Neither. But he *is* devilishly handsome.'

Anne Sophie smiled grimly.

'I was in a play with him. Years ago. The whole experience … was such an intense emotional melodrama. But in it, I made the best friends of my life, you see.' Cassie reached out and touched Anne Sophie's shoulder. 'And you're a … best friend too, you know, A. S.'

Anne Sophie turned around, walked away. Cassie was on the verge of calling her to come back but she couldn't. She just couldn't.

70. Sebastian

It was difficult, at first, to pin her down. Sarah, Alistair's sister. Sebastian said he'd call her. But he didn't need to, he saw her again after a drink with Alistair a few days later. She appeared like a fleeting apparition, on her way to some soirée, and he summoned the courage to ask her when they could meet. Just the two of them. She would be working at least four nights a week, she said, including the occasional Saturday. So they casually agreed to meet on a Sunday afternoon some time, that is, if she wasn't taken up with some family affair or a catch-up with her girlfriends. They settled on a Sunday a month later.

They met at Baker & Spice over coffee and crumbling shortcake. Sarah apologised for being so busy, folding her napkin and looking closely at him, as if trying to figure out where she might fit him in. She'd told him, over a game of snooker, that she wasn't too busy for him, but now, sitting across a table in a genteel café, he heard even more details of her active life. The hiking club. A day trip to Box Hill. The Epping Forest Oak Trail. A trek in Wales was also on the cards. Would he like to join her for tennis one day when the weather was warmer? Well, Sebastian thought, he could at least give it a go, even though he hadn't played for years. He couldn't tell her that he wanted to be with her, tennis or no tennis, win or lose. Instead, he asked if she ever felt tired, what with her long hours at work, her 'extra curricula' pursuits? No, she said, they energised her. He could see it in the lustre of her eyes, in the strength of her body, in the way she seemed to seize life with both of her elegant hands.

How he relished those slivers of Sunday. He took her to a concert and then a play but hardly heard a word. He was focused on trying not to look at her, trying not to fantasise about kissing her. They hadn't even touched, apart from the briefest of pecks on the cheek when they met and departed. It was enough to drive a man crazy. She didn't talk much, either, and he began to wonder if she was all horse-and-hound, the life of the body and not the life of the mind.

And so, one Sunday, standing in front of the Rosetta Stone at the

British Museum, he told her about Ptolemy of Egypt. The Stone had been *stolen*, he said, trying to make it sound more exciting. But Sarah wasn't impressed, indeed seemed faintly bored, by hieroglyphs, by one of the world's oldest records of human writing. Maybe it was her culture, he thought, growing up with history on every street, surrounded by, saturated with, old *things*. Did this make her care less for them?

'In the new world,' he said, 'such artefacts are astonishing.'

She looked at him sternly. 'In the new world there are old things too,' she said. 'I've seen them: carvings on a rock.'

Sebastian had to confess that he'd never seen the ancient treasures of his country. He felt suitably chastened.

Then they made their way to the café, among hundreds of tourists. Which made Sebastian feel even more like a tourist. Watching Sarah daintily sip her coffee (three sugars ... she clearly wasn't one of those anorexic girls you saw slinking down the street), he thought he understood what it was. The attraction. Of course he wanted to sleep with her, but what he loved was her sense of restraint. A kind of serenity that didn't feel forced, as though something was silent and sure inside her.

'The woman you told me about,' she said out of nowhere. 'The one you thought you were *too much* for.'

Sebastian nodded. Waited.

'Are you still in touch with her?' Then she flushed, bright red cheeks on her pale face. 'I don't mean to sound possessive,' she said. 'You're ... you're not mine to possess.'

He wanted to say: I wish I were. In every sense of that word.

But she was clearly rather rattled now, not serene at all.

'I asked because ...' Sarah stopped, started again. 'I think it's sad when love ends and people don't see each other anymore. When they have no idea what's happened to the one they loved.'

'I'm not sure I loved Veronika,' he said. 'I was attracted to her ... she was different from any woman I'd met. Unpredictable. Not all prim and proper like the hockey-sticks girls of my social circle. And ...'

He smiled, remembering they'd never even shared a bed.

'No regrets,' he said and looked at Sarah intently. 'Do you regret someone you loved?'

Sarah shook her head. 'I regret having my heart broken,' she said. 'If that doesn't sound like a cliché.' She waved her hand in the air. 'We all sound clichéd about love, don't we? Gosh. It was a few years ago now.

He was much older. He was famous and charismatic ...' She smiled. 'More clichés. Sorry. Anyway, what hurt me most was finding out how little I meant to him. I thought he was *the one*. All that. But he had other women I didn't know about. I was just one of his prizes. His trophies.'

Sebastian held her gaze. 'I wouldn't do that to you,' he said. 'Ever.'

Sarah coughed edgily. 'And I'm not so young anymore,' she said.

'Oh, you're positively antediluvian,' he teased.

'I'm thirty-four,' she said quietly.

Sebastian pondered. The older woman. Was this another cliché?

'And you're the loveliest woman I've ever met,' he said.

He was tempted to say that she was lovely on the inside as well as on the outside, but that would have sounded too suggestive. And besides, he hadn't met her on the inside. Not yet.

They finished their coffees in silence, and then she told him she needed to get home.

71. Cassie

She'd tried phoning Sebastian a heap of times, but her calls kept going to his answering machine. A robotic recorded message that she didn't feel like speaking to. In the end she opened her computer, ready to write that she was *dying* to see him, that she *desperately needed a heart-to-heart*, when she saw an email from Veronika. *Okay,* Cassie thought. *Let's see.*

It was a *really* long email. Cassie braced herself.

Dear Cassie,

You were right. Not just about my letter. The mawkish drivel. Oh my, those words stung, still sting, whenever I hear them in my head. I've done a lot of thinking since you left, and I'm not sure I can explain things, everything, my whole life, but if you'd be kind enough to read this, I want to give it a try. I've been lonely for years – and I say this not because I feel sorry for myself – but I'm beginning to think that I am not good at expressing how I feel when it comes to love. And that I might even 'perform love' for others. What a terrible thing to admit.

I think I did love Joshua. We were good friends when we were kids, when my family used to go and stay with Babička for our holidays in Starfish Bay. We did mad things together, like lying side by side on the road, listening for cars, and when we heard one approaching we'd jump up and run. We used to play pinball at the milk bar and then buy icy poles and sit on our bikes, licking the sticky stuff off our wrists. And we had quiet times, intimate times, when he told me about his mother dying young and how his father was violent. Terrible things, but he trusted me with them, and I think, looking back, that made me feel special. I think, in the end, I cared more about feeling special than I did about his suffering. And I abandoned him. He went to jail for two years because he started a fire in Starfish Bay. But he didn't do it. And I didn't visit him, not once. Then, years later, I ask him to come to Paris, just like that. I snapped my fingers and said, here, I want you, I need you, drop everything, come and rescue me. I thought about writing to him and telling him all this, but in the end, I decided he was better off without me in his life. I disappointed him, and I'm frightened I would do it again because maybe I'm selfish at heart, maybe that's all there is to me, and right now it's best for everyone if I just keep away from them and focus on my work.

And right now, I feel so sorry that our friendship ended the way it did. You were honest with me, and that's what good friends do, isn't it? Because they want their friends to be better people. Instead, I turned on my heels and walked out, calling you all sorts of names in my head. But you're a good person, I know that, I feel that, and if you can ever find it in your heart to be friends again … I don't even know where you are, but wherever you are, I'm sorry, Cass, I'm sorry.

Now I'm off to the laundromat. It's next to a little medieval church. If I press my ear to the wall, I can hear whole musical concerts. I think it's Vivaldi today. I wish you could hear it too.

Veronika

Cassie fired back an email, her heart beating fast.

Dearest Veronika,

I'm back in London. I didn't think you'd ever want to see me again. I'm sorry for being mean about your letter, and I'm sorry I left without telling you. I didn't leave because I was mad at you, but because Anne Sophie called me and said she missed me. She asked me to come back. You see, I'm selfish too. We're all a bit selfish, aren't we? And I couldn't tell you about Anne Sophie either because my happiness would have felt like slapping you in the face. I won't go on about anything now, just to say that I do love you, Ronnie, and I think your words were very brave and I hate the thought of you being so hard on yourself.

So please email me or phone me anytime, even two am, if you want to talk or just say hello.

Lots of love always Cassie XXX

Thank God for Dr Cohen. Cassie was so glad to see him again. It had been how many weeks now? She'd thought the break in Paris would do her good, in case she was getting too dependent on him, but now she realised she still needed him. That the butterfly wasn't yet free.

She didn't want to waste any more time or her money. Thank God he had a spot for a discounted client. She'd always hated the word *client*.

She settled in her chair, leaned forward.

'I know it's meant to be *free association* and that kind of thing,' she said, 'but there are *three* things I really need to talk about. If you don't mind, that is.'

He nodded. She thought he might be trying to hide a smile behind his big, bushy beard. He looked like Sigmund Freud, which Cassie thought was the *best* joke. But at least she hadn't fallen in love with him. She stared at the familiar, white-embossed ceiling, then back down at her Blundstone boots. He didn't respond. She fished a Tesco docket from her pocket.

'I've made a list,' she said. 'Firstly, we need to address the fact my brain is … receding … and I am becoming horribly forgetful. Next, a biggie, I think I am falling for my housemate. Well, she owns the house, and I guess I'm a mate. I don't want to move out or anything, but I don't know how to respond or what that means. The attraction, I mean. And number three on the list, I need to get into art school, and I don't know how to without a portfolio. I thought maybe we could work on my CV for a start. I don't want to go over any of the *unnecessary* stuff.'

She saw Dr Cohen take a mighty breath. 'You know, Cassie, it doesn't work like that,' he said.

She groaned. 'I know, I know. I just thought I'd give it a try. But if ever you want to give me a summary of what you think I should say in twenty-five words or less, for my application, I mean, I'd be really grateful. You're so good at being succinct.'

'Okay. Let's start with your forgetfulness,' he said. 'Maybe it's because you're attracted to a woman.'

When Cassie left the session, her CV remained a blank but she'd been equipped with advice on how to clear her thinking. Although by the time she caught the bus and couldn't stop picturing Anne Sophie, she couldn't remember if she was meant to buy a copy of *The Guardian Weekend* or whether she'd bought it yesterday. She'd also been equipped with a mantra: be brave and be true to yourself. Which was two mantras, really. And it wasn't all that helpful, was it? When she didn't know who that *self* might be.

That night, checking her emails, she remembered the self she *used* to be. Lucas had written to say he was working for a new mineral company in Perth and that he'd met *the one*, apparently. Cassie squirmed to remember how she'd thrown herself at him, how she'd swooned when he'd dedicated a song to her. Desperate for affection. Pathetic. And Gwen had written too … heard Cassie was living in London … what were the fashions like … Cassie couldn't care less about the fashions or the fact that Gwen had dyed her hair *blueberry*. Then another email popped up: Sebastian. He was working in the Civil Service … had just met a woman, and he thought it could be serious. He'd been working really hard but would love to catch up if *she* would.

Sebastian. Another man she'd thrown herself at. But she remembered their talk late into the night about his feelings for Veronika and how her heart had gone out to him. How he'd listened to her talk about Anne Sophie. Not much to tell him there, she thought, but *I would love to catch up*, she wrote. Because he was a friend, wasn't he? And she could use a friend right now.

She had a friend, of course, in Anne Sophie. But she wanted to sort out her feelings. And Anne Sophie would not be impartial.

72. Gloria

The view from the air! It took her breath away, peering down through wisps of clouds, catching glimpses of a hilly island dense with lush green foliage. It had been twenty years since she'd seen the place, twenty years since she'd been pushed onto a small fishing boat with her mother. She had told this story to others on the plane, the Friends of East Timor, all of them excited as she was at the prospect of meaningful work.

Looking down onto a brave new world, remembering the moment when she'd heard the news. She'd been ironing her skirt before school, watching TV: funny, the odd things you remembered. She'd seen images of joyous people running through the streets, and people carrying flags, waving, vehicles that looked like tanks rolling in. Army men in berets and baggy clothing. Small children, ragged and gleeful, and women weeping, or shouting out the liberation of their country.

Gloria could still see the principal's disapproving face when she'd glanced at the letter of resignation. Didn't Gloria understand that she was needed at the school, that 4D was making such good progress? When Gloria replied that the orphans in Díli needed her more, the principal had merely cast her eyes to the heavens, said *suit yourself*. Interpersonal had never been the woman's strong point. Leaving the school had been the easy part for Gloria.

The hard part had been telling her mother, who'd cried because her severe arthritis made it impossible to travel, and because she feared that her daughter might die of malaria or dysentery or dengue fever. *And I'm afraid you might never come back.* But then her face changed. She perked up. *You must look up your dear aunt, Filomena,* she'd insisted. Yes, Filomena. She would ring her and tell her Gloria was coming, that is, if she could get through. There would be a reunion. Her mother's eyes filled with tears as she smiled, then she'd nudged Gloria in the side, carried on about Gloria's cousin Estela, married with children ... I would love to be there, her mother had said, but Gloria must do it for her: have a reunion, be together as a family, the way it should be.

She'd told her mother she would be working in a convent, where she would be safe, cared for and pious, and where her mother could write to her as often as she liked. She'd written the address, in large black letters, and taped it to her mother's bedside table.

And now, sitting in a plane and clutching her bag more tightly, Gloria could picture the address she'd committed to memory. Her new home. She had no idea how long she would stay there. The woman beside her leaned into her. Gloria had already met her at the airport, exchanged a few words. Nicole: a nurse from Brisbane working for a group called Equal Health.

'Are you nervous?' Nicole said. 'I mean, you've never met these orphan kids before, have you? Do you speak the language?'

'I'm a bit rusty,' Gloria said. She didn't want to admit to being nervous. Scared, really. But excited, too, now that she was so close. Getting closer. To home. She didn't want to say more, preferring to sit with her feelings, trying to take in what she'd begun.

Nicole fumbled around in a pocket, fished out a pen and scribbled something on her boarding pass. She handed it to Gloria.

'My number,' she said. 'Trusty Telstra.'

She reached for a packet of cigarettes, offered one to Gloria.

'But it's no smoking on the plane,' Gloria said, pointing to the sign, hoping she didn't sound like a teacher. Relieved that she didn't have to say she'd given up, which would have made her sound smug. And anyway, giving up cigarettes was one thing, but what lay ahead of her was another big thing, bigger than anything she'd done.

She had imagined the smiling faces of unknown people who looked like her. She'd imagined them shaking her hand, welcoming the new teacher. She hadn't imagined a shabby, makeshift airport, sticky with humidity and thick with flies, nor had she imagined an Indonesian flag plastered on the welcome sign at the baggage terminal. Her training in Perth had not prepared her for the feeling of being overwhelmed, surrounded by throngs of people: nurses, architects, engineers and translators, a group of Portuguese nuns, a pair of Australian friars. She collected her bags and was assailed by a clutch of small children in grubby T-shirts offering currency exchange, rupiahs, American or Aussie dollars? *Boa tarde, Mana, di'ak ka lae? Taxi ba Díli!*

As soon as she stepped outside, she felt a wave of heat rush over her. She felt instantly heavy, befuddled with emotion. The snippets of Tetum, the dust, the smoky scent and liquid air seemed vaguely familiar, but she also felt the strangeness of the scene, of the place, as if she were returning to a dream set in some sort of eternal mirage. She looked around, hoping to see a familiar face, knowing that was crazy. And then she saw a man waving at her. He was holding up a small piece of cardboard with her name on it. He was smiling, threading through the crowd. A skinny man, diminutive, as if he didn't wish to take up any space. He stopped in front of her and smiled again: Gloria saw a few red-stained teeth and a long scar down the side of his cheek.

'New teacher?' he said in Tetum.

Gloria nodded. Anxious not to appear rude. But somehow her old language seemed stuck in her throat.

'Tiu Afonso,' he said.

He would drive her to her new home, he said. The convent.

He couldn't stop smiling as he took her bag, ushered her outside, then pointed to a derelict old car. It wasn't his, he explained, it belonged to one of the nuns, and he had promised to drive carefully. Gloria tried not to look alarmed. Was it safe? Was he a good driver? Was the car even capable of moving? But she must stop thinking like this, worrying about dangers ahead. She must simply squeeze herself into this junk of a car, her guitar case jammed up against her knees, and ... yes, the engine did actually start! And now she must hang on tight, bumping along on a potholed road but relieved that her driver, whoever he was – this tiny man with the huge grin – was driving slowly, his eyes watching out for traffic. An enormous white four-wheel drive went thumping past, two scooters zoomed in close, too close. There were so many people walking on the side of the road, their arms full of ... what was it? ... Gloria caught a glimpse of pineapples. Afonso turned on the radio. 'Slice of Heaven' boomed through the speakers. She had to note the irony. And then the ocean: palm trees and bamboo huts, rushing by in dizzying haste. Burnt-out ruins. Sad, burnt-out ruins, left to rot on the side of the road. Gloria knew what this meant: pro-Indonesian militias had set fire to the buildings, had razed some of them to the ground. The crumbling, vandalised walls.

Gloria was glad Afonso kept his eyes on the road. Glad that he kept silent. Glad that a familiar song was still pounding through the speakers, drumming out the sadness in her heart.

She saw a giant tarpaulin at the side of the road with UNHCR written across it.

As they neared Díli, the traffic thickened. Tin shed after tin shed.

Flaking colonial buildings. Lurid graffiti. *Departemen Dalam Negeri.* Gloria saw a dirty ute crammed with brave souls, some hanging off the back and at the sides. She remembered the busy market. The goats. She saw men squatting. She could smell their clove cigarettes when they pulled over to let a large van pass. So, not everything had changed. Was that something to be grateful for?

They drew nearer to the convent. The car pulled up with a rattle and a bang.

She struggled out of the car, put her guitar case on the ground. She wasn't prepared for the wreck in front of her eyes: peeling yellow paint, eruptions of cacti all over the walls, and a badly rusted roof. She stood stock-still, then gathered herself up: what did it matter, any of it? What mattered was the work inside. Her gaze went up to a giant cross, and she was hit by a sudden memory: a crucifix her grandmother had given her. Precious, made of pewter, not plastic. She had pinned it pride of place above her bed, but she'd pressed it so hard against the wall that Jesus' body, so delicate and finely moulded, fell off his cross. She'd used a reel of thread to tie him back on, but he was always falling off that cross, she was forever tying him back again. She tried not to giggle at the absurd memory.

Was she ready? She wasn't sure, but she knew she couldn't turn back now.

Afonso rang the doorbell, and they waited for some time. A young nun in a beige habit answered the door. She must have been Gloria's age. She was short and stocky, with a long face, deep-set eyes and an unexpectedly roguish grin. She gave her name as Sister Rita, then gushed at Gloria in English. *We are so pleased to meet you. Welcome, welcome.* She took both her hands and squeezed them. *Thank you, thank you. Obrigada. Obrigada. Come in, come in. Meet the sisters.* The vexing language problem, Gloria thought: her Tetum needed work, and her Portuguese was non-existent, although she could still remember some Indonesian, could even read it, if pressed, from two years at school before she and her mother had escaped. Indonesian teachers, Indonesian agendas. And Sister Rita's English was basic, of course. But they would try, they would have to try, to muddle through as best they could.

Afonso carried Gloria's things to her room. Sister Rita showed her where the girls lived – a weather-beaten Portuguese church with a giant bell outside. Classes took place in the convent, she said; the girls were fed rice and vegetables with every meal and helped prepare it with their own hands. Gloria passed through a corridor, saw various statues and shrines, rooms with ramshackle ceilings. She saw some nuns sorting and pounding corn in a large kitchen, and Sister Rita introduced them. Gloria tried hard to focus, but the names were a blur right now.

Then she was taken to an office, where an older nun was sitting at a desk, speaking on the phone: Gloria couldn't make out the language. She and Sister Rita waited until the woman ended her call, then rose to her feet with a burst of energy, rushed from behind the desk and hugged Gloria fiercely. Sister Julieta. She was all glee and cheerful eyes and she would be Gloria's supervisor.

She was shown to her room. It was in another yellow building at the bottom of a rather bare garden of shrubs and trees with yellow leaves: a bed, a mat next to it, a mosquito net, and a rack on which to put her clothing. Gloria suppressed a sigh. What had she expected? A five-star hotel? At least the nuns had access to a well and she wouldn't have to collect water from down the street in order to top up the water trough next to the toilet, like in some other places she'd heard about. The convent had a hand-water pump, a 'Sanyo', they called it. Another sigh suppressed. And just as she was thinking of, longing for, a shower but was too shy to ask, Afonso led her past a few container homes and haphazardly parked cars and a pigpen right at the end of the track to a well. She listened carefully as Afonso explained that she could shower but was warned that the water trickled and spat rather than flowed. No hot water. Not that I need it anyway, Gloria thought, sticky with the steaming heat. She must remember to keep her mouth closed as she showered and to swallow her toothpaste. She must remember why she'd come here. *Busa fuik, busa nain laiha*, he said. *Ignore the stray cat, we don't want to encourage it.*

She retired to her room, exhausted with this rush of information, this – what could she call it? – a guided tour. With the heat, the heavy heat, and with having to remember Tetum again, she was rustier than she'd thought. Of course, all of this 'expectation management' had been included in the training. She had to *keep an open mind and maintain a positive mindset.* She'd thought the training was meant for people who'd never been to Timor-Leste, but now she understood that it was meant for her as well. She lay down on her mat and made sure to keep away from the mosquito net to avoid getting bitten. Looking out the door through the gauze, she had a full view of the gutter. It stank of fish. A rooster crowed.

And then her life flashed before her eyes, the one she could have lived had she stayed, had she survived. Relief and regret mixed together. She'd been nostalgic about 'home' for years, but looking around her and smelling the fish, everything seemed so small, as if she were being sucked back in time. She felt a surge of nausea rise in her stomach, took a deep breath, told herself she was being soft, pitifully weak. And then something stirred, startled her out of her memory, out of her guilt. It was coming towards her: a scrawny cat with a thin coat, splotched with white and brown. It was filthy, mewing, making its way into her room, leaping onto the mat, curling up beside her. *Heaven indeed*, Gloria thought, and hoped she could soon fall asleep.

73. Cassie

Anne Sophie knocked on the attic door. She'd taken to knocking politely.

'Mind if I interrupt?' she said. 'What are you working on? Am I allowed to ask?'

'Leaves. With ink.' Cassie held up her nib and then picked up a thin brush. She couldn't decide, so kept them both in her hand. She had her ink pot and jars of water lined up in different shades of black and grey. 'I'm trying to work with ink,' she said. 'And … hey … just turn your head slightly. Move back a bit.'

'What? And fall down the stairs?'

'I want to paint you, silly.'

Cassie lifted the damp, streaked page from her easel and put it on the ground. She tore out another from her sketchbook. Anne Sophie stood waiting, bemused.

'Stand under the skylight,' Cassie said. 'That's it. Yes, turn a bit … yes, that's it … where there's a good bit of streetlight coming through.'

'So is this a portrait?'

'Why not? I'm done with leaves for the moment. And I graduated from trees in Paris.' She put her brush down for a second. 'Haven't the faintest clue, to be honest.'

'Well, just be quick, will you? My feet are killing me.'

'But you have to suffer for art!'

Anne Sophie smiled, blew her a kiss, and Cassie tried to stay calm. She dipped the brush, and with a quick flourish, she drew an outline. She braced herself, then made herself relax. She looked from the paper to Anne Sophie, back to the paper, loosening her body, her hand. Focused.

'Done.'

'Already?' Anne Sophie sounded incredulous. 'Thank God for that.'

Cassie motioned for her to come and look.

'What do you think?' she said, trying not to sound nervous. So much for acting on impulse.

Anne Sophie put a hand under her chin. 'Not half-bad,' she said. 'In fact, it's good. You've got my shape. My mouth.' She grunted. 'I need to sit,' she said. She bent down, untied her shoes and took off her socks. She eased herself into the only chair in the attic. 'Sorry,' she said and looked up at Cass. 'A tough day.'

Cassie moved closer. 'Tell me,' she said.

'A bloody awful day, actually. There was this woman with bowel cancer. Can't get her out of my head. She was angry, really angry. She's dying, and her son has only been to see her once in two months and she says he should have known she didn't have much time. He's busy with work, has two demanding kids. I wanted to say something … you know, maybe sometimes people need to be told … but she was so full of resentment, and I just kind of lost it …' Her voice was croaking now and sad. 'I said maybe it would be a good idea to say something to him. Tell him she needed him. And then she glared at me, almost spat at me to leave.'

Cassie put her arms on Anne Sophie's shoulders. 'I'm sure you did what you thought was right.'

'You don't understand, Cassie. You're supposed to just acknowledge the emotion and leave it at that. Not tell people what to do.'

Cassie felt reprimanded. 'I'm sorry, I didn't understand,' she said.

'And this chair's bloody uncomfortable.'

'I like it, actually,' Cassie said. Were they having an argument? Their first argument?

'You know, my mother could send us some things. Spruce up the attic. Or the *studio*, shall we say?' She removed Cassie's hands from her shoulders, rose from the chair. 'You should meet my mother,' she said. 'She lives in the Languedoc, near Montpellier. France isn't just Paris, you know.'

That irritated snap in her voice again. The tension.

'Are you inviting me?' Cassie said. 'Meeting someone's mother is … well, you know.'

She'd meant it as a joke, but Anne Sophie was glowering now, throwing her hands in the air.

'What am I going to do with you?' she said. 'What do *you* want to do? Tell me.'

Cassie tried to steady her breathing. 'What if it's not right?' she said. 'I mean, what if this is not right for me?'

'*I* don't know. So what? What if?'

'What if … it … I don't—'

'For God's sake, Cassie. It's not that hard. You just have to go where the joy is.'

Cassie wanted to move closer, she wanted to take this woman in her arms, but she just couldn't make herself do it.

'I've been thinking,' she said.

'Enough *thinking*. I want you in my life,' Anne Sophie said, softening. She opened her hands out.

'But I am ... in your life,' Cassie said.

'No. I mean more than that. I mean for real. I want you. I want to hold you and kiss you – take your nipples in my mouth – and touch you ... *all over*. It's killing me. Is that real enough for you?'

'Okay,' Cassie said quietly. 'For real.'

'You want me?'

'I want you.'

'For real?'

'For real.'

'Then will you let me undress you?' she said.

'Yes.' Cassie's heart was racing.

'I want to undress you with my mouth.'

Cassie felt a hot ache between her legs, all through her body.

'Is that alright with you?'

Cassie nodded.

'And then I want to make you come.'

74. Gloria

She ate in a hall adjoining the convent. There were others there, youths on some sort of retreat, it seemed. Sister Rita introduced them, then disappeared. They sat on the floor, prayed in a circle and ate rice and beans. Was her room comfortable? one of them asked in Tetum. Did Gloria have family in Australia? Gloria told them about her mother and the sadness of leaving, and a woman called Maria took her by the hand, told her about the new post office from where letters could be sent and sometimes even received. There was a machine, she said, to make the letters go faster. As soon as the meal was finished, Maria told her that breakfast would be served at seven. Through all this, Gloria nodded and smiled and used Tetum as best she could. Grateful for the hospitality, but ready once more for bed. For sleep.

But this time sleep wouldn't come, with all the thoughts whirling and buzzing in her head. Would she be able to manage forty little girls? Bigger girls, too, the oldest was fourteen. What had she brought with her? Knowledge gleaned from books, like Paulo Freire's *Pedagogy of the Oppressed*. She understood from reading it that pupils like hers should speak their own language, not the Portuguese that would soon be pushed onto them by the powers that be. She'd been given an instruction manual for Portuguese, but she would use Tetum words first, then the Portuguese version, and if the pupils liked, they could make the link with their own language. She would also teach them English, of course, as she'd been urged to do. She could begin by teaching simple greetings and pronouns, the basics.

And science, she must teach them science. She would help them investigate practical things like surface area, density, pulse rates, as the basics for learning land management, agriculture, economics. She knew nothing about these subjects, either, but she would learn along with her pupils once she had some English and the basic elements of numeracy and literacy under control. It could be done. It must be done, no matter how difficult the task or how slow the progress.

Hadn't Castro produced a miracle in Cuba? He'd sent literate high school students to educate the peasants in the districts, and literacy had blossomed as never before. A truly commendable scheme! Although she'd also heard about all the people suffering under Castro, and that news had certainly depressed her. But why did she need Castro when she knew that literacy campaigns had been the hallmark of the Fretilin years? When anticolonial leaders in Díli and Lisbon, developed their own pedagogy of liberation – of the land and the people. The Maubere Revolution.

There was no doubt that education was the path to freedom, the key to stability, prosperity, development. And she would be part of it. Right here, right now. She lay in bed and felt her heart beating at the prospect.

There was one more day left before she had to start teaching. She decided to familiarise herself with the area. Perhaps she would walk to the Church of Saint Anthony of Motael; she'd heard it was beautiful inside. She'd seen the place on the map and figured it wouldn't be all that far.

After the briefest shower in living memory, one that had barely cooled her down, she was feeling slightly queasy after a breakfast of tinned tuna and two-minute noodles. She could feel the beads of sweat running down her thighs. At least she'd known what to pack and how to dress: a sturdy hat, light long-sleeved cotton shirt and skirt below her knees. Modesty was imperative: that hadn't changed.

But other things most certainly had. She knew the place had been virtually closed to the world for over twenty years, throughout the struggle for independence, but now it seemed the world had come to East Timor. She could see, walking down the dusty road, that the place was full of men in different uniforms carrying automatic rifles. Men in sunglasses. They were staring out of big UN four-wheel drives, Thai, European, possibly American men, judging by their crew cuts. Australian military men. She passed some men playing cricket on the beach. *You beauty! Thanks, mate. No wuckers!* UN CIVPOL vehicles, vans, loud helicopters. But there were locals too, going about their business, peddling things fresh from the sea, offering her odd knick-knacks or approaching her on street corners trying to flog packets of Marlboro Lights or Portuguese bread rolls filled with sardines. They could see she wasn't a local; they must have sensed she had more money. Was it her clothes? Or the way she walked? She would have to take care. Yes, there were men staring at her, sizing her up. She had been warned.

She would need to figure out the bus. The route took her down the Esplanade, past the Motael Church. She wanted to go in and say a prayer but felt she should get back to the convent, after all. *Bondia, Bondia,* people said as she passed.

She didn't recall Díli, she'd been six years old when she left, but there were certain angles, splashes of light and colour that were somehow familiar. Faces, recognisable, remarkable, haunted. Might she be related to some of these people? There was a strange beauty to the water, too, and to the backdrop of the hills, some of them dry, others lush and verdant. She felt simultaneously at home and on guard.

And what would her students look like? She'd been told that they were smaller than they ought to be because of malnourishment, and she'd heard fragments of their stories before leaving Perth. Terrible stories. Some of them had seen their parents tortured or raped. Shot and killed. Some of them had been left behind when their families were taken to West Timor. Others had escaped to Díli, looking for relatives. Some had siblings who were taken by Indonesians to live with other families, and there were even some who had turned into scavengers and beggars. She would also be teaching children whose families simply could not afford to keep them, who were sent to be educated by the nuns. They would return to their families. They were not all 'orphans', strictly speaking. But she knew she must not ask them; she had been told this too. It would make them relive their trauma.

'And now we go to the classroom,' Sister Rita said.

Gloria followed. Apprehensive. It was her first day, after all.

She saw the pupils, *her* pupils, sitting in rows behind small wooden desks. They stood up immediately and recited in English, *Good Morning, Miss Gloria, and God bless you,* and sat down. *Dadeer diak ba imi hotu,* Gloria said, with the biggest smile she could muster. The girls were dressed in motley clothes of all colours, overalls and T-shirts with logos. Some of them looked about six years old, others about fourteen, and they were all looking up at Gloria. Some had bright and expressive faces, others looked distracted and moody. Gloria swallowed hard. She promised she would learn their names as quickly as she could. They seemed well behaved, sweet. Gloria let out a sigh.

But as soon as Sister Rita left, the girls began to shift in the seats, become a little noisy, then noisier, restless. Gloria saw a blackboard and chalk. Good, that was a start. She would begin with their names, then questions, with writing on the board, seeing what they could do, what letters they recognised, what numbers they could add and subtract. She felt her hands tighten and her head begin to spin. She conjured up the Maubere Revolution.

But as she looked around the room, she saw that there was hardly anything to use. There were no pens, pencils, paper or books. There was only the teacher, a blackboard and chalk. No-one had told her about this. They'd told her about the language, the weather and the food, and how students would need kindness as well as instruction. They'd told her that teaching supplies would be minimal. But *minimal* wasn't the same as *nothing*, not a bit. How could they not have warned her? She didn't know who was worse: the people who should have informed her or herself for being so ignorant. She thought of her school in Kardinya, with its bursting library of books, papers and pens for everyone, computer labs and sporting facilities.

She hung her head, held back tears, then looked up to see the students waiting. Waiting for her.

And then she thought: *Let's get to work, Gloria.*

It took a few hours to discover how much needed to be done. Some of the girls could barely read and write, while others were more proficient. But they all knew fragments of Indonesian, spoke to one another in their local languages, so Gloria divided them into groups and gave them different tasks and things to read. When they started chattering, giggling, nudging each other – when they acted like children, Gloria thought, what had she expected? – she took them outside to play. She let them skip and run and romp, release their energy, be free in their bodies, until – oh my goodness! Two wild pigs suddenly burst into the space and there were waves of shrieking and a flapping of terrified arms and a quick return to the safety of indoors. Gloria imagined her old principal frowning, denouncing the lack of civilised standards. She wouldn't tell her mother about the sudden arrival of the pigs; she didn't want to add to those maternal fears.

In the afternoon, they went to the church and sang. Gloria taught them songs from her childhood: 'You Are My Sunshine' and 'Waltzing Matilda'. They sang loudly, eagerly, these little girls in their long T-shirts and smocks, their hand-me-downs from some charity across the ocean. And yes, she would join them for mass on Sunday, she told them. They told her in return that they would wear their best dresses and plait their hair with ribbons, and they would ring the church bell.

'Ring the church bell?' Gloria said. 'How will you do that?'

They told her how they loved to run and jump to catch the bell, then fly up into the air. Gloria could picture them shouting and scrapping for their turn, saw the happy smiles as they ran, and their bodies went flying, flying above all their suffering.

Within a week, she was learning their names. Carolina, who constantly wet her pants. Another sign of trauma, like the frightened eyes, the sadness that would leap up in the middle of the laughter, the vacant stares through a window, as if looking for something that they knew in their hearts wasn't there. Lean, lithe Beatriz, who was always with Evalina, the two of them conspiring in the corner of the class, laughing at everything Gloria did. Constança, who was always cross and crying and interrupting the other girls.

And Gloria was learning, too, that there was always one more thing to ask for: more clothes for the girls, who wore the same clothes every day. Books, pens, pencils, paper. The bare necessities. She remembered, too, Sister Rita's longing for the goods she couldn't buy in Díli: Computers. Deluxe soap. Perfume. She'd seemed desperate for all three.

On the last day of her first week, Gloria took the girls out on a 'clean up Díli day'. They didn't seem to understand that the many plastic bottles littering the place were rubbish that needed to be recycled. The recycling would be sent somewhere. Gloria didn't know where. But it was better in bags than on the street. It was one more thing to teach them. She wished she could offer so much more, knowing everything they'd lacked: affection, food, footwear, medical attention. Forced to make a life, some of them on the streets, before coming to the orphanage.

And yet they knew, too, how to play and skip. They knew how to make joyful noise.

75. Sebastian

Six dates now, and he hadn't even managed a kiss. A record, surely. Was it because of the public settings, the awkward goodbyes, the quick dash for the Tube or a cab? The lingering daylight? Or maybe Sarah saw this as nothing more than friendship? Or dates with a cultural curiosity? Something to chat about with her girlfriends. He hated the word *girlfriends*: so adolescent, really. She'd said there was no special someone, but still ...

And then: she declared herself *free* one Wednesday evening. It felt like a minor miracle. He wanted to make a big effort. A restaurant at Claridge's, recommended by someone at work, but he already knew its reputation, of course. Old-world, impeccable.

The menu alone was enough to impress: Cornish lobster, duck breast, confit aubergine. Goat's butter pudding. But the prices were alarming: it would take a quarter of his monthly salary to pay for the lobster, confit this and duck that. But he smiled at the lovely Sarah, raised his glass of wine. Under the soft light of yellow lamps, sipping her elderflower drink, she looked both radiant and comfortable, as if she'd been to places like this since she was old enough to wear high heels.

Cutting his duck breast, keen to make conversation – why did she unsettle him like this? – he asked if she approved of the food.

'It's always excellent,' she said, then smiled. Flirtatious? 'But this is special,' she said. 'Being with you.'

Ah, he thought. The hook. His moment. He reached over the table and took her hand. Felt the softness of her skin. Saw the glimmer of her bracelet.

'And I'm glad to be with you,' he said. 'I can't stop thinking about you.'

There. He'd said it at last. Some kind of declaration. Her eyes were vibrant, as if willing him to go on.

'I think about you even when I shouldn't,' he said. 'Especially then. When I'm trying to drum up ways to stop the creeping encroachments of the European Commission ... or ... I don't know, checking the law on border controls in ... somewhere or other.'

And now I'm being pathetic, he thought.

Sarah was no longer smiling. He withdrew his hand.

'You remind me of my father,' she said.

'He must be good-looking, then.'

Jesus! Had he really just said that?

Sarah's face erupted into the biggest smile. 'He is,' she said. 'Extremely. And he's clever. Ambitious. With a soft spot for women. And I adore him. You should know that.'

Sebastian wasn't sure how to read this. Was she letting him into her life, at last? Or was she warning him about something that he wouldn't want to know?

'He was away a lot when I was growing up,' Sarah said. She brushed her fringe from her eyes, shifted in her seat. 'He's had quite a career, you know. He was in Northern Ireland and then Sierra Leone. He only returned from Kosovo last year.'

'He must have enormous responsibilities.'

Sarah nodded. 'And I hope they haven't broken him,' she said. 'He seems to wear them well, but you never really know ... what he might have seen. Or done. Or what came to pass, under his command. He simply hated writing those wretched condolence letters.' She went quiet for a moment, her eyes searching his. 'As a young girl, I'd bring him a cup of cocoa,' she said. 'To his study.'

Then she pulled back her shoulders, as if wishing to change the subject, and he was drowning in doubts now, flailing even more. Maybe this had all been a mistake. The intimate disclosure that seemed to be going nowhere. The ridiculously expensive meal. The hush of a fancy restaurant that only hefty amounts of money could buy.

'I'm glad you adore your father,' he finally managed to say. 'I ... I don't really get on with mine. He ... well, he tries to run my life. Wants me to be a huge success.'

Sarah raised an eyebrow. 'And you don't want success?' she said.

Sebastian swallowed. Was this another test? One that he seemed to be failing?

'I want to be good at what I do,' he said. 'Of course. It's a matter of self-respect, isn't it? But ... well, there has to be more than work, doesn't there?' He sat up straight, decided it was now or never. He looked directly into her eyes. 'I want to be with you,' he said. 'I don't mean just sex ... I mean ... Well, sex would be nice too, I—'

Well, that should do it, he thought. He'd made a right fool of himself.

A right colonial fool. But Sarah's face brightened and she placed her hand on his again, and he felt instant relief. Arousal.

'You've been the perfect gentleman,' she said. 'I was beginning to think you were too perfect. Shall we say next Sunday?'

'What about all day Sunday?' he said, emboldened now. 'Why not spend the whole day together? I'll come by, shall I? What's a civilised hour?'

Sarah frowned. 'It's just …'

'Just what?'

'I go to church on Sunday morning.'

'To church?'

'Yes. Are you a churchgoer?'

'Not really. Not of late.' He tried hard to smile. 'But … I'll come with you … if you like.'

Sarah leaned forward. 'Are you sure?'

He nodded. Unsure.

Church. It wasn't quite what he'd planned. *Nothing* like he'd planned. He had to stop himself from laughing at this prickly situation, at the irony, and most of all, at himself.

An organ. The smell of brass and the faintest hint of incense. Heavy wooden pews, dark beams, tiled walls of gospel scenes periodically stamped with crosses. Less ornate, in a way, than the Cambridge chapels with their elaborately stained windows, and different from the elegant simplicity of the riverside chapel of his school days. Different from the old limestone church on the highway where his great-grandfather had once preached. This church was more sober, more sombre somehow, than any of the others. Sarah standing next to him was singing quietly, holding the hymn book, not quite sharing it with him. She had a sweet voice. He tried mouthing the words. He hadn't thought this through. He looked around discreetly: older women, a few children, a handful of young women. One or two men. A baby crying on and off.

He knew by the earlier stares that he'd caused some sort of stir arriving with Sarah. He tried not to look at her. Wanting so badly to touch her arm, her neck, her hair, her breasts. He made himself pay attention to the preacher. *There was given to me a thorn in the flesh … We are all like sheep gone astray.* A sermon. Yawn. Sebastian didn't like being preached to. It made him feel … narky, irritated.

And would Sarah now be the subject of gossip, waltzing in with him like that? He looked around again. Maybe she'd dated someone from the church. She'd mentioned some of their activities, casually: fundraisers, sleep-outs, soup kitchens. Maybe it wasn't all that bad. A little more pomp and ceremony than he'd expected. A chalice. Incense. But *oh God*, it was interminable. The only thing that thrilled him was Sarah's body, her pure church body, standing next to him. A red sweater, blue blazer and jeans. Heeled boots. Her hiking gear, sort of, because she'd agreed to go walking with him after the service.

He didn't take communion. It felt too … it wasn't his thing. He wanted to shout out to the congregation: *I'm just here as the support crew.*

On their way out, he and Sarah shook the minister's hand. She greeted a number of people breezily. Everyone was staring at him again. It felt like running the bloody gauntlet.

They waited at the bus stop, ready to go off to somewhere to go on their hike to somewhere. He'd forgotten the details and it was getting cold – why was it so cold? – it was meant to be spring! His ears were beginning to ache.

'You survived the service,' Sarah said quietly.

'I played a game,' he said. 'Trying to figure out who was your old boyfriend.'

'The minister,' she said, straight-faced.

'Bit old for you? Although I'm sure he has great legs under that robe.'

She flashed her lively eyes at him. He wanted so badly to kiss her full mouth. But now she was looking up and down the street, waiting for the bus, no doubt. Damn bus. Damn hiking.

And then she touched his arm, looked him in the eye. 'I've changed my mind,' she said. 'I don't want to go hiking.'

Sebastian's heart began to sprint.

They climbed the darkened stairwell up to his room. He paused before they reached his door and lightly kissed her ear, brushed his lips against her mouth. He felt her body shudder. He leaned in to open the door and swung their bags onto the rack. She closed the door behind her, then turned to face him. And before he could make a move, try to kiss her again, kiss her all over, she pulled him towards her, pressed her body against him.

He held her by the waist and surrendered to her mouth until he took a breath, traced a finger around her lips.

'Follow me,' he said.

It was bitterly cold in his room, but he didn't care, she didn't care, as boots and jackets came off in a hurry. He reached forward and fumbled with a zip at the side of her sweater and then with the hooks of her bra, the buttons of her jeans. She slid off her knickers and she was naked now, shivering in his hands. She was beautiful, my god, she was beautiful, full breasts and curves and skin that the sun had never kissed. He watched her edge towards his bed and slip into his sheets. He followed, lay down beside her. At last. He felt hard. Bursting with virility. He ran his fingers through her hair and caressed her brow, cheek, chin, ran his lips along her collarbone and then bit her shoulder. He let his hand linger over her breasts until she took his wrist and led it to where she was wet and silky, to where he stroked her over and over. She tilted her head and gasped. Her limbs strained against his own. Then she dived down into the sheets and took him into her mouth. He was awed, ardent, wanting to be inside her now, and he turned to lie on top of her, his heart beating wildly. She pressed into him, their hips moving together. His balls tightened as she bucked and let out a high moan, the rising pleasure, the pure release.

He held her from behind, their bodies slack against one another, warm and loose and wonderful. So warm.

It was only later, drowsy in her arms, that he realised he hadn't asked. He'd been so eager, so ready, hadn't thought for a moment about contraception, but he was too embarrassed to ask. And anyway, it was too late for that now, much too late. Should he be worried? Did he even care? And he realised, lying beside her, feeling the warmth of her skin, that he didn't care at all. He only cared for this. For her.

76. Gloria

Gloria phoned her mother and managed to reassure her that all was going well, although the reception kept cutting out. It was hard work, she said, but important work, and the girls were learning bits and pieces every day. She didn't tell her mother about their traumas, or how she tossed and turned every night in an uncomfortable bed, survived on salty food. The rudimentary hygiene.

But she did ask her mother to ask her church to send books, pens and pencils, even toys. She would send a list via a fancy machine at the photocopy shop. A fax, she told her mother, and her mother thought her daughter was swearing and *you must go to church at once*. Gloria didn't tell her mother that, either. That she'd had no time for church. Had she visited Aunt Filomena? Or even just called? Her mother had given her the number. No. No, she hadn't called yet. She hadn't been able to reach her. But that wasn't true, if she was honest with herself: she hadn't tried to call at all. Or visit. She wanted to feel more settled first. She wanted ... well, she wasn't sure why she hadn't called when family was meant to be everything. When it would have meant so much to her mother. But right now, the thought of family hugs, a married cousin with children, tears of joy, any kind of tears ... it felt too much to deal with, on top of everything else.

Her father. Yes. It was time. Sister Julieta had explained to Gloria what she must do and accompanied her to the headquarters of the Timorese National Resistance Council. Then, to the Díli Diocese. They'd seen lists of people who had been arrested or killed. But no. Nothing. Concerned, compassionate faces. No answers. But how was that even possible when everyone knew everyone? Had all connections been torn asunder? Her father's name wasn't listed anywhere. Did that mean hope or desolation? Sister Julieta said she would light a candle.

Gloria had been at the job for three months already. She knew she needed a break. She needed to speak with some adults, in English. She'd written Nicole's phone number in her diary, knowing only that she was a nurse. But she'd been friendly enough on the plane. Welcoming. Nicole was surprised but delighted to hear Gloria's voice – *thought you'd died and gone to heaven* – and suggested they meet at a place named Uma Mutuk, meaning the burnt house. It was *the place to be*, apparently, full of *diplomats galore. And you won't get Díli belly either*, she exclaimed.

So here they were, exchanging stories in a restaurant. It was good to get out of the hot classroom, out of her ugly bedroom, and look at the small, pretty trees used for decoration, have some adult company. Nicole had brought along a garrulous New Zealander, Ned – a slight man in his forties with thinning hair who was working as *a translator for UNTAET. The United Nations Transitional Administration in East Timor*, he added proudly. He'd greeted Gloria, *Ita koalia Tetum? Ka Portugés, ka Inglés?* And then defaulted into Indonesian, assuming she was Indonesian, until she disabused him. He was fascinated by her story, said it was the best thing he'd heard all day, before ordering a round of beers and the whole fish with chilli.

Nicole had stories as well, working in an infant mortality clinic for displaced persons. *Heartbreaking*, she said, after witnessing a baby die that very day from a home-job cut of an umbilical cord. It was so damned noisy, too, with renovations next door turning the shell of a building into a maternity hospital. She moaned about the paltry supplies and the need for more midwives, but she was full of praise, *inspired*, by stories from doctors who had stationed themselves in the forest, kept themselves hidden during the conflict, tending to many wounded fighters. Their visions for a nationwide health system, eradication of tuberculosis, the whole bit. But *can my toilet situation be any worse?* she said, and then went on about the rotten food, the heat and missing her boyfriend. A bit of a moaner, Gloria thought, even if she was doing good work, and Ned was turning out to be a boaster, bragging about his UN pass, the fat salaries, accommodation with aircon and internet, access to the tax-free store where you could buy great spring rolls, patties and curry puffs, plus many cartons of beer. He told them about parties at the US embassy where you could sip cocktails, eat great pizzas and flush all the porcelain toilets you liked. Gloria didn't know whether that was true, but then she found herself warming to the thought of luxury. Not that she would say that, of course; she didn't want to sound like a pampered tourist. And now he was telling them about an Australian compound near the beach which had *five-star ocean views*, urging them to go scuba diving. Gloria shook her head. She didn't have the training. And besides, she thought, she had no desire to be under water when she was barely keeping her head above water on the land.

She'd been so focused on the girls, on how she might best teach them, care for them, negotiate the language situation, that she hadn't paid much attention to the wider world. Nicole told her about tensions between the locals and the UN, local prices going up, a housing crisis. Ignorant newcomers treating public places like they would back home, bikinis on the beach, kissing in plain sight. Not to mention all the big organisations who thought they were helping, like the World Bank funding school furniture but not the roofing; the Japan International Cooperation Agency fixing the electricity but refusing to fund emergency assistance. All the international do-gooders, Ned called them, but with no proper coordination.

'And what really gets me,' he said, 'is the attitude towards the East Timorese people. As if they need saving like the Kosovars, as if they aren't already extraordinary people with incredible resilience and courage. Against all the odds, they've won, they've achieved their independence.'

He knew the lay of the land, having been there for a year. Did Gloria want to join them? – they were off to the floating disco to meet some Peruvian dentists. She simply couldn't miss the drag-queen strumpet. Gloria declined. She didn't say that it wasn't her kind of thing; she used the old excuse of exhaustion. They all agreed to meet again some time. Look out for one another. That's what you did in Dili.

I must pray, Gloria thought. I must confess my sins. She hadn't been to confession since she'd arrived in this desolate place. She would confess for not visiting her family. But Sister Rita told her that Padre Vicente was away, doing pastoral work in a village called Maubara. Gloria was taken aback by the sound of the name. Her village. She knew the place was maybe a two-hour drive from Dili, she knew her Aunt Filomena was there, but she hadn't told the nuns about all that, didn't want to think about it now. She hadn't told her mother this, either: that she would go to Maubara when she was ready. When I have found your husband, she thought. My father.

She sometimes spent her evenings with Nicole's friends. Either drinks at the Venture Hotel, a novelty hangout made of shipping containers, or at the Castaway Bar, where they would listen to Timorese musicians play thrash guitar. Sometimes they gathered in their homes, cooked up fried chicken and noodles, and shared stories of death-defying moments with outrageous young taxi drivers who drove too fast and harassed them for far too much money.

And then, before Gloria knew what was happening, after the entertaining yarns and the music died, the stories became darker. Much darker. The stories of tongues cut out. The faces singed, and the limbs hacked off. Beheadings. Severed bodies. Rape. Electric shocks to hands and feet. The panic of evacuation, of people herded onto a barge and shipped off like cattle to Atauro Island. Mass starvation for those left behind. All in the name of independence.

Gloria began to wonder if it had all been worth it but knew she couldn't say that. She hadn't lived through any of those horrors, hadn't felt the passion for freedom. She had no right to say a word.

She focused instead on the daily things that needed to be done. The teaching. Washing her underwear in the sink. Jostling on the bus to buy food at the market. The country had been closed for so many years that most of the roads, like the one she travelled on now, were full of treacherous potholes that sent you bumping into the air. Locals carried their chickens in a cage; there was an occasional moaning goat. A shroud of dust would always hang in the air from the four-wheel drives and utes that sped madly by, stirring up the dirt. A persistent haze grew even thicker in the evenings on the beach, where the locals lit their fires to roast the day's catch. It should have felt picturesque, the sight of people cooking and chiacking, the ocean lapping behind them. But the haze, the dust of the day, all of it, brought on a regular cough.

One day she let the girls off early because she just couldn't make much sense in the heat. She roamed along the Esplanade, bought a stick of satay and ate it on the beach. She needed to keep a lookout, she knew, for shifty men on bikes and for restless teenagers lurking around. But there was something about being a native of the place that made her think she would know how to bolt if she needed to.

She wandered past the port where all the shipping containers arrived, saw people clamouring around the fence. What were they hoping for? Food? Building equipment? Maybe one of the containers would be full of exercise books, readers, pens, things she could use to give some proper lessons. She'd complained to Sister Rita about the lack of teaching tools, and the sister had replied that she'd been praying hard. Not very useful, Gloria thought. Not bloody useful at all.

She made herself keep walking, although she wasn't sure where she was going or why.

She could see the big statue of Jesus in the distance. The Cristo Rei of Díli. Nicole said she'd jogged five hundred steps to get there: a keep-fit regime, not a homage to a giant Jesus. Ned had told her about the magnificent view of the bay, the expanse of blue ocean, the sound of banana trees bending on a light wind. It was a gift from Suharto, that statue, for the Timorese people; it loomed large across the bay.

But right now, Gloria didn't want to pay homage; she didn't even want to see it.

She kicked a stone on the path, turned, and went back to the convent.

She made her way to the post office, hoping for some kind of letter, some news from the rest of the world. She'd already had one from Rosária, who'd told her about Friday film nights: she'd just seen *Ben-Hur* and next up was *The Robe*. Gloria found it amusing; her friend had always loved the classics. Rosária had also stopped hanging out with Martinho because he was *acting so important* since he'd graduated from the seminary. And she was *really stressed out*, helping her father prepare for the international food fair at Hillarys Boat Harbour. Scanning the pages, Gloria realised that she missed none of it. And she hadn't had time to reply.

Her mother still hadn't written, but a neighbour was going to help her, she'd said. Gloria had a feeling this could take months. She might even be back in Australia before her mother put pen to paper. The best they could do was listen to the crackles and the silence on the phone, try to splutter out some words, most of her mother's concerning her health and dire warnings about Gloria's fate. Nor had there been any news from her colleagues from the Kardinya school. They'd probably never heard of Timor-Leste.

She went to the big white building, the much-celebrated new post office. She expected something vaguely impressive, but it was just a counter with a man behind it, packed with people shuffling into different queues. She wasn't expecting to hear any news either, but still … she felt a rush of disappointment at being told there was nothing for her. No-one had written; no-one really cared enough to write. And suddenly she thought of Joshua. Their fleeting but lovely connection. He'd understood her feelings. The boy she had kissed. She felt a ripple of desire at the memory. She hadn't been with a man for so long, not even a secret one in Timor who she could safely hide from her mother. She winced, thinking of those clumsy encounters in her past. Only two, when she was studying, but even that would have been too many for her staunchly Catholic mother. But did they even count if she hadn't really enjoyed them? Had been excited, then deflated. Disappointed. Was that why she'd run away from Joshua? Because she somehow knew she wouldn't want to hide him?

She made herself wish the man behind the counter a good day, then left empty-handed and feeling a little empty inside.

77. Joshua

Six months back in Perth and he'd spent most of his savings. He'd paid off his trip to Paris, but he didn't want to think about that. He had to pay rent, buy beer and food. Not that the beer helped to drown his sorrows, and he didn't care much about food either, didn't really care about anything.

All that time at sea and all he had to show for it was a fucked-up meeting with a woman he cared about, who hadn't even bothered writing. He had to get her out of his head, had to stop thinking about her mum and dad, too. They'd been so good to him, but he hadn't once been to see them since he got back. He was just trying to keep his act together, lie low. Warra had noticed. The skulking around, the not-knowing-what-to-do-with-my-life kind of life. He'd given Joshua a bit of a lecture about staying positive, and Josh knew his friend had the right. Warra had stayed clean since he got out of prison, gone to TAFE. He was already an apprentice electrician, a year away from being the real deal. He'd given Josh a home and a bed on the floor. *It's all I've got, mate,* he'd said, but Josh didn't mind. He was used to making do, with trying not to feel sorry for himself.

He figured that Veronika was still in Paris, that maybe Cassie was still with her, and maybe that knobhead, Sebastian, was overseas as well. And who knew where Gloria was these days? He'd been over the seas, hadn't he, in a dirty, smelly, grinding job, and now he was back to where he started. Some days he felt like a foreigner in his own country, hating the glitzy shopping malls that seemed to be sprouting all over the place, hating the fake smiles of people working in the shops, hating the traffic and pollution.

And the hardest part of all was being out of work. He'd done a bit of bricklaying but hadn't been fast enough. A bit of carpentry, too, but hadn't been skilled enough. The Department of Social Security had turned into Centrelink, with people who'd told him he needed to *attend workshops to improve his interview technique.* They'd also asked him to name his *goals and four key competencies.* Josh had nearly laughed out loud. And at the end of his *assessment,* he was told to attend job training. It was *mandated,* apparently.

So he ended up in a place called a seminar room, full of hopeless people like him. Fat and skinny ones, dark-skinned and light-skinned, old and young, every one of them mandated. The woman running the show, dressed all official in a tight dark blue suit, told them she used to be an ESL teacher, but she could earn more money as *a cleaning trainer* for aeroplanes.

The Jobz Galore Agency, it was called. Josh wondered if someone was paid to come up with a name like that.

But it wasn't just any old cleaning, the woman was saying. She was standing up the front, holding a plastic toilet seat like she'd just won an Oscar.

'Stay on the dole,' she said, 'or earn respectable money doing this. Honest work to support yourself and your families. Night shifts pay more.'

She showed them where they had to clean in and around the aeroplane seats, inside the seat pockets, up and down the aisles. She demonstrated on a chair, and then on the toilet seat, with all kinds of brushes and products. She showed a slide of a toilet seat dotted with tiny specks, declared that it wasn't clean. Then held up her own seat again, and said, with a loud, proud voice: '*This* is clean.' Josh tried not to slip down in his chair. He had to pay attention, at least look like he was interested. Then the woman started passing round handouts with pictures of aeroplane seats and toilets, covered in ticks and crosses for *clean* and *unclean*.

'This is your bible,' the woman said, holding up one of the sheets. 'Lose this and you're out on your ear. Rule number one, be thorough. Rule number two, be quick. It all has to be done in twenty minutes. That's it. That's all you need to know.' She strode up and down the front, then turned to survey them all. 'So, how many of you are here for serious?' she said.

No-one put up their hand. The woman glared at them.

'So.' She frowned. 'Do you want to change your life? Want some good money? Hands up who wants five hundred bucks a week?'

Hands flew up. Josh kept still. He hated the whole herd-mentality thing.

'Well then, better pay attention,' the woman went on. 'I'm only doing it one more time.' She barked out the instructions all over again, with a crazy kind of energy, then gave them all a steely look. 'On your way out, you'll be given your time slot and entry badge,' she said. 'That's for your trial. You'll have to come to the international airport. Rear entrance. You'll see the sign. Be neat. Professional attire. No beards. No jewellery. Hair back. No cleavage. Yes, that's right, ladies, cover up your décolletage. And then you'll have to clean a real aeroplane. I said *a real aeroplane*. They're only taking six people. That's right, I said six. This agency only wants the best, and I don't want my trainees to be the ones to miss out. I want my trainees to be the best trainees. Who's gonna win, huh?' Most people put up their hand. 'That's it,' she said. 'You can all go home. Last one out's a rotten egg.'

They clapped. Josh sank in his chair.

He was glad that Warra was home. He was fixing up the garden, removing all the deadheads. He was often out with his family, spending time with them, so it was good to see his friendly face, receive his encouragement.

'Surviving them Centrelink people?' he asked.

Josh held up his badge and paperwork. 'I have a trial on Tuesday morning,' he said. 'As an aeroplane cleaner.'

Warra nodded. 'It's a start, mate,' he said. 'Good on you.'

Josh nodded. Warra could tell his heart wasn't in it.

'Want some grub?' Warra said.

Josh offered to make it. It was the least he could do. He threw together a giant stew, chucking in chopped potatoes and carrot, frozen peas, bits of meat. He'd make a vat of it and freeze it, and they could live on it for a while. Tonight, at least, it would be fresh. And they'd be eating together. It was good to have someone to eat with. His mate.

Over dinner, he told Warra he had no idea that Perth airport was so busy and how all the aeroplanes needed a thorough clean before they took off.

'Don't know why some people can't stay put,' said Warra. 'Save all them cleaners the effort.' He pulled a face. 'Hey, what's in this soup?' he said. 'Tastes like chopped-up boots.'

Josh found it hard to take any of it seriously: the training, the trial, the four key competencies, the toilet lid that needed to be sparkling clean. But in spite of himself, he was selected and recruited. The only thing he liked was talking to a bloke from Afghanistan, who'd thrown in taxi driving because the cleaning paid a lot more. A friendly bloke, who never complained or talked about his past and just got on with things. There were others there too, without English, newly arrived, who were grateful for the job and keen as mustard.

Josh managed to survive for a couple of weeks in what he felt more and more was an absurd kind of race: on standby once the planes came in, charge in and clean, then out of there in a flash. People left behind all kinds of junk: Josh found ticket butts, letters and chewing gum, books, even a bra. Found objects had to be recorded and sent to baggage services in black garbage bags. He passed them along like small, sad corpses.

He quit the cleaning job and let his beard grow. He slept in a lot, although it occurred to him that he wasn't really sleeping in since he didn't have anything to get up for. He found himself fantasising about getting rich quick, even thinking that his father had died somewhere, who bloody knew where, and left him a pile of money. But then Charlie would probably find a way to keep it all for himself.

Who knew where his brother was, anyway, he hadn't seen his picture in the paper for months. Last he'd heard, he was heading up some company to make some new-fangled instrument for cooking something or other. Which sounded like bullshit. He'd taken the rap for his brother, saved him from prison, so he could end up making money doing pointless stuff. But still. At least Charlie was doing something. And making money.

Josh had once heard on the radio that people wanted money for four different reasons, but he could only remember two: security and love. He understood the security part because everyone wanted to know where their next meal was coming from and have a roof over their heads and get medical help when they needed it. Wanting money for love was much harder to understand, if it meant wanting to shower people with gifts to show you cared about them. That wasn't love at all, Josh thought, although he wasn't sure what love really was or was supposed to be. If anyone asked him.

He'd also heard on the radio that walking was meant to help lift your spirits, make you feel less depressed. He knew enough to know that he was feeling depressed.

So one day, he made himself get out of bed and walk along the Swan River up towards Guildford. He started walking faster, and as he powered over Guildford Bridge, past the big old Federation pubs, renovated houses and neat little gardens, he felt a surge of anger rise up in his throat. Out of nowhere. Terribly. He wanted to pound something, smash something, throttle someone, see their gush of blood, and he was panting now, panting and hot, wanting to belt his father into a messy, stinking pulp and he was frightened now, by everything inside him, frightened and alone and shaking.

78. Felix

It was dusk. Felix sauntered through the Tiergarten, vaguely in the direction of the U-Bahn. He was due at the theatre at seven, but he did not wish to go. He wanted to linger, even if just for a moment, in the last slice of light, among the dappled trees.

It had been almost a year now since getting the company off the ground. More difficult than he'd expected – managing work and life with Max, concrete and the company. Each pulled at him from either side and threatened to tear him in two. There had been no time at all for dancing. And there was a thing … growing inside him, this ball of … frustration … like a juggernaut threatening to explode. His body tensed. He paced across a small bridge over the pond and caught a glimpse of a pair of lovers through the bushes, mouth to mouth, on a bench. He felt a swooning sort of agony. Max would be at the theatre waiting for him. *Jungle of Cities*. Felix would be late. His name was on the program. Assistant Director, it said. The small, printed biography held a coherent story. Felix wondered how he had come to inhabit such a dramatic disjuncture: to the world he was someone plausible, serious – but inwardly, he felt lachrymose, chaotic.

As he neared the gates, he heard the sporadic sounds of pigeons and sparrows. A raven swooped across the trees and rested on a branch. The theatre beckoned. But no, he turned off the main track towards the bird. Resting against the tree for a minute to catch his breath, he looked up at the raven who remained impervious. Felix pulled out his pocketknife. He wanted to channel this burning feeling somehow, carve something into the tree, but thought better and rolled up his sleeves and punctured his flesh. Ah. Beautifully sharp. A virtual paper cut. Nothing at all. And now his other arm. A rush of sweetness infused him before he registered the blood spurting and leaking all over the inside of his arms. Thankfully no-one was around. He licked some of it off. Pressed his forearms against the tree, now stained. He took out his handkerchief, wrapped it around one arm. Then the other. Blood pushed through. Why this lust for cutting? As long as no-one knew, what harm?

There was a time when he'd been filled with hope, even joy. Like the play in Australia – what – years ago now? Seemed like an eternity. He could see it in his mind's eye: the beauty of *Figaro*, people working together, inventing, making something to be proud of. Not the pressures he now faced with the company, the relentless need for viability, for audiences. He wondered if Veronika was still acting. He had liked her most of all. He hadn't seen any of them again, had barely been in touch. He'd meant to go back, he just hadn't got round to it. Perhaps they'd forgotten him anyway. Yes, he had once been filled with hope as he'd walked along the Domplatz, past the Ministry of Justice and Equality. A vision of how life could be. He stood there for some time. Until the blood dried. He put on his coat.

Day had been exchanged for night. He waited at the station. His arms throbbed. Perhaps he should try and get in touch with Veronika. The thought gave him relief. But how would he find her? The train rolled in towards him, swallowing up the tracks.

79. Sebastian

They all stood as he came into the room. Four people, who'd clearly been waiting for him to arrive. Sebastian gushed with apologies as a woman took his jacket, which made him even more flustered, tied up in embarrassed knots.

'I am terribly sorry I'm late,' he said again. 'It's entirely my own fault. I was working on something urgent last night and—'

'That's quite alright.' It had to be Sarah's mother, with her distinctly Scottish accent. Fair skinned, with hardly a wrinkle, and lively blue eyes. But her hair was dyed a brassy yellow, frozen into a stiff wave, and she was dressed like his mother had twenty years ago: a twin set and pleated skirt.

'These are for you, Mrs Cartwright,' he said, handing her a bunch of tulips and a small box of truffles.

'Do call me Elizabeth, dear.' She smiled warmly.

A man with papery bags under his eyes nodded. 'I must say I'm curious,' he said. 'What was it you were working on that was so urgent?'

He was wearing a tweed jacket, blue tie and a purple V-necked jumper. Balding, with fluffs of hair at the sides of his head.

'My parents,' Sarah said, and gripped Sebastian's hand.

'*Sir* Cartwright, a pleasure.' Sebastian shook the man's hand.

'Do call him Arthur,' Elizabeth said. 'And you know Alistair, of course.'

'Good to see you, old boy!' Alistair exclaimed. They shook hands.

They all looked at Sebastian again, as if wanting a more substantial explanation. 'The EU is preparing a treaty,' he said. 'Treaty of Nice. You've probably heard of it.'

He saw a sea of expectant faces. Had they heard of the treaty, and were just being *nice*? Offering him the chance to be important?

'Anyway ...' He cleared his throat. 'It's all about expanding the member states by ten more countries. Lithuania, Slovakia, Malta, et cetera. I received a call from the chief in our division, he requested some urgently needed analysis on some legal matters, the impact on Great Britain. We were, all of us, working round the clock, and I *am* sorry—'

'Oh, all that international law business,' Alistair said. 'We've got problems with our own bloody laws! You will know about the Afghan aeroplane hijacking a few months ago. The stand-off at Stanstead? Surely they won't let those hijackers stay in Britain?'

'A ludicrous law,' his father agreed.

'It needs amending, no doubt,' Sebastian said. Hoping he sounded authoritative.

The family was still standing. He wasn't sure whether he was meant to take the lead by sitting down. Or was that up to Sir Cartwright? The patriarch.

'Strictly speaking ... according to the law, they can stay in Great Britain,' Sebastian said.

'Ludicrous,' Arthur said, again, with a sweeping hand movement. Then he sat down, and the others followed suit.

'Oh, give the boy a wee drink!' Elizabeth cried. 'Poor thing!'

'Oh, please do,' Arthur chimed in. 'We've been so eager to meet you.'

'Oh, likewise,' Sebastian said. Was likewise *formal* enough?

Alistair winked at him. 'We're not quite as scary as the hijackers. It's a relaxed lunch with the family. Just feel at home.'

A dark-haired middle-aged woman with a thick waist scurried into the room. She wore a brown woollen dress with her hair tied in a bun, and a deferential expression. Alistair sprang to his feet. 'This is Carmita, our beloved Carmita,' he said and put his arm around her. 'We stole her from Spain.'

Carmita nodded demurely.

'She was our housekeeper in Mallorca,' Elizabeth said. 'And she was just so wonderful that we asked her to come and work for us here in South Kensington. And we couldn't do without her, could we? She's *family.*'

Carmita hadn't said a word, simply stood and nodded. She had expressive eyes and full lips. She leaned over and picked up a tray, offered smoked salmon and red wine, then fussed with the tulips and truffles.

'You have a lovely home,' Sebastian said. He wasn't sure if it *was,* actually. It was certainly large, with rigid Georgian symmetry, elevated ornate ceilings and a dark blue tartan carpet as far as he could see. Tartan! The furniture looked baroque, beautifully polished but unfashionable, and there was a glass cabinet full of crystal curiosities. Oil paintings of landscapes and portraits of dour faces; at least three grandfather clocks that he could make out. Three!

'Sarah tells me you're from Perth,' Elizabeth said, in her broad Scots accent. 'Australia?'

'Yes.'

'A very modern city, so I hear.'

'Yes.'

'Ach. So far awee.' She shook her head.

'We've all been to Perth in *Scotland*,' Arthur added, and everyone nodded, as if on cue.

'Mummy's from Ayrshire,' Sarah said, 'so Scotland's our second home. Loads of relatives up that way. In Ayrshire.'

'Oh, yes! So much fresh air in Ayr,' Elizabeth said.

Everyone laughed except Sebastian.

'Too much in fact,' she carried on. 'Goes to your head.'

They all tittered again. Sebastian was still feeling nervous. He felt he should say something; he didn't want them thinking he was nervous, or aloof.

'I hear Scotland's so beautiful,' he said, hearing himself sounding banal. 'I'd love to go there,' he added. Sounding even more banal.

'Time for lunch,' Elizabeth said and rose from her chair, the rest of the family following her.

Sarah smiled. Encouragingly, he thought.

Lunch was served in the dining room, on a huge oak table with lavishly upholstered seats. Gold-rimmed dinnerware. This was a relaxed family lunch? Sebastian saw multiple items of cutlery and tried not to panic. He knew what to do, but it had been a few years since he'd had such a formal meal. He reminded himself: Work your way from outside in. And then it came flooding back. Napkin on the lap. Soup bowl tilted away from you. Carmita served them soup as the family discussed the splendours of Spain and the Balearic Islands – the Moorish ruins and Gothic architecture, secluded coves and mountains, the blown glass, the wineries, the music of Catalonia. Sarah offered Sebastian some butter, and he heard his mother's voice: *Butter on the side plate first. Not straight onto the bread.* Then the conversation turned to Alistair's girlfriend, who lived in Sweden. Uppsala.

'So far awee.' Elizabeth sighed. 'But not as far awee as Perth.' She looked at Sebastian, pointedly.

He didn't know what to make of this. He sought refuge in the zucchini soup. Elizabeth turned to her son. 'And when will we get to meet your lass?' she said.

Alistair pondered. 'I don't know,' he said. 'Maja's still studying. Accountancy. Plans to come over for her summer break. Perhaps she'll join us in Spain this year.'

His father nodded with approval. 'Chartered accountancy. A fine career for a woman,' he said. 'It must be heaven – the two of you can talk numbers till the cows come home.'

Sarah nudged Sebastian. 'Mummy was a career woman too, you know,' she said. 'She worked for the Red Cross in Northern Ireland. They met when Daddy was stationed in Belfast.'

'Assisting Her Majesty's government in the maintenance of public order,' Arthur added.

'Romantic, don't you think?' Sarah said.

'Oh, I think so,' said Alistair. 'They should make a film about it.'

Elizabeth and Arthur exchanged a tender look across the table. Sebastian had seen a framed photo on the mantlepiece: Elizabeth in a slim white dress and beehive hairdo, Arthur with a full head of hair in a morning suit. He was not unhandsome, but certainly not as handsome as Sarah had led him to believe.

Sarah smiled at her father. 'Well, they haven't made a film,' she said, 'but there's someone on his tail, trying to get him to authorise a biography.'

Sebastian felt the need to acknowledge this. But not to flatter or gush. He'd met 'important' people before, but they'd never been the father of his girlfriend, or the woman he'd hoped would be. But before he could speak, Arthur was turning to face him.

'So you're a friend of Alistair's?' he said.

'Yes, Dad, we were at Trinity together,' Alistair cut in. 'Where Sebastian made all the girls swoon.'

Sebastian startled. 'I can assure you I did *not*,' he said. 'Alistair is being ...'

He wasn't sure what Alistair was being, and Sarah was looking put out. But Alistair was pressing on, regardless, about this *one* girl who Sebastian had kept hidden. Elizabeth gave Sebastian a disapproving look. A silence descended on the room. Thank God Carmita shuffled in to collect the plates, then brought in a silver platter with some sort of roast, and dishes of vegetables swimming in sauce.

Elizabeth cocked her head at him. 'Our cousin's forebears went to Australia,' she said. 'To a convict colony.'

'Well, yes,' Sebastian said, and cleared his throat. 'Some colonies in

Australia began as penal colonies. That's correct.'

'So are *you* descended from convicts?' Elizabeth asked. Deadly serious, it seemed.

'No, no. My great-great-grandfather was a free settler. An Anglican minister, in fact.'

Sarah nodded vigorously. 'I've found that people in Australia are quite proud of their convict heritage,' she said.

Her mother raised her eyebrows. 'Is that so?' she said, then turned to look at Sebastian again. 'Is that true, Sebastian?' she said. 'Are you proud to be a convict? Really?'

Sebastian nearly choked on his asparagus. 'Oh, no, *I'm* not from convicts,' he said. 'I am not a *convict*.' He tried not to sink in his chair. What was the woman on about? And why was she attacking him like this?

'Australia's a multicultural society,' Sarah said. 'A great success story, really.'

Alistair leaned into Sebastian. 'Mother's a little hard of hearing,' he said.

'Say what you like about multiculturalism,' Arthur said, rather loudly, 'but we need a common set of values.'

Sebastian gulped some wine. He needed to engage with this man: the man that Sarah adored.

'You've had a distinguished career, Sir,' he said. 'Arthur. What, in your experience, makes a successful general?'

Arthur's eyes lit up. He spoke at length, looking somewhere past Sebastian's ear, about twenty-nine years of soldiering, four wars and multiple operations ... tremendous amount of luck ... dealing with challenging problems ... delegating widely ... proving competence. Then he turned to his wife. 'And a good woman of course,' he said. 'It is on the shoulders of others that we prevail.'

Sebastian wasn't sure if this was admirable humility or a throwback to last century.

Then came dessert: crushed meringues with strawberries and cream. More talk about leadership, segueing into foreign policy, the EU, the role of the military since the Cold War. Sebastian tried to keep up, making what he hoped were intelligent comments, all the while glancing at Sarah, hoping for a gesture of approval.

But then Arthur rose from the table and announced that the men would adjourn to the sitting room for a drink. Sebastian wondered if the offer included a cigar.

Arthur poured the three of them a whiskey, kept talking apace about something different now ... *people chasing false gods* ... how so many people these days were *feverish, selfish little clods.*

Alistair grinned at Sebastian. 'He's quoting George Bernard Shaw,' he said. 'His favourite writer over a glass of whiskey.'

His father made a harrumphing noise, then suddenly leaned forward and slapped Sebastian's thigh.

'So, young man, what are your intentions?' he said.

Oh God, Sebastian thought, I am drowning in clichés. What on earth could he possibly say? Alistair groaned, told his father to *give the poor man a break,* but Sebastian knew he had to say something. Something to prove his worth.

'I won't do anything to hurt her,' he said. 'Your daughter, I mean. And my intentions are honourable, I can assure you.'

And with that, Arthur breathed what looked like a long sigh of relief before setting off on another lecture about the state of the modern world ... the loss of courage and integrity ... the value of sacrifice, faith, duty ... the need for military virtues ... but diplomacy as well, now more than ever ... had Sebastian considered a career in the diplomacy instead of the ... what was it, legal division of the Civil Service? He seemed like a bright enough chap. But he didn't wait for an answer, cranked up again, quoting some other military man, with talk of character, competence and communication.

Alistair rose from his chair. 'Are you quite finished, Father?' he said, then turned to Sebastian.

'I'll drive you home,' he said. 'You and Sarah.'

When they reached Sarah's flat in Pimlico, she invited him in for a coffee. But he was exhausted, he said. Honestly. He'd only managed to get to bed at four am and had set the alarm for ten, but there had been an outage in his building and the alarm hadn't gone off. He hadn't even had time to shave.

'All is forgiven,' Sarah said. And then she put her hands around his face and kissed him with an open mouth. So what else could he do but follow her up to her flat, where it seemed that her housemates were out for the evening. Sebastian had been there once before: it was a feminine space, white, with soft furnishings, candles, the sound of women's voices. But he'd never been alone there with Sarah.

'Is coffee okay?' she said. 'I don't have anything stronger.'

He sat down at the table, uninvited. 'Now why is that?' he said.

Sarah looked surprised at his question. 'Never needed alcohol, never wanted it,' she said. She looked at him intently. 'Do you have a problem with that?'

Sebastian sighed. 'Are you going to start grilling me, too?' he said.

Sarah paled. 'What do you mean?' she said.

He ran his hands through his hair. 'Next time, I'd like to be a little more prepared,' he said. 'Before I'm eaten alive like that.'

'Oh. Oh.' Sarah came and sat beside him. 'I *am* sorry,' she said.

But Sebastian was feeling sulky now. Everything he'd been holding back for the last few hours now came out in a rush: how her father had hinted that *my job isn't good enough ... have you thought of the diplomatic service, old chap ... your mother thinks I'm a convict ... I'm not a hero, like your father evidently is ...*

Sarah rose to her feet, kissed him on the forehead.

'You're the one I care for,' she said. 'Just you, as you are.' She walked her fingers over his chest. 'I am sorry,' she said. 'You're right, I probably should have warned you. It's just, they're my *family* and ... well, I don't know what it's like from the outside.'

Sebastian nodded, took her hand. 'I should go,' he said.

She began to unbutton his shirt. 'Make love to me again,' she said. 'Like last time.'

He kissed her deeply, and long, then drew away. 'I like my life with you,' he said.

80. Veronika

'You need to focus,' Antoine told her as he punched his coins into the coffee machine.

'I know,' Veronika said over the grinding sound. 'I'm just not myself these days, I could be coming down with *un rhume*. When will spring *ever* arrive?'

The machine spat out a café crème in a brown plastic cup.

Antoine handed the coffee to her. 'This will give you some … electricity.' He chuckled. 'In that last scene – you were like Sarah Bernhardt in a silent film.'

Veronika was disconcerted. Had she been hamming it up? Chekhov required subtlety, after all. Less Bernhardt and more Nina.

'I'm still lost,' she said. 'And I feel … to be honest, I feel pretty low these days.'

Antoine shook his head. 'But you are an actress!' He whirled his hands about the air. 'A shaman. A shapeshifter. A chameleon.' He prodded his finger into her chest. 'You can transform in an instant.' His eyes looked enormous up close, magnified by his glasses. 'I have given you a great role, so don't waste it, kiddo.'

He looked pleased, enjoying his little Americanisms. But Veronika couldn't even bring herself to smile. She couldn't believe she had been here nearly three years. And for what? She knew she needed to do something. Smarten up. She didn't want to disappoint Antoine or Philippe. Most of all, she didn't want to disappoint herself. She wondered if she wasn't having some sort of stage fright. She had heard that actors carry the imprint on their soul of all the roles they've ever played. Perhaps Phèdre had been haunting Nina and a cleansing ritual was in order. At least stage fright was a better than a breakdown. Was she having a breakdown? She couldn't be having one, could she, if she was aware of it happening?

But then as she and Philippe went through their scene in front of the class, she heard her voice changing register. She was jittery, less controlled, more emotional than usual. Maybe it was something in the lines themselves, or in the character she played. Nina, the young peasant girl.

The outsider. Or was it Philippe, throwing her off with his rather bloodless rendition of Treplieff, the young playwright? Or had Antoine's blocking and composition made her forget her lines? She'd memorised them easily enough, but once she had to move, gesture, *be physical*, she got muddled up, stumbled over her French.

She was relieved when the scene ended. Embarrassed by the faint, perfunctory claps from the class.

Antoine took her aside. 'You have to play the struggle, not the outcome,' he said sternly.

Sitting on the Métro, she remembered, she'd had stage fright once before. During *Figaro*. She'd almost forgotten. It had come over her out of nowhere, the inability to speak. Her voice just ... disappeared. Fainting under the lights ... the tight seams of her dress. The searing headache. Oh, the heaviness of it all. Charlie and Ana in the audience. A marriage proposal. Sebastian looking ridiculous. Joshua. The fire.

And there he was again. Would there be no coming back from him? Maybe she should write to him, after all. To clear the air. To say, I don't want to lose you forever, to not have you in my life. Your innocence. Your gentleness. And you want to be an actor, she thought. You don't know yourself at all. Joshua knew her. Joshua had cared for her until she turned him away. What would he be doing right now? Was he still at sea? Like me, she thought, all at sea, floundering in my work, my role, hardly able to squeak out my lines.

'Véronique!' It was Yaël, pushing her way into her carriage. 'I thought it was you!' She sat next to Veronika, still full of energy in her fluorescent sneakers, her spiral curls spinning out.

'Are you okay?' she asked in English.

'Stage fright. That's all,' Veronika said. Because she didn't want to pretend anymore, to make people think that she, that everything, was perfect. 'Weird, huh?'

Yaël smiled. 'Then let me tell you a story,' she said. 'A young actress was on tour with Sarah Bernhardt. She was boasting that she had never had stage fright. And the great actress said, *It will come with talent, my dear.*' Yaël leaned in, put her arm around her. 'There are ways of using this peculiar experience,' she said. 'Let it ignite you. Let it propel you into the limelight.'

Veronika was touched. 'You sound just like Antoine,' she said.

She'd had two letters from her parents, who, without actually saying it, were feeling upset that she hadn't been in touch. (She'd checked the last time … yes, well before Christmas.) Her sister had made her feel even worse because her last few emails had been full of laments about the children, lack of money, her *shit job* in a bakery … She'd moved back to live with their parents, but their mother was always telling her what to feed the children yet spoiling them with sweets and … on and on and on … Veronika had found herself thinking: ever thought about taking some control of your life, dear sister? Ever thought about taking contraceptives? She knew this was mean, unworthy. She knew she should feel sorry for Ana, but all she'd done was dash off some cheer-squad encouragement, her emails as brief as they were hollow. She just couldn't handle more misery right now. She'd have to face it soon enough when she went back to Perth. Start applying for jobs. Return to the old world she knew and which she hadn't missed at all.

She'd heard from Cassie, who had seen Gloria before she'd left Perth. Gloria had returned to her country, she'd said. She was teaching orphans, she'd said. It had given Veronika pause: were artistic ambitions less important than more practical ones? Humanitarian ones? Less noble? How could you pursue artistic dreams when there were mouths to feed?

There were no answers, of course, to such grand questions. And she knew what she needed to do. She had two more months in Paris. Her focus was the showcase. After that, she'd be going home. She decided she would let her return plane ticket expire if she landed a role in a French play, got sponsored by a corporation or married a wealthy Frenchman.

81. Gloria

Gloria knew she couldn't delay it any longer. It had been a year already. She also knew she could have returned to the officials. She had tried once before. She could have contacted someone high up in the church, asked for their records, consulted the new Commission for Reception, Truth and Reconciliation. But before any of this, before she filled out forms or spoke to people she didn't know, she felt impelled to *go home*. Many of her relatives had been killed, her mother had told her. But there was her aunt. Her cousins. Perhaps her cousins' children. She had to see for herself. By herself. She left the girls in the care of Sister Rita (and told them, quietly, to stop making faces) and caught a taxi. A taxi: such a luxury in this part of the world. But she had just enough money to afford it – there was little to spend it on, after all, except the occasional beer and a night out for dinner. And she wanted, needed, to take this trip by herself. And so when Sister Julieta insisted on coming with her, Gloria was vague on the details. She wanted to be alone with her thoughts, her past, her childhood home. She dissuaded Sister Julieta from accompanying her. It felt to her like something private, like prayer.

The teenage driver looked too young to drive and played rap songs loaded with expletives. He had unfamiliar dangling objects, and on the dashboard, plastic toys with big, oddly disturbing eyes. She had no idea where he'd bought them or what they meant, although she remembered that she'd never travelled in a taxi as a child; her family had been much too poor. And then she saw it: a small TV screen on the dashboard, playing a video clip of African women wiggling their bottoms. She looked away. Times have changed alright, she thought, and yet they haven't changed at all.

But when the taxi pulled up at Maubara, the boy-driver was meek and obliging. He only took half the cash she offered him.

The first thing she did was go straight to the beach. The beach of her childhood. She remembered the stretch of black-flecked sand, the lapping waves, the sun that made you drowsy. But it felt different now. Less carefree, less joyous. It was the sound, some ghostly sound that she couldn't locate, couldn't name. It was some kind of wind, something ceremonial, something dark, and she wondered if it was the souls of the dead, the massacred, making the island quake. Could that be possible? Whatever it was, she was moved by the sound, then found herself picking up a small chuck of driftwood and spelling out her father's name on the black sand: C-A-I-Q-U-E. As if it would help, as if it would spirit him back.

She walked through the scorched buildings and crumbling remnants of the old Dutch fort. It was bizarre to be back, to be filled with a strange kind of emptiness, seeing it all again. She roamed past a rusty gate half-hidden in a mesh of vines. She climbed the stone ramparts. The walls were overgrown with weeds. She saw an iron cannon she'd played on as a child, and she also saw, as clear as day, where the Dutch left their engravings on the turrets: 1756. It struck her now as absurd, this marking of territory, these claims of the powerful. The island had been carved up by the Dutch, then by the Portuguese, and then invaded by Indonesians. Who really owned it, anyway? She realised how close she had been, all those years ago, to the border of West Timor, where she and her mother had been driven to escape before they took the boat to Australia and were granted asylum there. Yes, there were strange splinters of memory, always on the move, from one part of the forest to another.

If she landed on Australian shores now, she'd be thrown behind barbed wires. Refused a date of release.

When she lay in bed at night, squirming with the heat, thinking back on her teaching day, the achievements and vexations, the tiny signs of progress, she would tell herself that she was simply too busy to ask them. That she lacked the energy as well. But now that she was here, in Maubara, now that she was closer to the father she loved, it felt right and true, it felt necessary, to move even closer. To find out the truth.

She spent the whole day asking. She stopped fishermen and men on bicycles clutching bags of fresh sardines. She stopped women weavers at the market hiding in the shade, peddling their creations: shells and coloured baskets made of seagrass. She showed everyone her father's picture and tried not to feel disappointed. Stupidly, she'd even stopped to ask children kicking footballs in the dust. *Ema bulak*, they'd all cried. Crazy person. Some of the children had run away from her. It wasn't what one did here, randomly ask questions to complete strangers. What had she expected? A swift and welcome solution? An answer to her missing father, her missing self, and to her mother's refrain that *he still has not come to me in my dreams.* Maybe she had lost her mind, after all. When there were people who could help. When she had family still there.

She saw the church in the distance. The church where they had gathered after the terrible raid. She steeled herself. Told herself she mustn't cry, mustn't get angry or feel afraid; that she had come here to see, to remember, to face whatever she might find. She'd been five years old, living in the forest with her family, when they'd come for them at night, and now it was coming back to her, the deafening noise, men in camouflage pushing them onto an open field, and guns, so many guns. Someone rushing her, rushing her mother, other people, into the church. They'd slept on the floor. How long had they stayed there? Weeks? Months? But she was only a child with no sense of time ... she wasn't even sure how old she'd been ... five or six? Her mother would never answer her questions. Had she seen their father before he was taken? Had she seen what they had done to him? Every time Gloria had ventured to ask, her mother had skittered away like a frightened animal.

And this is how it came upon her as she walked towards it: that simple church standing in front of the sea, a cracked, mouldy building, a bell at the side, half in shadow. It came to her now as it always came upon her: it was pain, not gratitude or thanks, that led her to bow down, offer prayers for relief, at the very least for understanding. She wiped the sweat off her face, brushed away flies and made her way inside. Maybe thirty people were sitting on plastic chairs for what must be midday mass. The walls were marked with mildew, and there was a simple altar with a dark green cloth. Modest statues on either side; large arched wooden windows. She tried to be quiet, respectful, but people turned around to watch her, as if they had sensed her presence, a stranger in their midst. She genuflected and made a sign of the cross. A few nods, some pleated smiles, but others looked sideways, askance. So many sad eyes, Gloria thought. What have they witnessed, or smelt, or touched? They must each have known someone ... the rounding up, the tortures and beheadings, the pitching of heads on forks. She pushed the images from her mind, watched as people rose from their seats, opened their mouths, began to sing. It was a melody she knew, with old Tetum words from her childhood, and she marvelled at the singing, the heads held high, the resilience, the endurance, like the little girls in their tartan bows and puffed sleeves, filing into church, standing tall, singing their lungs out.

Gloria didn't move from her place at the back of the church. One more song, and then the mass was over, people shuffling past her, nodding, wondering. She saw the priest approach her.

'A newcomer to our parish?' he said in Tetum. 'Or perhaps a visitor?'

'Gloria da Silva.'

'Ah. The new teacher in Díli.'

News travels fast, Gloria thought. The new teacher. Would she ever stop being new?

'Father Vicente.' He had a corrugated face, olive skin and salt-and-pepper hair. Thick glasses. His hands opened out. 'How may I help you?' he said.

She wondered what his eyes had seen.

'I am looking for my father,' she said and handed him her photo.

He stared at it for some time, then slowly lifted his head, looked her in the eyes.

'He is dead, isn't he?'

Father Vicente nodded. She felt her throat thicken.

'He was a good man, your father.'

A good man, she thought. A dead man.

'How did you know him?' she said.

'He was in the resistance army. He went into the forest. I brought food to all the men.'

'Is he … do you know if he's buried somewhere?'

Father Vicente shook his head. 'I'm sorry,' he said. 'You are not the first to come to me. So many people have lost their loved ones.' He reached out his hand, placed it on her arm. 'That doesn't make it any easier for you.'

He breathed in deeply, withdrew his hand.

'I can show you where it took place,' he said. 'If that is what you want.'

'It?'

He didn't take his eyes from her face. 'The massacre,' he said.

Is that what she wanted? Would that make it more real for her? Would it feel more or less painful to see the place where her father had suffered? Had he heard the sound of rifles? The shouts? Had he held his breath and waited to be dead?

She nodded to Father Vicente.

They walked towards the priest's old car, covered in the dust of the day, and he opened the door for her. His presence somehow helped. He had taken food to her father. He had known her father. Two good men, together.

It was another bumpy ride, but as she looked through the window, she was struck once more by the green. The intensity. She remembered the golden-green cliffs of her childhood until a storm rushed in and the sky grew dark and she would have to run for shelter.

They pulled up in a clearing and stepped out of the car. She saw a large building. Bruised-looking, smudged with graffiti that she didn't understand. An empty swimming pool with a desolate carpet of spinifex. Another building, bright white and stark, with a cross emblazoned on the front façade.

Father Vicente looked around, looked back at her.

'This is the place,' he said. Liquiçá. 'It was the afternoon. Your father was returning from a refugee camp. And then …' He pointed to the church.

She could feel her throat thickening again, her blood rising. 'It was the Indonesians, wasn't it?'

'No.'

'No?'

'Cousin against cousin,' he said. 'The Indonesian military forces set us against each other.'

He stood with his hands clasped in front of him, looking penitent.

Gloria searched for the right words. 'We call it …' She stopped. 'We call it divide and conquer.'

She looked around again. She felt the ugliness. The waste.

'It all feels so empty,' she said. 'So pointless.'

He nodded. 'It does,' he said. 'But we are never alone. Never.'

She turned to face him. This brave man, whose faith – at least it seemed – had never wavered.

'I'm not ready to go back to Díli,' she said. 'Do you mind if I walk around?'

'Of course not. I will wait for you.' He motioned towards his car.

Gloria wandered back past the old mansion, with its sad, waterless swimming pool choked with ugly spinifex. She kept her eyes away from the church, trying not to picture the bodies, the rifles, the moment. She climbed up a rocky slope, needing to walk now, needing to use her limbs. She could smell the salt of the ocean, climbed further, looked over the top of the slope. A statue. Gloria moved closer, saw the grubby hands of the Madonna and her bright blonde hair. It struck her now – the brightness, the western blonde Madonna – as ludicrous, almost obscene. She shuddered in the heat. What had she been hoping for? She knew that she should pray, pray for the soul of her father, for all the lost, discarded souls, but it felt like someone, some invisible hand, had packed stones into her ribs. Her father had been murdered in a church. All the beautiful life of him, murdered in a church. And how could she tell her mother?

They drove back to the village without speaking until Gloria could no longer bear the silence, the questions, the doubt.

'Was He there then?' she asked. 'God?'

'He was.'

'When my father ... was massacred?'

'He was there.'

'How do you know?'

'He was there.'

'So why didn't He stop the killing?' She leaned against the window, tears beginning to fall.

'I can't answer that question. I only know that the question has broken many people.' He turned to face her, quickly, then turned back to watch the road. 'Your work is hard in the school?' he said. 'Sister Rita tells me you need more supplies, and the girls ... some of them have seen so much that is wrong.'

'I do what I can,' she said quietly.

'Yes. You make repair.'

Gloria glanced at his kindly face.

'We need a school in Maubara,' he said. 'It's a walk from the town centre. Flat land, not too many trees.' He cleared his throat. 'But most important is a teacher.'

Gloria heard the implication. The invitation.

'The land overlooks the sea,' he said, keeping his eyes on the road. 'You could almost forget that terrible things happened there.'

She turned to look at him. A man who must have found some kind of peace.

'And you want me to be the teacher?' she said.

'There are many children who need an education.' He glanced at her quickly, then turned back to look at the road. 'I am not wanting to pressure you,' he said. 'I am asking you, right now, not to say no.'

A compliment, surely. But also daunting. No, terrifying.

'You have family here in Maubara?' he asked.

'I do,' she said. 'My aunt. I have other relatives. I know that many are dead … Like my father …' She could feel her voice breaking up again. And then she remembered a line from a poem she'd once read, a poem she didn't understand a word of but it had persisted in her memory … *so many, I had not thought death had undone so many.*

'And why aren't you with your family?' His voice was gently insistent.

She had been so busy with the girls, so taken up with all her tasks. She thought she would wait for her holidays, she wasn't sure when to contact them, why she hadn't done that yet when her mother had been so keen, she didn't know why she'd been so haphazard.

'Do you know Filomena Santos?' Gloria asked.

'She was at mass this morning. With her children and grandchildren,' Father Vicente said.

By now they had reached the village. He turned the car down a rather rudimentary track. Didn't he say he would drive her back to Díli? Gloria wasn't sure where he was heading. And then the penny dropped. Father Vicente was taking her to her aunt.

He pulled up in front of a makeshift building made out of large grey bricks. It had a tin roof in urgent need of repair. There was a chicken running around and a motorbike parked out the front. There were two grey plastic chairs. The usual, Gloria thought. The ubiquitous. But what would she say, now that she was here? Now that Father Vincente had more or less told her that this was the right thing to do. Would it be rude to arrive without warning? But her mother had asked her again, insisted that Gloria visit. More than visit: connect. It mattered, didn't it? Really mattered. And what might they say about her father? Did they even know about her father? Of course they would know.

Was that why she had put it off for so long? This visit. This connection.

Father Vicente stepped out of the car, but Gloria couldn't move.

She saw a man appear at the door. He was slight, of medium height, with a head of rather wild hair. She saw the two men speaking and then this unknown man smiling ear to ear. She heard him make a whooping noise, a noise of surprise, delight. Who was he? Her cousin's husband, maybe?

She stepped out of the car, ready to say something, hello, how are you, whatever came out of her mouth, but before she could speak, he ran towards her, wrapped her up in a hug. And then there were children, three children, their eyes wide at the sight of a newcomer. A stranger. The man pointed at himself, *Guido*, then waved the children towards her: *Salvador, Tiago, Miguel*. It was a rush, a blur, as he ushered them all inside, waved at the kitchen, as if to welcome it, welcome her: more plastic chairs and a large ashen oven and bench, and some sort of smell that Gloria couldn't name.

She looked through the window and saw two more children playing with a skipping rope in a courtyard. A gutter running through it. And there were three more of them, apparently, out with their mother *gone to market*. Some smiles from the children, some shy chatter that Gloria couldn't quite catch, then they rushed back to their skipping. Gloria couldn't figure out whose children they were. Surely not all Estela's children? How many was that? Eight?

She heard Tiu Guido calling out a name: *Filomena*.

And there she was: appearing out of nowhere, stepping into the kitchen. She looks like my mother, Gloria thought, and felt a pang of recognition, and guilt. A wiry woman, much thinner than Gloria's mother, wearing a green shirt and a tais. She had bushy eyebrows and greying hair, tied back. Black freckles on her face. Her wide smile just like Gloria's mother.

Gloria! Gloria! she said, her face lit up with wonder and surprise.

She buried her head into Gloria's chest and threw her arms around her. They embraced for what seemed like a long time, with tears and cries and then a shriek of joy as she drew away and rushed to the stovetop, fussing around Father Vicente, asking them to stay for dinner. The familiar priest and this unknown member of the family, come to see them, her face bright with joy. Then she insisted on showing Gloria around the house, gesturing, crying out and apologising, another rush of words, begging Gloria to stay for as long as she liked, there would be room, plenty of room. They had been expecting her. They had heard she was in Díli. Why hadn't she come sooner? Gloria apologised. She kept nodding and smiling. There were more tears. She was staying at the convent in Díli, but she thanked her anyway. How can I not thank her, she thought. How can I make up for the time when I didn't come to see her?

They stood outside, drinking sweet coffee from a cup, when a woman pulled up on a motorbike, with a little girl on her hip, two more balanced on the motorbike, along with several bags of shopping in mesh bags.

An impressive feat, Gloria thought, as she approached her, offering to help. The woman was wearing plain trousers and a yellow T-shirt, with her hair wrapped up in a scarf. She had warm eyes and a beaming smile. *Gloria is here,* her aunt called out. It was Estela. *Bem-vindo, di'ak ka lae?* she said to Gloria. Two girls jumped up and down. *Malae, Malae,* they said, with excitement. *Lae, nia la'os ema fuik nia ita nia familia!* Gloria knew enough to know the Tetum: *No, she's not a foreigner, she's like family, she's one of us.*

Tiu Guido said grace under a large picture of an effeminate Jesus tacked to the wall, and Gloria tried to make appreciative noises as she ate: old buffalo with rice, pumpkin and papaya leaves. She tried hard to make conversation. She was the cousin from Australia. A new teacher, Father Vicente explained to the children, who were noisy and distracted. Miguel was rattling some plastic object with rings, and Lara was helping herself to Mafalda's dinner. Estela tried to keep them all in line while Filomena was asking Gloria questions: did Gloria like Díli? Was her room comfortable at the convent? When would she like to stay over? Through all this, Gloria used Tetum as best she could. And she waited: waited to hear whether anyone knew about the death of her father. Surely, they would know. Surely, they would offer their condolences. But she couldn't, wouldn't, raise the subject. The subject. As if her father was merely a topic of conversation. So Gloria spoke about her mother instead: her good friends, her work with the church, and how proud she was of her daughter. Because she *was* proud, Gloria told them: of her education, her teaching, her coming home to help the children. She didn't tell them how much her mother worried about the dangers, both real and imagined, that might befall her only living child.

And then, out of nowhere, Filomena took Gloria's hand and held it tight. Asked her, in halting Tetum, if she had come to look for her father.

Gloria nodded. She tried to speak but the words were stuck in her throat.

'We would have told you,' Filomena said.

Was there an edge of rebuke in her voice? And why didn't she tell my mother? Gloria thought. Why didn't she set her mind at rest?

Guido cleared his throat. 'We tried to phone your mother,' he said. 'We ...' He looked across to his wife.

'She changed the subject,' Filomena said.

Gloria sat back, stunned, speechless still. All those years of torment for her mother. All those years spent wanting an answer. Wasted, pointless years. Or had her mother refused to give up hope? Thinking that if she didn't hear the words, then his death wasn't a reality. And what kind of thinking was that?

'It was two years ago,' Filomena said. 'He was a good man. A brave man.'

82. Sebastian

He'd been meaning to phone Cassie for some time, but what with one thing and another – work, more work, and Sarah, always Sarah, in his arms, on his mind – he'd finally got in touch. Cassie had suggested meeting at the Tate Modern, but when he turned up at the designated time and place, she was nowhere to be found. He'd left a message on her phone, but she hadn't called him back. He checked his diary for the details: he'd got them right, so she must have got them wrong. He felt a stab of irritation. It was just like her, he thought, so scatty, so spur-of-the-moment and who-cares-about-organisation. And he'd taken the afternoon off, especially. Still, he owed it to her, a friend who'd listened to his sob stories, given him warm hugs.

He took one more look at his phone, closed it, sighed. Looked up and – there she was! On the other side of the entrance. A tiny figure wearing the Trinity scarf he'd given her in Cambridge. She was jumping up and down, waving madly, and he waved back, suddenly delighted. She ran across the floor, swerving her way around people, and crashed into him with a fierce embrace. He was dizzy and laughing and lifted her up, whizzed her around. She tipped her head back, laughing too, taking deep breaths when he stopped.

'Cass!' He squeezed her hand. She kissed him on the cheek.

'My God! Sebastian Harper-Jones! It's *so* good to see you!'

Hurried explanations about the bungled meeting: she'd messed up the time (of course, Sebastian thought) and left her phone at home (why was he not surprised?) She was buzzing with apologies, stricken with guilt, but he *was* pleased to see her. *Really* pleased. In her bright red T-shirt and baggy pants.

'Your hair,' he said. 'You're not blonde anymore.'

She patted her mousy brown hair. 'I'm not a lot of things anymore,' she said and kissed him on the cheek again. 'You *do* look handsome, you old thing, just as handsome as ever.'

He patted his stomach. 'Well, I am glad you think so. I was concerned about the Heathrow injection. I was getting a pot belly for a while there. Had to get rid of it.'

She drew away, took his hands.

'So what are you doing, Sebbie? Tell me all about it. Everything. I want to know everything.'

He suggested coffee but she shook her head. 'Hey, last time I saw you, you had a horrible limp and some sort of issue with your neck.'

'Ah! Saved by physiotherapy. For a whole year after that. Did wonders. Still do a bit. Can't look at a game of rugby anymore, though, it leaves me cold.'

He took her hand again.

'Isn't this amazing?' she said. 'Meeting in the Tate Modern, I mean.' She threw her arms out wide and spun around. 'Isn't this place just awesome? So industrial. Brave architecture, no? Isn't it remarkable what they can do if they throw a bit of money at an old power station? *Controversial, though.*'

'Oh, I read about the construction shenanigans,' he said. 'I know all about that sort of thing. It was all I did for two years in Perth, after Cambridge.' He looked around the room. 'So have you been looking at the paintings?' he said. 'While I was waiting for you?'

She flushed. 'Sorry, Seb. I'm so sorry. I ... I saw heaps, actually. And the best of all was the Rothko 1959. Have you seen it? It's divine.'

'The one my niece could have painted?'

She slapped his arm. 'You're such a philistine,' she said.

'And I don't have a niece,' he said.

'Well, I adore the Rothko. It's calming. It lets me breathe. Deeply ... into something.'

'I know what you mean,' he said. 'I saw it last month. It's ... well, spiritual. It spoke to me. My soul.'

'Well, I never.' Cassie exclaimed. 'Next thing you'll tell me you've got religion.'

'I have, sort of. I've started going to church again.'

Cassie looked shocked. Appalled.

'I've met someone,' he said quietly.

'And she's clearly corrupting you!' Cassie bit her lip. 'Sorry, I shouldn't be so ...'

'No, you shouldn't. And I'm really happy, Cass. Sarah is lovely. She's *good* for me.'

She punched him on the arm again. 'You make her sound like a dose of medicine.' She took his hand again. 'Sorry, I shouldn't say that either. I shouldn't say a lot of things, should I? Anne Sophie's always telling me ... well, she's not always telling me, she actually likes to hear me talk. Most of the time.'

'Ah. Your housemate. The one you rather liked?'

Cassie smiled. 'It's happened,' she said. 'It took a few months for me to decide ... to know what I really wanted. To *feel* it, you know. But now it's good. All the talking and larking and making plans. And the sex. The sex is amazing!'

Sebastian couldn't help smiling himself. 'It took you a few months?' he said. 'You used to be such a fast mover. Remember how you pounced on me? During the play?'

She punched him on the arm again.

'Cassie.' He shook his head. 'You really have to stop punching me.'

'Maybe I punch because I don't know what to say,' she said. 'Or I'm scared I'll say the wrong thing. Or maybe it's just because I like you. Who knows? I've spent a lifetime not knowing what I want. All I did was rebel against my parents and make myself sick, and ... I love her, Seb. I can't stand to be away from her for more than a few hours, and I've never felt happier in my entire life. Even though I know that there should be more to life than one's personal happiness.'

Sebastian was happy for her. 'It's a good start, isn't it?' he said.

It had been wonderful to see Cassie. To talk. And wasn't the meeting so like Cassie herself? So unexpected, slightly zany. He loved that she was like that, just as he'd loved Veronika for being a little wild. Unpredictable. But he knew now he couldn't live with it; he wanted something that would last. *Someone* to last. He'd meant every word he'd said to Cassie about Sarah and so much more besides. Her lovely combination of confidence and shyness. Her lightness of touch with annoying or horrible people. The clarity of her big blue eyes. Her energetic stride: she was an excellent hiker. The way she listened to him attentively without fawning over him. But he hadn't told Cassie a word about the sex, of course. Because despite her blonde ponytail (how he and Cassie had laughed about that), despite her rather prim clothes and discreet jewellery, Sarah was passionate in bed. A little reserved at first, holding back, wanting his pleasure more than her own until he'd told her – gently but firmly – that he wanted to pleasure her. And even this was different too. It was more than mere technique. Thinking back to other women, he cringed with embarrassment for the shallowness of it all. Fun, sometimes, but shallow. But with Sarah, it was closeness that he craved. Wanting to know her more and knowing he wanted to keep her.

He turned to look at Sarah, rugged up in her coat, her profile soft and somehow yielding. He took her hand as they wandered towards his flat through the streets of Belgravia, and the word that kept returning was *compunction*. An old-fashioned word from the sermon. A word that pricked his heart. It was more than guilt, more than useless regret. It evoked a kind of grace. He caught sight of a starling leaping from the branch of a plane tree and knew it was grace that he wished for. Being a better person for Sarah. He loved the way she seemed *settled*. It didn't come from her family's wealth or connections but from something deep within her. He could hear her silence as they walked hand in hand. Was she reflecting, too? Was she wondering if he, *this*, the two of them, were right?

It was a long walk from Knightsbridge, so by the time they reached the Chelsea Embankment, they were weary, their faces glowing with sweat. The April morning was cold but humid. Cars zoomed past; Albert Bridge strung itself out in front of them. And then, unexpectedly, Sarah stopped him in his tracks and snuggled into him.

'I'm so proud of you, Seb,' she said, then pulled away to look at him. 'You're not an assistant anymore but a full legal adviser. You've worked hard, I know. You're dedicated.' She gave him a winsome smile. 'The salary raise won't hurt either, will it?' she said. 'I'll have to come with you to Huntsman to get you properly fitted out. She frowned. 'I'm sorry, I must have sounded like ... I didn't mean that about money.'

'Mean what, Sarah?'

'That money mattered to you.'

He was puzzled. He took her hand. 'Money *does* matter to me,' he said. 'I want to ... well, I want to make my own way in the world. Cut the apron strings and all that. Stand on my own two feet.'

Sarah looked away, then looked back into his eyes. 'I thought you might think that all I care about is money. Getting on in the world. And then I talked about getting you *properly fitted out*. I sounded just like my mother, just before she shipped me off to boarding school.'

'I don't want to ship you off anywhere,' he said.

He was building up to something, he knew. He thought that she was too. Her serious face. Her wanting to be honest.

'Did you listen to the sermon today?' he said.

'Of course. Did you like it?'

'I did,' he replied. 'There was something in it. It made me think about ... well, the fact that I'm not as good as I'd like to be. As you think I am.'

She pressed her hands into the collar of his jacket, straightened it out. 'Why ever would you say such a thing?'

'Because ... I haven't ... I've behaved badly with women. I've taken advantage. Been thoughtless, unkind.'

'So you're saying you're not perfect.'

'I don't mean that, no. I'm trying to say that I've always felt entitled. Not just with women but all my life. If I wanted it, I could have it. And I usually did.'

Sarah tilted her head to the side. 'Nothing to do with hard work, then?' she said. 'Or nothing to do with the fact that you're insanely attractive.'

'I'm serious, Sarah.'

She looked at him closely. 'Sebastian. What's brought all this on?'

'Because I want to be better for *you*.'

She shook her head. 'Don't make me into a saint,' she said. 'And you should want to be better for yourself, not for anyone else.'

'But I want to *deserve* you, Sarah.'

'You're saying the same thing in a different way,' she said. 'And in any case, all this talk about *worthiness*. You'd make a really good preacher.'

'Sarah! I thought you liked the sermon.'

'I don't like every one of them. They sometimes seem so earnest that I want to scream. Either that or get the giggles like a schoolgirl.' She gave him her generous smile. 'I do like you, Sebastian Harper-Jones. You interest me.'

'Interest me? That's a quaint way of putting it.'

She sighed. He thought for one moment she might slap him on the arm, but of course, she would never do that.

'It's because you're unformed,' she said. 'Don't look so taken aback, I mean that as a compliment. I mean ... like going to church. I know that you did it to please me, but now ... it's making you think. Isn't it?'

He felt as if she was looking right into him. 'Someone told me once that I had a vague notion of God,' he said. 'Maybe it's becoming less vague.

Maybe I'm becoming … something …' He took a deep breath. 'I love you, Sarah. I want you to marry me.' There. It was done. 'I don't have a ring, and we've only known each other for a few—'

She placed a finger on his lips. 'Yes,' she said.

He thought of that sapphire ring, and the woman who'd refused it, refused him. Who'd asked him about his notion of God. But that was in another life, and now it seemed he was a different person. Struggling to be a better one.

83. Felix

He wanted to do it alone. Far away, in another country. He thought, perhaps, of Japan. Of hiring a hotel room. No-one would know who he was. It would minimise the damage. But who would find him? Some room attendant? That would not be fair. Besides, he had no money to travel to Japan, to travel anywhere. And he hadn't an ounce of energy to plan a thing.

What was it he really wanted? To be outside of himself, that was it. Not himself. Something, someone else. Anyone. He could not fathom how he had come to be as he was: something limp, despicable. Alone. Living in Charlottenburg, with nowhere else to go when Max ended things. An apartment the size of a thumbnail. It was damp and dank when he arrived. He'd imagined spores settling on his lungs, but he couldn't catch the flu, not even a cold. The steely Berlin air in winter. Perilous. But no, he would not freeze to death. That kind of ending was too slow.

He would always be himself – that was the problem. And now Max did not want him. Why would he – what was there? After Felix had thrown it all in, all of it. His job, his car, and the theatre too. The company he'd had with Max. *Galileo. Mother Courage.* And the parties. Oh, the parties. But he'd bungled the money. It was all his fault. How had he got it so wrong? He still didn't know. The theatre. Max. He had been so sure. But now, it was not so.

How would he get through the next hour when his whole being was loathsome to him? And time – time was a bizarre endurance. The fact that he could breathe, that he was still alive, was a cruel joke the gods were playing on him. This was it. How could he erase himself? What relief he would feel if he could make it all go away? In the blink of a cosmic eye.

He rose, dressed and left his apartment, could scarcely put one foot in front of the other. He pressed on, bloodless against the cold. His body like a shadow moving down a dark tunnel. He reached the concrete bridge. The wind was a shuddering wall. He thought he heard a baby cry. No. Perhaps it was the raven. He longed, now, for some blissful concussion. For the elegant close of silence.

84. Gloria

Gloria knew what she had to do. She didn't want to sound newsy – I went to see my family, had a wonderful time, should have done it sooner. She didn't want to sound angry, either, although she felt a smudge of anger for her poor, self-deluding mother. Nor did she want to sound unfeeling; she simply needed to speak the truth. Simply? It felt like the most difficult thing she'd ever done, making that call, not wasting time, not letting her mother deflect or deny. It felt almost ruthless.

But her mother listened. And then she wept. And sighed. And wept again. She had always known, she said, and Gloria felt the anger rising again. She had always known how this would end. And then she wept some more.

Gloria said nothing. Simply listened to the sobbing on the other end of the line. And then her mother told her that she loved her. Gloria told her mother that she loved her, too. She hadn't told her that in many years.

Gloria found herself weeping, too, when she sang in church. She sang for her father. *A hero, a brave man*, Father Vicente had called him. Now he was a *matebian*, an ancestral spirit.

She knew she had lost something more than her father. She had lost the capacity for lightness.

Should she go to confession? Would that help? And what would she say to the man behind the screen? Father Vicente. Could she say she became impatient with the heat and the flies, with the girls who didn't always wash, with Carolina who still wet her pants, with the swarms of mosquitoes and the water that did nothing more than drip-drip-drip from a tap? Could she say that she was angry with her father because he'd taught his son to fight for freedom and now both of them were dead? Could she say that sometimes, in the dark of night, when she felt so alone and yet she was still here, she was still breathing and her heart was still beating ... could she say she felt ashamed to be alive?

She stood at the door of the church for a minute, an hour, she didn't know how long, until she turned her back, walked to the compound, went to bed and waited for sleep to drift over her.

Another weekend loomed, in which she would take a cold shower and eat a bread roll, feed the cat sardines, play a game with the kids. Maybe she would call Nicole and Ned, take a day trip to Areia Branca or One Dollar Beach, even Ulmera Beach, maybe have a swim, go out to a bar. But it was all too familiar. Too predictable. Ned would always get drunk. Nicole would always moan. *Nothing on TV*, she'd say, *can't understand a word of MTV Asia, or Argentinian soaps dubbed into Bahasa, or corny Portuguese game shows.* Although she'd met a South African doctor, she told Gloria, and things were *hotting up*. So much for the boyfriend back in Brisbane. Gloria hadn't even seen a TV since she'd arrived, let alone found romance, even for a night. She knew that people with the fancy jobs saw concerts of traditional Timorese dancers. They rubbed shoulders with important journalists and the political glitterati. Their stories were important, but she'd heard them all before.

She was lonely, not for friends, but for something more. That was the truth of it. And feeling old before her time. And then Joshua came back to her once more. Kind, lovely Joshua. Their heartfelt conversation. She craved his touch, his warmth, his understanding words. Why not … track him down? Just to say hello. Ask about his life. But how could she track him down? She had no idea where he was, what he was doing, whether he'd found someone to love. What was she thinking? But Ned could track him down, couldn't he? With his UN internet? Would that be legal, to ask him to find an address? For something personal, not official? She racked her brains for a possible location, but nothing came to her. It was all … hopeless, she was hopeless, she would … and then she remembered. Josh had been working on that farm. When they'd been acting in the play. But she didn't know the address, had never known the address. All she could remember was the drive from Perth and picking apples and being young. It had only been seven years ago, but it felt like a lifetime.

85. Joshua

It had given him a scare, feeling like that, all that angry stuff inside him. Wanting to destroy, even wanting to hurt someone, punch the shit out of them. It wasn't like him. Or maybe it was. Maybe he was more like Charlie than he thought. Maybe it took some kind of crisis to find out who he really was. Maybe he should see a doctor, get some pills to calm him down, take the anger away. But he already knew that pills weren't the answer because the question went deeper than that. Maybe he needed to talk to someone, but apart from Warra, there was no-one, and Warra would only tell him to pull his finger out, stop feeling sorry for himself, get some work, do something worthwhile.

Then words of Figaro, a fragment, came back to him: *I ... have had to deploy more knowledge, more calculation and skill merely to survive than has sufficed to rule all the provinces of Spain ...* Josh had come through a lot already. Yes – he would take a leaf from Figaro, his old character in the play. He would get his act together.

Monday. The first day of the working week. He remembered that much, at least. So he made himself polish his shoes, get dressed, brush his hair – which really needed a cut, maybe Warra would do it for him – and caught a bus to the city. He'd go looking in shop windows for *positions vacant* signs, kind of knowing it would be pointless. But at least he'd got out of bed.

He wandered aimlessly through the Murray Street Mall. He had yet to see one sign for a job; all he could see in the windows was a bunch of clothes and make-up and shiny jewellery. Pointless bloody stuff. And then he saw her coming out of Myers. It looked like Angela – Angela Vaček. Yes, it was her! She was checking inside a shopping bag, fishing out some paper. Should he say hello? Or turn tail and run? What would he say to her after all this time? He hadn't once been in touch. But then she looked up and saw him and a huge smile spread over her face and Joshua! she cried. I can't believe it! She hadn't changed a bit, and her hair was still glossy, with a few strands woven back and pinned at the sides, just like Veronika's.

Joshua! Oh my goodness, it is you!' She put down her bag and hugged him. She smelled of roses or some kind of flower. Then she drew away, red-faced and smiling, and looked him up and down.

'Just look at you!' she said. 'What a smart young man. How *lovely* to see you!'

And then a rush of questions … what was he doing these days … working in town? On a lunch break? Josh tried to answer but she didn't seem to be listening, her face so eager, like a little kid.

'I am *so* glad to bump into you,' she said. 'There's a letter arrived for you, it came a good while ago. I wasn't sure how to get in touch with you and Veronika didn't know where you—'

'A letter?'

'From East Timor. From Gloria. She was one of the girls in that play, wasn't she?

Gloria. So she must have made it home. He remembered how much it had meant to her. And now writing to him? What was that all about?

Angela broke into his thoughts, talking ten to the dozen, telling him about Ana and the children … *living with us … Michal doing well … they'd love to see you … have to dash before the shop closes … come for dinner … collect your letter.*

She took his hand, and Josh found himself back in the orchard. Her cooking. Michal's encouragement. The kindness. He wasn't sure if Ana would love to see him, though. And still not a word about Veronika.

'Dinner would be great, Mrs Vaček,' he said shyly.

'Angela, remember? Are you free on Sunday?'

He felt overcome. There, in the busy street, where she'd looked so pleased to see him, hugged him, invited him home, the letter, a feeling that welled up in his heart …

'I'd love to come,' he said. 'Thank you.'

'Is six o'clock okay? For dinner?'

'Perfect.'

'Michal will be *so* pleased to see you.'

Walking up the hill towards the house, he felt wistful, even a little nostalgic, as if he were returning home. Except that it wasn't his home; it was a house, owned by someone else. But still, it had been a kind of home for a while. A refuge. Like the packing shed on the farm. And then he remembered the letter again and felt a warm glow spreading in his chest.

Gloria had taken the trouble to write. Whatever she had to tell him, she had taken the trouble to write.

It was only later, trying to get to sleep, that he realised he'd failed on his mission of trying to find a job. He turned over in bed, trying not to dwell on it, trying to think of Sunday and dinner with the Vačeks and the fact that he'd been invited. That people wanted to see him.

He'd put on his best shirt. He'd even ironed it, although he hadn't managed to remove all the creases. Still, he was trying, trying more than he'd done for weeks. And Warra had cut his hair for him, teased him about a date.

'No way,' Josh said. 'It's my old boss, Michal, and his wife.'

'From the farm?'

Josh nodded. He didn't need to say: the people who gave me a chance.

'What happened to that daughter of theirs?'

Josh didn't blink. 'They've got two,' he said. He couldn't bring himself to say her name.

'I mean the one who broke your heart,' Warra said quietly. 'When you came back from Paris. I could tell.'

'Maybe I broke hers as well,' Josh said. 'Anyway, I don't want to talk about it.'

'You never do, mate.' Warra placed a hand on Josh's back. 'Leave you to it. Have a good evening.'

But what if she's there for dinner, Josh thought. What if she opened the door and saw him standing there? Would she laugh at him? Pretend he wasn't there? Be all French and self-important? He knew he'd been tough on her, and maybe she deserved it. Maybe she didn't. But if she *was* there at the dinner, if they got the chance to be alone, he would say that he was sorry for what happened, for not listening, for leaving in a storm. He would try to clear the air. And then leave it at that.

It had been a long bus ride, but it was worth it just for the view. The valley was beautiful at twilight, casting its shadows over the trees. A flock of galahs flew over his head, and it made him feel lighter, glad that he was visiting the Vačeks. With or without Veronika. A pair of kids met him at the door: the girl had fluffy red hair and a little button nose and she was hugging some sort of stuffed toy. The other, a boy, was wearing Spider-Man pyjamas and wielding a plastic cricket bat. Ana's kids. Cute, both of them. He thought he should say hello or ask them their names or whatever you asked little kids, when Angela appeared behind them, gushed at him, made him blush, welcomed him to their home. She introduced the kids: *Meredith and Benjamin, my grandchildren, Ana's pride and joy.* The little girl gave him a shy kind of smile, the boy whirled his bat in the air, and then both of them ran away.

'They're a handful sometimes,' Angela said, 'but we love having them here, and Ana ...' She linked Josh's arm through hers, started walking. 'Ana's a good mum. It's easier now that they're older, of course. I remember when ...'

She didn't mention to Josh anything about being an uncle, so she must have known that Charlie wasn't the father. She just went on, talking about her own children when they were young. Ana, then Veronika. But nothing about Veronika in the here and now: where she was, what she was doing, who she might be with.

As they moved to the kitchen, Josh could smell the richness of butter and beer. He saw Michal standing at the stove, his back towards him.

'Michal!' Angela cried. 'Look who's here!'

Michal turned around and his eyes glowed. He rushed towards Josh like a long-lost friend, shaking his hand, patting him on the back. He looked older, greyer, but the welcome and warmth hadn't changed.

'It's been too long, young Josh,' he said, shaking his head.

'Yeah. Sorry I didn't come sooner, Mr V, I've ... I've been away. And ... you know, doing lots of stuff.'

Michal looked a bit puzzled, then smiled again, said *good for you,* and told Josh *to take a gander* at what he was cooking. Sizzling things in a pan.

'Looks great,' Josh said.

'Schnitzel. I remembered how much you liked it.'

Josh felt really touched. Wished he hadn't said that he'd been *doing lots of stuff.*

'Michal *insisted*,' Angela said. 'And I'm doing the veggies. Potatoes, carrots, cauliflower. I remembered how you loved your veggies.'

'I wouldn't touch Dad's cooking if I were you. Not unless you want your stomach pumped.'

Josh knew that voice. Ana: loud, assertive. He followed it into the living room, and there she was, sitting on the floor in Ugg boots and surrounded by piles of Lego, with two spaniels sleeping next to her. Fred and Ginger, same as always. But Ana looked older in a tired kind of way, worn out, really. Josh remembered how he used to be a bit scared of her.

'How have you been, Ana?'

'Good,' she said without looking up. She began to gather the Lego, throw it into a plastic box.

'You've moved from Geraldton?' he asked.

'Yeah. It sucked.' She finally looked at him. 'She's not here. She's still in Paris. She'll be back soon, though. In case you're *wondering*. In case Mum hadn't told you.'

Josh was embarrassed. What was he supposed to say to that? And was he meant to ask about Charlie? Whether he kept in touch. Whether he ever saw the kids? But none of these questions seemed the right ones. It was a relief when Ben came tearing through the room and asked him to play some cricket. *Please*, he said, and Josh saw Ana's face light up.

'Your manners are definitely improving, Ben,' she said. 'But there's no time to play now. It's dinnertime.'

Josh felt a tug on his trousers. Looked down to see Meredith peering up at him, her face scrunched up with something to say. She had red curls, like Veronika. The same bright eyes.

'We played with a slinky at kindy,' she said, 'and we got all tangled up in it.'

Josh didn't know if this was fun or not.

'It was like being inside a rainbow,' the little girl said.

So definitely fun, then, Josh thought. She was a cutie, this one, and he loved that she could talk to him so easily.

'And what was at the end of the rainbow?' he asked.

'We thought it would be gold,' Ben chimed in. 'Nana told us there was gold.'

'But the teacher said no,' Meredith said, waving her hands in excitement. 'She said there was no gold.'

Ana hauled herself off the floor, gave Josh a smile.

'Their teacher's a bit of a killjoy,' she said.

'What's a killjoy?' the boy asked.

Ana suddenly made a grab for him. 'Mummy!' she cried, then tickled him round the waist. 'When she's in a bad mood.'

She didn't look so tired anymore.

It didn't sound all that bad, the way it came out of his mouth over dinner when they asked him questions. The fishing liner, the bricklaying, the carpentry and cleaning work. Right now, he was 'between jobs'. Someone at the agency had sent him a few options, he told them. He'd been earning a decent living, he thought. He wasn't a disgrace, after all, and they didn't treat him like one. They listened to him, heaped seconds and thirds onto his plate, filled him in on the orchard. It was a real conversation, the warmest he'd had for a long while. Ana left her meal half-eaten to put the kids to bed ... *her greatest joy,* Angela said ... *they're growing up just fine* ...

Work and food and children, but not a single mention of Veronika. It was odd, Josh thought, but he was relieved just the same.

And then Angela mentioned the letter. In the flurry of talk, Josh had almost forgotten it. But when she handed it over, it was definitely for real, he suddenly found himself speechless. His name on the front; a red flag with black and yellow and a white star; Gloria's name on the back. His hand trembled when he put it in his bag, then headed for the door. A hug from Angela, a slap on the back from Michal, and even a hug from Ana and a *nice to see you again, come and see us sometime* ...

All the way home in an empty bus, he kept thinking of the letter in his bag. He could almost see it through the canvas. He would wait until he was home, make a cup of Milo so he didn't drink more beer and hope that Warra had gone to bed. He would take the letter into his room and keep it all to himself.

Dear Joshua,

I hope you don't mind me writing to you like this, out of the blue. It's been a few years, so I hope I'm not intruding into your life. I have no idea where you are, but someone I know who has internet connection managed to find the address of Veronika's parents and I thought maybe they knew your address because I remembered you worked for them on their farm. Sorry, that's a long-winded way of saying that I was hoping to find you. To say that I still remember our connection with great fondness and would like you to know that I made it back to Timor-Leste. My homeland now. You seemed to understand how much it meant to me, and so I would like to tell you about my life. And should this letter ever find you, to find out about your life, too.

He felt a wave of longing rush over him. She had taken so much trouble to find him, to give him something of her life. Wanting to know his life, too. He heaped in two sugars, kept reading. It was a very long letter.

My country is independent now, you might have seen it on the news, and there is much work to be done. I am teaching in an orphanage, forty girls who have seen terrible things but who want to learn. It's hard work, but there is also much joy in watching them grow stronger. The main problem is the lack of adequate supplies, although my mother just sent me a parcel from her church with books and writing material, but I'm not sure that the Famous Five series will be all that relevant to these girls! I'm staying in a convent – don't laugh! The heat is unbearable, the food is always salty, there are constant blackouts, I have to coat myself in mosquito repellent. At least I don't always have to eat off the floor! I don't have a fridge or a comfortable bed. I've never been so happy in my life.

I have been asked to start a new school, run by the Carmelites, in my old village. You might remember me mentioning Maubara. We don't need a new building, as there are plenty of derelict buildings that can be fixed up with very little money, and there will be plenty of local people willing to help because that's what they do in this place. It somehow seems right to go back to Maubara, although I haven't quite decided. The prospect is rather daunting.

I have also learned that my father is dead. It wasn't unexpected, but I still hadn't given up hope. That's the problem with hope. We must always hold on to it, but it makes loss so much harder to bear. But I am glad to be here. I'm beginning to feel like I belong here, although I have to learn more Tetum, get used to the different ways of doing things, like boiling water on a kerosene stove before I drink it, sleeping with a mosquito net and living on two hundred US dollars a week. But these are small things when the big thing is work.

So thank you for listening, Joshua. You were a good listener for me back in Perth. I will always remember how attentive you were, how kind. And for what it's worth, I want to explain now why I pushed you away. It was because I knew my mother wouldn't let me be with a guy who wasn't Catholic. It had nothing to do with not liking you, not caring for you. So please forgive me for being cruel to you. I didn't mean to lead you on, I would never have done that to you. Anyway, confession time over – I haven't been to confession in months! I hope that you're happy with your life. If you have the time and inclination,

I would love you to write to me and tell me where you are, what you're doing, whether you have someone special in your life. Maybe you even have a child by now!

With very best wishes,
Gloria

He was stunned. He was in tears. Beautiful, unstoppable tears.

86. Veronika

So here she was, at one thirty in the morning in the middle of May, in the tiny theatre on Rue Marie-Stuart, in full costume: a long white dress that came up to her neck. She was ready to tear it off and lie down. Everyone except Philippe had gone home, and she was supposed to be sobbing on cue. She was already wrecked, felt like she was on the verge of something ... of breaking down. Antoine was muttering about something not being quite right, and her mind was going blank. Did she really care, anymore, when something wasn't quite right?

'Antoine, it's very late,' she said. 'Philippe and I ... we're both exhausted.'

She was relieved to see Philippe nodding. Poor man, playing the suicidal Treplieff. She could see it had taken its toll.

'Okay, okay, okay.' Antoine told them to *prenez un pause* while he spoke with the lighting man.

Philippe muttered *putain*, several times, and left to take a pee.

Veronika sat in one of the theatre seats, pulled the script out of her bag. She knew her part backwards. Perfectly. She would remember the fucking lines for the rest of her fucking life. But she would look at it again. Maybe there was a clue, something she'd missed. She had to make one last effort to be better, to please Antoine. She scrambled for the right page and saw the script scribbled in pencil in the margin. She scanned it quickly:

I was afraid you might hate me ... My life used to be as happy as a child's ... Why do you say that you have kissed the ground I walked on? You should kill me rather ... I never knew what to do with my hands ... I am a seagull—no—no, I am an actress ... Now I am a real actress. I act with joy, with exaltation. I am intoxicated by it, and feel that I am superb ... I feel the strength of my spirit growing in me every day ...

She felt Antoine towering over her.

'What was your emotion at the beginning of the scene?' he said.

Veronika kept looking at the page. 'Distraught,' she said.

'Yes. The physical act is in the stage directions. Sobbing, sobbing against his chest.'

She wanted to stamp her feet. 'We've been through this,' she said.

'Start again.' He clapped his hands.

Veronika sighed, made herself look up at him. 'But it's not even been five minutes,' she said. 'I have things to do tomorrow. And I'm tired, Antoine.'

'*Ça ne m'intéresse pas.*'

So what else could she do? She went back onto the stage. She started again.

Antoine leapt up beside her. '*And I dream every night that you look at me without recognising me* ... That's your line ... She has been away for years. She comes back to visit her first love. And then this part, *C'est où on a un petit problème.* Here we have a problem. Why can't you embody these words? In this little section ... it's like you're not really there.'

Philippe returned, leapt onto the stage. Everyone's leaping, Veronika thought, and it's not getting me anywhere.

'I don't need you, Philippe,' Antoine said. 'Not yet.'

'Give her a break, Antoine! Can't you see, we've had enough?'

Antoine turned to face Veronika. 'Answer my question. Why are you not *there*?'

'I don't know *why*, Antoine.'

'But you *do!*'

'And if I do?'

'Then you can *fix* it.'

'And what if it can't be fixed?'

She felt on the edge of tears now, thinking of Joshua and all that she'd lost, of Cassie so far away, of Sebastian in love, of Gloria doing good things, and now this ... not getting it right, wanting it to be right, wanting to be the best she could be. It mattered. It was everything: to get it right. And she didn't want to cry, not here, not now, not ever.

'What if I've done everything I can to fix it and it makes no difference?' she said. 'And what if I've been guilty and wretched and hateful and there's nothing to be done?'

Antoine shook his head.

Philippe cried out: '*Nina! You are crying again, Nina!*'

No. Veronika would not cry. She would not sob on cue. She would do no such thing.

Antoine watched the scene come to an end, then walked around, holding his head in his hands. He turned to Veronika again.

'She is triumphant!' he declared. 'She has the strength to endure. So while poor Treplieff is lost, the final emotion for Nina is one of spiritual triumph.'

Veronika glared at him. 'And what about the love and the hate?'

'Ah.' Antoine's eyes lit up. 'She loved him but loves him no longer. She has been in love for a long time with the love they once had.'

'*Antoine! Je peux aller maintenant!?*' The voice was annoyed, vehement. The lighting man yelled that he was leaving. Antoine turned away towards the lighting box, began to ask him some questions. Veronika went backstage for a glass of water. Philippe was sitting in front of the mirror, turned to look at her.

'I know the stage is ... what do I say?' He frowned. 'The stage is a false intimacy. But I will confess to being a little taken with you. And Nina. You are a fine actress. I am safe to say this, now that I hear you will be leaving us. It was my privilege to play this part with you.'

Veronika felt on the verge of tears again. But she thanked him. She was a good actor. He had told her. And she felt it in herself, that she had learned, she'd been dedicated, she'd worked and worked and now ... she was good. Better, much better. But she also knew that she was already far, far away. That in her mind she had already left.

She returned to the theatre, collected her bag from the seat. Antoine was still there, but she merely gave him a quick curt nod. She began to walk away, down aisle of the theatre, out into the foyer. She would walk home, back to her cramped little studio. She would have a farewell drink with Yaël. But Philippe was calling after her. He emerged from the wings and came towards her.

'Véronique!'

She felt a hand on her shoulder. It was Antoine.

'You were very good, back then,' Antoine said.

Philippe wiped the sweat from his brow. 'Leave her alone,' he said quietly.

'I have been hard on you,' Antoine said.

Veronika nodded. She wanted no more of this but with the two men either side of her, she dared not move. Antoine slipped his arm around her waist.

'Get your hands off her!' Philippe said, pushing Antoine aside. Antoine shoved him back and reached for Veronica's hand, gripped it. 'Maybe a little too hard.'

'Go, Véronique! Leave! Leave! Don't let this ... man ...' Philippe made a fist at his teacher. The two men hurled expletives at one another. She rushed through the side exit.

'Go!' she heard again. Stern whispers. *Salaud!* The guttural sound of spit. A moan. She hoped they wouldn't kill one another. She could just make out Antoine's voice.

'But you see ... I only took her on because I made the promise to someone. He paid for her to come, so I could make her one of the best actresses of her generation.'

'You did what?' Philippe grunted.

It was preposterous. Like a line out of a bad movie. Veronika dropped her bag and bolted back into the theatre.

'What are you talking about?' she cried. 'Who is this *someone*?'

Antoine halted, looked full of misgivings. 'A friend of yours.'

Philippe was hunched in a seat, shaking his head.

'I thought you had left,' Antoine said. Then he threw up his hands. 'Simmons. Charles Simmons. He paid for you to come here but said I must not tell you. But you—'

She somehow managed to turn back through to the exit and rush into the street, to walk until she started to run. Past all the shops and dingy buildings, the graffiti, yanking up her long skirt, her Nina skirt, striding now, past the Métro signs and empty squares, past beggars and street cleaners, all the way over the bridge, the Notre Dame from the back, sinister as a pouncing spider.

She didn't sleep at all. Not for a minute, a second. She tried to think but nothing was clear, nothing made sense ... why would he ... *Charles* Simmons. The very thought of his name made her feel sick, made her turn over and over in bed, her cramped makeshift bed that she'd made love in with Josh ... Josh ... had *he* known about this ... did anyone else know she was a *kept* woman ... Why? Why? Was Charlie trying to make it up to her? To Josh? Was he really in love with her? And what kind of love was that? Was *she* even at fault for Joshua's imprisonment? She couldn't make her thoughts settle, couldn't put them in a simple straight line. All night. All night in the dark, images rushing back to her, through her, turning her inside out.

She slumped out of bed. Six am. She would book a flight to Perth. There was no point, absolutely none, in performing the play. Performing. In Paris. Or even going to London and trying out for a repertory company, where having attended the Pierrot studio would surely be a bit of a calling card. She just couldn't. She felt like everything, all of it, her desire, her ambition, her need to be better, was all one horrible, hurtful lie. And maybe she'd taken the place of someone who deserved it more than she did. How could she have been so blind, so stupid? Here: have a newly minted scholarship, Veronika! Yes, you! The woman who's hardly done any acting worth talking about. Who thought she was better than other people, so clever, so arty, too good for Josh, too good for Sebastian, too good for Ana. How was she any better than Ana when she owed everything to a man?

She turned on the kettle. She sipped tea. She tried not to think any more.

She opened her laptop. How quickly could she book a flight? Fly away, far away from the scene of her humiliation. But Charlie might be in Perth, mightn't he? But then she'd heard from Ana that he liked to go overseas a lot. He could be anywhere.

An email from Cassie popped up. Veronika just knew it would be brimming with shining good cheer. She wasn't sure she could handle that. Even when Cassie was feeling low, she somehow made it sound like she was on a high. That life was worth living. And sure enough: life with Anne Sophie was *going swimmingly*. Ha! Veronika thought, who said *swimmingly* these days? Or was Cassie becoming a posh Londoner? She read on:

And guess what?? We're opening a shop on Portobello Road. Anne Sophie has started an ethical jewellery import business. She flies to Mombasa every month to buy jewellery from women who work with recycled materials. They do really well out of it, and people can't get enough of it.

I've started painting again, seriously, I mean, but I've still got a long way to go. I was enamoured with ink but now it's gouache that steals my heart.

You must be close to flying home. Didn't you say your student visa would expire soon?

Then gushing with news about Sebastian. A swanky job in London. A woman called Sarah.

He's fallen in love, for real ... Anne Sophie and I went to dinner with Sebastian and Sarah in a restaurant with chandeliers and snooty waiters and the best chocolate mousse I've ever eaten in my entire life, after the prawn salad, that is, and the dainty entrées before that. Sebbie had told us before that he and Sarah were paying, which was really nice of them, and even though Sarah doesn't drink, she's not one of those people who makes you feel like you're morally spineless if you like a tipple now and then. Well, we had more than a tipple, the three of us, and we all got on famously and then ... wait for it! Seb told us that he and Sarah are getting married and that Sarah's keen to have a baby. Anne Sophie told me later that she really warmed to both of them, how Seb was so thoughtful and funny and how Sarah is what the English like to call a brick, all good nature and dependable. Except that makes her sound like she's hard and boring, and she's actually soft and sweet but not in a sticky kind of way. We all exchanged numbers and said we should do it again.

A brick. The woman sounded like a typical well-heeled Brit, probably horse-faced and with a braying laugh to match. Veronika pulled herself up. She really was being a cow. Was she jealous? Well, she was, just a little. Not because Sebastian had fallen in love, but because he seemed to have found some certainty, had grasped the future with both hands, while she sat empty-handed, staring through the window of her cramped little studio, watching a concierge dragging a rubbish bin through the courtyard. Did she really belong here, in Paris? With her flawed French, the absence of friends, her tourist's eye view of the city?

She returned to Cassie's email. More about how Sebastian had *really changed. He isn't a pompous prat anymore, he's warm and kind and open to thinking about new stuff.* Cassie hoped Veronika didn't mind all this talk about Seb, she was sure everyone had moved on, *even if we don't always know where we're moving to.*

Veronika rose from her chair and turned on the kettle. She felt pleased for Cassie and knew she should feel pleased for Sebastian, too. Why not be happy for other people if you couldn't be happy yourself? But then again, wasn't there something too final about Sebastian and Sarah? Something that sounded like a closing of a door, even if the room wasn't to your liking.

ACT FIVE Real Selves

[2002–2003]

'... you've seen our play
What it's worth you best can say,
In one respect it's true to life.
All the fuss, the hubbub – strife,
In the end – for all they say
Are but follies of a day.'

– Pierre Beaumarchais, *The Marriage of Figaro*

87. Veronika

Táborák at the orchard. Standing in front of the bonfire, Veronika's eyes were watering from the smoke. At least they weren't tears, she thought, pulling back her shoulders, trying to make herself better because she didn't feel afraid of the fire. That was something, at least, to feel proud of, standing in the clearing with her family and their friends, toasting their sausages on the fire. Michal, Angela and Ana, and some of Michal's Czech friends from childhood. Two older couples who had once known Babička. Ben and Meredith were running amok, Ana shrieking and chasing Ben who was running after Meredith who was dressed as a witch. Meredith's black cardboard hat fell off, then she tripped over it and began to cry.

'There, there,' Veronika said. She bent down to inspect the child's knee. 'Let me kiss it better.'

She picked her up gently and carried her towards the house. Seeing the girl's face swollen with tears, her nose a streaming mess, Veronika understood: *It's all too much. I can't do this anymore.* But she would not, must not, think about that now. Her failure. The humiliation.

Three years in Paris. Almost a year since she'd been back. Would the hurt ever leave her?

She took Meredith into the bathroom and washed her face with a warm flannel. She cleaned her knee and placed a bandaid over the graze. None of this stopped the child from wailing, feeling sorry for herself. Veronika wanted to say *it's just a fucking graze, Mez, you're not going to die,* but instead she took her by the hand and led her to her bedroom. A doll's house shoved up against the wall, looking a-shambles. An upside-down green chair, a pair of purple sneakers strewn about, an open satchel spilling with crayons. Veronika thought, why is she still crying? Will nothing stop her crying?

'What's wrong, Mez?' she said, trying to sound patient.

The child's face was ruddy with tears, as plump as a cherub's, as she looked up at Veronika. She had her grandmother's fiery red hair.

'Am I going to be burnt?' she whimpered. 'Like a steak?'

Ah. So that was it. 'It's *at* the stake, Mezzie,' she said. 'And no, never, we would never do such a thing.'

Meredith was wide-eyed. 'Ben said it's witches' night tonight and they burn all the witches and now I'm a witch,' she said.

Veronika bent down to her, then took her hands. 'You're *dressed* like a witch, you're not a witch,' she said. 'And what Ben was talking about … It's only a custom. A way of doing things in another country called Czechia. It's called *pálení čarodějnic*. We light the fire to protect us from evil spirits.'

Meredith nodded. 'My socks are itchy,' she said.

Veronika pulled down the child's socks, unzipped the black costume. Had Meredith understood? Or had she suddenly become bored by the drama of it all? Who knew how little kids thought? She took her to the bathroom to brush her teeth, then *time for bed.*

'Bloody hell, Ron. I thought she'd been abducted.' It was Ana, puffing at the doorway, hurriedly closing the door, then looking pleased at her daughter. 'No such luck, I see,' she said, and sat down on Meredith's small bed.

'What's up?' Veronika said.

'I'm hiding from Ben,' Ana said, and sighed. 'And I think Dad's drunk and that old guy, Karel What's-His-Name, you know, the husband of Babička's friend Jana, well, he keeps on at me about finding a job. Like parenting isn't a friggin' *job*. I wish he would POQ.'

Veronika watched as Meredith began cuddling her favourite doll.

'I was just explaining *pálení čarodějnic* to Mezzie,' she said.

Ana groaned her way up – she was so unfit these days – and pulled open a drawer, found the child's nightie. Meredith held out her arms, let the nightie slip over her head, asked her mother in a muffled voice to *tell me a big story.*

'*Prosím pohádku.* Let me see. Hop into bed first,' Ana said, then tucked her child in snugly.

Veronika found it puzzling. Her sister cursed the children in one breath, then bathed them with love in the next.

'You know the bonfire outside?' Ana said to her daughter. 'Well, the bonfires were even bigger in a city called Prague. My nan came from there. Aunty Ron's nan.'

'Where is it, Mummy?'

Ana brushed her child's hair from her face. 'It's a magnificent city, far away, where I once lived for a while. Babička – your great-grandmother – was born there. It looks all higgledy-piggledy from afar, with a hundred pointy roofs, just like in a story book. Up close all the shops are painted different pastel colours and they look like doll's houses. There are narrow alleyways and wonderful cafés called *kavárny* where there's music and there's a statue of Saint Wenceslas on his horse in the town square, just down the road from the Grand Hotel Europa. Imagine that, little one. It sounds beautiful, doesn't it?'

Meredith nodded.

'And there's a magic clock in the centre of the town,' Ana said. 'It's called the Orloj and it's the oldest ticking clock in the world. It shows you the position of the sun and the moon. And the streets are cobblestoned and lit with lamps that look like enormous lanterns. And there's a giant church on the other side of the bridge and inside there's a rose window that shines out in all directions, like a kaleidoscope.'

Meredith frowned. 'Why is there a bridge?' she asked.

'So people can walk across the river,' she said. 'It's called the Vltava and it's very long. The people are very proud of it. And there are artists on the bridge who will draw your picture for a few coins. And trams which are like trains only they go down the middle of the street. And there's a market. In the old town, there's a special house, like a big hall, with incredible golden rooms and patterns on the walls and paintings of beautiful ladies and you can hear music there, too. So yes, magic. All of it.'

Meredith nodded, sleepily. 'Can we go there?' she said.

'One day,' said Ana with a faraway look, 'when I was in Czechia, they called me Anástazie Vačková.'

'Why?'

'Because I am a woman. Vaček is for a man. But here, it doesn't matter. We keep Grandpa's name.'

Veronika was intrigued. Ana had never told her about her time in the Czech Republic, let alone the gender of grammar in her own surname. But then Veronika had never asked: she thought that Ana would find it too painful. And besides, if she were honest, she hadn't cared to ask her sister about anything that mattered. In the days when they didn't like each other, when Ana had been openly hostile and Veronika had treated her with contempt. But since she'd come home, Veronika felt differently. There was something touching, something admirable, about Ana's tending to the children. It was hard work, relentless, and sometimes her sister screamed with frustration and exhaustion, but there was no doubting the truth of her love for red-haired Mez and sturdy Ben.

Ana leant over and kissed the child's forehead, then looked up at her sister.

'She looks like you,' she said, quietly.

'Was my daddy a prince, Mummy?'

Veronika waited.

'Yes. He was a prince,' Ana said, then stood up from the bed. 'One down and one to go,' she whispered.

As they walked towards the door, Veronika took her sister's hand.

'I liked your pictures of Prague,' she said. 'I'd like to hear more sometime.' They returned to the *táborák*, where they found Michal, Karel and Jana, with Ben curled up on Angela's lap. So, the others must have gone, Veronika thought, trying not to yawn. It was time for bed, she thought, wishing she could be tucked up like Meredith, had someone to tell her stories, take care of her. Then she made herself snap out of it. Told herself not to be a damn baby.

She sat down next to her mother, gently stroked Ben's forehead. Jana said she remembered Veronika's grandmother; she had been a good friend. Another story, this one a story of escape. How Babička and her husband Ludvik had one night in a spa town, Karlovy Vary, before they escaped to Moschendorf. There was a photo of them somewhere, Jana said, but she didn't have a clue where it had gone. She turned to Veronika; her face lit up. 'In the photo she looked so happy,' she said. 'That I remember. She and Ludvik holding up two giant spa wafers. A West Bohemian specialty, you know. Your *babička* said it was the last thing they ate in Czechoslovakia, and that it had been snowing. And she remembered the taste of cinnamon.'

Jana moved in closer, and Veronika caught the scent of something floral. Youthful.

'Your *babička* had a ... a sweetheart, you know,' she said, her voice quavering a little. 'Before Ludvik. Her father didn't approve of him, either. A bookbinder. Lived in Josefov. Ivan Winterberg was his name.'

Ivan Winterberg. Veronika let the words roll round in her head. A sweetheart. A forbidden romance. Star-crossed lovers. She'd had no idea.

'So did Babička's father put an end to it?' she said.

Jana shook her head. 'He was caught by the Nazis,' she said. 'Shipped off to Terezín. He died in a labour camp.'

344

Dawn. Veronika sat under the wisteria sipping tea. A blush and honey sheen across the sky. The squark of a bird. More autumnal by the day. The leaves of the plum trees would soon show their colours. It was the only peace she could get before Ben and Meredith woke up and all the chaos began. Her father was already up too, planting or pruning.

She let the tea warm her, let the feeling come. The feeling of being split between two places. As if she hovered between the orchard, in the wooded hills overlooking the Swan Valley, and walking the hurried boulevards of Paris. She missed the fascination of passageways, the immaculate parks, all the seductive enchantments promised by the City of Lights. It was one of those moments when she could remember Paris without hurting. She had improved her acting, she really had, without the need for someone else's approval. The integrity, the loss of ego, the loss of thought, those moments when she became someone else. And she'd owed it all to Felix, in the beginning. She'd tried to get in touch with him several times but hadn't succeeded. But he'd led her to Paris, in the end. To the galleries, the opera. Cassie.

She remembered how, on one blustery afternoon mooching around the Père-Lachaise, she had the feeling she would die in that city, as she'd once imagined. She might blow about the world like a tumbleweed, but she would surely end up there and find a sense of belonging.

She took another sip of tea, set down her mug. She was being fanciful again. It was time to move out. Get on with things. What had she been doing since her return from glamorous Paris to familiar, provincial Perth? Working at the pub, which stank of beer (what did she expect: Chanel Nº 5?), and where she'd had a couple of pointless flings with customers. Nice enough, but pointless. Babysitting for one of Ana's friends. Going for runs through the fire trail, all the while trying to figure out what to do next. A blankness. A blankness filling in.

Her mother had encouraged her to start auditioning, but Veronika had merely said she'd get around to it sometime. Her mother, her father, Ana, all of them had asked about Paris, but all she'd shared was a picture-postcard story. It was easier that way. The thought of auditioning, setting foot onstage again, made her guts churn with shame. It had all been so tainted by Charlie. She'd even felt too frightened to appear in a play, dreaded the thought that he would turn up to see her. Not that he would: he was living in Florida, Ana told her, with some woman he'd met on the internet. An heiress. Aviation empire, apparently. They were *doing business* together. So he was out of the country, hitched up with someone grand and still making piles of money. He was out of her life, but she still couldn't bring herself to try acting again. It wasn't rational but it was how she felt. Perhaps she had lost something vital. The passion. Maybe one day, who knew when, she'd get back to it.

Ana had seemed upset by Charlie's email, which had arrived just days ago after months of no contact. But Veronika had found it hard to muster any pity. Her sister was still pining for the creep, it seemed. Which wasn't rational, either. But Ana had never been rational. And she'd hidden things; she had known all along it was Charlie who started the fire. She'd never tell Josh she'd known. At least she'd come clean to her parents about the kids' real father. She and her sister, bound together in a kind of unholy, unspoken alliance. Because of course she couldn't tell Ana about Charlie sponsoring her lessons. Charlie. Her mentor. Her *bête noire*. Her nemesis. Any number of roles she could cast him in, but always the dastardly villain of the piece.

She was trying to make a joke in her head. Trying.

And then another story came back to her: Babička's sweetheart, who'd been caught by the Nazis and died in a labour camp.

So many secrets, Veronika thought. She looked up at the early morning sky, still tinged with the pearl-pink of sunrise. Count your blessings, isn't that what people said?

88. Joshua

Gloria's letter had been sitting on the mantlepiece since April – for more than a month! – and he still hadn't written a reply. How could he possibly reply, when she was doing such awesome things, being so courageous? When he still had no job, no plan, and still with some anger simmering inside him. He needed to move on to something better, something with purpose, like Gloria, beautiful Gloria.

He'd used excuses when he'd come out of detention: how the world had seemed strange, bizarre, everything sprawling out in all directions, so that he'd never found his rhythm. And what was a rhythm worth anyway, when you got into one, only to slip off it again? But now he needed something to hold onto, some solid core that he must have lost when he was just a kid. His mum with no hair, aged beyond her years. His father's looks of disgust; his terrible fists. Was that why he'd taken the rap for Charlie? Not because he loved his brother, and not because he was a saint, no way. Had he wanted something to define him, give him meaning? Or had he wanted to be a knight in shining armour for Veronika? Who after years of not seeing him, not bothering with him, had been wearing a white dress with no zip, just pinned together, and he'd caught a glimpse of her naked flesh. He'd been inside her. He'd felt so close he thought he would die. Her skin almost blue in the light, her freckles like tiny shadows. You had to look away or you'd look too much.

He turned over in bed. What was he doing, thinking, yearning for Veronika?

Warra would know the answer. Warra would rib him and say *you're just horny, mate.*

He remembered the darkness of Gloria's eyes. Her broad smile. That kiss. The craving welling up inside him. Should he write back to her? Find out if she still had feelings for him? But she couldn't let her feelings show, could she, with her religion that divided people into groups and one of those groups, the one he belonged to, was less worthy than the other. But he couldn't stop remembering her lively mind, her interesting stories, the sensational way she sang, a rich voice that flew into high notes and transported him. There was defiance in her singing. A vibrancy. Her generous spirit ... and there was this other thing, this thing that made you want to tell her anything. Whatever garbage came into your head. He'd reeled at how much he'd shared with her, so quickly. And now she was doing good in some difficult part of the world. She was a good person. A precious person.

He felt tears running down his face.

Was it that you wept, and when you wept, you felt different after? And how after that, you could remember the good things? The boat, yes. His father took him out as a kid. When he was sober. He'd been terrified at first. Hated it. But then his dad had taught him how to read the wind, the sea, how to manage the sheets, tie the knots, how to tack. Gazing up at the Milky Way, like when he was a kid, he'd felt boundless. He'd seen the Southern Cross, the Seven Sisters, all to himself. And then he'd thought of stardust. That's where we're all from, someone had told him, and how there were the same number of atoms in the universe as there had been five seconds after the Big Bang. Almost fourteen billion years ago. And they just kept playing musical chairs. Changing. Rearranging. And then he'd seen it. A bright shadow: dolphins, luminescent, next to the boat, jumping, bending stripes of silver, moving in the darkness.

What crazy things he was thinking right now.

And what did it matter if he couldn't be with Gloria? He could, he should, write to her, tell her how much he admired her work. Offer sympathy for the loss of her father. They'd bonded over that as well, two people without fathers. But at least she knew what had happened to hers, even if it was the worst. Not that he would ever say that to Gloria. He would never say anything to hurt her. Her letter had made him feel so much better. Soothed him. So different from Veronika, who'd kept him on edge, made him feel happy one moment, then dumped him on his head the next, left him feeling hurt, all messed up. But Gloria was kind. She had a flame of goodness in her heart. If he wrote to her, he could tell how he, too, remembered their moments with such fondness, and how even though they were only moments, they had lasted, they had lived inside him.

He could even say that he would like to see her if she ever came back to Perth. But only if she felt happy with that idea. He hoped she'd feel happy about it. Or at the very least, that she wouldn't tell him not to waste her time. Not that Gloria would come right out and say it like that. She was much too thoughtful. Sensitive. He could ask her, couldn't he? It wouldn't hurt to ask.

89. Veronika

Her mother wiped her hands on her apron, smiling at Veronika. Told her she'd seen a job advertised in the *West* for the Perth Concert Hall. A customer service and sales representative. Wouldn't it be fun, working in a box office?

Veronika nodded, then winced. 'Sounds like a glorified name for *ticket seller*.'

'Ana's going to enrol in a course,' her mother said.

'Good for her,' Veronika snapped, then immediately regretted it. 'No, I mean *really* good for her. She hasn't said a word to me.'

'It's a course in business management,' her mother said. 'She'll be accepted as a mature-age student, but she needs to sit some tests first. She ... could do with some help with writing essays. It's a long time since she left school.'

Her mother pulled her apron over her head. 'I think she feels a bit reticent about asking you.'

'Why? I don't understand.'

'Well ...' Her mother moved towards her, placed a hand on Veronika's forearm. 'Ana knows she needs to move on,' she said. 'I mean, she's been living here for a few years and ... well, the children are growing so fast and needing new shoes and clothes every other month ... and the cost of the bore water for the orchard, it's going sky high. Your sister ... she doesn't want to keep depending on us.'

Veronika understood what her mother wasn't saying. She felt a ripple of shame rush through her.

'I'll find a place to live,' she said, trying to keep her voice steady.

Her mother took Veronika's hand. 'Can you afford it? I mean ... I know we haven't asked you for board, but ...'

'I'll check out the ad for that job,' Veronika said. She tossed back her head. 'At least I'll be close to a stage.'

Her father stood at the doorway, looking tired, greyer. How had she not noticed the tiredness?

'I've been knocking for a while ...' he said. 'I wasn't sure if you'd be home.'

'As you can see, I am,' she said, straining to smile. She gave him a hug, asked him to come in.

'I start a new job tomorrow,' she said. 'Working in the ticket booth at the Perth Concert Hall.'

Michal nodded, several times over. 'Ah. Well. Good on you,' he said. 'Your mother ... she'll be pleased, too.'

'It was time, Dad. I ... I'm sorry I stayed for so long.'

He went to speak, but she turned away, busying herself with the kettle.

'Nice digs,' she heard him say, '*bezvadný dům!*'

She turned to face him. 'You mean the peeling paint, chipped cornices and those rickety French windows.' She scratched her head. 'It's really cheap, and it's close to everything.'

Although she hardly ever went out. North Perth was only a short amble from restaurants and pubs, an art house cinema she loved and the best underground bookshop. But she couldn't afford any of that. She saw her father pick up a book, inspect the spine, put it back on the table. Saw him looking at all the boxes still waiting to be unpacked.

'No tea, thanks,' he said. 'I just came to see if you needed a hand. Any jobs for me to do? I can see the blind on the front window is coming off at the side. I can drill it back in if you like.'

'Aren't you impressed by the heights your daughter has ascended to? Such palatial splendour ... *fantastický*, no?'

Her father grimaced. 'Don't say that, love,' he said. 'You should feel proud of what you've achieved. Your mum and I certainly are. You're the first one in the family to go to uni, and then a scholarship to Paris, for heaven's sake, all that living like a great lady. And now a job at the Concert Hall!'

She remembered the interview: they'd been struck, apparently, by her communication skills; her knowledge of the performing arts. And they thought she'd be *terrific* over the phone, with *that voice*. The voice that once played Medea, she thought, and motioned to the French doors.

'Shall we sit outside?' she said, then led the way to the tiny backyard. 'Have a seat, Dad.'

They sat down on upturned milk cartons, next to a burnt-out barbecue.

'Those leaves will need raking up,' her father said. 'Got a rake?'

Veronika felt on the verge of tears. 'I've failed,' she said.

Her father shuffled forward.

'I've failed at being who I wanted to be,' she said.

Her father didn't speak. She didn't even know if she wanted him to speak. But then she heard him sigh, stretch his back, settle down again.

'You know you look just like Babička,' he said.

'You mean miserable and lost?'

'Not at all. Not a bit. And I don't just mean the eyes and cheekbones either. I mean that your *babička* was tough. She went through so much, you know. The horrors of the Red Army, she saw them with her own eyes. Then when she and my father left, they thought communism wouldn't last and they'd soon be reunited with her family. She didn't see them again for decades.' He swept the air with his hand. 'I have her to thank for everything. She was a class act, Babička, a real fighting spirit.'

'So I should stop feeling sorry for myself?' Veronika said.

Her father looked her in the eye. 'What do *you* remember about her?' he said.

Veronika tried to picture it. 'Lots of things, really. Like how she drank so much Slivovitz and managed to stay coherent. How she read to me and how ...' She suddenly stopped. 'I remember when she was dying,' she said. 'When I sat by her bed and she told me ... she told me she was waiting for the silence. It made me wonder if that's where we go when we die. Into the silence, into nothing.' She returned her father's gaze. 'I used to be afraid of the nothing,' she said, 'but now I think ... that nothing is my life, and it can't get any worse than that.'

Michal sat there without moving. It felt like a long time before he spoke.

'Your mum told me that you don't want to audition for plays,' he said softly. 'Don't you want to act anymore? It used to be your life.'

Veronika brushed away a tear. 'It's not that,' she said. 'It's just. Everything. I ... It's just people. I let them down. Disappoint them.'

'Like who?'

She inhaled deeply, exhaled. 'It doesn't matter,' she said.

'Like young Josh?'

Veronika was taken aback.

'Your mother figured something was going on,' he said. 'She saw the way he looked at you ... when you came to dinner, asking if you could use the orchard for that play you were doing. And then all the time you were swanning about on the farm, she saw ... and, well, since you've been back, you've never once asked about him. Your mother noticed that, too.'

Veronika folded her arms, hugged her shaking body.

'He came to dinner,' her father said. 'We kept waiting for him to ask about you, but he never did. You were such good mates when you were kids. How ... how did that happen?'

'It happened,' she said, dully. 'And ... look, Dad, I really don't want to talk about it. I know you mean well, but ... and in any case, he's not the only man I've let down. Do you remember that man from the play? Blond hair. Well built. Good looking?'

'Simon?'

'Sebastian. He didn't work out, either.' She shook her head. 'He actually proposed to me, Dad. Can you believe that? It seems so funny now, but ... well, I really hurt him.'

'We all make mistakes,' her father said. 'Let people down.'

There was no way in the world she would speak of Charlie. The fraudulence of Paris.

'Sometimes, Dad ... sometimes I feel like I'm coming apart. That nothing's worked out.'

'You mean you haven't worked it out,' Michal said. 'Not yet. But you will, love, I know you will.' He leaned forward, hands on knees. 'Babička used to say that we make our own life, and we do the best we can. I know it sounds corny, but it's true. And she had the right to say it. She was always coming out with these little gems.' Then his face suddenly brightened. 'You know what, Ronnie? Why don't you talk to Karel and Jana?'

'What do you mean?'

'You know ... interview them. Find out about Babička. You could make it a project.'

'A project?'

'You could write about Babička's life. No-one's ever written it down. It would be a kind of family history, you know.'

Veronika said nothing. What would be the point? A small book, a small gesture, photocopied for a few family members.

'People need to know,' Michal said. 'So many Australians, they know nothing about migrants except maybe some bad stories. Or they turn us into something they can put on their mantlepiece, to show off to the neighbours.'

'You should write it yourself, Dad,' she said. 'You know a lot more about

Babička than I could ever know. You lived with her for decades.'

'I sure can't forget when I was a teenager,' Michal said. 'She could be a pain sometimes, you know, pushing me to make something of my life.'

'Like you're doing to me right now.' Veronika didn't feel angry or even resentful. She knew that she deserved the pushing.

'Why not think about it, love?' her father said. 'Write about Babička, the bravest of women, and the pain-in-the-arse mother. Well, that's what you think when you're a young man. She was different for you, and different for your mother, for her friends.'

Veronika reflected. 'Like a play,' she said. 'Different voices.'

'I couldn't write a play to save my life,' Michal said. 'But maybe *you* could.'

Then he rose stiffly from the milk crate, looked around the yard. 'I'm going now, Ron, and I'll come back in a couple of hours with my tools, a shovel, some paint. I'll get stuck into this place. I'll pinch some of Angela's herbs, too, and get some cuttings from the garden. I'll make the place look *nadherny*.'

Veronika turned on the kettle, settled down to wait for her father to return. To make the place look *lovely*. Pushing her to make something. Urging her to tell a story. Well, Babička's friends will have stories, she thought, stories I've never heard before, that maybe no-one's heard before.

She opened her laptop, opened her emails. Junk mail galore: how to make money, obscenely expensive skin cream, donations for some wildlife fund, weight loss … Cassie's name. Dear Cassie. She hadn't heard from her in months. But then I haven't been in touch either, she thought, because I have nothing worth putting into words.

Dearest Veronika,

It's been simply forever! Where does the time go? It was much better when you were just across the English Channel only a Eurostar away. Now you're too far away! Not fair!! I really do miss you. What are you doing? Have you settled in Perth by now? And are you starring in any plays? And how is your family? Your last email, gosh, you sounded a bit glum, so I hope you're feeling better. All that sunshine and the beaches and the hedonism. Speaking of which … any love on the horizon? Anne Sophie and I are still going strong, I can't imagine my life without her and she tells me the same thing.

We're coming into spring at last. I feel positively naked without my coat and I just love it. My art is coming along quite well, really well, in fact. I had a small exhibition in Camden and sold two ink drawings. A. S. calls them my 'swirly pictures'. Why do people like the swirly ones? They're not as good as my paintings. Still selling jewellery, enough to stay afloat, more than enough, actually.

I've been keeping up with the Players. Did you know that Gwen is pregnant!? She doesn't know who the father is, and she doesn't seem to care! Gosh, I would be caring. What if the father turned out to be a serial killer, or worse, voted Conservative? She's living not that far from you, maybe you could see her sometime, I think she might be a bit lonely. And Lucas has bought a house, some sort of duplex somewhere horrible, sent me a photo, he's terribly proud of it. Closer to home, we went Sebastian and Sarah's wedding. Stunning ceremony, beautiful choir. I wore my first ever fascinator! (But A. S. said it looked like a lampshade.) We drank loads champagne. And A. S. had me in hysterics, impersonating Sarah's stuffy relatives. Sumptuous in all, but the speeches were too clean. Anyhow, apparently they're trying for a baby.

Have you been in touch with Joshua? Did you two ever make amends? But I don't have a clue about Gloria, she's still in East Timor, I gather. Anyway, life goes on. Wouldn't it be fun to see one another again?

Please write to me soon and tell me everything. I miss you heaps.

Cassie XXX

PS. Can you believe we used to bicycle around Paris in miniskirts holding up an umbrella at the same time? I couldn't imagine that now – as guess what?? I wasn't going to tell you because it's still early days but I'm absolutely BURSTING to tell you. I'm pregnant!!! Anne Sophie and I are over the moon!!! I'm feeling a bit puffy but A. S. tells me I'm glowing. I so, SO want you to meet the baby, and Anne Sophie too, I know you'd really like her, I just know you would. I would love to get us all back together, the Players, maybe a reunion in the orchard. What do you think? I could email everyone, and then after the baby is born, we could all meet up somewhere. What do you think? Tell me it's a great idea!

Cassie was having a baby! Veronika scanned the email again, zoomed in on the giddy PS. It seemed unreal. Impossible. Her flighty friend grown up and settled, giving birth, raising a child. Gwen, too, having a baby. Ana's babies growing up. Sebastian trying for a baby. Had the world gone mad with all this ... breeding? Oh, she knew it was a big deal for Cassie, of course it was, and probably for all of them, but she couldn't really see what all the fuss was about. Mothers always complaining about the sacrifices they made for their children. Or else they couldn't stop boasting about the genius of their precious offspring. Ana could drive her up the wall like that ... *Ben is such a good speller; Meredith draws such beautiful pictures* ... And as for Cassie's reunion idea: Veronika shook her head. What could she possibly have in common with pregnant Gwen and duplex Lucas? And imagine seeing Sebastian again ... she'd feel mortified ... ashamed. What on earth would she say to him? *I hear you're trying to have a baby, all the best with that.* I went to Paris to improve my acting skills, to lose myself in other people, but it was all a big mistake, founded on a lie, and now I don't know who I am anymore. And would he even care? Maybe he would. Maybe he really *had* changed, as Cassie said, become a better person. Maybe because he was happier. Maybe that's all it took. Well, it must have helped, anyway. And she was happy for Cassie, she really was. She was probably the best friend she had. The only friend, if you didn't count Ana.

So she replied straight away, sent Cassie her love and best wishes, commented on her painting success, all the while trying to picture her friend with a bulging belly. She added some news about her own life: her new job in the box office, starting tomorrow; her sister aiming to go to college; and some flashes of thought about writing a play. To honour Babička, really. Maybe starting with her youth, then her migrant experience in Australia. Just a vague idea at this stage, and she would have to talk to Babička's old friends while they were still alive, or their minds were still working properly. Did Cass ever worry about getting old? Veronika had looked in the mirror yesterday and seen, to her dismay, how her skin had slackened and how tiny lines had appeared around the corners of her eyes, around her mouth. *And I swear that my boobs have shrunk, Cassie! But then I remembered my grandmother saying that any more than a handful was vulgar.*

90. Charlie

Conch fritters and fried green beans. And now Peggy was telling him that razzleberry pie was ready. Was she trying to make him fat? Peggy and Amy, tapping their fingers at the table, waiting for him, but he said to start without him; he wasn't hungry anymore. And he couldn't pull himself away from the lurid screen, either. Vivid as acid, the picture was, sucking him in like a black hole. Cable TV. So many channels it was nuts. Kind of thrilling, mind you, switching from one bizarre scene to another.

He paused for a moment on a greying white guy evangelist standing in a stadium. *This is the voice of the world tomorrow and we are all saved!!* he bellowed to the crowd. Charlie couldn't bear it.

He flicked over to a soap, *The Bold and the Beautiful.* He knew that one. No way. Taylor dying. Ridge in tears. What a poonce. Taylor. He felt a bit sad for her. Who wouldn't want a piece of that bird? That bitch Brooke will finally get her chance. *Boring*!

A shopping channel next. Cucumber shredder. What sort of knob would buy that? Another shopping channel. Exercise equipment. That was more like it. A busty woman with a tight butt lifting herself up and down a machine and a man, nuggety as a walnut, carrying on about some powder. I should work on my abs, he thought, but I don't want to end up looking like a shiny walnut.

Next. News. CNN. Jesus. Bombs gone off in a Bali nightclub. Christ. More US troops killed in Afghanistan. He turned away from the screen for a minute. Different coloured lights flashed behind his eyelids as the rasping voice of the presenter carried on. More disaster.

Charlie was worried about the mines. Fuel shortages. Ore disappearing. Worried about embezzlers edging their way in while he was away. Should he quit trying to run things over the phone, get out of the mines, go into business with Peggy, with her family?

He switched off the remote, feeling so damn weary. The prickly reality of things sinking in. Was it such a bad idea, hooking up with Peggy? She was damned smart, a strategic manager in that mega company. You'd think she was just a daddy's girl but looks can be deceiving, as they say. The stack of sandy curls, earrings as big as hula hoops, a little thick with the make-up, sure, but she was pretty and voluptuous, knew how to dress, bright silky tops and strappy heels, gold bracelets that clinked. And she knew a thing or two about running a mega company. He'd seen her in action. In the boardroom. And she wasn't all shoptalk, either. She sang him ditties in the car, driving along the boulevard, taking Amy to school. She was a swimmer, loved to tango. She was perky and funny and she sat on his knee and told him not to mind the lovebugs, the humidity, the retirees on their scooters. All he needed to do was leave Down Under for good 'cause *who couldn't be happy living so close to Disney World?* But should he make the leap? He might have been living in the most humungous house in Rose Isle, Orlando, with marble floors and three spa baths and the widest view of Lake Rowena, but it wasn't his. None of it. And Amy – a carbon copy of her mother in miniature, but with darker hair, a whiny thing – she wasn't his either. None of it was his. Or him.

He switched off the TV and sank into the sofa, feeling like a fake. No, he had to stop that. Had to.

'Honey, your pie's getting cold.'

He'd met Peggy through Platinum Introductions. It had cost him five thousand dollars for an ageing woman called Pam – a calm voice, counselling degree, and a *certificate in matchmaking* (who knew?) – to find him *someone suitable.* Five thousand gave you three dates but no guarantees. He figured it was the only way to weed out the gold-diggers. The clingers-on. He needed someone with as much money as him. Or more. It wasn't like there'd been a shortage of supply. But he just didn't know who he could trust. After all that drama with Ana, that leech, it was the only way. And who would have guessed, Peggy Miller, an heiress no less, really liked his picture. Seventy-three percent compatibility, according to the questionnaire.

They'd first met in Istanbul. *Halfway,* she'd joked on the email. Not halfway in the slightest. That would have been Honolulu, he pointed out, but she'd been there a dozen times already. So he booked the cruise down the Bosporus. They'd wined and dined at 360 Istanbul before they flew over Cappadocia in a private helicopter. They talked about meeting next in Kerala. But she wanted it all. Immediately. Without the wait. She had a kid, *the cutest little jit,* who was going into fourth grade. Amy had her nanny, but she couldn't just take a vacation, could she? There was Dragonfly Aviation. A busy schedule. She was needed. And so he'd packed up and flown over in a wink. Some sort of *extended stay,* without going into the logistics. It was harder to win over Amy, though. He'd really tried. Braved the crowds and took her to Adventure Island Water Park at Tampa Bay. They'd even seen the *gators.* But she kept going on about her dad who was living in Mexico, mentioned the *yummiest churros* and the National Palace where she'd seen pictures of men and horses and battles on walls and art all over a staircase. Did they have that in Australia? No, he'd said, and it made him feel like a dud. No National Palace. No churros.

He didn't know much about kids, but he couldn't help remembering those tiny babies resting on his forearms, kicking their miniscule feet, wailing. Eyes barely open. Mind-blowing little creatures, they were. And for a fleeting moment in time, he'd been *Dad.* The surge of love. The pride. A family. A family that was his. Only to be taken away.

Peggy had been to the aeronautical university. She talked a lot about something called *avionics* and global cargo and said they were thinking about moving into manufacturing for aerospace, not just aeroplanes. Dragonfly were doing well, not like Eagle Air, which had to be bought out by the government of Brunei. Would Charlie do it? Would he make the leap?

'Charlie, what are you doing?' Amy's baby voice. She was standing at the door. And then her mother's voice.

'Y'all better get here quick, or this pie will disappear.'

Charlie finally got up, wandered out of the TV room, via the kitchen and out onto the patio. He would pass on the pie.

'Honey ... *Charlie,* sweetheart, are you okay?'

He didn't want to talk. He just wanted to look out at the lake turning dark, see it almost disappear, then maybe disappear into it too. He wanted to mull things over. He wanted to be on his own. He thought about that woman. The one who slipped from his grasp. The one he thought of when the day was too long, or when he was stuck in the Florida sun, in some kind of ten-lane traffic jam on State Road 528, sick with the stinging scent of asphalt. Or when he saw some pretty picture that Amy drew. Some mottled, multicoloured finger painting she pulled out of her bag. That's when he thought of her.

The woman who had something he didn't understand. The flouncing about on stage, the crazy costumes, all that pretending. Christ, life was hard enough without trying to be someone else. Still, it was the thing that seemed to keep her going, that kept her fire alight. What had she told him that night? That she wanted to go to Paris to be *better.* Well, he hoped she was better, after he'd paid for her fancy classes. He remembered now, all those phone calls he made to find a French director called *Antoine*. The information had been easy enough to obtain. Charlie's Mauritian friend from horseracing made the call to France; Antoine had hardly deliberated before he named a sum. There were conditions that Antoine accepted. And Charlie wired the money up front: a whole three years' worth of 'scholarship' and a bit extra for the Frenchman.

All that effort to support her career, but then he'd looked out for news of Veronika starring in some play and hadn't found a thing. Maybe he should tell her … no, maybe not. She'd pound on his door and tell him how much she hated him. Passion. That's what she had, what she maybe still had, and he'd never come close to her again, breathe her in, dream about taking her to bed.

What could he do now about that old flame? He could contact Ana again. She would know where her sister was, what Veronika had done with the scholarship he'd arranged for her. Coming to think of it now … digging up old bones … maybe not such a good idea. He'd already sent her a sort of olive branch at Easter time. Ana might reply and give him some information. And where was his brother in all this? Where was he now, how had *he* ended up? Damn it, I even miss my dad, Charlie thought. How could he miss his father? He didn't know how, but he did.

Yes, he'd had moments when he felt they had bonded; like he had made him proud, like he enjoyed Charlie's company, even. But then when Charlie failed at something, tripped up or talked back, when his mother didn't make his dad happy, there was a beating. A black eye. A swollen and bleeding lip. He remembered his mother, the ironing board, his father coming at him. His chest red and burnt with the imprint of an iron. He'd taken it out on his brother. Sharing around the beating, pounding him to a pulp when he felt like a piece of nothing. That felt like justice. Balance restored.

He wasn't so bad. At least he'd not laid a finger on Peggy. She didn't wind him up or complain if he didn't come to eat his key lime pie or take Amy to school.

And still he came back to Joshua. Where was he? That poor, scared kid who'd taken the rap for his crime. He owed him one, for sure, but his brother would never take it, he knew. He was just like Veronika. Two people who hated him.

And what damn good did that do?

91. Sebastian

Sebastian checked his phone. Still no message from Cassie. He had a feeling, though, that she might ambush him at any minute. He looked out onto the hazy London skyline. He could make out the dome of St Paul's and the turrets of Westminster Palace. A magnificent blue sky, and the oak trees fresh with leaves. People wearing shorts, picnicking, taking off their shoes, basking in the feeble sun.

A familiar voice. *On time! How great is that?*

Really? Fifteen minutes late, he thought.

Cassie plonked down next to him, kissed him on the cheek. She was wearing a floppy hat and a retro kind of dress smothered with bright patterns. Her hair had grown down to her chin. She looked ... what did she look like? Jubilant. Triumphant. And peppering him with questions straight away, about life in Hampstead, and was it *bucolic* and how was Sarah liking it, and yes, she was feeling fantabulous.

'Shall we walk?' he said. 'I need to move.'

He saw Cassie flash him a look of concern.

'Too much of the peaceful life,' he said.

And so they began their walk down the winding dirt path through the Heath, past the lawns and into the thickened trees. They swapped stories: Cassie raving about the jewellery market, Sebastian explaining, insofar as he was allowed, the business of the foreign office. Counterterrorism, Afghanistan, the vexed question of a legal war. He heard himself rattling on, trying to sound more important than he actually felt.

'Sounds tough,' Cassie said and shot him a smirk. 'I'll stick with the jewellery.'

They took a seat on a park bench in front of a pond. It was set deep amid the oaks. Willows dipped in the water and herons skirted the muddy banks. He heard Cassie sighing, deeply, as she looked out onto the lake.

'It was on a day like this that I fell in love with Anne Sophie,' she said, then suddenly turned to him with a stricken look. 'I am so glad I never slept with you,' she said. 'I would have fallen horribly in love and it would have been a dreadful torment to know that you really loved Veronika.'

Sebastian had no idea what she was talking about. But then he often didn't, with Cassie.

'What's brought all this on?' he said.

Cassie shrugged. 'Anyway, I'm glad that Sarah makes you happy. She *does* make you happy, doesn't she?'

'Yes. Yes. Of course she does.'

He fell silent again and gazed at the pond, at the lilies dotting the surface, a dragonfly landing on the water. He felt Cassie take his hand, squeeze it tight.

'Are things alright between you two?' she said. 'Honestly?'

Damn the woman, he thought. Cassie was a mind-reader. A kind, sweet mind-reader.

'Honestly not,' he said. 'Sarah's ... well, she's had some bad news. She found out she has something called polycystic ovaries. It means ... it means she's having difficulty conceiving.' He looked down at Cassie's hand in his, felt the warmth of her beside him. 'It's been almost two years now,' he said. 'It's all been a bit of ... well, an ordeal. I've been feeling very down about it. More and more.'

Cassie took away her hand.

'How do you think Sarah feels?' she said.

Sebastian felt annoyed. 'Well, of course it makes her ... oh, angry and depressed and then full of hope, but ... well, no-one ever asks me how *I* feel.' He tried to keep his voice steady. 'I agreed to move to Hampstead to reduce the stress ... to improve our chances ... but none of it's worked. And Sarah, my God ...' He shook his head. 'She's tried every treatment under the sun. Hormones, herbs, acupuncture. *Chanting.* Cupping. Would someone please tell me what the fuck is *cupping*? And the bills! You should see the cost of all of this nonsense! And she's obsessed with the timing of her cycle. And well ... it all makes me feel like she just wants me for my sperm.' There. He'd said it. He'd never told anyone before, even Sarah. Especially Sarah.

Cassie nudged him in the side. 'Sebbie, don't be silly,' she said. 'I've seen the way Sarah looks at you. She loves you. You can't fake that, you know.'

Sebastian threw his hands in the air. '"*One life! One life! That's all I have!*" she moans at me. "*The thought of not being a mother ...*" This is how she goes on and on and well, I do my best to support her and *I'd* love a child, I really would, but no-one seems to care about that.'

Cassie was silent, staring into the pond. Then she turned to him with a smile. A smile! 'Have you thought about IVF?' she said.

'I *hate* fucking needles. Just the thought of them.'

'But *you* don't take the needles, Seb. That's Sarah's job.'

'And she's ... getting on,' he said. 'That's another problem. She'll be thirty-six next month.'

Cassie took his hand again. 'Poor Sarah!' she said. 'I *am* sorry. I am really sorry.'

He leaned forward, covered his head with his hands, then removed them. Sat up straight. He felt that familiar anger rising inside him again, as if he were about to break.

'I can't bear it,' he said. 'I love her, Cass. I really do. But all her talk about timing and bleeding and uterine lining, it's really ... it's hardly an aphrodisiac.'

He suddenly sprang from the bench. 'Let's get a drink,' he said.

They walked for some time, he didn't know for how long, towards a pub that he knew they would eventually find. London was full of bloody pubs, the Fox this, the Bloodhound that, and he badly needed a drink. He'd come specially to see Cass, someone to talk to about all this mess, but she hadn't exactly lavished him with sympathy. *Poor Sarah*. And now she wasn't saying a word, either. Cass: silent? Maybe a drink wasn't such a good idea. Maybe she wanted to get back to her beloved Anne Sophie and ... well, *he* needed a drink. That's all he knew right now.

The pub was crowded, people coming in and out, jostling, gesticulating, as he sat with his lager in front of him, a pint already half-guzzled. Cassie had insisted on orange juice. Was she on some kind of health kick, another one of her faddish ideas, along with her jewellery and her paintings and her silly hat perched on the table? And now she was rattling on about her paintings and plans to visit Anne Sophie's mother for Christmas and something else about new furniture. He tried to look interested. He stood up to get another pint ... *no more orange juice, thanks, there's only so much sugar and vitamin C a woman can take*. When he came back with his lager, she started up about something different ... the Players ... some crazy idea about a reunion ... had he kept up with the Players ... Lucas had started a new band ... last mail full of happy news ... released a single that had made it on the indie charts. Well, good for him, Sebastian thought, grimly. He couldn't even remember what Lucas looked like.

Suddenly she stopped talking. Looked at him intently.

'Maybe you should just stop worrying about it,' she said. 'Anxiety reduces the chances of conception.'

Sebastian took a hefty swig of beer.

'It's not *my* idea,' Cassie said. Persisted. 'There's a lot of research that says—'

'And how do you propose I stop being anxious?' he said. 'And don't go on about meditation and yoga and all that ... *quackery*.'

Cassie didn't flinch. 'Have you talked to Sarah about how you feel?' she said.

He shrugged.

'Well, that would be a good place to start,' Cassie said. 'If you want to save your marriage.'

Cassie the self-appointed guru. It was enough to make him scream. They sat in silence for a while, Cassie staring into her orange juice as if she might find some inspiration from the glass. Then he heard her clear her throat.

'I'm pregnant,' she said.

Sebastian jolted. She reached across the table, put her hand across his arm.

'I'm pregnant,' she said again, her bright green eyes looking right into his. 'A donor. A bit of a process, but we got there eventually.'

He felt a rush of indignation. 'You could have had *my* sperm, you know!' he said.

Cassie's mouth fell wide open. 'What the fuck, Sebastian? What the fuck are you on about? How do you think Sarah would have felt about that?'

Sebastian shook his head. 'Of course. I'm sorry. I'm ...' What was happening to him? A fluster of emotions. And now he was saying dumb things. 'Too much beer,' he said. He looked at his watch. 'I'm meant to be meeting Sarah and my brother-in-law in an hour or so, so—'

'A Norwegian stevedore,' Cassie said. 'Nice looking in the photo. Loves mountain biking. Clean medical history. Prepared to meet the child when he turns eighteen. Plays the fiddle. Always fancied a musical child. Intra-uterine insemination.' She picked up her glass, set it down again. 'Thanks for asking,' she said.

And now it was all too much again, too much. He felt offended. Outraged. Get yourself some sperm. Put it in a tube. Mix it up with an egg, shove it in the oven and bingo! A baby. Just like that. He leaned closer to Cassie.

'I'm curious,' he said. 'Did you find him in the phone directory? Or was it like online shopping where you just add whatever you like to the basket or … maybe like a drive-through? Hm … I'll have the baby boy, thanks, with a serving of fries.'

Cassie stood up, her face flushed. 'You haven't changed at all, have you?' she snapped, and flashed him a look of disdain. 'It's always about *you*.' She shook out her purse and some coins hit the table. She slapped on her hat and stomped out of the pub.

Sebastian sat there for a minute, astonished, his head reeling with beer and the sting of her words. She'd walked out on him. She hated him. Well, he'd been a prick, hadn't he, a first-class prick. He'd been … he leapt up, bolted after her, saw her walking a block away, ran panting after her, calling after her, *Cass. I'm sorry, so sorry …*

She stopped, turned to face him. He saw that her eyes, her beautiful green eyes, were brimming with tears.

'I'm so sorry, Cass,' he said again. 'I … It was just your timing …'

She sniffed. 'I thought we were friends,' she said. 'I thought you would be happy for me.'

'I am, I really am.' He took her hand, willing her to forgive him. 'I was mean and cruel and … you're right, I need to talk to Sarah.'

Cassie nodded. She didn't brush away his hand.

'Do you know what you're having,' he said.

'A boy. We found out yesterday. My scan. Fourteen weeks.'

He felt stupid. A bit tipsy. Sick of the way he kept botching things up.

'I actually wasn't going to mention any of it,' Cassie said. 'Because of you and Sarah.'

An ambulance rushed past, and Cassie came closer. 'But … the baby will need a bloke around. A role model, you know.'

He could just make out her words above the blare of the siren.

'A role model?' he said, incredulous.

'Yes,' Cassie shouted, then waited for the noise to rush away. 'Even if he *is* a real *prick*. A bloody pain in the arse.'

She laughed. Which made him laugh. Which made him feel she was a good, dear friend. Then she took his hand, held it tight.

'Talk to Sarah,' she said.

'I'm off to Brussels for a week,' he said. 'The timing's not right.'

'No excuses, Sebbie. Talk to her.'

92. Gloria

Gloria had steeled herself. She had thought she had seen it all in Díli, but nothing could have prepared her for the blow. Her mother, Sofia, looking so old, so broken, lying in a stark white hospital bed. Her beloved mother. Did she recognise her daughter, at least? Was that a glimmer in her eyes that said hello daughter, my dear daughter, my Gloria? Her mother couldn't speak, couldn't even eke out some garbled words, and all Gloria could do was hug her carefully, kiss her gently on the cheeks. Put a red and green necklace around her neck. *Sea grass*, she said, woven by one of the women in the Díli market.

Díli. Her girls needed her, she would miss them, but her mother needed her more. I will stay here as long as I have to, she thought. Her mother. The woman who stifled and vexed her, who was full of sighs and fears, who prayed to a God that Gloria was no longer sure existed. But her mother had carried her to safety. She'd lost a husband and a son. And the last time they'd spoken, her mother had told her that she loved her. Gloria knew this to be true.

A stroke. The doctors weren't sure about recovery, the nurses told her. They said it would take a few months to know. Some speech might return to her. Some mobility. In the meantime, she must stay in hospital, be monitored and medicated, receive physiotherapy and speech pathology. All these words, Gloria thought, hopeful words, words that urged her to keep up her spirits, for her mother's sake, as well as for her own.

She'd been living in her mother's flat but after a week, she needed to get out. It was dark and dreary, and there was too much of the past in it, too much sadness in the photos and the tinny ornaments. She'd asked around for a place to stay.

Her old Timor friends had a few leads but they didn't come to much.

Rosária offered her a sofa at her place, but Gloria wanted something more stable. A room of her own.

A former colleague at Kardinya, a PE teacher, had a spare bedroom, but Gloria remembered Scott's rather lecherous eyes and couldn't bear to think of that bedroom. She did ask him, though, if there was any relief teaching on offer, and he said he'd speak to someone at the school. In the meantime, she hoped that her credit card would hold out.

And in all this time, visiting her mother, shopping for food, sleeping fitfully, if at all, she felt the strangeness of being back in Perth after two years away. Much stranger than her return to Timor-Leste. People's movements, people's cars, were too fast; buildings were too wide, too tall. The big bright lights in offices never seemed to switch off. So many shops stuffed with luxuries. She wanted to stop people on the street and ask them if they knew how much they had, if they wanted to give any of it away. But she didn't do that, of course. Instead, she flushed the toilet in her mother's flat, and felt both grateful and vaguely unreal. She felt unreal, too, in the supermarket: hundreds of cans of soup and kidney beans, rows and rows of bottles of this and sauces of that. Mega-packets of rice. Whole aisles of chocolate bars. It made her feel slightly queasy, as if she'd eaten too much in one sitting. She found herself eating small helpings and trying not to feel guilty.

And then there was Joshua. He had written to her a month ago and she still hadn't written back. His letter had filled her with trepidation. She'd been pleased by his interest in her life, by his sympathy and affection, but she also understood that he was lonely. That he seemed to be asking something of her that she wasn't sure she could give. She was lonely too, of course she was, but she had her work, her life in Timor, and now this ... her mother. She worried at first that she'd sounded too eager herself, too needy, in her letter, but she hoped she hadn't given him the wrong impression. Led him on.

And yet. It was always in the night that the feelings came back. Her days were busy with visiting and doctors and a quick bit of shopping, with the sadness of realising that her mother wasn't getting better – but in the night Joshua would return to her. He'd told her in his letter about his new job, stacking shelves in a supermarket, and although she didn't know where he worked, she found herself dreaming of the local Coles, gazing down the aisles, hoping for a chance encounter. He'd also given her his phone number. She could call him any time, he'd said, if she was ever back in Perth. *It would be so wonderful to see you, Gloria, I think about you a lot.* But she hadn't phoned him. She hadn't even started punching in his number, then making herself stop.

And yet. She wanted to see him. She longed to see him. Head in one place, heart in the other.

Someone was there. Rosária's mother, Mrs Gomes. She was sitting beside the hospital bed, muttering prayers. It had felt like decades since Gloria had seen her last at the *Kore Metan*. She recalled high-school sleepovers at Rosária's, netball matches and church fetes and homework-buddy marathons. Mrs Gomes had always been a devout, censorious sort. *She's not dead yet*, Gloria almost said, but stopped herself.

'Hello, Tia Carmen. Hello, dear Mum.'

Gloria kissed her mother on the forehead. Her mother's face was grey and bony, but her eyes shone up at her daughter. She looked … not blank, really. Calm. Maybe the prayers had brought her some comfort, after all.

'Thank you, Mrs Gomes,' Gloria said. 'For all you've done.'

The woman patted her on the arm.

'Wonderful to have you back, Gloria.'

'Just as well you were there,' Gloria said. 'When … it happened.' She was feeling guilty. She put her hand on her mother's. 'I don't know what would have happened, Mrs Gomes … with Mum living on her own, you know, and I can't bear to think—'

'She'll be glad you are home,' Mrs Gomes said. It will make all the difference.'

Gloria nodded, smiled thinly. She felt another pang of guilt: looking down on this woman for being so pious, so sanctimonious, but here she was, Mrs Gomes, sitting by her mother's bed. She looked tired. Worn down. She packed up her prayer cards and picked up her bag.

'Don't go,' Gloria said. 'Please.'

She felt a sudden panic about being alone with her mother. There had always been a nurse, or someone hovering in the background. Another patient, someone's family friend. She didn't know if she could face it.

'She is better now,' Mrs Gomes said. 'She's had the oil of unction.'

As if that would magically resolve this terrible situation. Don't go, she'd pleaded, but the woman was going, gone, and all Gloria could do was sit on the edge of the bed and try not to cry. Her head was a jumble. She was tongue-tied. She closed her eyes. And then the questions flooded in. Is she comfortable? Is the light too strong? Does she need the toilet? Does she want the TV on? Is she tired? Am I tiring her? How do I entertain her? *Should* I entertain her? Tell her stories? Maybe she wants to speak. Maybe she doesn't know she can't speak? Maybe it's too much for her. What if she's frustrated? What can I say that won't sound petty? I can't do this! *How can I do this?* Gloria opened her eyes and summoned all her hope.

'I love you, Mum,' she said.

Gloria had visited her four times now but had never once seen a doctor. She'd tried to make an appointment, but it never seemed to happen. A meeting scheduled the day before but then the doctor had cancelled, some kind of emergency. She'd met different nurses: nurses to take her mother to the bathroom and wash her, nurses to take her mother's blood pressure and give her some pills. She'd met a social worker who'd given Gloria a pile of papers she could hardly bear to look at. Information about how to get her home fitted out. Pictures of benches, bars, mats and lights and ramps. But still she needed to speak to a doctor. Surely that wasn't impossible?

She went to the desk and asked to speak to a doctor. Make another appointment, at least. But the ward clerk merely waved her off and returned to his computer. What was he doing? His pinched-looking face seemed to be squinting at the internet.

'Please,' she said.

'Not possible right now. Don't know when. Sorry, you'll have to wait until ...'

Gloria was furious. Okay, so it wasn't Timor. There was Medicare, clean floors, the reassuring smell of disinfectant. It was a western capitalist democracy, but *for crying out loud!* Was it too much to ask to see a doctor? To be treated like a human being?

'I need to speak to a doctor! *Now!*'

The young man looked up at her, bewildered, then shrugged his shoulders.

'Look, I'm busy at the moment,' he said.

'And I said now! Right now!'

If only I was a rich fucking white man, she thought.

The young man sighed. 'Okay, calm down, calm down,' he said. 'I'll see what I can do.'

And I'll see your face in a pulpy mess, Gloria thought. Calm down, calm down ... her mother had been here for a week and this kid who barely looked out of school was telling her to calm down! She watched as he picked up the phone, folded her arms, waited. Finally, the young man put down the phone, told her that the registrar would meet her in her mother's room. That she would be with her *shortly*.

Then he turned back to his computer, as if Gloria was done and dusted.

The doctor didn't look much older than Gloria. She wore a headscarf and white scrubs and was holding a file bulging with papers. Blood tests and scans, Gloria thought. People's lives literally in the woman's hands. The doctor had a gentle manner, a soothing voice, and Gloria felt her body loosen. And she didn't have the energy to shout anymore.

'Just as well your mother received quick medical attention,' the doctor said, and proceeded to describe what Gloria already knew: a *blood clot ... weakness on the left side ... treatment for the blood flow ... vision loss.* Did doctors always do this, she thought? Talk about the patient as if she wasn't there.

'But what can be done?' Gloria said. 'I mean ... to help her?'

'Exercise,' the doctor said. As if it was the simplest thing in the world. 'Extending knees, stretching shoulders.'

She handed Gloria the pile of papers. It didn't look simple at all!

'You will have to do these at home,' the doctor said.

'At home?' Gloria felt her heart seize up. 'So soon?'

'No, not immediately. Your mother will need to move to the rehabilitation hospital first.'

'For how long?'

'We don't know exactly. A few weeks maybe, until she's stabilised. She'll be monitored there, and she'll receive the very best treatment. Therapy – for her communication and motor skills. For her mobility. The technology is excellent. Then there will be a home-based program. Which is where you come in.'

'Home-based?'

The doctor nodded. 'There's a lot you can do with her. But if you're working, you may need to hire a carer.' She pointed to the file. 'The instructions are very clear. But ... you need to understand that many stroke survivors don't always recover physically.' She looked at Gloria's mother, then back at Gloria. 'The emotional part of the recovery is just as important. It helps if ... you're close, you know. I believe you've been in every day to see your mother.'

So somebody knew, Gloria thought. Someone must have passed it on: daughter visited, no change, daughter visited, no change.

'Any more questions?' the doctor said.

Her throat thickened. 'Can I ... I mean, it's just me,' she said. 'It's just me, looking after my mother.'

The doctor looked tired. 'Your mother is lucky to have you ... Not everyone ...' She stopped. 'But you must look after yourself, too. Call in some carers. Have breaks. Go out with friends.'

Gloria nodded, dumbly, grateful for this professional advice, for this touch of compassion. For not being patronised or dismissed. She thanked the doctor, watched her walk away, leaving her alone again. She turned to look at her mother, who was mercifully asleep. She sat down beside her bed and tried not to think about what lay ahead. For her poor, dear mother, and for herself.

And then, without thinking, she began to sing, softly, slowly, with some kind of faith in her heart.

Ita hotu Maromak nia povu. We are all God's people.

93. Veronika

The building was what was called brutalist: stark, uncompromising. With wall-to-wall red carpet and vaulted ceilings. Her manager, Nathan, was lean, middle-aged, with neat brown hair and a shiny forehead. Starched shirt and highly polished shoes. He took his job as box office supervisor uber-seriously, and she was doing her best, even though she didn't feel motivated. And he was doing his best to be helpful – really helpful, showing her how to balance and reconcile receipts and ticket sales; advice on dealing with difficult customers; parking details; learning a computer program that tracked all the transactions through a *patron database system*. She had no idea that *ticket seller* was so complicated, and so exasperating as well.

But she wouldn't be there forever, and it would pay the rent. At least it wasn't the stinking pub. At least she could breathe. And it was a twenty-minute walk from her new place. She could even ride her bike there if she wanted. And if she fancied, she could meander along the foreshore at lunchtime, imagine herself floating away along the Swan River, all the way out into the Indian Ocean. Yes, she could float away to Madagascar. They spoke French there, didn't they? Madagascar, now that would be nice …

She'd had a tour the day she started. The other staff were friendly, welcoming, but as soon as she found herself in front of a computer, she was either panicking about what to do or sighing with boredom. The repetition of answering calls, facing the screen, putting on a nice smile for whoever turned up. Did that count for emotional labour? She'd read about it. Being paid to smile.

Had Nathan sensed her lack of motivation? Her disenchantment? One day, during her afternoon tea break, he'd found her standing outside the back of the building, in the wind tunnel of St Georges Terrace. *You get to seat a whole concert hall, you know, now isn't that something?* he'd said. He told her she could attend concerts, if she liked, once the spare tickets had been *approved*. She might even be given a ticket if she was doing a late shift and the Perth Concert Hall wasn't full. They liked their customer service representatives to know the program, he said. It was like tasting the wine if you worked at a cellar door: you could recommend with conviction once you'd sampled. But she would have to wait until her probation was over. *Probation?* It made her feel like a criminal. Still, she liked the idea of a ticket. There were symphonies, jazz orchestras, rock concerts, opera, even stand-up comedians.

It got her thinking about Babička again. A stage; a performance. What had Babička told her, when Veronika was sixteen or so, about the pressure to *assimilate quickly*. Right now, Veronika wished she could *assimilate* into the life she used to have: *young and carefree*, wasn't that the cliché? Thinking that life was a banquet she could feast on. That a dazzling future awaited her. And now … were there any remedies for a trampled heart? *Trampled*. Was she being dramatic again? Melodramatic? Was her life really so bad? It wasn't glamorous Paris, but at least here, back home, she wasn't living under false pretences.

She missed Cassie, too, but Cassie had her own life, shacked up and happy with a woman. Out of reach. Veronika longed for one of Cassie's heartfelt, page-after-page emails. And she longed for a pair of feet that didn't ache.

94. Joshua

It had been a long five hours, stacking all those bloody shelves, with a lousy fifteen-minute break, and his back was aching something awful. But turning over his pillow, dosed with Panamax, all he could think of was the news: the store manager asking him to be the night manager because he was *such a good worker*, apparently.

But do we really need all that stuff on the shelves, Josh thought. Surrounded with masses of cans, bottles, jars, packets, shiny labels spruiking miracle cures for this and that, hundreds of different soups and soaps, even different strengths of toilet paper. The vitamin aisle was just plain ridiculous: hundreds of bottles, there must be, for totally useless stuff. Growing stronger hair or bigger biceps, helping you relax, helping you perk up; a brand-new, pepped-up *you*. The make-up section was the worst, though: skin cream for women at forty dollars a pop, thirty dollars when the specials came around. Dozens of lipsticks, liner stuff for the eyes or lips, stuff to make women's lashes look longer or thicker. *Alluring*, the packet said. He had no idea women used all this stuff, or thought it mattered. *The surplus economy*, Warra called it.

Josh knew that his job was pointless, but it also helped him to survive. Since survival was the name of the game. And becoming night manager would mean more pay, maybe a slightly better way to survive.

He heard his phone beeping. Who the hell? Maybe it was Ana. He'd phoned her once. Just to say hi and see how the family was doing, but she'd been too caught up with the kids. He wouldn't have minded seeing those kids and … well … He groped for his mobile. Didn't recognise the number.

'Hello? Who's this?'

'Joshua. It's me. Gloria.'

Bloody hell! How long had it been since he'd written to her? Two months, maybe even three? He'd stopped counting.

'Gloria?'

'I'm in Perth,' she said.

'Right. Okay.'

Silence.

'So ... I'd like to see you,' she said. Just like that. And then she sighed. Sounded a bit uneasy. 'I don't mean I came to Perth to see you ... I mean ...'

He didn't have a clue what to say.

'I've come back to look after my mother,' she said. 'She had a stroke. And ... well ... she's not getting any better.'

'I'm sorry,' he said. And he really was. He remembered his own mother. The long, slow fade, and then she wasn't there.

'Is your mum with you?' he said. 'I mean ... are you her carer or what?'

'She's still in hospital.'

Her voice sounded so trembly, and his heart went out to her.

'But she'll be coming home at some point,' she said. 'There's not much more they can do for her. She'll get some help at home, but ...'

He could hear what she wasn't saying.

'You're going to look after her at home?' he said.

'Yes. Of course.'

'But what about your work? In Timor?'

He heard her sigh. 'It will still be waiting for me,' she said. 'When ... when ... I don't know when.'

Her voice was sounding even tremblier now, and he thought she might start to cry. He didn't mind if she did; it sure sounded like she had a lot to cry about right now.

'Can I ...' He wasn't sure what to say. 'Can I ... help in any way?'

He heard her catching her breath. Damn this phone. The distance. He wanted to hold her, wrap her up, just hold her.

'You know what would help?' she said. 'I know it's been a long time, but ... you were kind to me, Josh, really kind, and—'

'Where do you live?' he said, as though it was the most important question in the world.

And so she told him and he said he'd come right over and she said he didn't need to and he said he did, he wanted to, and he would be there in half an hour.

'I'm in my PJs,' he said, stupidly.

She giggled. 'I bet they've got stripes,' she said. And she giggled again.

It was the strangest feeling, standing at the door. She didn't look any different: those big brown eyes and curly hair and a smile as wide as the ocean. Her glow. And so he just couldn't help himself, couldn't stop himself, he took her in his arms and held her, held her close, and she was crying, sobbing, into his chest, great big sobs, as if she couldn't stop. And then they faded into hiccups and sharp breaths and then she drew away from him. He didn't want her drawing away, he just wanted to hold her, feel her warmth. The closeness.

'I'm sorry,' she said. 'I've wet your shirt.'

'No ... you haven't. It's fine ... Gloria—' He couldn't really speak. He found himself stroking her hair, that lovely curly hair, and he didn't want this to stop. The touching.

'I'm a wreck,' she said, her shoulders slumping. 'I shouldn't have asked you to come. It's so late, what was I thinking?'

'I'm glad to be here. Honestly,' he said.

He couldn't stop looking into her eyes.

95. Gloria

'It's terrible,' she said. 'My mother can't speak, can't walk, she can't feed herself ... she ... it's awful, Josh, just awful.'

'And you'll be looking after her?'

She nodded. Sniffed.

'And your work in Timor,' he said. 'You'll go back there some day. I know you will.'

She felt ... what did she feel? That he cared, really cared about her and what she was going through. With his boyish face, that unruly hair, the curve of his upper lip. She liked the way he leaned back, giving her some space, but she wanted him to hold her, too, wanting no space between them. He was looking at her keenly, and she had no idea what she might say next.

'I'm sorry I didn't answer your letter, Josh. I—'

'It's okay. I understand ... You have important things to do in your life.'

She met his kind eyes again and felt her heart grow bigger.

'*You're* important to me,' she said. 'You've always been important. You ... will you hold me again? Please.'

She didn't know she was going to say that. Although she must have known. She must have known what she wanted. He took her in his arms, and she felt him breathing, felt herself breathing, the two of them together. Then she felt him brush her cheek with his mouth and soon his mouth was on her mouth and she was kissing him back ... tongues meeting, bodies pressing and *come to bed*, she said, *I want you so much*.

She took him by the hand and led him to her bedroom. Her old bedroom, now her new home for who knew how long. She didn't know how she would cope with her mother. She didn't know how long she would have to care for her, or when she could get back to Timor. There was so much unknown, and all of it troubling, all of it scary. But this, here, with Josh, felt sacred and inevitable.

She opened the top drawer of her mother's dresser and retrieved her *morteen*, the precious glass and copper beads, her sole heirloom. They still shone a beautiful red. Joshua touched them with fascination, put them round her neck, and took her hand again. Feeling the warmth of his hand in hers, she wasn't troubled or scared anymore. She would hold him close, bring him into her body, and know it would be real, that *they* were real, and that whatever lay ahead, they would lie in one another's arms and feel content. Even happy.

96. Charlie

Evenings, Charlie liked to stand on the veranda, looking out onto the water.

Peggy opened the flyscreen, walked towards him, put her arm around him.

'Honey,' she said, all sweet in his ear, 'are you living here for good now? 'Cause people are asking.'

Charlie had nothing to say. She wanted certainty, and he didn't want to tell a lie. He was done with all that.

'You better figure it out sooner or later,' she said. 'Amy's gettin' real attached to you.'

Charlie frowned. 'I'm not so sure about that.' He wasn't sure about many things right now.

Peggy released her hand, looked him in the eye, then sighed.

'I'm beat,' she said. 'See you in the morning. *I guess.*' She pinched his cheek and pressed her lips against his head, then turned and disappeared into the house.

Sweet Amy.

Charlie sat down, his eyes adjusting to the dark again.

If he stared long enough, he could make out shapes in the distance. Houses. The jetty. The thicket of trees. Something else indistinct ... he couldn't be sure of that, either. Something moving. Funny how it all looked so different at night, so quiet and unsettling. The darkness. Shouldn't it be the same in the daytime? He was being stupid. Irrational. He skipped a breath. Felt some kind of pressure at the top of his chest, like an animal crouching over him, pushing him down. He couldn't shake it off.

Then a fleeting image of his brother in prison. His damaged hands.

Where had it come from – this vision? When he'd never once been to visit.

'Joshua,' he said out loud and gasped for air.

He could feel it. What was it? A panther? A bear? This thing out there was still stirring. He gazed into the darkness again, losing himself.

Then a howl. A plaintive howl resounded across the water and almost hit him in the nose.

He would leave his old life behind. But how could he move to Florida without doing something for his brother? Some money. More than some, a lot. A whole lot. He would do that. He would see him again. He would help him out. Charlie put his hand over his chest, wished he could reach out, touch his brother.

97. Sebastian

He'd tried. Several times over breakfast this morning he'd tried, and each time the words had stayed lodged in his throat. Then it was off to work because work could always distract him. But sitting at his desk, staring at the screen, he'd begun to wonder if he'd made a mistake. Let himself think what he'd never allowed before. That he and Sarah had made a mistake. Getting married when they hardly knew each other. And now two years into their marriage and it felt like things were unravelling. Their perfect life in a beautiful house in a quiet, privileged nook, and she was unhappy. Desperate.

'What are you reading there, darling?' Sarah emerged from the steam of the shower and reached into the arms of her dressing-gown.

She sounded relaxed for a change. That was something.

He cleared his throat. 'When thou hast done, thou hast not done / For I have more.'

'And what hast thou done, pray tell?' She looked at Sebastian, amused.

He fumbled for a second. 'Original sin,' he said.

She came towards him, fresh faced with damp hair, leaned over to where he was reading in bed. She gently prised the book from his hands.

'Ah. *The Metaphysical Poets*,' she said. 'Easy bedtime reading?'

'I like Donne,' he said. As if she'd been accusing him of something.

'Do you want to keep reading?' she said. 'Or?'

'Or what?'

'Original sin?' She loosened the belt of her robe.

'Actually, I'm incredibly tired,' he said, and tried to smile. Then he plumped his pillow and reached over to turn off his side light. 'A full-on day tomorrow. Back-to-back meetings. And I have a lot to prepare before I go in.'

'That's alright,' she said quietly.

He heard her rustling with bed clothes. She was probably putting on her pyjamas. The passion killers. As if passion wasn't already pretty much dead and buried. She slipped into bed, then snuggled into him from behind. He wanted to fall asleep, but he could feel her thinking, almost as if she were speaking aloud.

'What is it?' he asked in the dark.

'When you were away in Brussels,' she said. 'I really missed you. Every day you were away ... felt like a sort of bruise ...'

He felt his chest tighten.

'That's nice,' he said.

'Nice?'

He felt Sarah stirring behind him. Disappointed. With him, with their marriage, with those months and months of trying and failing. He made himself turn around to face her. Sarah. His wife.

'I realised how kind you are,' she said softly, looking into his eyes. 'How much you do for me. All the little things. The big things. Like moving here. The appointments. My ... moods. I know I've not been easy.'

He stroked her cheek gently. 'I want to make you happy, Sarah,' he said. 'But—'

He could see her waiting. He had to keep going. Cass had told him.

'I know how much you want a baby,' he said. 'And I understand ... well, I think I do ... how much all this is hurting you ...' He took a very deep breath. 'But sometimes I feel like ... I feel ...'

'That the sex has become so mechanical? I know. I—'

'It's more than that, Sarah.' Should he tell her? What if there was no going back? What if he'd come all this way to find her, this woman he loved, only to ... 'I sometimes feel that I'm just ... well ...'

'A sperm donor?'

She cupped her face in his hands, gazed into his eyes. 'I said I missed you, Seb, so much that it hurt. And I don't ever want to lose you. I understand how you must have been feeling but I thought ... I thought if I didn't talk about it, everything would somehow ... I don't know ... magically resolve itself.'

He drew her close.

'We'll work it out, won't we?' she said.

He heard the resolve in her voice.

And then she drew away, lifted up her hair, took his hand and guided it towards her spine.

'Feel the bump at the top?' she said. 'It's called the zeal point. The

Ancient Egyptians believed it's a spiritual gateway – the mouth of God in fact – through which the soul can be released.'

'Then let me kiss it,' he said.

And so he kissed her there, and around the back of her neck.

'I want to kiss you everywhere,' he said.

He couldn't tell her about Cass being pregnant. By now, likely heavily pregnant. That would have to wait. But they'd made a start, at least, and a start was so much better than unravelling. He kissed her lips, and she kissed him back, hungry now, it seemed, for wanting him. It felt like wanting him for himself.

98. Cassie

Cassie had just stepped off the bus, on her way home from Dr Cohen's. Waddled off, really. They'd been workshopping some of her fears around motherhood and how it would be alright if she was just *good enough* and then ... oh my God! Out came a gush of warm water between her legs. Was her bladder playing up again? No, no, surely not ... it couldn't be happening ... three weeks early ... that was good news, wasn't it? At last! She wanted this baby out, wanted to be able to sleep again, wanted to feel her organs back in their right place. It was happening! Oh shit! What to do? She didn't have her phone with her. She hadn't even packed her hospital bag. She kept walking towards the house, hoping, praying that Anne Sophie was home. Fuck. Help. Fuck.

She walked three more blocks. Cramps. Cramps in her pelvis. Like shudders. Like hammers. Fuck. Help. She wanted to throw up. Sit down. Should she stop someone? Ask them to take her to hospital? How would she make it? *She would make it.* She began to recite a poem she learned in primary school. And then *Figaro*. Lines from *Figaro* came to her ... *Cause a public scandal! Make us the talk of the castle!* But then another pang below her abdomen. And there she was! There must be a God, she thought, it was Anne Sophie, driving down the street in her green Mazda. A miracle!

Cassie leapt into the middle of the road, waving her arms, and Anne Sophie screeched to a halt, her face aghast.

She rolled down the window, looking furious.

'Cass, what the hell are you doing?'

'It's time!' Cassie wailed.

'My God!' Anne Sophie leapt out of the car, and they hugged in the middle of the road. 'Get in, get into the car!' she cried, hoisting Cassie's rear into the seat, then running to the other side, jumping behind the wheel, drove off muttering and gasping and throwing worried looks at Cassie.

'He's pressing against my spine!' Cassie moaned. 'I swear this kid is going to be enormous! *Enormous!*'

They pulled up in front of the hospital, where Cassie had done all her scans, and as soon as she saw the entrance, said she felt a strange sense of comfort.

'I need to find a parking spot!' Anne Sophie shouted. Not comforting at all. 'You need to go in by yourself. Through there! Emergency!'

'But I can't walk ... my back is so sore ... don't leave me, please don't leave me.'

Anne Sophie undid her seatbelt and placed her hands on Cassie's bump. There was a loud toot from behind.

'Just hang on a tick, will you, little one. Hold on a bit longer? Your other mum needs to park the car.' She kissed the bump, took Cassie's head in her hands, and kissed off the tears, kissed her cheeks. 'You can do this, Cass. I'll come and find you. I love you.'

Cassie slumped out of the car and waddled as fast as she could to Emergency. There were crowds of sad-looking people sitting in the waiting area, a queue at the desk, someone with a bandaged head being wheeled past, and Cassie shouted out for help, and a nurse with a clipboard walked up to her, calm as you like, how can she be so calm, can't she see I'm in pain ... I have to get this damn thing *out*! Maternity. The nurse was walking her to Maternity but it was taking so long, every step an agony and hospitals must take up whole suburbs ... lifts, levels ... ushered into a ward full of groaning women.

And then nothing. Placed on a bed and told to wait. Wait for fucking what? Where the hell was Anne Sophie? A nurse put something round her wrist, checked for something, the lord knew what, and then, thank God, the midwife. Nancy, dear Nancy, and Cassie cried with relief. *Hello, love. A keen one, innit? Can't wait to see his mum.*

They wheeled Cassie into a room by herself, placed her on the bed, put her feet in stirrups. She felt like a horse. Where was she? Anne Sophie? Cassie cursed herself that she didn't have her phone. Oh God, what where they doing? Ouch! What was Nancy doing down there? Then Nancy moved away and covered her with the sheet. Torture again, her whole body clenching. Everything seemed to be contracting. Time. Space. Air. And then through a sweaty blur, she saw a familiar face. It couldn't be. Of all the times in your life but yes ... it was him ... Sebastian! God almighty!

'What are you doing here?' she heard herself shout. 'I want to die! Please ask someone to kill me! Will you kill me?'

He came to her side. He looked so clean. So sparkling and shaven.

He was wearing a suit. Cool as a cucumber. She let out an ugly cry. He looked worried, bent down towards her.

'Anne Sophie called, and I happened to be close by,' he said. 'She had a minor accident in the parking lot. But she's on her way now, she won't be far behind.' He took Cassie's hand.

'I'm going to die,' Cassie moaned, looking up at him.

'You're *not* going to die, Cassie!'

'But I *want* to die!'

Oh my God, it was her, at last … Anne Sophie, rushing in, cardigan flapping about.

'I'm here! Cass! Darling! How are you?'

Cassie could hardly speak. The midwife put on an oxygen mask. Anne Sophie kissed Cassie's free hand, then held it tight. Smiled at Sebastian.

'I can't believe it, can you?'

And now what was Nancy doing? Telling her not to push *just yet*, measuring her every bloody second, and then more pushing and clenching, more oxygen. But then something happened. Something made her body take over. It was visceral. Profound. Something was moving, something was surviving, making its way into the world and she felt it all over, knowing it was coming and there … oh my, my, oh my God, this mucky thing in her arms and it was him. He was here, lying on her chest, and she stroked his little head and held him to her heart.

99. Sebastian

Sarah told him that morning that she would try something she'd seen them cooking at the Club: wild mushroom risotto in truffle oil. She'd promised him *pudding* too, caramelised pineapple with something or other. Was it chocolate sauce? Sebastian felt hungry, just thinking about it. He arrived home, climbed up the stairs and found her in the kitchen, chopping mushrooms to the Spice Girls, getting the words wrong. *I know what I want, what I really, really want.* She hadn't seen him. He surprised her with a *boo* and a kiss.

'Smells amazing,' he said. She was in her yoga clothes. In a chirpy mood, it seemed.

'I've only just started.'

He was glad to be home. Glad of the prospect of a delicious meal made by his lovely wife.

'I'm starving,' he said. 'And it looks amazing, too.'

Sarah turned down the music and warned him not to get too excited. That risotto took forever. He took off his tie, poured himself a glass of water and pulled up a stool.

'I like watching you cook,' he said. 'You look in your element. A true professional.'

He was throwing out compliments all over the place, trying to soften the inevitable.

'How was your day?' she asked, merrily shredding some cheese.

Now. Now was the time to tell her.

'The usual,' he said. 'Although ...' He took a sip of water. 'Although Thursday was unusual.'

'Hm? How so?' She began to hum to the Spice Girls, put cheese into the risotto. Was she even listening to him?

'Cassie's had her baby. A little boy.'

Sarah turned to him, her cheesy fingers in the air. 'When?'

'Last Thursday.'

'Why didn't you tell me? You'll have to send her my congratulations.'

She rinsed her hands, then retrieved some leeks from the fridge. 'And some flowers,' she added.

Sebastian swallowed. 'This probably sounds a bit weird,' he said. 'But … well, I was actually there. At the birth.'

'At the birth?' Sarah's voice was brittle, and his heart sank. She proceeded to split the leeks with a knife. He could see that her hands were shaking. 'How … how did that happen?'

'I got this call from Anne Sophie,' he said. 'She'd reversed into an expensive car in the hospital car park. It was a pretty bad dent, apparently, and the man was irate, threatening her, and then she had to wait for the police. Anyway, long story short, she phoned me to rush to the hospital and offer some moral support. For Cassie, you understand.'

He was burbling, he knew, but he also knew the worst was yet to come.

'By the time she got there … Anne Sophie, I mean … she was a complete wreck. She said the damage would cost her a bomb and—'

'You were at the birth,' Sarah said again. Icily.

She placed the leeks into an oiled pan. She wiped her hands on her apron, then switched off the CD player.

'That's a relief,' he said, stupidly. 'You can't really call that music.'

'Did Anne Sophie make it to the birth?' Sarah said.

'She did, yes.'

'And?'

'It was very emotional,' Sebastian said, pushing his hair back. 'For everyone, I mean. The child was … tiny and … pure … and lots of dark hair and … well … Cassie was happy and exhausted. I got back to work after lunch. The others hadn't even noticed I'd gone, would you believe it? I'd missed a whole bloody meeting with the arbitration team. It didn't seem to matter.'

He had wanted to tell her more. He had wanted to tell her that he'd been in tears, gazing at Cassie's baby. That he'd felt like nothing else mattered more in life than this. That all we really needed to do was take care of one another. Live each day as if it were a miracle. But how could he say this to Sarah? How could he say that people all over the world would go on having babies and that two people wouldn't and there was nothing they could do? How could he say anything to help her?

A pot of broth was simmering. He sipped his water; she stirred slowly. He couldn't tell what she was thinking, or what she might say, if she eventually chose to talk. He felt like getting up, taking a shower, something to break the tension.

'I'm tired,' she said finally, still stirring the broth. 'I'm tired of hearing about other people's babies. The new girl at work, off on maternity leave already, and a hugely pregnant woman in the foyer who looked so smug and—'

She slumped down onto the kitchen floor. My God! He sat down quickly beside her.

'What matters to me is you,' he said, finding some words at last. Not knowing if they were the right ones, whether he'd blundered again, whether he would always be stumbling in the dark. 'You, Sarah. Only you.'

She took his hand and smiled into his eyes. The saddest smile in the world.

'I know,' she said. 'I know.'

'What matters is us,' he said. He wiped a tear from her cheek.

'Us,' she said and leaned her head on his shoulder.

100. Veronika

She tiptoed into the auditorium, just as the orchestra had finished tuning their instruments. Discordant; even squeaky. It was the first time she'd managed to watch a performance, so she'd almost forgotten what to do: keep still and silent, simply watch and listen. It felt like a peculiar emancipation: to be, but not be seen.

She saw the conductor flourishing his arms, his hair flopping wildly ... so distracting. But then the violins began and she felt an ache in her heart. Immediate, deeply moving. And then, as the timpani joined in, breaking the spell, her thoughts began to wander. Maybe she should have been a violinist instead of an actor ... there was more emotion in the violin than in any part she'd played ... but didn't all art aspire to the condition of music? Who'd said that? Someone she'd once studied, Walter Someone-Or-Other. His name escaped her.

And why was it always a *he*? All those classical roles she'd played. Not that men didn't know how to write about women: she'd been astonished at Euripides' Medea, at her rage, her passion for revenge on a heartless man. And women wrote plays, of course, and won prizes. Lillian Hellman the most famous of all, and hadn't some woman, Margaret Edson, won the Pulitzer? Veronika had even read the play, *Wit,* confronting and brilliant and moving, but she'd never seen it performed. She'd never seen a single play written by a woman.

So why shouldn't *she* write a play? Not that she aspired to the condition of greatness but simply to pay tribute to another woman. Her *babička.* All the big moments of her life: the wars, the experience of migration, what was lost and what was found. All the small things of her life, like catching three buses to the Boans food hall so she could feed her family *real* food. Making her own butter, spreading it thickly on rye bread. Her first Australian expression that Veronika remembered: *bloody hell.* When Babička hadn't even known what it meant! And the funny stories she'd told her, about a playwright who Veronika found out years later didn't even exist. A fictitious genius called Jára Cimrman, *the greatest Czech figure of the modern age.* And Veronika's favourite doll – a name-day present from Babička. A woman who was stuck in the bush but yearned for the forests of Czechia. For the *enchantment*, she called it. It became one of her favourite words.

The clash of the percussion brought Veronika back. A pulsing rhythm, a crescendo, and then the plaintive notes of a viola solo. It made her sad, the sound, made her think of Babička's lost lover. She'd found some information on the net: the Gestapo arrests in Prague, the deportations. Did Babička know what happened to the man she was meant to marry? How had she felt when she lost him? Did she ever think of him, even long after she was married, had a child, and made a new home far away?

How should you write about all that? The *feelings*. Veronika already knew that Ivan would matter, too, as much as her grandfather, her *dědeček*, who died before she was born. And would she herself play a part? Maybe. Maybe not. Maybe it was better not to be looked at, and it would give her more control. To at least put words into the actors' mouths, until the director had his own way. Her way.

She drifted back to the music. The oboist reminded her of Sebastian: something in the profile, the rigid posture. It felt like a lifetime ago. But what if she had married him? A changed man, Cassie had told her. What kind of life would she have had?

And then she thought of Charlie and her heart burned with shame.

But there was also the joy of Cassie's baby. An excited call from Anne Sophie, *we've called him Oliver, from* Oliver Twist, *because the midwife in the hospital was Nancy,* and then Cassie on the phone. *Not a wink of sleep. He's gorgeous. It's my real life. This is it! Just the beginning.*

The second movement. It was bouncier, she could hear the lilt of the strings, the laughter of the flutes. It was possible to be happy.

Cassie had asked her to visit Gwen; she was doing it tough, like Ana had done. Veronika couldn't picture moody, avant-garde Gwen with a baby, couldn't really picture any of them with a baby. Would Sebastian and his Sarah finally have one? She hoped so, she really did, although she couldn't help thinking that the desire to reproduce was at some level just plain egotistical. Wanting to perpetuate your own precious self. But then again, Ana's kids were lovely, and you had to admire her, taking back her life, and loving her kids so intensely. The love was real; how could anyone deny it?

And Josh. Dear, sweet Joshua. He'd actually phoned her, out of the blue, telling her he'd *reunited* with Gloria. *A beginning,* he'd called it, but she could hear in his voice that he hoped it would last. She'd always loved his gentle voice until it turned angry. Which was what she deserved. But he'd sounded at peace on the phone, living with a woman she'd once called *that refugee*. How could she have been so cruel, so ugly? So young. Couldn't she forgive herself for being so young? She was glad that Gloria hadn't heard those words, and she hoped that Josh would never tell her. Maybe one day she would pay them a visit. Be happy for them, and really mean it.

And maybe she could get in touch with Felix, tell him about the play that she wanted to write. He could give her some advice in his quaint English. But where would she find him? Maybe Cassie would know; she'd kept in touch with all of them.

The Players. That had now been ten years ago. Hard to believe, Veronika thought. How mad they'd all been, jumping into the creek, kissing on the sly, the extravagant, outlandish costumes, the strutting and declaiming, Sebastian on bended knee. How they'd laughed together, helped each other, felt proud of what they'd made. How the audience had clapped and cheered and made them feel special. Full of joy eternal.

The music was over. *A revolutionary symphony*, Nathan had called it. Yes, Veronika thought. It had been.

An usher, a young girl, came to stand beside her. She had tears in her eyes.

'I thought I'd die with the sadness,' she said. 'And then it made me feel happy ... and alive.'

Veronika would write that play. She would create that joy eternal for her family, for all the people in the audience, people she didn't know, would probably never know. But that was the magic of theatre: a gift to strangers, who would leave a heightened, even exalted, space and return to their ordinary lives. They might have been moved, provoked, somehow changed. Even transported, made anew. She would never know that either, and yet it wouldn't matter at all. In the end, what mattered was making and who you might become in the making.

Acknowledgements

I acknowledge, pay my respects, and express my profound gratitude to the traditional custodians of the lands on which this novel was written: the Darkinjung People of the New South Wales Central Coast; the Birrabirragal People and Gadigal People of the Eora Nation, New South Wales; and the Whadjuk Noongar of the Perth Hills, Western Australia, where some of this book is also set.

Sincere thanks to the magnificent team at Fremantle Press for their dedicated work on my novel: in particular, I thank Georgia Richter for believing in this book and for her great diligence, judicious editing and for her excellent humour, and Kirsty Horton for her fastidious fact-checking. Thanks to Alex Allan, CEO and the marketing team led by Claire Miller for their tireless efforts.

I am deeply indebted to my cultural consultants and sensitivity readers for Timor-Leste: the remarkable José da Costa, for sharing his story with me and for his invaluable insights and comments, and for his translations; and Vannessa Hearman for sharing with me her extraordinary knowledge of Timor-Leste, for her careful sensitivity reading, as well as suggestions on drafts of sections of my work. I also wish to thank language guardians and sensitivity readers whose input has also been crucial for my project: Alex Jay Lore, Hailey Zhu, Jiřina Hrabcova, Dominik Hržina, Sara Heft, and Roberto Prato di Pamparato.

Thank you to Gabriela Baladova of the Czech and Slovak Association of WA for providing me with an abundance of readings, stories and contacts. I thank Honi Edmondson for sharing her immigration story with me and for her candid insights on Czech experience in Australia. Thank you also to Nonja Peters and Michael Leach for their superb scholarship and for offering helpful leads.

It has been an enormous pleasure to work with Susan Midalia on an earlier version of this manuscript. I thank her for her outstanding skill, tact, wisdom and generous attention to my work.

For their insights, comments and suggestions on earlier drafts of my work, I heartily thank Catherine Cole, Catherine Heath, and Linda Funnell. I am grateful to Emily Schlick for checking and tuning and Katherine Waghorn and Anne Ryden for their proofreading. Thank you also to Rita Kalnejais, Bem Le Hunte, and Francesca Smith for some wonderful creative jam sessions.

I have benefited from fruitful discussions with friends and colleagues, including Anna Kamaralli, Michelle Cahill, Nigel Parker, Jane Bergeron, Michael Pigott, John Rees, Helena Kadmos, Daniel Oi, Natalie Biletska, Jenny Wong, Jason Cannon, Isabelle Russell, and Elizabeth Cowell.

Special thanks to Claire Potter for her energising support and friendship and always fascinating conversations on writing.

I am indebted to Emmanuelle Chaulet for a hugely helpful conversation about the French theatre scene and acting training in France. I thank orchardists Michael Padula and the Padula family for allowing me to visit their orchard and for kindly sharing with me a wealth of information. Thank you to the Timor-Leste Studies Association and the staff at Hotel California and Hotel Esplanada, Díli. I also thank the Carmelite Sisters of Maubara for their warmth and hospitality during my time in Timor-Leste.

Parts of this novel were written in Paris and in Cathar country at La Muse Artist's community, Labastide-Esparbaîrenque, in France. I am grateful to John Fanning and Kerry Eielson from La Muse for their support during my stays and for creating such a fecund space for the imagination to grow.

I owe a debt of gratitude to Norah and John Kalnejais and the Kalnejais family for allowing me the writing space at Killcare cottage to work on this novel. It has been simply amazing to be by the Bouddi National Park as this fictional world came to life. The close-knit community at Killcare, Hardy's Bay and Wagstaffe has become a home away from home.

Heartfelt thanks to writers I admire enormously, Bem Le Hunte and Melinda Harvey, for their generous cover quotes.

I also express my gratitude to the School of Arts, English and Media at the University of Wollongong.

Thank you to the following people for their encouragement and unfailing support: Gail Jones, Cynthia àBeckett, Jeremy Hastings, Cheryl Hardacre, Catie Fearman, Wendy Cole, Mike White, Avril Vorsay, Lissy Abrahams, Nina Levy, Cally Brennan, and Claudia Canny. I thank RIGPA, Sydney community.

I am also grateful to have been the recipient of an Emerging Writer in Residence Fellowship at the Katharine Susannah Prichard Writers' Centre, Greenmount, Western Australia.

I thank my family: my mother, Jane Pike, for instilling in me a love of theatre and for living such an expansive 'theatrical life', and my father, Glade Pike, for his ever-practical help and kindness. I thank my truly marvellous sister, Sheelagh Wilson, for illuminating conversations and constant support, and my wonderful brothers, Anthony and Mark, for their sense of humour and for suggesting axolotl T-shirts.

This novel is dedicated to the memory of a dear friend, Tina Chen Visage, who suffered much and left us too soon, but whose intelligence, munificence and wisdom will never be forgotten. This novel is also dedicated to my beloved partner, Mark, whose magnanimity, immense patience, and unwavering support has meant everything.

The following works were used in the research for this novel:

Bailey, Jonathan B.A., Richard Iron, and Hew Strachan. *British Generals in Blair's Wars*. London & New York: Routledge, 2016.

Bethencourt, Francisco, and Adrian Pearce, eds. *Racism and Ethnic Relations in the Portuguese-Speaking World*. Oxford: Oxford UP, 2012.

Cabral, Estêvão, and Marilyn Martin-Jones. 'Writing the Resistance: Literacy in East Timor 1975–1999.' *International Journal of Bilingual Education and Bilingualism* 11.2 (2008): 149–69.

CAVR. *Chega! The Report of the Commission for Reception, Truth and Reconciliation in Timor-Leste (CAVR), Executive Summary*. Díli: CAVR, 2005.

Chaulet, Emmanuelle. *A Balancing Act: The Development of Energize! A Holistic Approach to Acting*. Gorham, ME: Starlight Acting Books, 2008.

Chekhov, Michael. *To the Actor: On the Technique of Acting*. New York: Harper and Row, 1953.

Chubbock, Ivana. *The Power of the Actor: The Chubbuck Technique*. New York: Gotham Books, 2005.

Cigler, Michael J. *The Czechs in Australia*. Melbourne: AE Press, 1983.

Czech and Slovaks in Western Australia. WA: Czech and Slovak Association (pamphlet), n.d.

Davis, Russell Earls. *A Concise History of Western Australia*. Warriewood: Woodslane, 2012.

Descotes, Maurice. *Les Grands Rôles du Théâtre de Beaumarchais*. Paris: PUF, 1974.

Fergusson, Ben. *An Honest Man*. London: Abacus, 2009.

Gare, Deborah, and David Ritter, eds. *Making Australian History: Perspectives on the Past Since 1788*. Melbourne: Thomson, 2008.

Gregory, Jenny, ed. *On the Homefront: Western Australia and World War II*. Nedlands: UWA Press, 1996.

Hainsworth, Paul, et al. *The East-Timor Question*. London: I. B. Tauris, 2000.

Hagen, Uta. *Respect for Acting*. Hoboken, NJ: John Wiley and Sons, 2008.

Huneke, Samuel Clowes. *States of Liberation: Gay Men Between Dictatorship and Democracy in Cold War Germany*. Toronto: Toronto University Press, 2022.

Leach, Michael. *The FRETILIN Literacy Handbook of 1974: An exploration of early nationalist themes.* In proceedings from Timor-Leste: The Local, the Regional and the Global, 5th Timor-Leste Studies Association conference. Ed. Universidade Nacional de Timor-Lorosa'e, Díli, 9-10 July, 2015.

Marek, Vera. Interview by Ales Raich. *J. D. Somerville Oral History Collection*. State Library of South Australia. Full Interview Transcript. 8 Jul. 2000.

Megalogenis, George. *The Longest Decade*. Melbourne: Scribe, 2006.

Peters, Nonja. *Milk and Honey – But No Gold: Post War Migration to Western Australia 1945–1965*. Nedlands: UWA Press, 2001.

Traube, E. G. *Cosmology and Social Life: Ritual Exchange Among the Mambai of East Timor*. Chicago: University of Chicago Press, 1986.

Wise, Amanda. *Exile and Return Among the East Timorese*. Pittsburgh: University of Pennsylvania Press, 2006.

Quotes from the following texts appear in this novel:

Baudelaire, Charles. *The Painter of Modern Life and Other Essays*. Trans. Jonathan Mayne. London: Phaidon, 1964.

Beaumarchais, Pierre-Augustin. *The Barber of Seville and The Marriage of Figaro*. Trans. John Wood. London: Penguin, 1964.

Chekhov, Anton. *The Seagull*. Trans. Marian Fell. Auckland: The Floating Press, 2016.

Donne, John. 'Hymne to God the Father.' *Divine Poems, Devotions and Prayers*. Ed. John Booty. New York: Mount Vernon, 1953.

Nietzsche, Friedrich. *This Spake Zarathustra*. Trans. Thomas Common. New York: Boni and Liveright/Modern Library, 1921.

Racine, Jean. *Phèdre*. Paris: Belin–Gallimard, 2019.

Shakespeare, William. *Hamlet* (French). Trans. François Victor-Hugo. *Oeuvres Complètes de Shakespeare*, Tome 1. Paris: Pagnerre, 1865, 101–199.

Shakespeare, William. *Twelfth Night*. London: Arden (Third Series), 2008.

Shakespeare, William. *A Midsummer Night's Dream*. London: Arden (Third Series), 2017.

Permission granted to use quotes from the following:

Lines from *The Four Quartets* by T. S. Eliot, published by Faber and Faber Ltd, reproduced with permission.

Lines from *The Waste Land* by T. S. Eliot, published by Faber and Faber Ltd, reproduced with permission.

First published 2024 by
FREMANTLE PRESS

Fremantle Press Inc. trading as Fremantle Press
PO Box 158, North Fremantle, Western Australia, 6159
fremantlepress.com.au

Cover images by stocksy.com/2973961/hurt-woman, patternbank.com/
svetlanakononova/designs/564284513-peacock-in-dark-tropical-garden
Cover design by Nada Backovic, nadabackovic.com
Printed and bound by IPG

 A catalogue record for this
book is available from the
National Library of Australia

ISBN 9781760993061 (paperback)
ISBN 9781760993078 (ebook)

Fremantle Press is supported by the State Government through the
Department of Local Government, Sport and Cultural Industries.

Fremantle Press respectfully acknowledges the Whadjuk people of the
Noongar nation as the traditional owners and custodians of the land
where we work in Walyalup.